DISINTEGRATION

S.E. Soldwedel

This is a work of fiction. Names, characters, organizations, places, events, and incidents are either products of the author's imagination or are used fictitiously.

Copyright © 2019 S.E. Soldwedel
All rights reserved.

No part of this book may be reproduced, or stored in a retrieval system, or transmitted in any form or by any means, electronic, mechanical, photocopying, recording, or otherwise, without express written permission of the publisher.

Published by Inkshares, Inc., Oakland, California
www.inkshares.com

Edited by Steffen Kønsen
Cover design by S.E. Soldwedel
Interior design by Kevin G. Summers

ISBN: 9781947848948
e-ISBN: 9781947848436
LCCN: 2018937929

First edition

Printed in the United States of America

PROLOGUE

I CAME TO your Earth with a N'horran criminal and the spoils of his crime. He called himself Arak Matar. Antithetical to his species' peaceable ways, the N'horr were happy to relinquish him to me.

When my prisoner-turned-partner and I arrived at your planet, I masqueraded as one of you. My name, today, is Darek Marseh, but I have taken many over the centuries. I am Alitán and have powers of which you humans can only dream. I can manipulate your primitive minds, make you see what I desire you to see. I insinuated myself into your societies. I influenced hearts and minds and, once I had the ears of the leaders of men, I exerted my will.

You were too close to making the same mistake as had my own people, ages prior. It was my duty to prevent you small, fragile beings from achieving disaster. And all without revealing my true nature.

It was impossible.

You would not relent, and I grew weary of my failed machinations. I could have killed you all. In fact, if technological progress continues unchecked, my people demand that we eliminate the culprits.

As if that would not have revealed to you my nature. As if exterminating the lot of you would not have been "interference."

Such hypocrisy.

I refused my directive. Instead, Arak Matar and I turned your world into our playground. We revealed ourselves. We integrated the aforesaid "spoils" into your societies. These corren men were the hybrid offspring of Arak and human women. You may wonder how the humans got to the N'horran homeworld. You put them there when you launched a generation ship at your nearest stellar neighbor. The craft traversed a wormhole and arrived before it had even departed.

This strange confluence set me on my course.

I brought back your own bastard children. Accidents of lust. Exceptional combinations of N'horran and human strengths. I turned these correns into an army that struck mortal fear into your human hearts.

It served you right to be so afraid, contemptible little ants that you are. Filled with such hubris. Running amok. Trapped in your tiny bodies on your ruined little world, orbiting your small sun. Yet feeling so large. So important.

Not so, my little darlings. Not so.

It was your own fault that I declared myself your emperor and allowed Arak to put millions of you to the sword. Although, you did us far better by eliminating billions of yourselves in the bedlam that ensued our introduction. You self-obliterated with scores of nuclear weapons. You called the atrocity "the Blight" and rued the day we arrived.

But if you had never reached for the stars, the stars never would have come for you.

BOOK I

ONE

A'ARILON RAY SHOT up from his nightmare into a sitting position. He made no sound. His dark red irises were barely visible around his dilated pupils.

Anjali Hastings sat at the edge of the bed in her green and black Allied military uniform. She yelped at his sudden arousal and stood up, eyeing him.

"Oh, fuck . . ." Ray sighed. He put his head into his hands. Sweat rolled down the golden-white skin of his back.

Anjali put her cinnamon-colored hand on his leg. He grabbed her wrist, acting out of instinct with a craze in his eyes.

"Hey!" she cried. "Take it easy . . ."

Only just noticing her, he furrowed his bony brow. "Sorry." He let go.

She rubbed her wrist and looked at him with reproach, but he took no note. He looked around his quarters. The ocher-hued clouds of Venus shadowed the room, consequences of the artificial sunset. Solar shades regulated each day to twenty-four hours.

Anjali sat again, regarding Ray with her big, expressive brown eyes. "Same dream?"

He nodded without looking at her. "Always the same dream."

She flipped her thick black hair over her shoulder. "We're due to leave in a few hours."

Ray rubbed his face, tracing his harsh, bony features. Corren features, all, except for the smooth bridge of his nose. It was absent the ossified protuberances sported by the rest of his kind. Even corren-human hybrids, dubbed "variants," had them.

"Come on . . ." Anjali said, pushing his leg, stirring him from his thoughts. "Don't let him haunt you like this."

She moved her hand atop his, a picture of contrast in both color and size. Her dark skin had deepened with regular exposure to sunlight. To bask in the sun was a luxury of life on Venus. On Earth, they could only dream of seeing its light.

"You'd be haunted, too, if you knew what I do."

She patted his hand. "Arak Matar is pure evil. We all know it. You just know it a little more."

He rolled his eyes and sighed. "What time do we report?"

"Twenty hundred." She kissed him. "You sure you're okay?"

"Yeah, I'll be fine." He kissed her forehead and rose from the bed. "I'll meet you in the arboretum in a half hour."

His voice was dull and monotone. He shut the bathroom door behind him.

She waited a moment, staring at the barrier between them, frowning. She knew it was futile to press him about his feelings, but she dismayed at his preoccupation. Leaving his quarters to do her own preparations, she adopted a neutral expression. She had no desire to advertise her distress.

***

Ray pulled on his gloves as he walked. His Allied compatriots had never been fast to extend him a salute. They reserved quickness for fellow humans. Ray's race made him an aberration and the humans never failed to remind him of it. Seeing "that corren" in strange, all-black enemy armor incited sideways looks and whispers. Hatred for the Confederation ran deep, and correns came from the Confederation.

Outside the arboretum, Ray paused. The metalliglass floor, walls, and ceiling provided unobstructed vistas in every direction. Overhead, the sky was clear. The sun was setting. The western thunderheads and smaller wisps drifted in ruddy contrast to the darkening east. Night and stars remained hidden behind the curtain of fading daylight. Beneath his feet, opaque ocher clouds churned. He entered the botanical space. It brimmed with color, but the pervasive palette of Venus muted everything. Anjali waited by a weeping cherry tree. A vestige of Earth, before the Blight. She wore the same Confederate armor as Ray, her crest hidden, too, beneath a thin, opaque patch.

"You're late, Raymond."

"We've still got time before we report," he replied.

"You know Heston has his eye on you. On us. He's been looking to get us shipped back to Earth since we got here . . . says we're not doing any good. You fucking off and dragging your feet doesn't help us out."

Ray frowned. "I wasn't dragging my feet, I just got caught up. It's not easy wearing this shit again, revisiting this part of my life."

"You need to get your mind right," she chided. "You need to be harder."

"Harder. They raised us to be hard, Angie. Unfeeling killing machines. You want me to be that again?"

"Of course not," she snapped. "But you can't swing all the way soft. There's still a war on. There's still fighting left to do. I need to know I can depend on you. Heston needs to know it, too. We need to prove our usefulness to keep our spots."

"Well, we're about to be put to better use, by his measure," Ray replied. "But I really don't like this." He brushed the covered Confederate insignia with his fingers. "I can feel it in my gut."

"We don't have a choice," Anjali responded. "We follow orders. That's how it works."

Ray looked at her. "Whose idea was this, Anj? His?"

"I don't ask why, Ray."

"What about the great Fleet Admiral Hastings. Would you make an exception for him?"

"You know the answer to that," she answered, visibly irritated. "Daddy's command of Earth's navy doesn't afford him sway over us. And I don't have any over him."

Ray shook his head and grunted in disgust.

"Let's go," she demanded. "We don't have time to be moaning like children."

She walked out of the arboretum and toward the hangar.

Ray sulked and followed. "Who says we haven't made that one mistake already?"

"I don't want to go back, Ray," she warned.

"You don't think he's already punched our ticket?"

She lapsed into silence at his sarcastic retort. She took a step and then stopped, forcing him to halt or collide with her. She turned and put her hand on his chest.

"We could defect . . ." she whispered.

Ray brushed her hand down to her side, intertwining their fingers. He warned her with a look. "Treason," he whispered.

"Are you so worried about that?" She extracted her hand from his grip and rapped her fingertips on his breastplate. "Humans treat you like shit."

"You're human . . ."

She smiled. Her big brown eyes were warm. "My kind in name, not nature."

Ray exhaled through his nose, keeping his voice down. "I don't want to go back there, either."

Thoughts of Earth induced dread in everyone.

He looked down at her coy face.

"And the Reds would never take us back; Daedalus and I are pariahs. We deserted. How can we go back? Arak would never let us live. He and Marseh would have us publicly flayed, castrated and slowly, very slowly, executed."

Anjali opened her mouth to speak, but he put his finger to her lips. He frowned.

"We can either be killed by the Reds in retribution," he continued, "or by the Allies as traitors . . ." He sighed. His shoulders slumped. "There's no choice. Let's go."

He walked to the door. It slid open to reveal the hall between the base and the hangar. He stood in the opening, letting Anjali pass. They walked the rest of the way in silence. Ray concentrated on the endless sea of clouds rather than his thoughts. The sulfuric acid-laden wisps were the last glimpses of Venus he ever expected to see.

General Heston waited at the hangar door with Colonel Robinson and Major Pruša, flanked by two MPs.

"A'arilon," Heston said in a caustic tone. The general's relative dearth of height allowed Ray to tower over him by close to a foot. Anjali, too, stood taller than her superior.

Ray flared his nostrils and narrowed his eyes. He saluted.

"Commander Hastings," the general added with a subtle twist of his mouth. He looked at them both with a hint of disdain. "If we're done with the hand-holding . . . With me."

Ray glanced at Anjali. She shrugged at him and he rolled his eyes in response. They followed Heston, Robinson, and Pruša through the airlock doors and into the hangar. Anjali stopped to straighten her uniform.

"Come along, Hastings," Heston urged as he waddled farther into the large bay. He led them to a Confederation cutter-class ship. "You'll remove those patches once aboard. You have to proudly present that insignia for this mission—"

A small vehicle drove by, nearly clipping Heston. His kilt blew in the breeze.

"Damned, crazy—I think she was aiming for me!" he sputtered. He shot the driver a menacing glare as he gathered his wits.

"Should we detain that woman, General?" asked one of the MPs.

"A few more inches and that could have been satisfying," Anjali whispered to Ray.

"I'm glad you've never said that about me," he replied with a beleaguered smile.

She chuckled.

"No, no . . ." Heston said to the MP, "just . . . take note of her. Interview her later. Ship her back to Earth if she doesn't appreciate her post." He frowned and turned his attention back to Anjali and Ray. "Where was I? Oh, yes. So, we got her working."

"You mean Daedalus got her working, sir," Ray interrupted.

A perturbed scowl crept over Heston's face, but he checked it. "Lieutenant Daedalus worked closely with an entire *team* of human engineers, Lieutenant Commander. You'd do well to remember their contributions. Commander Gage, in particular, was instrumental in our success."

"Is that why you assigned him to Klippeborg? As a thank-you for a job well done? I'm sure he appreciates being back on Earth."

The general ignored the sarcasm.

"This is what you're piloting," Heston said, motioning at the stolen enemy craft. "All those simulations we had you do . . . were based on the controls for this cutter."

"You don't think they miss it?" Ray asked.

Heston frowned. He turned a redder shade of brown.

Colonel Robinson interjected. "We found her derelict in space, Commander, just beyond the Mars orbit. Floating there . . . two dead crew aboard. No sign of struggle. Hull intact. So, we brought her in. I shouldn't need to tell you things you already know."

"You didn't find it at all suspicious . . ." said Ray, crossing his arms, ignoring the colonel's admonition.

"We've had her for a while now," Heston picked back up, ignoring Ray's bait. "Your corren kin has been over the ship with a fine-tooth comb and everything's to his satisfaction."

Heston looked at Anjali.

"The three of you logged extensive hours in the flight simulator Daedalus developed. I'm satisfied. And so should you be. All command coding is intact. Those credentials should get you into Overground."

"Should?" Ray asked.

"Yes, Commander," Robinson insisted, his tone sharp. "Should. There's no guarantee. But we've hatched a good plan and we're confident. You should share our confidence."

Ray's expression soured.

Heston responded in kind.

"Your crew is already on board," he said. "They've been prepping while you two were . . . otherwise occupied." He cast an unveiled, disgusted expression at Anjali.

She kept her composure.

Ray, though, could not excuse the insult. "Respectfully, sir, mind your face when you look at her."

He brushed Heston as he passed. Anjali followed up the gangplank.

"Lieutenant Commander A'arilon!" Heston bellowed. "You are *done*! Your commission in the navy was a *charity*. Your exchange in *my* army is a gift! You got a second chance you never deserved . . . there won't be a third!"

Ray turned on his heel and rounded on the small, fat man. Heston shrank backward.

"Then take me off this mission," Ray demanded with quiet menace. Robinson and Pruša could barely make out the words.

"Dammit, A'arilon," Pruša complained, but Ray ignored him.

"Well, ah—" Heston stammered. He wilted beneath Ray's intense aggression, stupefied by the breach of decorum.

"Throw me in the brig, you sack of shit. Court-martial me!" Ray pressed, not raising his voice. He took a step back and held out his arms. "Better yet, execute me right here."

"That's quite enough, Commander!" both Robinson and Pruša demanded in unison.

Ray stepped toward Heston, who retreated a step lest they touch.

"You think we're all as stupid as you," said Ray. He cast a glance at Pruša for good measure. "Anyone without shit for brains could smell the stink all over this."

Heston adopted a low, even tone. "Get on that fucking ship or I *will* have you executed, right here, you insubordinate *fuck*!"

Major Pruša stepped toward Ray. "Lieutenant Commander, get on that ship. You overestimate how much of an asset we think you are. We won't hesitate to drop you."

Ray crossed his arms. "Looks to me, Major, like all you do is hesitate."

"Take aim at this traitor," Heston ordered the MPs, his voice calm to the point of sounding bored.

The MPs trained their rifles on Ray.

The entire hangar crew stopped what they were doing to watch the standoff. The crewman who had almost run down Heston brought her cart to a halt. She rested her arms on the steering wheel and placed her chins atop them.

Atop the gangplank, Anjali put her fingers inside the collar of Ray's breastplate. She gave him a gentle tug. "Raymond," she said in an even tone.

"Get on that fucking ship. NOW!" Heston bellowed.

Ray tensed and shrugged off Anjali's hand, but he turned and took to the ramp. She double-timed to match his pace.

"Have you lost your mind?" she whispered.

"No," he replied. "Just testing a theory. And I'm not happy with the conclusion. We're not coming back from this. Can't you see that?"

"I'm just following orders, Commander," she said without meeting his gaze. "Perhaps you should do the same." She chewed her lower lip and glanced over her shoulder at Heston. He widened his eyes and gave an almost unnoticeable, but sharp, shake of his head.

Ray and Anjali entered the cutter and the ramp raised behind them, sealing the hull.

Heston turned and glowered at his charges. "You MPs, dismissed."

After they had walked off, he looked up at the colonel.

"He's much smarter than he looks," said Robinson.

Pruša nodded, frowning at the same time. "Vile snake. Let's just hope Hastings' appraisal of him is a sober one. If we sent them off with him in charge just 'cause she's sweet on him . . ."

"All we can do now is wait and see, Major," Heston replied. "But I have faith in Commander Hastings."

He looked around the hangar at the idle workers. He locked eyes with the stout female crewman.

"Get back to work!"

TWO

RAY WALKED FROM the hold into the common area of the ship, where the crew sat assembled for the mission.

"Gentlemen," said Ray, looking around the compartment. His eyes settled on Second Lieutenant Ada Bennett, "and lady."

She gave Ray a slight nod.

"Lieutenant Commander Hastings is my second-in-command," he continued, gesturing at Anjali.

He noted the three other officers in his crew, two commissioned and one not. There were only four noncommissioned grunts. It was an incongruous amount of command experience.

He began calling roll.

First Lieutenant A'arilon Daedalus looked up when Ray called his name.

They had never served together in the Confederation. Daedalus had defected first, and Ray followed independently. The humans assumed that a bond akin to actual brotherhood existed between the two correns. But the men had been born in different batches and they barely associated. No matter how close they might become, Daedalus always undermined it.

Streaks of black scar tissue mottled the hulking, chalk-colored corren's face. "Hey, brother," he replied.

"What did you name this tub?" Ray asked.

Daedalus cracked a slight smile. "Don't talk about her like that, Raymond. This is *Filomena*. She's a lady. Treat her with respect."

Ray cocked his head to the side and raised an eye ridge in response.

"I heard a lot of shouting out there," said Daedalus.

"Pay it no mind," Ray said.

Private Adams raised his hand. "With all respect, sir, why are we doing this?"

Ray opened his mouth to dress down Adams, but Daedalus beat him to it.

"Shut up, Private."

"Hey!" Ray barked. "Stow it! All of you! None of us are here to speculate. You've all been fully briefed. You've been told what you need to know. We have a mission to accomplish, and its success is the only thing that concerns you. Am I clear?"

The crew responded in unison. "Sir!"

All except Daedalus, who crossed his arms and scowled.

Ada answered when called. The light-skinned woman stood out among the brown crew. She acknowledged Ray with a nod and a "Sir."

"Sergeant Major Vasily Rozhenko," Ray called next. He worked his way down in order of seniority.

In a thick Slavic accent, a seven-foot-two-inch cyborg answered. But for the metal surrounding his one synthetic eye, his face was mostly flesh. Half of his bald head was capped with the same durable alloy. An epicanthal fold hid the upper lid of his natural eye. He extended his mechanical right hand, which dwarfed Ray's sizable appendage. The corren accepted the gesture, both amused and discomfited to feel small.

"Hello, Commander," said Rozhenko. "I am hearing of you. It is pleasure finally we are meeting."

"Oh yeah, he's just so renowned," Daedalus muttered. He gazed out the porthole at the activity on the hangar floor.

Rozhenko ignored him and leaned over to speak into Ray's ear. "That corren. You are working before with him? I am knowing him just one hour. Already, is quite unpleasant."

"Imagine how I must feel," Ray answered with a smile. "I've known him much longer than you."

Rozhenko replied with a beleaguered smile. Daedalus made a face and pantomimed speaking in a bitchy manner.

"Sergeant, excuse me," Ray said, turning his attention back to the entire crew. He called out, "Corporal Gehsan Patrick ibn Malcolm."

Patrick replied with a perfunctory "Sir" at the sound of his name.

He studied Ray, fascinated to be in the presence of both correns. Their existence in the Allied Nations bordered on myth. He'd never before seen the creatures, except in pictures. In the flesh, he found them similar to humans but taller and more muscular. Denser. And with such grotesque, bony facial features. Patrick heard the rumor that Hastings and Ray were lovers. He couldn't understand how she found that attractive.

Corporal Smythe answered his name when called, his voice tinged with resentment.

Private Adams ran his hand over his bald head and answered when called. His assignment to the mission had left him confused, ignorant, and distraught. Yet, despite his penchant for being vocal, he followed his orders.

Private Norris was the last to be called. Ray knew that the man was toxic, further evidenced by the way everyone avoided him.

How did I get saddled with this mess of rejects? Ray asked himself.

"Commander Hastings and I'll take the bridge," he said aloud. "As you were."

Rozhenko sat opposite Daedalus, nearest the four fellow noncoms. Stretching out his overlarge body, the sergeant muttered to Adams.

"Corren reptile has personality of snake."

"But this 'corren reptile' has great hearing, Sergeant," Daedalus replied without looking up.

Rozhenko shifted uncomfortably. Adams opened his mouth to speak but Rozhenko intercepted him.

"Shut up, Private."

Adams closed his mouth. He moved to the most solitary seat in the room.

Ray's voice came over the comm, counting down to takeoff. The engines of the ship roared to life. The landing struts withdrew, causing the ship to levitate above the hangar floor. Ray looked out the window. He noticed the general running for the safety of the airlock. Heston looked over his shoulder. Ray gave him the finger.

Once all personnel were clear, the bay doors opened. Ray fired the aft thrusters. He guided the Allied Naval Vessel *Filomena* into the atmosphere. Running his long, deft fingers over the controls, the vessel cut upward. He had to hand it to Daedalus; the simulator had been a perfect representation.

Despite the ways the Allied military fell short, the training to use the cutter had been so comprehensive. But such clinical, technically superb training revived Ray's doubts.

The *Filomena* transmitted an Allied transponder signal to fool the Confederate satellites. Sensor camouflage spoofed the dimensions of an Allied cargo ship. Ray hoped the ruse went over as well in reality as in theory.

He waited. His shoulders tensed. He expected a swarm of speeder- or stinger-class vessels to appear and shoot them down. But no Confederate craft appeared.

Ray refused to consider it good fortune. Doubts nagged at him like a distant tolling bell. He punched in the necessary coordinates and the *Filomena* accelerated beyond escape velocity. Her prow pushed through the upper atmosphere and into the vacuum of space. At top speed, the Allies headed toward Overground. They had hours until arrival at the Confederation space station.

He laid his hand out, palm up on the space between his and Anjali's consoles. She clasped his hand. They intertwined their fingers.

She looked at him and flashed a wan smile.

He sighed and looked at the viewscreen, considering the vast darkness ahead.

THREE

ON EARTH, CARINA Duvais took stock of the medical provisions. Her blaster dangled in the holster on her left hip. She went over her mental list of Manon's requests. Vaccines, hypodermics, painkillers, bandages and salves, sutures, antibiotics, and so on.

Each item in the medical case meant one of Carina's patients might get sick, remain in pain, or even die of sepsis. She felt ambivalent raiding the pantry to pay mercenaries for steel and ammunition. But she admitted to herself the grim truth that some would die even with medicine. She exited the supply closet laden with the large, sturdy case.

Tuah Bell looked up, knowing better than to ask any questions. She couldn't infer the actual truth, but what she supposed wasn't good. Carina walked by without a word but brushed her right hand across the head nurse's backside. The med bay doors closed. Tuah returned her attention to the injured and dying soldiers, smiling at Carina's surreptitious touch.

Pablo Sotillo saw Carina ahead of him in the corridor and hastened to catch up.

"Not now, Lieutenant," she said without looking at him.

"A pleasure to see you, too, Captain."

She continued walking, mouth shut, eyes forward.

"I heard Andersen's been after you."

"What he does doesn't matter to me," she replied.

"So, you're saying he's handled?"

Carina stopped and put down the case. Squaring herself with Sotillo, she studied his scarred, rugged face. Every time she looked at him she saw Falco—how she imagined the boy might look, now, sixteen years later. The resemblance was uncanny. It unsettled her, but she refused to give Sotillo any vulnerability upon which he could prey.

She wanted to ask if he had a brother, but knew better. She couldn't show any interest in his life, lest he take it as interest in him. If Falco's surname had been Sotillo, she didn't want to know how one brother wound up in a slave colony and the other in the Allied military.

"What are you after?" she asked.

"Same thing as everyone else, I figure."

He smiled in a way that might have been charming, but Carina was immune. She knew a predator when she saw one. She'd encountered countless men like him up to the moment she found refuge in the army. Even among the ranks, they existed. Sotillo was proof. She'd killed more than a few such men, and relished every death.

She cast him a sour expression.

"But you've made it clear, I know," he held up his hands in a feigned gesture of respect and understanding. "And I've got an outlet . . . it's just . . ." a wolfish grin spread across his face, "your pussy would beat Gardiner's asshole any day of the week."

"Mind your mouth, Lieutenant," Carina snapped. "Talk to me like that again and not only won't I fuck you, I will fuck you up. I won't even call the major."

Sotillo smiled. He was unabashed and undeterred, but willing to accede. He smoothed his hands against his trousers. He adjusted his genitalia without shame. "Apologies, Captain. I let my dick do the talking just now."

"Don't waste my time, Pablo; I've got important things to do."

He picked up the heavy case with ease, making a show of his strength. He handed it to her. "Yeah, I'm sure you do."

Carina took the case and resumed walking.

He let her get a few steps ahead of him before calling after her. "Carina . . ."

"You don't get to call me 'Carina' any more, Lieutenant," she said without turning around. "Go fuck the major's asshole."

He stopped in his tracks and she kept walking. He glowered at her back.

"Even better, *Captain* . . . because I *am* gonna fuck you, you stuck-up bitch," he muttered. "Whether you like it or not."

Well out of earshot, Carina turned the corner and found René Duquesne waiting for her. The master sergeant wore a lightweight mechanical rig that augmented his strength.

He saluted. "Capitaine Duvais."

"Monsieur Duquesne," she replied, curt but polite. She offered a wan uptick of the corner of her mouth. Carina preferred to work alone, but Colonel Van Sinderen insisted René meet her black-market connection.

Two MPs guarded the ladder to the detention level, the most compromised and malodorous point in the entire base. A breached bulkhead exposed the complex to the sewer tunnels. It made any manhole cover, municipal maintenance duct, or train tunnel an access point. The guards stood aside. René descended first and moved out of the way. Carina dropped the medical case and he let it fall to the floor. She climbed down as he picked up the case.

René had set up as significant a defense of the breach as he could manage. His meager supplies included trash, force fields, and improvised explosive devices. The measures would dispel anyone who tried wandering through the hole but provided no guarantee against dimensional jumping; the Confederation technology allowed almost instantaneous point-to-point movement. It could only project the user a few dozen meters but was enough to penetrate from the street or the tunnels. Yet, without accurate coordinates, it was risky. A jumper could materialize inside solid matter, leading to instant death or maiming. René strewed the corridors with detritus for that precise reason.

He instructed Carina to follow his steps exactly. In their nondominant hands, subdermal chips emitted a frequency. It oscillated to match the force fields, letting them pass through unharmed. They passed empty cells on either side of the debris-strewn corridor. Beyond the breach stood Manon Derouard. A hood concealed her face. At her side, her robotic counterpart loomed. René paused at the sight of the six-foot woman and her seven-foot-tall android.

"Vite, René," She urged. "Où sont tes couilles?" *Where are your balls? "You need to lead, so I don't blow us up."*

He frowned at the insult, starting toward the cloaked woman and her robot. Carina fell in behind him. When they reached the breach, Manon doffed her hood.

The likeness of the two women struck René. The texture of their hair, though not the hue. Carina's was the color of rust; Manon's chestnut. They shared the same full lips and exquisite shape of their eyes. Carina's were green; Manon's blue. Crude streaks of violet face paint decorated the mercenary's cheeks, making her eyes seem purple. She was shorter than Carina, a paler brown, thinner, with a longer neck. The shapes of their faces differed. Their noses were not quite the same. But René was certain they were sisters.

Yet Carina had only ever spoken of Michèle and Agnès. He knew that Michèle had drowned during the girls' escape from Tripas, and he'd met Agnès in Marseilles, where he first encountered Carina, sixteen years ago. Manon was not Agnès. Michèle was dead. The sudden existence of a fourth sister confused him. He wanted answers but held his tongue; it wasn't the time.

"Bonsoir, Karin," said Manon.

René's ears pricked up to hear Carina so addressed.

"Manon," Carina replied.

The robot towered over them in silence. His blank white eyes betrayed no sign of consciousness. He could well have been an inanimate fixture, but the lack of dust on his person gave him away.

Manon gently touched his metal arm. "Jack," she said, soft and pleasant with French inflection. *Jacques.*

Without a sound, not the whirring of a servo nor the clicking of gears, Jack moved. He picked up the five items behind him and placed them in front of Carina and René.

"Fifteen kilos of steel and a variety of projectile ammunition," said Manon in French. She, too, enjoyed the break from speaking English. *"The ammo count isn't exact. About a hundred kilos. Maybe more, maybe less, but thereabout."*

Steel and ammunition, and their raw materials, were some of the few monies recognized by the world outside the military. Practical things, like medical supplies, were another. Military credits spent fine in military canteens, but fiat money did nothing for those in need of something fungible.

Too long since he'd enjoyed the company of a woman, René eyed Manon with ravenous hunger. She was stunning. Manon looked him in the eye and smiled the smile of a woman who knows she's beautiful and knows its effect. René's heart fluttered. Blood rushed below his waist.

"Et notre paiement?" she asked. Her gaze fell to the medical case. She scratched the shaved side of her head.

René closed his eyes and took a breath, jarring his brain back to the matter at hand. He held out the medical case. Jack deftly took it.

"Everything you asked for," said Carina.

"As expected," Manon replied. *"When should be our next rendezvous?"*

"I don't have any more supplies for you," said Carina. *"I'm sacrificing people who will probably die anyway . . . so you can have this. But I can't surrender anything else. I don't know how else we can pay you."*

Manon smiled again. She donned her hood. "D'accord. *Well, if something occurs to you,* chérie, *let me know.* Au revoir."

Without further word, Manon and Jack turned and disappeared into the darkness.

"She called you Karin," said René as he and Carina stood alone at the breach.

"So what?"

"Pourquoi?" *Why?*

"C'est mon prénom." *It's my name.*

"Then why do we call you Carina? You've been Carina since I met you."

She looked at René from beneath her creased brow and sighed. She didn't like it when people pried. But, beholding his guileless face, her own expression softened a little. She closed her eyes.

"I don't like talking about my life, René. You already know more about me than I want anyone to know." She rubbed her stomach. "I don't ask you about your life."

"But I'd like it if you did," he insisted.

She looked at him, then closed her eyes again. She shook her head and flared her nostrils.

"Fine," she replied. She hit him with the full force of her smoldering, gray-green eyes.

"You want to know something about me? My father named me Karin. When I was on Tripas, there was another slave, a boy, who called me cariño ... 'darling' ... and I didn't like how it sounded. So masculine, so I told him to call me cariña, *but then I didn't like the inflection. So, he dropped it.* Voilà. Carina."

René wanted to know more. *Who was the boy? Where was he now? Why continue to call yourself by his pet name after so long?* He knew that he'd already pried from her more than she wanted to share. He dared not push for more and risk provoking her nasty temper.

Carina picked up the steel and retraced her exact steps through René's minefield. She stopped when she realized he'd not followed.

"René," she said in a low, even tone. In the quiet corridor, there was no need to raise her voice.

Nylon straps connected the boxes of ammunition in pairs. He put one pair over each shoulder. When he reached Carina, he smiled at her.

"What you just told me . . .I didn't know *you* ever liked men."

"Je n'aime pas les hommes, René," she assured him. *I don't like men.* "Remember that," she added.

"What about Manon?" René asked.

Carina screwed up her face. "Elle est ma *sœur.*" *She's my sister.*
"Non, non. *I wonder who Manon likes."*
"Why do you care?"
He smiled again. "Je pense que je suis amoureux." *I think I'm in love.*
"Idiot," she replied. *"Your dick may like her, but don't call it love."*
Yet she smiled.

FOUR

RAY PUSHED ONE of the illuminated panels. "I've missed this interface. The design is so much more intuitive than ours." He winced at his praise of the Confederation and glanced at Anjali.

She barely nodded, staring straight ahead. She wasn't listening.

Earth loomed on the viewscreen like a ball of wet clay. From their vantage, it seemed impossible that anything could exist on the planet.

"It used to be blue," Anjali mused. "I've seen the stills . . . watched movies in the library, from before the Blight. God, Ray, it was beautiful. I can't believe it's the same place."

This time, Ray barely nodded. He kept his eyes forward. He ran his finger up and down the smooth bridge of his nose.

"It's so worthless now," she said with a disappointed twist of her mouth, "but we keep fighting over it. If you'd asked me what I'd be when I grew up, it was always a soldier. I never thought about anything else."

She looked at him.

"What else is there?"

He replied with a slight shrug of his right shoulder, without meeting her eyes.

She interlocked her fingers and pulled her arms back, stretching. Her breastplate rode up her chest. The bodysuit beneath stretched along with her.

Ray glanced at her, scanning up from the boots that ended just below her knees. He stopped at the inside of her right thigh. Rather than mull her words, his mind went to salacious things.

"Fuck," she sighed.

The utterance hijacked the incipient fantasy. He returned his attention to the console. Their destination neared.

"Reversing thrust," Ray announced to the crew. "Once your restraints release, gear up and be ready by the time we dock."

The ship's proximity sensors rang out.

"Overground," he muttered to no one. He looked out at the gargantuan structure in stationary orbit. It grew in perceived size as they sped closer. He looked at his monitor. "Moments like these, I get it. The yen for a benevolent god. Breaching the security perimeter in three . . . two . . . one . . ."

The cutter's interior lights dimmed and then turned red. Overground scanned the stolen ship. Confirmation or destruction awaited them in fewer than thirty seconds.

Ray looked at Anjali. "I love you, baby."

She smiled at him but felt a reply would be trite. She turned away, refusing to maintain eye contact. A subtle, rueful twist played over her lips.

Ray frowned. His stomach knotted as he looked at the back of her head. The warning lights turned green, then returned to normal. He set the autopilot to direct the vessel into port. As he rose from his seat, his magnetic boots tethered him to the deck. Anjali grabbed his hand. He halted, looking expectantly at her.

"You know how I feel about you," she said.

He made a thin line of his mouth and said nothing. He extracted his hand, and she followed him from the bridge.

"Look lively," Ray barked at the assembled crew.

The sight of them in their helmets and armor somewhat allayed Ray's misgivings. They looked impressive. Especially Rozhenko, with his staggering height and mass. He wielded a giant Gatling-style pulse gun encircling the mouth of a plasma cannon. His cybernetic enhancements made the feat of strength possible. No normal human could raise such a weapon.

The cannons were the only Allied arms that Confederation armor could not withstand. The war might have been less lopsided had the Allies possessed sufficient large, fresh corpses and resources enough to cybernetically reanimate them. As it was, sentries and the weapons they wielded were in short supply. Rozhenko was, himself, an aberration: the lone casualty whose consciousness survived resurrection.

The ship entered Overground. Through the common room windows, the docking bay interior replaced the view of outer space.

"You three," said Ray, "Bennett, Norris, and Smythe. Stay with the ship. Corporal, Private, you have the helm and tactical while we're gone.

Remember your time in the simulator. Lieutenant, check in with us at the specified intervals. Mind the comm. If shit goes sideways, remember your duty. You have the ship."

"Wait . . ." Ada began.

Ray shot her a look that brooked no dissent.

His unit comprised the most insubordinate soldiers he'd ever encountered. He rued again that he'd been robbed of handpicking them. Mouthy independents did not make a well-oiled machine. Mouthy independents made for sloppy units and dead soldiers. He refused to recognize any correlation between their dissent and confusion and his own.

Ada shut up. One corner of her mouth dipped downward before she corrected her expression.

Anjali, Daedalus, Rozhenko, Patrick, and Adams gathered with Ray at the airlock.

They donned their helmets. With an ocular command to the heads-up display in their visors, they set them from transparent to opaque. The airlock equalized the pressure between their environments. It blasted them with jets of compressed air. When the lights around the hatch turned green, Ray opened it. He stepped into the short, transparent tunnel. At null gravity, it bridged the gap between the ship's airlock and the station's interior.

Amid the bustle of the hangar, the six interlopers began their raid.

FIVE

"SIR, THEY HAVE arrived," said Kurgan Derovias. The black-clad centurion bowed in the presence of his Lord.

Arak Matar sat atop an ornate wooden throne, its back to his audience. His long black cape spilled over the edges of the chair. It pooled upon the polished, black- and red-veined marble floor. Where the cape folded over itself, its vermilion lining blared against the darkness like puddles of fresh blood. He clenched and unclenched his fists, each nearly the size of a human child's head. Black gauntlets bedecked his arms, polished to a glaring shine and trimmed with intricate red enamel leafwork.

He raised his right arm and ticked his hand ever so slightly in dismissal.

Derovias again bowed and departed. The door slid closed.

Alone again, Arak enjoyed the silence.

Enveloped in darkness and cold, his breath plumed into small clouds before disappearing from view. While he could make his subjects uncomfortable without help, he wanted a visit to his chambers to be unpleasant. All the better to be more intimidating, instill more suffering with starkness and lack of light and heat.

Atop the mahogany table sat a battle helmet. A human skull broken into large pieces had been refashioned into a mask. Two long metal fangs jutted from the upper jaw like vicious tusks. They tilted the face upward. It stared at Arak. An axe blade protruded from each side of the helm, afront the ear holes. Spikes honed to a fine point burst from the V-shaped crack that split the skull's crown. They ran in single file, decreasing in length as they approached the nape.

Arak leaned forward and took the helmet in his big hands. He ran the pad of his right thumb along the ridge of the left eye socket.

"Do I still haunt you, Jack?" he asked the vacant skull. His lips curled into a malevolent sneer.

He placed the helmet atop his head. Few of his charges and fewer of his enemies ever saw his face. His long, braided black hair cascaded down broad shoulders made broader by armor and cloak. He gazed for a moment at his muddled, indiscernible reflection upon the marble floor. Rarely did he look upon his own face. By design, his rooms were devoid of mirrors.

Turning, he moved with grace and agility that belied his soaring height and dense musculature. He strode to his chamber door. His heels thundered upon the stone. The door hissed open and closed behind him, framing him in black.

Uron Irva'a and Kurgan Kir, stood guard to either side of the doorway. Ishtafan Alesh and Tolon Inishi awaited him in the hallway with Derovias.

The five centurions bowed to their master. Arak Matar. Governor of the Americas. The Lord of Blackwing.

The Allies called him "the Butcher."

He inclined his head at his charges. Derovias stood aside while the other four flanked their Lord. Arak strode away with regal mien. His cape billowed behind him. Booted footsteps trod in unison upon the metal floor. Derovias trailed.

As the sextet reached the adjoining corridor, Arak stopped and looked at his men.

"While we must . . . allow them to escape with the cargo . . ." His labored voice crunched like trodden gravel, a side effect of the black scar that traveled from his right clavicle to the lobe of his left ear. "We have only one . . . stipulation . . . who must survive."

He licked his lips.

"Aside from the human woman . . . and your two traitorous kin, kill whomever you wish. Maim the woman, for all I care . . . so long as she *lives*. Just be sure," he looked at each man, "to leave enough of them standing . . . to complete their mission."

He searched the centurions' eyes for doubt or dissent.

He trusted Alesh and Inishi, forcing them to hold his gaze only briefly. He lingered long on Irva'a, whose own red eyes looked back without wavering. Next, Arak looked at Kir with the same intensity. Kir's eyes were an aberrant yellow, his skin a deep golden-brown. He did not falter beneath the intensity of his Lord's silent challenge.

Last came Derovias. He looked into Arak's hateful, amber-colored eyes, suspended in blackness, surrounded by the human skull that hid his master's scarred visage.

Derovias didn't flinch. In fact, it was all he could do not to smile.

Arak's deep, rich, guttural voice resounded.

"Do not . . . make this easy for them."

SIX

RAY APPROACHED THE end of the tunnel. The station's interior door opened. He stepped through. His team followed.

Condensation dripped from the dank walls. The uninhabited hinterlands of Overground's outer ring comprised only cargo holds, machine rooms, and laboratories. Ray halted and held up his fist. His charges stopped, and Daedalus came up beside him. Each man gave an ocular command to his heads-up display and their visors became transparent. Ray studied Daedalus' vermilion eyes, noting the amber coronae that ringed his pupils. Daedalus stared back. Ray's eyes, devoid of amber, were a deep carnelian red and unlike any corren eyes Daedalus had ever seen.

The two men conveyed their tacit understanding. Where there should have been a receiving party, conspicuous absence instead greeted them. Daedalus issued another ocular command, opening a private comm channel.

"Nobody home."

"What do you make of it?" asked Ray.

"I prefer it. You want them here? Have a little chitchat? 'Gee, Ray, what are *you* doing here?'"

Ray frowned.

"Everyone knows who you are, *Raymond*. With that nose? You're the only one of your kind."

"Fuck off, *Reggie*," Ray replied.

Daedalus scowled, more at the human name than the dismissal.

"Just be alert," said Ray. "This is already a bad sign. Take up the rear. We need to press on."

They reverted their visors to opaque black. Daedalus fell into formation and Ray took point. The beacon upon Ray's shoulder lit up to guide him, as if he were a calm, welcome Confederate. Each Allied intruder's beacon lit up, except Patrick's. His visor measured his stress response and determined that the threat level demanded stealth.

"You nervous, cupcake?" Daedalus said over the shared comm.

Everyone looked to see at whom Daedalus had directed the remark. Their eyes fell upon Patrick. His heart thumped yet harder.

"Turn it on manually, Corporal," Ray ordered. "Control your breathing."

The interlopers stopped at the intersection. Ray looked out for unwelcome company. He waved his charges forward and disappeared around the corner. As they pressed farther, the grates beneath their feet yielded to a solid floor. The lighting became a uniform green, sufficient for the beacons to shut off. Even Patrick's; he had calmed himself, and automatic control resumed.

At a large, heavy door, the Allies stopped.

Ray looked at Patrick. "Do your thing, Corporal."

Exhaling a calming breath, he reached into the pouch on his belt and withdrew a device provided for the mission. He plugged the mechanism into the door's control panel. The gadget cycled through possible codes, hunting for the one that would defeat the lock. Mere seconds passed before the door hissed open.

Ray cocked his head to the side. *Too easy.*

Anjali thought to ask after Ray, but she held her tongue. She knew better than to disturb him when his wheels were turning. The two of them stepped inside the lab. She motioned for the others to wait while they secured the room.

Patrick put the device back in his pouch.

A quick survey revealed only one human doctor slouched, oblivious, before a computer. Anjali beckoned the rest to follow. The doors hissed closed behind Daedalus.

The bay held a few hundred specimens. Daedalus looked at tube after tube, most of which contained a large humanoid body. He angered to see correns being grown at a more rapid pace than their natural-born kin. Spurred to physical maturity without ever having breathed open air.

Ray entered the doctor's periphery. The man looked up to see himself reflected in the black visor.

"Oh!" he exclaimed. He shook like disturbed gelatin. "What are you doing here?"

Aside from other doctors and what humans and Ingili provided brute labor for menial tasks, no one came to the labs. An encounter with Marseh's personal guards would liquefy the bowels of most men.

Ray raised his index finger to his visor, perpendicular to where his mouth would be.

The doctor slid from his stool and backed away. "Please! Please!" he wrung his hands. "I didn't do *anything*, I swear!"

Ray took another step.

"Okay, okay," the man said, flushing red, holding out his hands in desperate protest. "Yes, I . . . ah . . . *watched* something I shouldn't have, but that's all! Really!"

Daedalus moved to the head of the group.

"It just gets boring down here sometimes!" the doctor shrieked.

"Don't toy with the human, Raymond," said Daedalus over the comm. "Attack."

"No! Wait!" the doctor protested.

Daedalus removed his helmet and slammed his own bony visage into the human's face, caving it in. The sound of breaking bone filled him with sadistic pleasure to the point of mild arousal. He threw the unconscious body to the floor like a toy that no longer held his interest.

"Pathetic little creature . . ." he said, readjusting his genitals.

He turned his attention to the computer monitors. Though technologically proficient, he was no hacker. It chafed him to ask for help, but he called to the nearby Patrick.

"Corporal, to me," Daedalus ordered. "Make yourself useful."

Patrick reported without hesitation. Though reluctant to be in Daedalus' company, he wouldn't refuse an order. "Sir?"

"Find us what we're looking for," said Daedalus, indicating the computer.

"Which is?"

"A human, fully mature. Narrow down our search, at least."

Patrick nodded, sat down on the stool, and began infiltrating Overground's network.

Ray pored over the lab. Narrow catwalks skirted the stasis and gestation tubes aligned in sets of two parallel rows. Machinery lined the walls, all for one or another genetic engineering purpose. And all beyond his purview and understanding.

Light seeped up through the green liquid of the tubes. Most held correns. A few stood empty. The rest housed a diverse array of organisms in varying stages of maturity. Patrick's fingers darted across the keypad. Specs for each organism popped up on the monitor. According to the records, only one tube held a mature human organism.

Daedalus put on his helmet, clapped Patrick hard on the back, and walked toward Ray and Anjali. They stood observing the menagerie.

"It's in Tube 42, this side, this row," said Daedalus, but no one replied. He remembered that he had muted his comm. He un-muted it and repeated himself. Struck by a sudden thought, he halted and spun around. A smile played across his lips.

"Where are you going?" asked Ray.

"We need a way outta here," Daedalus replied without turning around. "I'm planning ahead, brother."

He walked back to Patrick, who remained at the terminal.

"Get me a map of this place," Daedalus ordered.

"The lab?" asked Patrick.

"No, dipshit. The whole station. Can you do that?"

Patrick frowned. He turned back to the monitor and began typing. After a few minutes of searching, being thwarted by the firewalls, and then defeating them, he brought up a detailed schematic of the outer ring. They included the docking bay and all access tunnels large enough to accommodate their ship.

Daedalus smiled. "Can you get more?"

Patrick sighed. "Probably. It's been a cakewalk so far . . ."

"Get it, then," said Daedalus.

The ease with which Patrick infiltrated the station's information architecture disconcerted him. Daedalus didn't care. He crossed his arms in self-satisfaction at his good idea. Patrick couldn't access anything beyond the outer ring.

"This is the best I can do."

Daedalus looked around the workstation for a data stick. He found one and handed it to Patrick. "Take it all."

With another sigh, the corporal downloaded the schematic. He ejected the stick. Daedalus snatched it away, sliding it into a pocket of his jumpsuit.

"Sir, you should know—" Patrick began.

Daedalus shushed him. He was not interested. He walked toward Ray and Anjali, whistling. At the sound of his tune, they halted preparing the tube for transport. Ray flipped up his visor and frowned.

"You're happy. That has to be bad news."

Feigning shock, Daedalus raised his hands in mock defense. The correns shared a smile. The alarm sounded and their smiles vanished. The lights went out. Their beacons remained off, informed by their stress responses.

"This is what I mean!" Ray yelled.

Daedalus stood mute: half-guilty, half-dumbfounded.

"Rozhenko!" Ray hollered. "Patrick, Adams, form up!" He slapped down his visor.

"I didn't expect that," Daedalus said, mostly to himself.

With a grave face, Anjali shook her head at him. She flipped down her visor and night-vision brought her surroundings into view.

"Help me with the tube, Lieutenant," she ordered.

The liquid within the container had congealed. The substance conveyed oxygen in both its solid and liquid states. It gelled to restrict movement during transport. Over the comm, she ordered the rest of the group to secure the cargo. Rozhenko, Adams, and Patrick arrived to assist Daedalus in lifting the vessel.

Patrick faced the bay doors. He regarded the container with a dubious look. "I told you this was way too easy—"

An energy blast screamed across the room. It passed between Daedalus and Anjali, striking Patrick. The impact spun him in place, sending him crashing to the floor. He cried out. His left shoulder smoked. The smell of cooking meat wafted up from him. He thrashed upon the floor, growling in excruciating torment. His armor melted into and mingled with his flesh.

Anjali's armor bubbled from the heat of the blast. Only Ray's and Daedalus' armor were genuine Confederation issue. The rest wore Allied armor made to look like the enemy's. The interlopers suffered its inferior protection against superior Confederate weaponry.

"Hold your fire!" ordered Derovias. "You'll hit the tanks."

"Did I hit the tanks?" Alesh retorted. "No. I hit the man."

"Hold . . . your fire," Derovias demanded. He curled his upper lip to reveal his uncharacteristically long and sharp eyeteeth.

Daedalus ducked behind the rows of tubes and crept toward the entrance. He crouched low and waited behind the last tube for the chance to pounce. From his hiding place, he could hear the centurions arguing whether to advance or to seal the doors.

Patrick's pained gasps monopolized the otherwise quiet comm link.

"Seal them in," Derovias demanded.

Daedalus took a deep breath. He jumped from his hiding place with both guns blazing. He darted across the walkway, firing at the centurions. They returned fire. He dived. A blast flew past his feet, striking a computer bank. Sparks flew. The machines belched smoke.

"Seal the fucking doors!" yelled Derovias.

He and Alesh backpedaled into the corridor.

Daedalus tried again to mount an assault. Covering fire from Irva'a and Inishi forced him back. A blast struck the tube behind which he hid. The vessel cracked. The fissures sonorously multiplied into faults, plinking musically before shattering in a crescendo. The green liquid spewed forth, splattering Daedalus. The organism within spilled out with the deluge, flopping on the floor in its death throes.

The bay doors closed.

"Adams!" Ray ordered. "Get the device Patrick used to get us in here."

Adams hurried to where Anjali tended to Patrick. With a sheepish look, Adams rifled through Patrick's pouch and retrieved the device. Ray tried to reopen the door, but it refused every permutation from the device. He walked to Patrick and Anjali.

"I need you to open that door, Corporal. Get us out of here."

"I knocked him out," Anjali said. She held a hypo-vial of tranquilizers.

"Dammit!" Ray spat. "Why? We need him! We need a way out!"

"That's the only door," Daedalus rasped, diverting Ray's attention.

Ray calmed himself, though he remained furious at Anjali.

"That doesn't make it the only exit," he said, looking around. "There has to be a utility duct; I refuse to believe *this* is what they planned for us. There's got to be a solution."

"Who has plans for us?" asked Adams.

Ray frowned behind his visor. "They have to make a show of resisting us, at least."

Anjali frowned back from behind her own opaque shield.

Rozhenko looked at Adams, confused. Adams opened his mouth to ask again but thought better of it. He shrugged and turned away.

"There." Ray pointed to a vent in the wall. "Up near the ceiling. Adams, Hastings, only you'll fit. The rest of us'll prep the cylinder."

Ray jumped onto the counter nearest the duct. He ripped the vent cover from the wall with one hand and threw it to the floor. Grabbing Anjali's hand, he hoisted her up and into the duct. He did the same with Adams. The human felt infantilized by the ease with which Ray manhandled him.

In the cramped, dirty duct, Anjali muffled a cough with the crook of her arm. She pushed herself along. Cockroaches skittered away from her. She suppressed her revulsion and pressed on. She stopped to peek through a duct cover. Adams came to a halt behind her. He admired the curve of her buttocks.

"Do you see anything?" he whispered, stifling his own cough.

Anjali locked eyes with a rat standing on its haunches barely a foot away. The rodent squeaked and ran off in the direction it had come.

"No," she answered.

She took the vent cover in both hands, popped it free, and pulled it into the duct. She slid the cover aside, pushing it into the junction down which the rat had absconded. Poking her head out, she peered around the hall.

"All clear," she said.

She slid out headfirst and placed her palms against the wall. Pushing away as she fell, she gracefully flipped and landed on her feet with her gun drawn. Adams followed closely behind. He landed with less grace. They ran to the door. Adams gripped his pulse rifle. He scanned the avenues of attack.

The charred control panel spewed sparks.

"Shit," Anjali muttered, frowning at the damage. "I've got to blow it."

Adams sniggered.

"You're a child, Adams. Go. Take cover behind that bulkhead. And be alert! They may not be far off."

Adams ran behind the jutting bulkhead. Over the comm, Anjali warned the rest of the party to back away from the door. She looked over her shoulder. Adams peeked at her.

"Don't watch me, Private. Watch our six."

Adams pressed himself against the wall. "Oh, I'll watch your six, Commander," he said to himself. "Gladly."

Without eyes on her, Anjali withdrew a keycard from her bodysuit. She flicked open the smoldering control panel, revealing a slot. She inserted the card and dashed behind the bulkhead opposite Adams. Seconds later, the door exploded into the lab with a white-green flash.

Adams peeked out again.

"Sit down, jackass!" Anjali chided.

The explosion's backwash billowed over them. Anjali went to the door, swiping at the smoke to reveal a hole into the lab. She noticed she'd left the secondary controls exposed. Glancing at Adams, she found his attention diverted. She flipped the busted panel back into place.

"Let's hope it's big enough," she said.

"Never had any complaints," Adams replied, joining her.

"Shut *up*, Private," Anjali demanded. She turned to him with such vehemence it shocked him. "You do *not* talk back to your superior officer. And you do *not* address me with innuendo. When it comes to you and me, I do the fucking. And I promise you won't like it. Get me?"

Daedalus emitted a low whistle, indicating that she'd dressed Adams down on the group channel. The young private blushed. He couldn't hold her smoldering gaze.

"Yes, sir," Adams replied.

She shook her head at him then ducked through the hole into the lab. Ray, Rozhenko, and Daedalus waited with the heavy tube. The doctor lay upon the floor, bleeding from his broken face.

"Hastings," Ray said to Anjali, "Patrick's on you. Adams, stay put. And stay sharp. Pick up the slack when Daedalus comes through."

Anjali flung Patrick over her shoulder and carried him from the lab.

The hole was barely big enough for Daedalus to back through alone with the tube. He kept the cargo steady as he backed into the hall, stepping over the section of the door that had survived the blast. He held the tube by the tips of his fingers to keep from rending his flesh on sharp, twisted metal.

"You couldn't have blown the damned door outward?" Daedalus complained.

"How could I have done that from out here?" Anjali snapped.

"How *did* you blow it, anyway?" he asked.

"Just do your job, Lieutenant," she replied.

The base of the tube came through the opening and Adams immediately grabbed it. Daedalus gasped as his workload lightened, giving him a moment to breathe easier. Adams felt the strain right away.

"This sucks," he complained, exhaling heavy breaths as sweat poured from his brow. "It's fucking heavy."

"Shut up, Private," Daedalus ordered.

Rozhenko and Ray fed the tube through. They gritted their teeth as it scraped dangerously against the metal. They fed it until Ray alone held on. Though weaker than the cyborg, the corren was more than strong enough. His greater agility and flexibility made him the better candidate. Once Ray was through, Rozhenko awkwardly followed, leading with his plasma cannon. He retook his position next to Ray. Adams eyed the tube, looking at the deep gouges in its transparent side.

Ray shrugged. "They said what, not how. Move."

They followed Anjali. Patrick's limp body dangled in her fireman's carry. Daedalus and Adams backpedaled as she led the way. They moved into the long corridor leading to the airlock. Each bulkhead jutted five inches taller than the grated floor.

"Watch your step," she warned.

Adams' eyes widened, looking back in the direction they had come.

"Company!" he yelled.

He let go of the tube. Swinging his pulse rifle by its strap, he brought it to his hands in a practiced, fluid motion.

"Shit!" Daedalus blurted. He struggled to keep hold of the canister but managed the weight.

Adams fired at the pursuing Red Guardsmen. Daedalus, Rozhenko, and Ray scurried to take what cover they could behind the bulkheads. They set down the tube.

Anjali dropped to one knee and bowed. She rolled Patrick over her head and released him gently to the floor. She drew her weapon, lay on her stomach, and took aim, adding to Adams' barrage. Struggling to get a good shot, she rose to one knee. A blast struck overhead and sparks rained on her. Instinctively, she raised her arm as a shield, though it offered no protection.

She retreated behind a bulkhead.

"How many?" Ray yelled, his back to the action.

"They keep coming!" Adams yelled. "This better be worth it!" He peppered the onslaught but needed three shots in one spot to penetrate the Confederate armor. "A little help? I can't hold them!"

Ray nudged Rozhenko. "Get out there, Sergeant."

He obeyed without a word, hauling his cybernetic bulk into the fray. "Take cover!" he shouted, hefting the huge plasma cannon.

Adams scurried to safety. Rozhenko fired the Gatling portion of the weapon. He mowed down the Confederation forces with six thousand pulses per minute. A grenade skittered near his feet. Anjali dived after it and hurled it back to sender. The concussion grenade dazed the Confederates, making easy work for Rozhenko.

Remaining prone at his feet, Anjali doubted she could reach shelter. He stepped over her, allowing her to rise behind him. Two blasts struck Rozhenko's chest. He staggered backward, colliding with Anjali. As she stumbled from the cover of his big body, a Confederate rifle blast struck her in the chest. She crashed to the floor. Her helmet banged against the grating. She groaned and cursed herself, then cursed General Heston.

Ray yelled out to her. He clambered over the tube and dived behind the covering fire provided by Adams and Rozhenko. The cyborg remained unfazed despite taking hits. From behind the bulkhead, Daedalus added to the Allies' barrage.

Ray slid to his knees. He fumbled with the straps of Anjali's breastplate. He tried to pull the armor from her body before it melted. Then he noticed it was merely scorched.

"Stunner?" he asked, incredulous.

Anjali coughed. She tried to dispel the fuzz inside her skull. "Just lucky."

He vacantly yanked at the straps.

"I'm fine," she said, slapping at his hands. "Stop it!"

Silence washed over the corridor.

"Report!" Ray yelled, rising to his feet.

"Clear!" Adams reported.

Anjali tried to rise. She made it to one knee before a dizzy spell overtook her. She put her hand to her head and swayed, falling onto her backside.

"Are you all right?" Rozhenko asked, offering his big hand.

"I'll be fine," she answered.

He pulled her to her feet. She staggered. He steadied her.

"There's bound to be more," Daedalus warned. "Big man mowed 'em down but more are coming. Mark my words." He stood by the tube. "Let's go, people. Time's a-wastin'."

Ray gave Anjali a dubious appraisal. His concern nearly nullified his frustration with her. He joined Rozhenko, Adams, and Daedalus. They hefted the tube anew.

"Norris, prep the ship," Ray ordered over the comm.

"Roger that, Commander," Norris replied. "Preparing for launch. What's your ETA? Over."

"One mike," Ray replied. "Over and out."

The Allies moved as fast as they could under the strain of their cargo. They passed Anjali, who took up the rear to cover them. She backpedaled, stooped, with her pistol raised. She yanked Patrick's unconscious body along by his collar. The dead weight drained her, but she kept up her gun.

At the tunnel to the ship, she holstered her blaster. She picked up Patrick and took point. Ray relinquished his hold on the cargo, to remain as the last line of defense. Rozhenko absorbed the weight. He kept pace as Daedalus and Adams backpedaled toward escape. The airlock rolled open to reveal the helmeted Corporal Smythe.

"Welcome back, gang," he said over the comm.

Anjali foisted Patrick into Smythe's arms.

"Tend to him," she ordered.

She directed the cargo onto the ship before rejoining Ray.

"Back inside, Hastings!" he barked. He fired his pulse rifle.

An enemy blast slammed into the doorframe. She flinched. Crouching, she returned fire, but her pistol was useless at long range. She returned to her feet and tugged at Ray's arm. He wouldn't budge.

"This is *not* the time for a last stand!" she shouted. "It's time to go!"

"If they advance, you don't get away!" he growled. He fired with surgical precision, cutting down each man stupid enough to round the corner. "Get back on the ship!"

"Don't be stupid!" she demanded, pulling at him. It was as futile as trying to uproot an oak tree with her bare hands. Guilt washed over her. It clouded her judgment. "Why are you doing this?" she whined, distraught and frustrated. She came around to face him, trying to push him through. "Go, dammit!"

"I'm not an idiot, Angie," he replied.

She looked up at him in distressed confusion. A bright blue flash of Confederate weapons' fire erupted. She screamed. Agony ravaged her face. The sharp note ripped through Ray's ears over the comm. His face slackened in disbelief as she slumped into his arms. His rifle clattered to the floor. Anjali howled and moaned in pain.

Ray opened his mouth to give voice to his despair, but no sound escaped.

He pulled her into the tunnel and lay her down. Retrieving his rifle, he fired upon the advancing Confederates. He struck one in the side of the neck, obliterating the unprotected flesh. Green blood spattered the next man. The target's head teetered to the right and tipped backward, dangling like a hood. The body crashed to the floor.

Inside the cargo bay, Daedalus, Rozhenko, Adams, and Smythe—having discarded Patrick in the common room—seated the tube into its collar.

Anjali's armor dripped molten metal onto her jumpsuit. The heat-resistant fabric put up meager resistance. It smoked as it burned. Ray clenched the trigger and another guardsman fell. The Confederates ceased fire. Anjali's skin began to cook. She passed out. Her agonized moaning ceased.

In the hold, Daedalus wiped a bit of slime from his breastplate and flicked it to the floor. He made his way to the cockpit.

Ray stood rapt. The idle guardsmen and centurions parted. Arak Matar strode into view, flanked by Kir and Derovias.

Arak pointed at Ray. The long, thick digit tapered at its end like a talon. Layered metal plates girded each knuckle of the Butcher's gloved hand. Though separated by more than ten meters, Ray felt the claw upon his chest. It bore through to his heart.

"Get out of my seat, Private," Daedalus ordered Norris. The human hurried to make room for his gruff superior officer.

Arak's red-lined black cloak billowed despite the still air. His black braids writhed. Ray looked at the Butcher's mask, at the skull that haunted his dreams.

Time slowed.

Malignant amber eyes gleamed within the hollow sockets of the death mask. Ray was enthralled. Reality fell away. A guardsman fired. To Ray's muddled senses, the discharge made no sound. It crept through the air like a blue sun in miniature.

Daedalus moved to disengage the dock. He noticed the airlock remained open.

Outside, time ground almost to a halt.

"What the fuck is going on out there?" Daedalus demanded over the comm.

The voice and the smells of melting fabric and burning flesh roused Ray from his trance. Time sped back to normal.

"Raymond!" Daedalus shouted. "Hastings! Report!"

Ray threw his arms up in front of his face. A futile, instinctive gesture. He crammed an astounding amount of thought into the moment between discharge and impact. He closed his eyes. He clenched his teeth against certain death, pushing outward with his hands, as if to dispel his doom. The blast struck. His face contorted in reflex, but he felt no more than a mild jolt. He opened his eyes to see the blue energy dissipating along his arms. It never touched his armor. It faded into nothing against an invisible shroud.

The surprise in Arak's eyes warmed Ray's soul. Without wasting another moment, he backed into the tunnel and sealed the door to the station. As it closed, Ray saw Arak grasp the throat of the gunman.

Inside the tunnel, Ray snatched up Anjali. He refused to ponder his miraculous survival.

"Reggie!" he yelled into the comm as he stepped onto the ship. He sealed the airlock. "Get us out of here!"

Daedalus grimaced again. *That name.*

"Nice of you to show up, Raymond," he replied over the shared channel. He brought the ship around.

Ray set Anjali on her belly. He ripped the compromised armor from her back, wincing as it burned through his glove. Drawing his knife, he cut the bodysuit from nape to collar and peeled it from her torso. Her flesh bubbled like melting cheese. Intense heat radiated from her. He threw her unconscious, half-naked form over his shoulder. Running to the cargo bay, he set her down again.

The tube that held their purloined, living cargo stood in its collar. Ray's fingers darted over the controls. The opaque, mint-hued gel slowly reverted to translucent, hunter-green liquid. He draped Anjali over his shoulder, climbed to the catwalk and, once more, deftly put her down.

When the gel had fully liquefied, he opened the lid. He lowered her into the tube. The viscous goop brimmed over the lip and oozed down the outside. With Anjali ensconced, Ray closed the lid and sealed it. The liquid filled her lungs. Her unconscious body spasmed, reacting as if drowning.

He jumped to the floor and checked the controls. The readout adjusted to indicate two lifeforms. It upped the oxygen to accommodate, absorbing the intrusion without complaint. Anjali convulsed until the liquid saturated her bronchioles. Her sympathetic nervous response gave way to the parasympathetic. Her body grew still.

Rozhenko came into the bay as if hassled. "What is it you do, sir?" he asked, sheepish. He tried to make himself small, like a bear pretending to be a mouse.

Patrick stood behind, clutching his wounded arm.

Ray said nothing.

"That thing is for holding two?" the big Russian pressed.

"Back off, Sergeant!" Ray snapped. "Did they choose all of you for your fucking mouths?"

An impact shook the vessel and Ray reeled.

Rozhenko steadied himself against the doorway. He grunted. Without another word, he headed back into the main compartment. He passed Ada.

"Well?" she asked.

"He was not appreciating . . . such inquiry," Rozhenko reported.

Patrick looked at Anjali, nestled in the stasis tube with the naked male. The unconscious pair intertwined like lovers.

"Here's hoping I don't kill you both," Ray said. He punched in the sequence of commands provided by Heston.

The liquid again congealed into opaque gel, hiding Anjali and their stolen prize from view.

SEVEN

DAEDALUS SPED TOWARD the closing hangar doors. They would seal before he could reach them.

"Dammit!" he growled.

"Punch it!" Rozhenko prodded.

"Will you shut up?" Daedalus retorted. "If I punch it now and those doors close, we die in a big ball of fire. You want that?"

Rozhenko shook his metallic head.

"Then shut up and let me fly." He accelerated.

"You speed up!" Rozhenko protested in his stilted English. "You said—"

"Shut. *Up!*" Daedalus screamed. "I said, 'Shut up!' Do you see those speeders on our tail? Sit your big tin ass at tactical and be useful!"

The Allied Naval Vessel *Filomena* sped toward the bay doors. The gap had grown far too small for her. Rozhenko looked at his tactical display and uttered a string of curses in his native tongue. He tried to steady himself as weapons' fire jarred the ship.

"We will be getting smashed by door, just like you say—" he worried.

Daedalus grunted. "Shut. Your mouth. Or I'll cork it . . . with my fist."

As the door seemed too close to avoid collision, his fingers darted over the controls. The aft belly and forward dorsal thrusters fired at once. The ship pitched ninety degrees. Daedalus fired the aft engines and the craft nose-dived. She rocketed toward the floor of the voluminous docking bay.

Daedalus watched one of the speeders fly through the small opening in the bay doors. The other crashed headlong. It exploded in a bright flash.

"That's two down," he said, bringing the ship level. "Way to go, *Filomena*, baby." He patted the console like a pet.

"Yes, but now we are being trapped," said Rozhenko.

Daedalus rolled his eyes but said nothing. He piloted the *Filomena* through the hangar, veering into a service tunnel. Rozhenko looked out the front viewscreen. Dubious strain wracked his face as they sped through the narrow tunnel.

"You are knowing what you do?"

"I downloaded station specs while we were in that lab," Daedalus replied. "I knew this would go south, so I got a map."

Rozhenko's expression brightened. He cast his ornery pilot an approving glance.

"Don't get wet about it," Daedalus sneered.

***

Ray looked at the control panel of the stasis tube. The readout remained optimal. The dark green liquid converted to an opaque, mint-hued gel. He couldn't discern the bodies within. The ship shook and he staggered again. En route to the bridge, he passed Patrick and paused. The corporal's normally olive complexion was ashen. His shoulder mangled and charred, mingled with the dull melted armor.

"Bennett!" Ray yelled.

Ada appeared in the entrance to the cargo bay.

"Tend to the corporal."

"Of course," she replied.

The corren squeezed past her. His crotch brushed her backside and her breath caught in her throat. She exhaled and rolled her eyes at herself. There was never a wrong time to be aroused.

Ray continued toward the bridge without a backward glance. She banished the thought of him and focused on Patrick.

"Let's go," she ordered. "Med bay."

***

Daedalus struggled with the controls. He tried to evade the remaining stinger. The close quarters of the tunnel left scant room to maneuver.

"Report," Ray demanded, bracing himself as the ship rocked from weapons' fire.

"We are not escaping," Rozhenko replied. He ham-fistedly prodded the tactical controls, attempting to fire aft. "They trap us. Stinger on tail and no room for maneuvers. I mean, enemy ship has not much teeth, but is fast . . . and dedicated."

"Get up," Ray ordered.

Rozhenko stepped aside.

Sitting down, Ray's fingers danced over the controls. "Where we going, Reggie?"

Daedalus scowled and muttered to himself before replying. "We're in a service tunnel that runs the entire ring, connecting all the bays."

"Who is this 'Reggie'?" Rozhenko asked.

They both ignored him.

"So we're just gonna fly in circles?" Ray replied.

"Look, I wouldn't be doing this if I didn't think there was a way out. That's where I'm heading. We're barely a klick away."

"Trusting they are not knowing this," piped Rozhenko, "and are cutting us off."

"Even if they do, what do you suggest?" Daedalus snapped. "Surrender? You may not have noticed, big guy, but they're trying to *kill* us."

"So what we do?" Rozhenko asked. He took an empty seat.

"Feast your eyes, sweetheart," Daedalus said.

Two speeders headed toward them.

"Doesn't matter," he added, "we're here. Clench your asses, gentlemen."

Ray fired at the speeders. Daedalus pulled the opposite move from before to bring the *Filomena* perpendicular. He punched the aft engines. The *Filomena*'s tail scraped the tunnel floor. Ray flew from his chair. Rozhenko's head slammed against his console with a metallic *donk*. Ray dropped a mine and one of the speeders exploded.

The remaining speeder found itself on a collision course with the stinger. The stinger destroyed its compatriot. It emerged from the fireball, flames licking its shields, guns blazing. Daedalus fought the controls. The ship scraped the wall. Rozhenko hit the floor as Ray climbed back into his seat. Learning, he strapped himself into the harness. The stinger sapped the *Filomena*'s depleting aft shields.

"Aft shields at 60 percent," Ray reported.

The stinger rocked them again.

"Are they ever giving up?" Rozhenko complained in childlike despair as he deposited himself anew in his chair. The harness could not accommodate his bulk.

"They could have toasted our deaths by now," Daedalus said. "We *should* be dead. They're toying with us." He paused. "Or maybe I *am* just that good."

"It's our cargo," Ray replied. "They let us take it. They didn't want to damage it on the station . . . they don't want to damage it now."

He deployed a series of mines. Small explosions immediately shook the cutter.

"Got him," said Ray.

"No way they let us take," Rozhenko protested. "If is so important, why do they?"

"Unfortunately, Roz," said Ray, "I don't have the luxury to reason that out right now."

"Gimme two forward torpedoes, on my mark!" said Daedalus.

"Ready," Ray replied.

"Mark!"

Ray loosed the torpedoes.

Two bright flashes shot from the prow. They struck the inner hull of the space station. It exploded in an orange flash. The vacuum starved the flames and they vanished.

Daedalus piloted the cutter through the breach. A self-satisfied smile played across his scarred lips.

"We are home free?" asked Rozhenko. "We will be taking off now. Warp speed."

Ray looked at him. "Warp *speed*?"

"I watch old program in library," Rozhenko replied. "There is Russian character and I wonder: I talk like this?"

Daedalus' smug face reverted to dour solemnity. He set course to Venus. Overground shrank in the rear viewscreen.

"This was way too damned easy," Ray muttered. He shook his head.

"Look," Daedalus replied. "I'm not about to say any of that was 'easy' . . . but I'm with you. We shouldn't be getting away like this. Hell, we never should have gotten in. We *should* be dead."

"Please to not be saying this," Rozhenko begged.

Ada walked into the cockpit. "Mission accomplished?"

The proximity alarm beeped.

"Not yet," Ray answered. "Pursuing ship, unknown class . . . coming fast!" He turned to Daedalus. "It's Marseh."

"Pizdyets," Rozhenko swore in disbelief.

Ada frowned. She slid into the last open seat and strapped in.

"Of all the ways to die," Daedalus offered, "getting blown to bits in space has to be one of the best. If you don't vaporize, you suffocate and flash freeze."

Ada rolled her eyes.

"We're not dead yet," Ray said.

Weapons' fire flashed around them, jarring them in their chairs. The enemy ship cut across their bow. Its hull markings were easily discernible but corresponded to no language nor insignia they had ever seen. Its build was unlike any Confederation or Allied ship.

"It *is* Marseh," Daedalus said with hushed reverence.

"If he is even real," Rozhenko countered. "I mean to say, you are seeing him, ever? He is myth."

The ship jolted against the barrage.

"Does that feel like a myth to you?" Ada snapped, scowling.

He shut his mouth.

"Take evasive action, dammit!" Ray exclaimed.

Daedalus' face tensed. "What do you think I'm doing?" His fingers played over the ship's controls. "Changing course to Earth. If we stay in the open, we're done. Maybe we can shake him in the debris field."

The orbits of defunct satellites, derelict spacecraft, and other detritus blanketed the planet, hindering conventional weapons lock.

"Gun it, come on!" Ray implored. "We're going top speed and he catches us," he snaps, "like that?"

"This heap won't go any faster!" Daedalus protested. "Most pilots are only as good as their ship, and this thing's a lumbering piece of shit," he winced and patted the console, "Sorry, *Fil*. I didn't mean it, baby."

He looked Ray in the face.

"I'm flying her like a stinger. If it weren't for me, we'd already be dead."

"Don't get too full of yourself," Ray warned.

"We are being hailed?" Rozhenko dared to speak.

"No," Ray replied. "He's not here to talk . . ."

He let go a barrage of blaster and torpedo fire as Marseh flew across their bow. Every shot missed its mark. Marseh fired another volley. Ray braced his hands on the console to keep from smashing his head. The emperor's ship came around for another pass. It taunted the *Filomena* from within feet of her shields.

"He's too fast!" Daedalus complained. "I can't evade him. He's dodging the debris like it isn't even there!"

Ray released a batch of mines.

Marseh gunned the belly thrusters, kicking his ship straight back. The mines barely missed. Anticipating the sudden change of trajectory, Ray fired two torpedoes. They struck the keel of Marseh's ship but were absorbed by the shields. Marseh's ship tipped forward. The craft sped at them. It passed over top of the *Filomena*, dropping a series of mines. They detonated along her dorsal hull.

A monitor above Ray's head exploded, showering him with sparks.

"We can't take much more of this!" he yelled. "Dorsal shields at 5 percent!"

"We're leaking fuel!" Daedalus replied, exasperated. He watched the hydrogen meter plummet. "There's no way we make it back."

"We *have* to get out of here!" Ray implored.

His console showed no remaining torpedoes, nor mines. The blaster battery neared empty. It drained as the ship's fuel leaked into space.

"And go where?" Daedalus snarled. "This tub can't go half a mile, let alone half an AU! We are *fucked*."

He swiped his hand across the navigation panel. The *Filomena* yawed to port. She dived into Earth's exosphere. Gravity overtook them.

Marseh fired an electromagnetic pulse. It engulfed the Allies' ship. The impact propelled the *Filomena* forward and knocked out her primary systems. Daedalus fought with the controls. It took a moment for the system to reboot, but only life support came on. The ship spun out of control. She hit the mesosphere and spun back the other way, careening downward. The air around the hull glowed yellow and orange.

Stolid, pinned to their seats, Ray, Daedalus, Ada, and Rozhenko watched their descent. The viewscreen flashed shades of gray: ground, sea, sky, ground, sea, sky. Dark earth and darker oceans loomed larger with each rotation.

Ada blacked out.

Autopilot came on. Daedalus regarded the panel in amazement. The ship righted herself. She had a destination: Nova Spes, the contentious Atlantic landmass off the west coast of Ireland. The seat of power of Arak Matar. They were being guided there.

The controls indicated insufficient power for the Emergency Landing Protocol. If it failed to engage, impact would kill the entire crew.

Daedalus strained against the g-forces. Frantic, he tapped at his console, diverting power from life support to the ELP. He went under. Ray followed into oblivion. His head smacked against his console, releasing a stream of blood. Rozhenko remained alert longest. The mechanical portions of his brain were unfazed by the gravitational forces. Yet his organic parts succumbed to the stress. The computer governing his existence induced unconsciousness.

The *Filomena* slowed as the Emergency Landing Protocol activated. Her nose lifted. She yawed ninety degrees to defray impact across the longest surface. The maneuver executed too late. The cockpit filled in an instant with dark green fluid. It flooded from hidden outlets at every angle. The crew's unconscious bodies shuddered as the liquid filled them. It gelled within and around them.

The ship plowed violently into the ground. She rolled end over end along her long axis, then landed on her belly. She slid, turning prow first from angular momentum, churning mud and earth. The hull screamed. It rent at the seams. Momentum carried the craft forward, chewing the ground. She decelerated.

Eventually, she stopped, nose buried in mud and drier earth beneath. The ship protruded from the ground at an angle. The torn hull ripped apart.

The aft section fell to the ground.

Smoke belched from the burned-out engines.

EIGHT

MARSEH PILOTED INTO his private hangar. The ship extended its landing struts. Directional thrusters hissed as they stabilized the craft. The controls confirmed a firm dock.

He shut down the ship and opened the canopy.

To the attendant, Marseh appeared to have made no move. Yet the emperor stood beside the jumpsuited corren, towering over the tall man by more than two feet. The attendant flinched at Marseh's ability to teleport, but it was a trick of the mind. He had climbed from the cockpit, yet, better than a good illusionist, he thwarted perception of movement and time.

The attendant bowed. He directed technicians to examine the emperor's ship.

Marseh strode toward the doors. They opened to reveal Arak Matar. As Marseh passed, Arak followed.

"Emperor," he said. The address carried a hint of derision.

"Don't coddle me with titles, old friend," Marseh stated.

"As if you'd tolerate me calling you by name," Arak replied. "I carried out your orders, *Highness*."

Marseh looked at him. "Very good."

The advantage in height afforded Marseh the small pleasure to look down upon his insubordinate charge. The Butcher's helm hid all but his hateful yellow- and red-flecked eyes. He had learned a few of Marseh's telepathic tricks, but success depended upon a perfect confluence of factors, surprise paramount. The emperor would not be caught by surprise. He had no fear of his pupil ever breaking through.

They reached a set of doors, which opened automatically. Arak kept pace.

"We've not spent this much time together in years, Governor. To what do I owe this unexpected pleasure?"

"I want to know why you ordered me to let them go," Arak demanded. "That abomination of yours, which masquerades as one of mine . . . he was with them. May he *rot*. I want to know what they took from that lab."

"If it was your business to know, dear friend," Marseh began. He stopped and turned to Arak. "I would have told you. Still, I very much appreciate that you carried out my orders so dutifully."

"This was the last time," Arak threatened.

"Would you threaten our supremacy out of mere spite? We are on the brink of winning."

"We've been on the brink of winning for eons. They always find a way to survive. What good has doing things your way done for us?"

"I'd prefer to inherit their lands intact than lay them to further waste," said Marseh. "What would you like to do? Secede? Can you and your loyalists fight me *and* the Allies at once?"

"Can *you* fight us?" Arak shot back.

"I've never taken you for a fool, old boy," Marseh replied. "Don't disappoint me now, after all this time."

He walked away. Arak ceased to follow. He watched Marseh disappear around the curve in the hallway. Glowering behind his mask, the Butcher turned on his heel and stalked off.

***

Marseh retreated to the inner ring of the station to a byway devoid of traffic and public facilities. Near the station's off-limits fusion reactor, he kept his avatars. He placed his hand upon the wall, which receded and slid aside. Stepping through the trick door, it closed behind him. He walked the length of a short corridor that opened into a small bay.

Five front-loading tubes filled the space. Two held gestating versions of the adult bodies in stasis within two of the other tubes. The fifth tube was empty. Marseh ran his fingers over its controls and stepped inside. The container filled with fluid. He waited until the liquid filled his lungs, then retreated from the flesh. Without Marseh to animate it, the unconscious vessel twitched in reflex, then grew docile.

Unfettered by a physical form, Marseh projected himself elsewhere within the inner ring. He went to where only he and his most-trusted paladin, Asharan Lután, had access. The private bay housed a lush habitat brimming with greenery. To accommodate the inhabitants, the bay spun independently, generating gravity over 10 percent greater than Earth's.

Marseh revealed his shapeless self. He coalesced from vibrant particulate into an apparently solid form. He approached whom he came to see.

"Shaula," he said aloud.

She ceased to pick fruit and turned to face Marseh.

Sitting next to her, a soot-gray, tiger-sized cat with white jowls flicked its long tail. She scratched the large feline behind its ears, inciting a thunderous purr.

The woman had stunning, wide-set, sapphire-blue eyes. A hallmark of Waardenburg syndrome. Her sandy-brown hair coiled into tight, natural curls. Her rich, unblemished dark-brown skin made her eyes stand out even more. She stood shorter than most humans, with greater muscle mass and bigger, denser bones. Consequences of growing up in higher gravity. Physiologically human, her homeworld was hundreds of light years from Earth. It orbited the principal star of Lambda Scorpii. Long before the Blight, the Arabs called that star Shaula.

She looked at Marseh. A translation collar registered the vibrations of her vocal chords. While Marseh could read thoughts and implant replies, she didn't appreciate the intrusion and he humored her. He'd taken a shine to Shaula more so than to any of her kith. From that affinity, he devised a role for her in his machinations.

"Hello, Darek," she replied. The translation collar converted the clicks and vocalizations of her language, a distant descendant of Xhosa, into English.

"How are you feeling, dear child?" he asked, looking at her midsection.

She put her hand to her belly, atop the growing womb. "I feel pregnant." She smiled. "But it is not unpleasant. I do not feel limited." The translation collar wouldn't speak in contractions.

"I come to tell you that our plan has been executed."

Shaula's expression darkened. "So, he has been taken?"

"Yes, love. I am sorry to have robbed you of him, but I made him for this purpose. I never imagined that I would find you. Nor that you two would discover a mutual affection. I am glad for you both, of course. But he has a role that he must play . . . if anything is ever to change."

"I know that," she said, and not petulantly. She seemed resigned. She looked at Marseh with her bright blue eyes. "Do you think he will succeed?"

"I hope that he will."

"And will he survive?"

"I hope that he will."

Shaula twisted her mouth and shook her head. She looked away. Marseh was a god to her. Her last memories of home were of being implored to escape, being hustled into the sleeping pods. She recalled nothing thereafter. Why had she survived when, by Marseh's account, whatever had attacked her worlds had been so merciless? She could find no logical reason that a handful of beings should escape the slaughter of billions.

"I have a mission for you, my dear, should you choose to accept it," said Marseh.

She looked at him again, cocking her head to the side.

"I would like you and Lután to go to the surface. Determine if Commander Hastings has survived and recover her to me."

Shaula's eyes widened. She tried to manage her panic. "Why would she not have survived? What has happened?"

"Everything has gone according to plan," Marseh insisted. "There was no way to force them to the planet without crashing them there."

"They have crashed?" She couldn't reserve her panic anymore.

"Please, child, be calm."

"Where is Sargas, Darek? Is he dead?"

Marseh said nothing.

"Darek, tell me if he is dead."

"I don't know, Shaula."

Her eyes widened with dread.

"We won't know until we can make some kind of contact," said Marseh. "That is why you must ascertain Commander Hastings' whereabouts. I want you to know, first, whether Sargas lives. The tube in which I put him, to pass him off as freshly grown, it can withstand a lot. And, as you know, he is nigh indestructible. And you, albeit less so, having engaged in activity to pass his nanobots into your body . . .

"While I wish neither to lie to you nor to provide false hope, I expect that he survived. At least Ray or Daedalus should have devised how they could survive the crash. We chose our candidates well."

"Fine," Shaula said. "I will go. I want to know, for myself, where he is. And I want to go *now*."

"Soon, my dear. Soon," Marseh cooed. "But, first, we must prepare."

NINE

THE CENTURIONS GAVE a quick bow. Arak Matar caught them off guard at the speed with which he approached his quarters.

"Come with me." He pointed at Derovias.

As the doors to his quarters slid closed, Arak turned to the centurion. "Did you monitor the emperor's flight like I asked?"

"Yes, Lord."

"And?"

"The emperor incapacitated their vessel and left them to fall to Earth. They crash-landed on Nova Spes, to the west of Orchard City."

"So they are on the planet, either alive or dead." Arak stood quiet for a long moment. "Alive, I reckon. Assemble a party of five centurions, Derovias, excluding yourself; I want you here. Have them await me in my hangar. I'm going down there."

"Lord," Derovias began. The obeisance intended to soften what followed. "What of the emperor's orders—?"

Arak slammed his hand upon the table.

"To hell with the emperor's orders! Do not speak to me of him!" He paused. With a breath, he regained his composure. "But . . . be discreet. Go."

"Yes, Lord." Derovias bowed and hurried from the room.

Arak removed his helmet and placed it on the table. He ran his fingers through his long, braided black hair and stalked about. In the next room of his lavish quarters, three human women lay together on the enormous bed. A fireplace crackled, warm and inviting. The room belied the stark, fearsome persona he advertised as his public self. No one saw him there except his concubines.

They rose from the bed and approached him.

"Hello, lovelies," Arak said, trying to soften his gruff voice.

The women serviced him, and he chose to ejaculate into his favorite. She shuddered at the idea of becoming pregnant and losing her place, but there was no room for dissent.

"Leave me," he commanded.

They vanished through another door to the quarters they shared. Arak pulled up his breeches. He replaced his armor and waited for Derovias to return.

As he refastened his cape, he stared at the fireplace. He concentrated not on the jumping flames, but upon something between them and himself. Something invisible and ethereal that he could sense but not see. He closed his eyes and clenched his jaw, breathing out through his nose. His eyes shot open to the sound of the door chime. He left the bedroom to meet Derovias in the cold, forbidding antechamber.

He turned his back to the door. "Enter."

Derovias obeyed. His eyes fell upon the back of his master's head. The fearsome helm stared from the table.

"They are assembled, Lord."

"Excellent," Arak replied. "Have them await me there."

Derovias bowed and left.

A smile played across Arak's thin lips. He emitted a glottal chuckle.

"What finds you in such fine humor, N'horr?"

The voice came from everywhere at once. Unspoken, it had been implanted. It filled Arak's head. He ground his teeth and turned slowly until Reyevas came into view.

"I've warned you not to refer to me in that way."

Reyevas bowed in deference. "Forgive me, Lord. It's not as if your correns know what it means. Are not the original crop long dead, by now?"

"Regardless," Arak said. He dismissed the comment with a wave. "I wish not . . . to encourage their curiosity."

"Prudent as always, Sire," Reyevas conceded.

A form-fitting mask obscured his entire face, but for his blank, white eyes. A respirator covered his nose and mouth. Wires threaded through the skintight cap that covered his entire head. In the middle of his forehead, at the hub of all the wires, sat an orb that looked like a black opal streaked with white. Reyevas had never explained the jewel's purpose, and Arak never asked. He deduced it to be a talisman of wisdom or telepathy: a third eye.

"What do you want?" Arak asked. "I felt you spying on me, in my chambers. Do you enjoy watching me fuck? I don't appreciate the intrusion."

"I wouldn't expect modesty to be a concern of yours, Governor. My only yen is to wish you well on your journey to Earth."

Arak grunted his displeasure. He walked within a foot of Reyevas, who stood just shorter than the surly Butcher.

"Spare me. Why do you play these stupid games? You take me for a fool."

"Forgive me, Lord, but you misunderstand me," Reyevas protested. "I would never confuse you for a fool. Shall I go?"

"No, you shall not," Arak ordered. He grabbed Reyevas by the collar. The metallic armor that covered his entire body seemed somehow organic.

Though an apparition, Reyevas deceived Arak's senses. The Butcher perceived the incorporeal figure to be solid.

Arak snarled. "I want to know what possesses you to come and go as you please. Without heed of consequence. I want to know . . . your purpose."

"I serve only you, master," sniveled Reyevas. "I meant no intrusion, Lord. I apologize."

Arak unhanded him.

"You truly think . . . I'm so simple. So mad with ego that I couldn't conceive of anyone more powerful than I. Do you forget Marseh? Every day, I have constant reminder of my own . . . inferiority. You don't fear me. This act you put on . . . to prey upon my mania . . . is transparent. Pathetic."

"Then why do we dance, N'horr?" Reyevas asked, the supplication gone from his voice.

"Because it entertains you? I know . . . what you are, Alitán. You forget that Marseh once looked just like you. Are you his spy? Do you expect me not to be . . . *unnerved* . . . by your intrusions? Nor for me to be annoyed . . . by your obsequious bullshit? Only an idiot trusts a soothsayer."

"His spy," Reyevas laughed. "Oh, dearest N'horr, you couldn't be more mistaken. I expect only that you act exactly as you would. And I expect things to work out to our mutual benefit."

Arak curled his lip. He waved Reyevas away.

Reyevas disappeared in the same manner Marseh so often employed. Arak took full notice of the similarities. Particularly the men's ability to warp perceptions. He doubted that either could teleport without aid of technology. He supposed, though, they could become invisible through a trick of the mind. It enraged him that his could be so deceived.

He cast his misgivings from the forefront of his thoughts. Donning his helmet, he left his quarters.

The doors to his private hangar rolled open with a mechanical whine. Five centurions awaited. They bowed. He strode past them en route to his ship.

Kir approached. "Sire, I think that, perhaps, defying the emperor is not the best course—"

Arak glanced over his shoulder. "I don't recall asking, Kir, for advice."

Kir paused for a moment. He failed to relent. "Still, my Lord, I think it unwise to—*GRRK*!"

Arak lashed out. He grasped Kir by the neck with one hand, dragging him until they faced each other. The Butcher then lifted him from the floor.

"You disappoint me so much," said Arak. His voice was calm, without a hint of anger. He clenched his teeth from the effort of hoisting Kir's large, heavy body. As he tightened his grip on Kir's throat, an emotion close to sadness played across Arak's face. It remained hidden behind his mask.

Kir's legs swayed back and forth as he suffocated. He clutched at his master's arm.

Arak summoned his anger and lifted yet higher.

"Never speak to me of the emperor," he growled, "nor his wishes!"

He threw Kir to the floor. The centurion landed in a heap, gasping for air. He coughed bloody sputum.

Arak rounded on the others. They cast their eyes downward.

"Have any of you . . . suggestions for me?"

They said nothing. Their eyes remained averted.

"Pick him up," Arak ordered. "Restrain him belowdecks."

Alesh and Inishi retrieved Kir, who rubbed his throat with a feeble, shaking hand.

"That was unwise, brother," Alesh said, his tone just above a whisper. It was something between a taunt and an admonition.

Arak opened a comm channel within his helmet. "Derovias."

"Yes, Sire?"

"I require another, better centurion. Kir . . . has disappointed me."

"Of course, my Lord. Whom shall I send?"

"Yourself."

TEN

THE HULL OF the *Filomena* popped and hissed as it cooled. Smoke continued to belch aft.

Darkness flooded the ship's innards. Rain pelted the craft. Thunder echoed within the fuselage. The cocoon in the bridge liquefied and drained. Auxiliary power came on at barely a trickle. It was just enough to cast faint blue light from the cockpit terminals.

Daedalus shot up at the deafening crash of thunder. He coughed up stasis liquid in agonizing fits until his lungs were empty. Pain shot through his skull. He winced until it passed. He put his hand to his face. It came away sticky with remnants of the fluid that had saved his life. He examined his fingers in the pale light. The gel looked black against his alabaster skin.

He rubbed his fingers together and looked around. No one else had awakened. Viscous water puddled at his feet. A stream trickled into the cockpit from the deeper confines of the ship. At the sound of gurgling, Daedalus looked over to see Ray. He slumped over the tactical console, unconsciously vomiting. Blood mottled his forehead, but he had no visible wounds. Rozhenko and Ada began to convulse. A chorus of purging catatonics surrounded Daedalus.

It surprised him to have regained consciousness first. Ray's healing factor was far superior. Daedalus had countless scars. Ray had none. His ability to mend superficial wounds was freakish, even among correns.

Ada sat contorted in a difficult but not impossible position. Daedalus recalled twisting her into some challenging shapes back on Venus. He palpated her spine for evidence of trauma. Ascertaining her to be unbroken, he seated her more comfortably. He turned his attention to Rozhenko and was rougher with the big man. He sat him in an ideal position to spew.

Daedalus looked around, wondering what next to do. He placed his hand atop Ray's head. It was an affectionate, brotherly gesture. Suddenly self-conscious, he withdrew the loving touch.

Ray stirred like a stubborn child but didn't wake. The endless nightmare of Arak Matar held him fast.

The battered and misshapen interior hull bulged inward. Daedalus turned his dense, muscular body sideways. He shimmied into the common room, smelling and tasting iron. A small fire crackled along the starboard wall. He recognized the almost appetizing aroma of burnt flesh and the foul odor of burnt hair. Though adequate, his natural night-vision remained inferior to light-aided sight. He reached for the beacon on his shoulder and found it broken. He threw it to the floor in disgust.

Sliding his feet along the floor, he made for the emergency supplies. Despite his care, his foot caught something soft. He tripped, grunting as he fell. He put out his hands to break his fall and something sharp sliced open his left palm. He sucked in a breath and then cursed. The smell of burnt flesh gave way to nearer odors of feces and iron-rich human blood. Turning over, Daedalus groped about with his good hand for what had tripped him. He felt something putty-like and tepid. It groaned.

He snatched his hand away.

Rising to his feet, Daedalus continued to the emergency storage with newfound conviction. He popped open the compartment, where two blankets tossed about in the crash piled on the floor. He tore a strip from one and wrapped it around his injured hand. He fished a working beacon from a tangle of two spare jumpsuits.

The auxiliary systems whirred, diverting power. The deep hiss of the fire-suppression system followed. Glancing over his shoulder, Daedalus watched the thick white fog snuff out the flames. Oppressive darkness took over the room. He flicked on the powerful beacon. Sweeping the beam, it revealed the two long tables, one lodged in the ceiling and the other in the floor. The crash had rent the interior hull, strewing mechanical debris everywhere. It collected more toward the prow than the tail. The babbling stream ran its course to the cockpit.

Daedalus traced his light across the floor where he'd tripped. A human hand, limp at the wrist, protruded from a pile of wreckage. He moved the beam downward. The body ended at the waist. Its legs and hips were missing. The torso rested against the table stuck in the floor. With a quick extrapolation and flick of the wrist, Daedalus shined the beacon on the missing legs. They rested against the wall next to the cockpit entryway.

"Help me," Adams rasped, his voice muffled.

Daedalus swallowed hard and knelt down. He cleared the debris from atop the private's ashen, pain-twisted face.

"Help . . . please."

"Shhh," said Daedalus. He cleared the last of the ship innards from atop the dismembered man.

He straddled Adams and frowned. Putting his right hand around the private's throat, Daedalus squeezed. Adams tried to struggle. He took few a feeble swipes at the corren's arm, then went slack. Daedalus got to his feet. He dragged the corpse out of the way, screwing up his face at the smell of exposed and lacerated viscera. The dark stream running to the cockpit ran darker with blood and excrement.

Turning full circle, Daedalus checked for survivors. His light fell upon two charred, unrecognizable bodies. He forced his way up the incline, through the medical bay and toward the cargo hold. The control panel hung from the wall, spewing sparks. The doors stood ajar. Water trickled through.

Wedging his hands in the narrow gap, he pushed the doors apart. He winced at the pain in his left palm. Material from within the bay rolled through the opening, forcing him to jump out of the way. When the landslide subsided, he felt a hand on his shoulder. He spun around with his fist raised. The visor hid Patrick's face, but the slight frame and shoulder wound gave him away. He had stowed himself in one of the med bay crash pods.

Daedalus flipped up Patrick's visor.

"Please don't hit me," said the corporal.

"Shit," Daedalus replied, shaking his head. "I can't believe you're actually alive, cupcake. Good for you."

"Anybody else make it?"

Daedalus shook his head. "All the grunts bit it, except the tin man."

Patrick thought of his fellow noncoms. He felt nothing but a vague chagrin at their deaths. The forced and inauthentic sensation is what caused him real qualm.

Daedalus moved into the cargo bay.

The aft wall opened to the black sky. Rain poured in from outside.

Ray startled awake, eyes wide, pupils dilated. His heart raced, pounding against his chest. He gagged and spewed the last vestiges of fluid from his lungs.

Once he stopped retching, he put his hand against the crick in his neck and panned the bridge. He discovered Daedalus missing. Ada and Rozhenko sat unconscious with fluid dripping from their mouths.

Ray exhaled a heavy sigh. He escaped into the bowels of the ship. Ada revived, catching his exit in her periphery.

"Reggie!" Ray called from the common room.

"Cargo bay!" came the shouted reply. "You fucking asshole . . ." carried far more quietly behind.

Ray heard it loud and clear.

He made his way aft and pulled through the cargo bay doors. Ada followed. Together, they swept their lights across the room. At the center of the bay lay the tube. Empty. Its contents—Anjali, Sargas, and the liquid—voided.

Ray's pale golden face drained of what little color it had.

Daedalus swallowed the lump in his throat.

Ada felt Ray's rage pierce her skull like an awl. She winced against the pain and put her hand to her left eye. It doubly surprised her because she could not typically read corren emotions. First Daedalus, and now Ray. She wondered if her powers were growing. She hoped they weren't.

Ray growled. "Anjali!"

He scoured the room, throwing items aside. Crates and debris clanged against the walls of the hold as he tore the room apart. Daedalus turned his back to the rampage. He stood in front of Ada with his arms outstretched, shielding her from flying objects. Something heavy struck him in the back. He frowned but he held his ground.

A loud, long, metallic creak split their ears, but Ray was oblivious in his fury. The ship lurched, throwing Ada forward. Daedalus stumbled backward as the *Filomena* fell from her precarious slant and landed flat. The impact threw Ada into Daedalus' waiting arms and he gently pushed her away. She couldn't believe that he and Ray had remained standing.

Through all of it, Ray never paused. He crashed through every obstacle like a juggernaut until, suddenly, he stopped.

"Anjali!" he exclaimed in elated satisfaction.

He spied her near the breach in the hull. She sat with her knees to her bare chest, decked from the waist down in her tattered bodysuit. But then Ray saw the pair of bare male arms encircling her abdomen. The naked male legs sticking out to either side of her. Anjali's unconscious head lolled against Sargas' shoulder. Their closeness stoked Ray's ire.

He seethed. His shoulders bunched. His arms hung away from his sides, tense and bent at the elbows. His adrenaline spurred his fingernails to grow into talons, and the bones protruding from his face became more prominent.

His limbic system prepped for battle.

He growled. It grew into a bellow. A wordless, animal wail.

Sargas rose to his feet, naked as a newborn.

Ray reached for Anjali's slumping form, hoping to snatch her away. Sargas grabbed the corren's wrist and, aided by the momentum, threw him from the ship. Ray scrambled to his feet, covered from head to toe in gray slop. He clambered back into the ship. Sargas betrayed no misgivings about his nudity, gave no sign of fear. He awaited the impending second challenge.

Ray swung at Sargas' head. The tall, brawny man deflected the blow as if the corren moved at half speed. Ray jabbed his talons at Sargas' exposed abdomen but was again thwarted by quick reflexes and uncanny strength.

"I'll rip your fucking dick off," Ray snarled.

Sargas grabbed Ray by the wrists. He pushed him backward, step by step. Ray clenched his teeth as he resisted but couldn't overpower the man from Overground. It took everything the corren had to avoid a second expulsion.

"Stop!" Ada yelled.

"Stay out of this!" Ray hollered.

Daedalus grabbed Ada's arm and pulled her away. "What are you gonna do? Talk 'em out of it? It's gonna take force, Ada. Force you don't have."

"Oh, fuck you," she replied, shaking off his grip. Despite his gracelessness, she couldn't argue.

Rozhenko made his way into the cargo bay, pausing just within the doors.

"Oh, hey!" he whispered, upon noticing Patrick.

"Sarge," winced the corporal.

Daedalus tried to impose himself between the combatants.

"Don't meddle where you don't belong," Ray warned.

Daedalus shook his head and chuckled. He stepped back. Ray returned his full attention to Sargas. Daedalus punched Ray in the face. Sargas let go at the same moment. Ray tumbled sideways, falling to the floor. He tried to rise to his feet, but Daedalus kicked him in the head, laying him on his back. Sargas watched, stoic. Daedalus straddled Ray and threw a left, then a right. He delivered blow after blow, switching to his elbows after his knuckles split apart.

"You gonna stop?" he blared.

Ray put up his hands in surrender. He clutched in vain at Daedalus' left arm and grasped for purchase.

Ray spat blood. "God damn you." Green gore covered his face from scalp to chin.

"Give it a fucking rest and get your head about you," Daedalus demanded. He stood. "Absent fucking Mother, Raymond. You lovesick psycho. She's *fine*."

"You goddamned bastard," said Ray between ragged breaths.

"Don't make me beat you to death," Daedalus warned. "Leave it the fuck alone."

Ray's red eyes glowed with anger. "Why the fuck . . . do you even care . . . about this *shit*?"

Daedalus shrugged.

"'Take this bullshit mission or be executed,' they said." He ran his raw, rent, bloody hand through his hair. "Live another day or die now. Those were my options. And you know what? I thought about running anyway. Because *fuck* the Allied military—"

"You watch your mouth!" Rozhenko objected, aghast.

Daedalus looked at the cyborg and spat on the floor.

"But I *wanted* to raid Overground," Daedalus said, turning back to Ray. "I thought it would be an adventure . . . even though it stunk of rot. And it's been *quite* the adventure."

Ray sneered with malevolent contempt. "So, then. What now, *boss*?"

Daedalus jabbed his thumb at Sargas. "We're gonna get his bare ass to the nearest brass. What else is there to do?"

"This is cargo?" Rozhenko asked.

Daedalus drew breath for a salty reply, but Sargas preempted him.

"Cargo. Hardly."

"You talk!" Rozhenko exclaimed.

"More than can be said for you," Sargas retorted.

Rozhenko muttered in Russian. He side-eyed the naked man's exposed genitalia.

Daedalus looked over his shoulder at Ada. She didn't bother with the side eye. Her expression confirmed sheer admiration.

"Don't ogle the thing, girl," Daedalus chided. "It's barely bigger than mine and he's, like, half a foot taller."

She blushed and glared at him.

"Um, guys . . ." said Rozhenko.

They returned their attention to Sargas, who smiled at them. It unnerved Rozhenko, but Daedalus smiled back in his own weird way. He extended his hand. Sargas looked at it for a moment, deciding what to do. To them, it looked as if he didn't understand the gesture. But then he grasped Daedalus' mitt and shook it quite naturally.

"This is awkward," Daedalus said. "But, then, what about this has been normal? You got a name?"

"We should escape this ship," Sargas replied. He walked toward the prow. He trod the metal debris with his bare feet as if it were feathers.

"That's not a name," Daedalus replied to his back. "But fuck it. Who needs manners? I'll just call you 'Asshole.' Cool?"

"Hey, where . . ." Rozhenko demanded of Sargas. "Where the hell do you go?"

Sargas didn't reply.

Daedalus, Ada, and Rozhenko followed him into the common room.

Ray got up. He rubbed his hand down his battered face and emphatically flicked his blood onto the floor. Sifting through the junk, he found Anjali's boots. He remembered the spare jumpsuits in the supply closet and went to retrieve one. He left her in the cargo bay, alone and unconscious.

"Hey! Asshole!" Daedalus called out, stumbling through the debris. He withdrew the bigger of the spare jumpsuits from the closet. He handed it to Sargas. "It's only got two legs, but try stuffing your dick into that."

Sargas remained taciturn. He stepped into the garment as if getting dressed were second nature. The black and red Confederation jumpsuit was a tight fit, despite its ability to stretch within a few inches to suit the form of its wearer. The garb's extremities ended just below Sargas' elbows and at the middle of his shins. Though too small for a permanent solution, it sufficed.

Daedalus chuckled. "You look ridiculous. Asshole."

"So, there are clothes but are no boots in this closet?" asked Rozhenko.

"I didn't see any boots," Daedalus replied, "and, seriously, you think they'd fit this prick? He's almost as big as you." He looked at Rozhenko's mechanical legs, poking out from his jumpsuit, bootless.

Ray came into the common room. "We need to get out of here. It's not smart to stand around in a Confederation ship, in Confederate uniforms . . ."

"Unless, of course, we're in the heart of Confederation territory," Daedalus retorted.

"I don't think we are," Ray answered, morose and monotone. "And they'd out us as frauds, anyway. The two defectors and a party of humans? We need to leave."

"We're on Nova Spes," said Daedalus. "I can tell you that much. The autopilot brought us here."

Ray's face healed before their eyes.

"Wherever we are," he said, "we need to get as far away from this wreck as possible. Get outside and get our bearings. If we're in Allied territory, we're lucky, but we still need to avoid getting shot on sight in these uniforms."

He snatched up a blanket and the other jumpsuit from the floor. He stalked back into the cargo bay. It surprised him to see how much Anjali's back had already healed. As he dressed her, he wondered what kind of magic was in the stasis fluid.

"I'm sorry, baby," he said quietly, kissing her forehead.

He put her helmet on her head, wrapped her in the blanket, and picked her up.

The group climbed out of the ship onto the muddy ground. The rain had stopped, but the soft earth hindered their gaits. A rotted and dilapidated barn greeted them as they congregated under the dark night sky. Its roof drooped into the shape of an impish grin.

"I hate it here," Patrick sighed.

"Who doesn't?" Daedalus replied.

"I was so excited to be posted to Venus," Patrick lamented. "My wife was applying for a civilian gig."

"I hate to break it to you," Daedalus replied, "but I doubt it. Your wife's probably been warming some other man's bed since the night you left."

Shock played across Patrick's face. It melted in momentary despair before snapping back with angry vigor.

Ada jumped in before he could speak.

"You are the biggest asshole I've ever met," she said to Daedalus.

Daedalus jerked his thumb over his shoulder at Sargas. "No, honey. He's the biggest asshole you've ever met. Look at the size of him."

Patrick took off his helmet and threw it to the ground. He growled in anger.

Daedalus smirked. "I know, sweetheart. I'd be mad, too, if my wife was fucking around. But, then, I'd never be stupid enough to get married."

"What the fuck is your problem?" Patrick howled.

"Did you hurt your pussy in the crash, Corporal?" Daedalus goaded.

"Enough!" Ray bellowed. "We don't have time for this shit!"

Daedalus winked at Patrick, who sputtered in impotent frustration. He was on the verge of tears. Ada picked up his helmet and handed it to him.

"You need to develop a thicker skin," she said in hushed tones.

"How can you just excuse that?"

"I'm not excusing it," she replied, "but not everyone is gonna be nice to you. Especially not him."

"He reminds me of my sergeant in Basic. That fucking prick. I hated Basic. Motherfucker broke us down. Said every nasty thing he could think of . . . but I took it. I thought, when I got through, when I was a real soldier, that shit would stop."

"You should have gone to the Academy," she replied. "You're too smart to be a grunt."

Patrick frowned at her, incredulous at her assumption that he could have taken a different course.

"I'm nobody, Lieutenant. I'm a 'fugee. Grew up in a camp. No sponsor. I took the only route there is for people like me."

"And that's admirable," she replied. "But you have to know that most men in the service, even the officers, are like him," she nodded toward Daedalus. "Childish. Stunted. Insecure . . . cruel."

She rapped her knuckles against Patrick's breastplate.

"You need to be armored, Gehsan."

It touched him that she remembered his name. He had forgotten hers right after Ray called roll on Venus.

"Consider the source," Ada continued. "When someone like him insults you . . . it isn't about you. It's about him. He has the problem. Not you."

Patrick looked down at his muddy helmet.

"Thanks," he muttered.

A thought dawned on Rozhenko.

"Hey," he said to no one specific, "what if Reds are sending to investigate crash?"

"No one's sending anything," said Daedalus. "Do you know how much shit falls out of the sky each day? It's a fucking junkyard up there."

With Anjali cradled in his arms, Ray checked the horizon for signs of settlement. In the distance, he spied some low-rises and a mammoth CO_2 scrubbing tower. Dried blood mottled his face. He tensed as Daedalus approached. A tic of rage spasmed his mouth and cheek. He looked at Daedalus, who said nothing.

Daedalus cocked his head to the left and blinked once. Slowly. Deliberately.

Ray sneered and turned away.

"Hey!" he shouted to the group.

He gently hoisted Anjali onto his shoulder. She didn't wake.

"Shape up and move out! We got a hike ahead of us."

ELEVEN

CARINA HAZARDED A glance over her shoulder and massaged her short, curly, rust-red hair. She sighed. The door to her quarters opened automatically. It slid closed behind her.

A small, downcast lamp provided the only light. She threw herself into her chair, then hopped right back up, making a face. Reaching into her back pocket, she withdrew her flask. She shook it. A high-pitched slosh replied, and she threw the vessel at her dresser. It landed with a hollow, tinny thunk and skittered across the surface.

Pulling off her boots, she kicked one of them across the room. She peeled off her socks and massaged her feet, picking the lint from between her toes. Sliding down in the chair, she stared at her dark ceiling and sighed again.

"Fuck this planet and all its horny boys."

She unbuckled her gun belt and disrobed to her undergarments. In the bathroom, she traced the crude scars on her abdomen with the fingers of her left hand. She washed her hands and face and stared at her reproachful reflection. It was obvious why Andersen and Sotillo and countless other men lusted after her. But it did nothing to soothe her ire. She didn't care that others found her beautiful. A stream of pejorative thoughts hounded her. A constant, bullying interior voice nagged at her in her native French. It followed her back into her room.

You're just a pretty shell around a horrible person, Karin.

Scowling, she pulled on her olive-colored leather breeches and her black boots. Rare and durable, her cowhide clothes were some of her most treasured possessions. She refilled and screwed closed the flask, slipped it into her pocket, and grabbed another gun belt, buckling it around her waist. Her antique but lovingly maintained .44-caliber Mateba revolver hung against her left thigh. She drew the gun and checked the cylinder.

She put on her shoulder holster and slid her blaster into the soft leather pocket under her right armpit, affixed her Bowie knife and two six-round speed loaders to her belt, then donned her black leather jacket. Grabbing two handfuls of loose bullets, she dumped the currency into her jacket pockets. She withdrew a few pieces of metal from the satchel Manon had given her.

For a rainy day, she thought.

The nagging, bullying part had a retort, as always. *You're taking food from the mouths of your fellows, Karin. Selfish salope.*

"How about you shut the fuck up?" Carina said aloud.

Unhooking her respirator from its place near the door, she carried it into the hallway. The bright light hurt her eyes. She squinted and winced and headed toward the lift. It hurried her to the surface. Her boots echoed across the dark, quiet lobby of the old building. Before the Blight, it had been headquarters of the Dorance Corporation. As she walked toward the doors, she tracked her reflection in the surprisingly intact, well-kept, polished granite floor.

At the exit, towering armed sentries in hunter-green armor stood guard. A dark blue quill topped their Romanesque helmets.

"Halt, Captain," said one of the sentries. Its voice was hollow, lifeless, metallic.

Carina stopped. She shivered to think that the dead men's programming denied them any autonomy.

"You carry ten kilograms of contraband."

"Check your orders," she replied. She hoped Van Sinderen had entered her departure into the general orders. The sentries would not let her leave without confirmation. "I'm authorized to take this scrap off base by Colonel Van Sinderen."

The sentry said nothing. It parsed the orders queried from the wireless network. "Confirmed. You may proceed."

The two giants stepped out of her way. The front door read her chip and opened for her. She slid her respirator over her nose and mouth.

Carina never wore her military colors in public. The citizenry hated the Allied occupiers. Earth remained a soldier's most-dreaded assignment and every resident's living nightmare. But it was better to serve than to be a civilian. She enjoyed warm showers, nonhuman meat, and climate-controlled shelter, among many things civilians might never know. Her commission in fact lowered her likelihood of violent death, but dying mattered very little to her.

If anyone deserves to die, it's you, Karin. Who leaves their little sister to drown?

"*If I'd saved Michèle, Agnès would have drowned instead!*" Carina exclaimed.

She tucked her head between her shoulders in embarrassment. While unintelligible to most, speaking to herself in French didn't look any less crazy. She looked around, but the street was empty.

"*What the fuck was I supposed to do?*" she added quietly.

Better. You should have done better.

Her mouth twisted in grief. Her eyes watered but she refused to cry. *It's bad enough I'm talking to myself,* she thought. *I am fully nuts.*

No, said the nagging, tormenting part of her, *you're not crazy. You don't get off that easy. You need to answer for what you did.*

"*I did my best!*"

Your best? Pathetic. Why do you *get to walk around while Michèle's bones litter the ocean floor? Why do* you *get to live?*

Carina closed her eyes and composed herself. She had grown so weary of the constant internal fight. She had chosen death in Marseilles. She should have died.

Would have been better if you had.

She bristled at Earth's drab palette. It felt like shades of gray were the only colors she'd ever known. Drawing her flask from her pocket, she pulled down her respirator and took a long draw. She put away the container but left her respirator hanging. Graffiti blared dejected messages of hopelessness and rage from every surface. On the broken concrete in front of her, painted in red, it read: "The End Is Here."

"Cute," she remarked, flipping up her collar.

She continued down the street on high alert. Her fierce eyes fixed upon the sign hanging from a three-story building with a brickwork façade. The old, wooden advertisement swung from two rusted chains. They creaked in the gentle breeze. The faded blue paint was peeled and cracked, but the name was clear: "The Pendragon."

The door creaked on its big hinges. Its dust catcher swooshed against the marble threshold. The pub was a foreign world of laughter and merriment, with familiar dashes of violence and depravity. Only its two ersatz antique doors barred the crueler outside world. She pulled her respirator from her face and sauntered to the lone vacant stool.

"Be still, my beating heart," said Seamus, the bartender and proprietor. "Carina Duvais. Beautiful as ever."

"Save your charms for a lady," Carina replied, loud enough to be heard over the din. She gave him a close approximation of a smile.

"May the lady one day recognize her own confusion," Seamus said, winking.

"Doubtful," she retorted.

"So, what can I get my most comely customer?"

She rolled her eyes at him. Seamus offered a cigarette. She waved it away. He shrugged, put one to his lips, and lit it.

"You know what I want," she said. He grabbed a bottle of whisky from the wall and poured it, neat, into a glass.

His eyes lingered on her for a moment before he walked away to tend to other customers, all of them men. Aside from the prostitutes, Carina was the only woman present. Manon was likely the sole other unowned female to ever visit the bar.

Carina twisted her mouth. She drank.

When Seamus came back, her glass was empty but for one sip.

"You're almost all right," she offered.

Her face danced through a range of awkward expressions. She felt a hot rush of blood to her cheeks and looked ruefully at the amber liquid.

"I should finish this."

"If you don't want it, just leave," Seamus replied. "That one sip isn't holding you prisoner."

She scoffed. "Nous sommes tous les prisonniers."

"What's that?" he asked, annoyed. "Something about prisoners? Speak English, Carina, will you? And speak for yourself."

She shot him a dead-eye stare. "Of course, no . . . not you, Seamus. I forgot. *You're* no prisoner. You," she pointed, glass in hand, "are a jailer."

She drained the last sip.

"You done?" he asked.

"Non." She tapped the bar with her index and middle fingers. "Un autre, s'il te plaît."

He refilled her glass. "That, I understand."

She drank and shrugged. "Look, I'm tired of eating shit. I need a steak. Vegetables. Fruit. Food. Actual food."

"And I should provide these things because you're so nice to me?"

She shook her head and then gently shook herself. The metal in her bag jingled. A bar patron glanced over his shoulder at her. She snarled at him. He turned away. She lifted her eyebrows at Seamus.

"How much did you bring?" he asked.

"Ten kilos." As the sentry had informed her.

"In that case, follow me," he said.

They walked, with the bar between them, toward the back. A large, dark-skinned man guarded a closed door. Seamus smiled and nodded. His guard stood aside and opened the heavy wooden portal. Inside the private room, a seasoned, elderly man with a kind face awaited orders. His mustache matched his salt-and-pepper hair.

"Hasim, put on a steak for Lieutenant Duvais. Give her the full complement of vegetables, too, and a starch of some kind. And, please, a bowl of fruit."

"Rare, please, Hasim," she requested in Arabic.

She and Seamus sat down at a large, heavy wooden table. Hasim hurried into the kitchen.

"Hasim makes a mean steak. I'd love it to be fresh, but it's tough to get a live cow. I can get my hands on one, maybe two slaughters a year and I have to freeze the meat. You kinda have to take what you can get."

"Seamus . . . they feed me literal shit at the base. Sterilized, processed, high-protein fecal matter 'steak.' I don't care if the poor cow was killed and frozen a century ago, I'm tired of eating recycled excrement and drinking purified piss."

"You're still better off than most everyone else," he replied. "Most people out there, with no steel or lead, don't even have recycled shit to eat. You can't eat it hot from somebody's ass. Look on the bright side."

"You seem to be doing just fine."

"Are you suggesting I eat shit out of people's assholes?"

"Don't you?"

Hasim emerged from the kitchen. He placed a bowl of fruit on the table and returned to tend to Carina's meal. She grabbed an apple and took a big bite.

"Tell me why you brought me twenty-two pounds of steel. For you, steak is an ounce for an ounce. How much meat can you eat?"

She glared at him.

"That's not a euphemism," he insisted.

She gave him a leery appraisal. "Right . . . I'm grocery shopping. I need about eight kilos of meat, and as many fruits and vegetables as the rest will cover."

Seamus nodded. "It's not going to be much in the way of fruits and vegetables. You should have brought more steel, Carina."

She frowned at him for making her feel guilty.

He shrugged, unaware of the subtext. "I'll have Hasim make up a care package." He went into the kitchen.

Carina tucked into her steak and savored the taste of blood on her tongue. The beef was hot, buttery, and juicy. She imagined eating like this every day and it made her angry that she couldn't. The whole meal and her drinks would cost her, albeit at a discounted rate. Despite that she gave Seamus a hard time, he still favored her. She would throw in some bullets to cover the difference, but the more she enjoyed, she could bring even less back to base for the others.

She shrugged. A small amount of guilt still nagged at her, but not enough to go without the treat. Mercifully, her bully saw fit to stay mum. Perhaps she, too, was enjoying herself. As good as it all was, the water was especially delicious. Carina smiled.

Seamus set down a bottle of Scotch. "Have as much as you want. It's on me. I'll be at the bar." He closed the door behind him before she could even say "thank you."

She finished her meal alone, downing four fingers of whisky in the process. For dessert, she alternated between the apple and a pear.

Hasim brought what Seamus had demanded. Withdrawing the steel from Carina's pack, he replaced it with the wrapped, frozen meat. Another pack held the fruit and vegetables. He hefted each individual piece of metal. Looking at her, he shook his head.

"*How much more?*" she asked in Arabic.

"*At least twelve bullets,*" he replied, his eastern Saharan dialect different from her Algerian.

Carina fished in her pocket for loose ammunition and pulled out a handful of mixed-caliber rounds. She put them in his hand. She fished out a few more and deposited them, too, in his cupped palms.

"Voilà. Est-ce suffisant?" she lapsed back into French.

"*Yes, it's enough,*" came the Arabic reply.

"Shukraan, Hasim."

"*You are most welcome, Miss Carina,*" he said in Arabic.

She grabbed the provisions and the bottle and went back out to the bar. Seamus stood behind it, drying a glass.

"You look . . . drunk," he said. "How long until you're back on duty?"

"I don't feel drunk. I got long enough."

A shrill scream pierced the din.

"Shit," Seamus said. He put down the empty glass.

Carina poured some Scotch into it as he stepped out from behind the bar. He was shorter than her but taller than most. Thin, but taut and muscular, he had no trouble parting the morass to deal with one of his prostitutes and a troublesome john.

You should stop, she thought to herself as she drank.

Atop the stool, back to the bar, she ignored the other patrons while she watched Seamus at work. She had thought she wanted to tune it out, that she didn't want to overhear, but she had to know what people could do. What they *would* do. She didn't catch it all, but she refused to blind herself to reality.

To best know how to deal with Seamus, she needed to know him. The real him.

He returned to his place behind the bar. "That went well."

Carina's lip curled. "So glad for you."

TWELVE

RAY LED HIS party across the muddy earth.

Rozhenko took the left flank and Daedalus the right. Anjali slept in Ray's arms, wrapped snugly in the blanket. Ada and Patrick brought up the rear, just behind and to either side of Sargas, still unaware of his name. Mud caked his bare feet. It kicked up onto the legs of the ill-fitting bodysuit. He towered over everyone but Rozhenko. In the proximity of the two giant men, both Ada and Patrick looked minuscule.

Within the first half hour of their trek, they reached a highway and followed beneath it. The standing remnants of the big road loomed above them. Whole sections had fallen to the ground in disrepair.

Ada looked at Patrick. "Are you okay?"

A gentle breeze blew over them. It barely moved the wet, mud-caked portion of her long, light-brown hair that stuck out the back of her helmet. Patrick's wounded left arm hung at his side.

"I'm brilliant. Got a barmy arm, thinking about my wife fucking around. Aces."

Ada frowned at him.

He caught her expression out of the corner of his eye. He sighed.

"What do you think, Lieu? It hurts like hell. As soon as we get to a med bay—" He made a chopping motion. "If we get to a med bay."

In the diffuse light he could see her freckles.

"Look," she replied, "it's superficial. You're not gonna lose it."

Patrick held her gaze. His deep-set brown eyes hid beneath his brows.

"That's nice of you to say, but don't bullshit me. Sir." He couldn't remember her name. He sighed. "I don't even know your name."

"It's Ada. Ada Bennett."

"I'm sorry I forgot," he replied. "I know we've already met, but it's a pleasure."

She offered him an anemic smile. He half-smiled back.

"This guy could use a real name," he said, jerking his thumb at Sargas.

"Yeah, but what?" Ada said.

Without any communication, the three of them slowed, acting in subconscious concert. Rozhenko and Daedalus noticed the change and slowed their own gaits.

Ray, sensing the distance without seeing it, glanced over his shoulder. "Keep moving, people; we need to make good time."

Ada and Patrick picked up the pace and Sargas followed. He knew they would need a moniker for him. He wouldn't abide "Asshole" or "cargo" or "the organism" for much longer, but he couldn't very well tell them he had a name. He couldn't disturb the illusion that he'd been born only hours ago.

"I would like a real name," he stated.

"Oh, so you don't like being anonymous?" Patrick asked. "When Lieutenant Giant Prick asked you your name, you had nothing to say. But you can walk and talk like any full-grown bloke. You've got to have a name."

"Yes," Sargas replied, "you've indicated that one must have a name."

"And you care what we think," Patrick said, nearly laughing.

"What do you want to be called?" Ada asked.

Sargas tilted his head to the side and regarded her thoughtfully.

"You know any names?" Patrick asked. "You know a lot of other things."

The organism took the opportunity to introduce his own moniker.

"How is 'Sargas'?"

Patrick laughed sharply. "'Sargas'? Are you kidding? What the hell is that?"

Sargas made a disappointed face. "It is a binary star . . . in the constellation Scorpius. You think it's a bad name."

"Oh, no, mate. It's a fine name," Patrick chuckled. "But you sure you don't wanna tack 'the Magnificent' on the end there?"

"You mock me."

"Maybe there's a better name for you than 'Sargas,'" Ada intervened. "How about we think about it for a little while? There's no need to settle for just anything. But we'll call you Sargas for now, okay?"

"Sargas . . ." Patrick said, wiping his eye with his dirty hand. He winced as the filth burned his sclera.

"You pick up pace," Rozhenko ordered. "And be bringing *it* with you."

"I am not an it."

"Sarge," said Patrick, "meet Sargas."

"What the f—uck?" Rozhenko held the "f," drawing it out. "'Sargas'?"

"He's kidding," Ada said. "I mean, we're just calling him Sargas for now."

"Sargas . . ." Rozhenko said, shaking his head.

"Why so forthcoming now, Starman?" Daedalus pressed. "Huh, Scorpy?"

"I am neither your subject nor subordinate," Sargas replied.

"So, what exactly are you trying to say?" Daedalus replied, stepping toward the man.

"Stop. Everyone," Ray said, not raising his voice. All heard the threat in his even tone. "Just stop." He turned to Daedalus. "Don't antagonize the thing."

Ray then addressed Sargas.

"And whether you like it or not, you are *my* subordinate. I know why you were made; for what purpose." He subtly tilted his head toward Anjali.

Sargas narrowed his eyes.

"And," Ray continued, "while this all might be a rude awakening for you, this is how it is. Just give me one thing. Comport yourself like a soldier."

They stared at each other for a long moment. Sargas nodded.

Ray resumed walking. He was strong, and Anjali was light, but carrying her became more of a chore the farther they went. He returned her to his shoulder to give his arms a break.

"All of us should be acting more like soldiers and less like children," he said. "We crashed. Men died. But our mission doesn't end until we deliver him."

The troop fell in with expressions ranging from chastened to relieved to solemn. Daedalus, however, just looked annoyed. The first signs of settlement appeared around them. They walked below the highway, hoping to avoid attention. Daedalus climbed the embankment, trying to remain out of view. He assessed the scene and scuttled back down the slope.

Water dripped from above. It splashed in dirty pools below.

Patrick smacked his lips. "I don't mean to complain, sir, but I'm thirsty."

"Yeah, I second that," said Ada.

"We don't have any water," Ray said, setting down Anjali.

Ada and Patrick sat, dejected, at the base of the embankment. They licked their lips, desperate for moisture.

"I can barely breathe," huffed Patrick.

"Try to relax," Ray replied. "The low oxygen is wearing you down."

"Gah, don't these helmets have filters?" asked Ada.

Daedalus shook his head. "Aside from mine and his," he indicated Ray, "the rest are knockoffs. We already had the visor tech and the comms, but the brass didn't give me time to reverse engineer the better, smaller respirator."

Patrick screwed up his face, as he thought hard for a moment. "Wait a minute. You mean . . . we all would have died if the hull had breached? We went out in the field without functional suits?"

"Stop whining," said Daedalus. "Do you know how cold space is? You wouldn't have survived a hull breach very long, even with a functioning respirator. Not after the atmosphere escaped the ship. Your suit isn't even insulated. You'd freeze to death before you'd suffocate."

"Are you fucking kidding me?" Patrick blurted.

Ada put her hand on his leg to calm him, but the others ignored his outburst.

Patrick continued his harangue to his audience of one. "It tastes like somebody took a shit in my mouth."

"That's just gross," she replied.

Ray tapped Daedalus' shoulder and beckoned him away from the group.

"What's up?" asked Daedalus.

"I want your tactical opinion."

"We've got three and a half humans, 'Sargas,' and how far to go?" Daedalus asked.

"Roz at least has mechanical backups," said Ray. "I'm not even sure he has lungs. He seems unfazed by the weak air."

"But cupcake and cream puff? They're weak, Raymond. You're carrying your girl and I can see you're tired. How far will we have to carry those two?"

"They'll make it through. The surface is survivable; millions of humans live without respirators."

"But how useful will they be if we get ambushed or attacked? That's my point. They're dead weight." Daedalus spat on the ground.

"We're not leaving anyone behind," Ray answered.

"What's the point of serving in a military full of weaklings? All they do is put us at greater risk."

Ray said nothing. He looked at Sargas, who stood alone. Sargas shifted his gaze from the humans to the correns and back again.

"What do you make of him?" Daedalus asked, jerking his head at Sargas. "*Do* you know what his purpose is?"

"I don't know shit," Ray admitted. "But I think he's more than we bargained for. A soldier organism should barely be intelligent. It defeats the purpose, giving them more than a basic understanding of directive. None of the genetically engineered organisms I've ever faced had any brains," he said. "He's too smart."

Daedalus nodded. "Yeah. I get that, too."

"And you know what else bugs me?" Ray added. "Shouldn't he be giving us a lot more resistance?"

"Like . . . ?"

"Like, he knows we're not Confederates. He must know everything that's happened isn't what he was programmed to expect upon waking. So . . . why be so compliant?"

"You think it's a trap."

"You said it was too easy. That we should be dead. We fell out of the fucking sky, Reggie—"

Daedalus flared his nostrils.

"Through the atmosphere." Ray ignored the warning look. "We crashed into the ground . . . and most of us survived? Explain that to me."

"Maybe there *is* a god and maybe he loves us," Daedalus said. He rolled his eyes.

"Yeah, right. Maybe his name is Marseh."

"Oh, come on," said Daedalus. "You think the emperor can thwart gravity? That he's made of magic? Manipulator of life and death? Now, I want to kill something just to prove I can."

He glanced over his shoulder at Sargas. Their eyes met and held. Daedalus' brilliant red- and amber-flecked eyes considered the big man. Sargas' gray eyes were similarly calculating.

"Bastard gives me a bad feeling," Daedalus said. "You know, the one that makes me violent."

"Like you've any other inclination," Ray said. He rubbed his jaw.

The cuts inflicted by Daedalus' fists had already healed. His hands still bore the wounds inflicted by Ray's face, though they were mending.

"Just rein it in," said Ray. "He's not ours to fuck with. The brass want him."

"Chain of command," Daedalus spat.

"Yeah, chain of command." Ray shook his head. "Show a little less disdain and you might make captain again."

"And what about you, eh? You *ever* gonna make full commander?"

"Be careful."

Daedalus scoffed. "Fuck off, Raymond. That stick up your ass is so insufferable sometimes. All I'm saying is you've got the same contempt when it suits you. They treat us like shit, remember? Always have. When we defected, they locked each of us up for over a year. You think I liked being called 'Reggie' by those fuckwits? Or by you?"

"I don't want to reminisce about bad times," said Ray.

Daedalus rolled his eyes again. He turned to walk away.

Ray grabbed him. "I need to know I can count on you."

Daedalus looked with disgust at Ray's hand until he relinquished his grip.

"Don't worry about me," Daedalus replied. "Just keep your own head. I wouldn't have to beat you down if you didn't lose your mind."

They rejoined the rest of their party. Rozhenko opened his mouth but Ray shot a look that silenced him.

"We need to keep moving," Ray ordered. "If we're gonna bed down, it's not gonna be here."

He picked up Anjali's swaddled body. She nestled into him.

"We need drinkable water," Ray declared.

"So you *are* thirsty," said Patrick.

"No," Ray frowned. "For you."

"How *aren't* you thirsty?" Patrick asked, exasperated and incredulous.

"We don't get thirsty," Daedalus replied.

"But *how*?" Patrick pressed.

"There's moisture in the fucking air!" Daedalus snapped.

Patrick, cowed, shut his mouth.

They waded into Holst's Hollow. The highway diverted northward and they left its cover. Ramshackle, decrepit buildings littered the sidewalks. Broken windows peered at the streets. The ominous silence pulled tighter the group's already taut nerves. Ray and Daedalus slowly approached the corner and peered around it.

Someone flitted across the thoroughfare. Ray's ears twitched as he strained to listen. Though barely audible even with his exceptional hearing, he recognized the patter of many pairs of feet. Shadowy forms zipped into a building down the road.

A blue flash lit up the darkness. A fleeting dawn of weapons' fire. The azure blasts glimmered on the metal frames and reflected in the broken glass. Loud pops of old-fashioned bullets joined the unmistakable whine and blue tint of Confederate weapons' fire.

"What the hell is going on?" Ada demanded.

"Shootout," answered Daedalus. He smiled with unabashed joy.

"We can't be caught in the middle of this," said Ray.

"So, what do we do?" Rozhenko replied.

"There's a building across the way. It's some kind of rally point. If the humans are using it to escape the Reds, that's where we want to be."

"They've got projectile weapons!" Patrick warned. "We'll be shot on sight!" He rapped his knuckles against his breastplate. "This shit's no match for bullets! It's fucking useless against energy weapons!"

"Corporal, hold your shit," Daedalus ordered.

"We either move," said Ray, "or we wind up under a Red boot. They take us prisoner or execute us, and our mission fails. That's unacceptable. This is our only shot. We're going."

Another volley of blue light—brighter, closer—lit up the street. The pops of projectile fire lacked the volume and frequency of the energy salvos.

"The Confederates are winning," said Sargas.

"We have to move, now!" Ray demanded. "Rozhenko! Round that corner and lay down some cover!"

The cyborg grasped his plasma cannon. He marched into the intersection, his already brutal face yet more grim. He fired from the instant he cleared the corner. Ray pushed Daedalus toward the rally point, then shoved Ada and Patrick to follow. They raced behind Rozhenko with Sargas close behind. Ray hefted Anjali and brought up the rear. He careened backward through the door to the rally point, shielding her.

"To the back!" he insisted to the others. "Move!"

Rozhenko backpedaled inside. He returned his cannon to its place on his back. Patrick tripped, falling on his face. In fluid motion, Ray threw Anjali over his shoulder and, with his free hand, grabbed Patrick by the collar and dragged him behind the counter. The jostling rendered Anjali fully alert.

"Get up! Get up!" Ray demanded and Patrick scrambled to his feet.

Ray put Anjali down and she moved under her own power. The Allies flooded toward the back room.

A dim, faltering candle lantern swung from a frayed cord in the ceiling. It cast its fickle light on the face of a young boy. He froze, terror in his eyes. Behind him, an old, empty refrigerator stood tipped on its side.

It revealed a ladder shaft. The hatch was welded to the bottom of the appliance.

Daedalus took a step toward the boy, who screamed.

A loud click, followed by a symphony of cocked hammers, gave Daedalus pause. He couldn't see into the room, but he now knew it was full of unfriendlies. A tarpaulin crinkled beneath his feet.

"Another step and I end you," warned a deep, old voice with a distinct Scottish accent.

The boy scurried to the trap door and down the ladder.

"Weapons on the floor," said the voice.

"Just kill them now!" said another voice, a woman's. She was silenced with a hiss.

Ray and Ada dropped their pistols. Patrick sloughed off his pulse rifle and let it fall to the floor. Rozhenko gently set down his plasma cannon. Tentative, wary humans crept into the guttering light and retrieved the discarded firearms.

"They've got a fucking cannon, Edmund!" one of the humans yelled. "It's too heavy!"

"Leave it," the old voice replied. "Step forward. Come into the room, so we can see you."

Anjali held up her hands and stepped toward the light.

"I'm unarmed," she said. "I'm human . . ."

"That doesn't mean anything," said the female voice. "You," she said to Daedalus, stepping into the light. "Drop your fucking gun or I will waste your big, stupid ass."

The weak light gleamed against her silver hair, but her face was young. She pressed the muzzle of her pistol against Daedalus' breastplate, over his heart.

"You go ahead and take it, love," he said, smiling. "I'd rather not make any sudden moves." He winked at her.

A man stepped out of the shadows, carelessly waving his gun. "You big, ugly fuck. Who do you think you are—?"

Sargas, fleet and without effort, snatched the gun right from the man's hand.

"Don't—!" yelled Ray, but too late.

A hail of bullets rang out, and Sargas fell backward to the floor. The gun clattered from his hand.

"Fuck!" said Ray, peeling his helmet from his head. He dropped it on the floor. "Fuck! Fuck, fuck, fuck." He put his hands to his head. "Oh, fuck . . ."

"Hold your goddamned fire," said the older man, Edmund. He stepped into the light. "You," he said to Ray. "Look at me."

Ray turned to him.

"I think I know you," Edmund said. He pulled down his hood, revealing a bald head and an old face, covered with a silver beard.

"You just totally fucked us!" Ray blared.

"You fucked yourselves!" said the young man whom Sargas had disarmed.

Ray bared his teeth and tensed.

"I'm sure I know you," said Edmund. "Avix Emera."

"Who the fuck are you?" Ray growled at the sound of his original name. He paused. There was a glimmer of recognition, but nothing close to recollection.

"Edmund!" yelled the mouthy young man. "What are you *doing*? Look at his uniform! Look at his *face*!"

The old man held up his hand. The young man fell silent.

"I knew you—" Edmund began. He stopped short at the sound of breaking glass.

From against the wall, he grabbed a mop handle. He smacked the candle from the lantern. Darkness fell upon the room. The embers cascaded down the wall, snuffed before reaching the floor.

It took but a moment for Ray's eyes to adjust. Some of the humans were already down the hatch. Edmund, somehow unencumbered by the darkness, shepherded Anjali down. He grabbed Ray's wrist. The grip was unnaturally strong. He pulled Ray in the direction of the trap door.

"We need that body!" Ray said of Sargas.

"No time for that! Climb!" Edmund demanded.

Ray climbed downward but hesitated. A heavy boot cracked against his nose.

"Climb, motherfucker!" hissed the loudmouth human male, who then turned to see Edmund pulling Daedalus toward the ladder. The corren sloughed off the grasp.

"We need that body," Daedalus said, looking at Sargas.

"Just say the word, Edmund, and I'll waste him," said the man.

"Shut up, Bjorn," Edmund replied.

Daedalus could see in the dark. He pounced to where Sargas lay, surprised to find a smile beaming up at him.

"What are you smiling at? Is this a joke?"

"It's good to be alive," said Sargas.

Daedalus pulled him up. "You're just full of surprises."

They heard voices from the front of the store.

"Seems clear," said one.

"Look at the floor, idiot," replied another, indicating footprints in the dust. "Check the back."

In the back room, Edmund hissed at Daedalus and Sargas. "Go, dammit. Now! Climb or die!"

"We're all dead unless we can rig some kind of booby trap," Daedalus replied. "Let me get that cannon."

Edmund eyed him dubiously.

"No fucking way," Bjorn replied.

"And some grenades to kill those Reds who just came in here," Daedalus added, looking at Bjorn's bandolier.

"Bjorn," said Edmund. "Go welcome our guests with a bang."

"Gladly," Bjorn replied.

THIRTEEN

MARSEH SPLAYED UPON his throne, deep in thought. His left hand played against his face. His booted feet rested upon the dais.

At times, he liked to occupy one of his bodies and spend significant time constrained by its corporeal bounds. He believed it helped him understand humans, correns, and Arak Matar.

The door chimed.

"Enter," Marseh said quietly, but his voice carried.

No one could accurately describe the sound of his voice. It took on whichever timbre most effectively bent the will of the listener.

A paladin guardsman entered. With a deep bow, he addressed Marseh.

"Emperor, Governor Arak has left the station in his personal cruiser. Per your orders, we did not interfere."

"Thank you, Skal. Monitor where and when they land. Keep me informed."

"Of course, Lord," Skal replied. He bowed again before leaving.

Without moving from his seat or diverting his gaze, Marseh spoke out. "Do not lurk, Reyevas."

From near a column to Marseh's left, Reyevas stepped from the shadows. While he had stood just shorter than Arak during that encounter, he now stood equal to Marseh's nearly nine feet.

"What is it now?" asked Marseh.

Reyevas' white eyes lit up, indicating a smile hidden behind the respirator that covered his face.

"You know, Darek. You can hardly call your stewardship of this planet a success."

Marseh's features arranged themselves into an expression of mild annoyance. "Our masters wanted the humans' technological progress thwarted, their population reduced to a manageable figure. These things have happened."

"I'd hesitate to call them manageable. And that poor planet. Such a cost, Darek."

Marseh laughed quietly and without amusement. "I would have liked to see *you* do differently."

Reyevas said nothing.

"You've been here, now, for weeks and still haven't told me why," Marseh said. "What have you done to be consigned to this wayside star system . . . which I, of course, have so horribly mismanaged."

"It amuses me that you think my presence is result of a penalty."

"Both I and Arak arrived here as punishment. Who would come here of their own volition? For whom would being here be a reward? At least the N'horr know how to peacefully coexist, but humans lust for conflict like their lungs lust for air. They grew like weeds, unworthy of attention until, in less than a cosmic blink, some of them threatened *all of us* with catastrophe."

Reyevas shook his head. "Is all of your time among these anxious, simple creatures to blame for your wearisome delivery?"

Marseh looked from beneath his heavy brows at Reyevas. "If I'm such a problem, then why not eliminate me? If you know I'm vulnerable to you, why not kill me while I occupy this body? Is there some other way we can die?"

Reyevas recoiled in genuine disgust. "If I were to force myself into the vessel you occupy, we both would surely perish."

"How do you know?" Marseh taunted. "Have you ever tried it?"

"We're forbidden to occupy a sentient body! You know this! It would kill the host and possibly even us, and that's with a lesser species. I have no desire to murder you, Darek," Reyevas replied. "And neither Arak . . . nor even the correns and humans."

"That's not an answer."

"Of course I've never tried it!" Reyevas exclaimed. He paused for a moment. "Have you?"

Marseh smiled, again without mirth. "No, my friend. Of course not. They conditioned us very well to fear possessing a sentient being. But would it not make sense for an immortal to flirt with his only means to die?"

Reyevas pondered Marseh with a wary eye. "I'm not here to kill you," he hissed, waving away the unpleasant digression. "I've told you why I've come."

"Yes, you have, but I tire of your intrusion. If you are here only as an impediment, I will take great pleasure in eliminating you."

"Would you commit that sin, Darek? Are you *so* low that you would violate our highest law?"

Marseh shook his head and opened his mouth in a silent laugh. "Perhaps I've spent too much time with a corrupted N'horr and with these callow humans. I feel so . . . corporeal." He smiled his lipless smile. "And you know these corporeal beings can't help but give in to their baser urges."

"You spend too much time in your body," Reyevas declared. "You've been away too long. It's cruel for them to deny you any contact . . . but, and I apologize for this remark, we are not here to concern ourselves with your feelings. I accept that it is no treat to be critiqued, but we all have our masters."

"I do not accept you as mine."

"You don't need to," Reyevas replied. "Just don't stand in my way."

He vanished without waiting for a retort.

Marseh probed for any lingering trace of his counterpart, but found none. He relaxed, satisfied that his perception was keen enough not to be thwarted. Cocking his head to the side, Marseh paid attention to sounds he heard, not with his ears but his mind. He sat down upon his throne and abandoned his body. It could survive without him. Its involuntary nervous system would breathe in the absence of his consciousness. It would die only if starved or denied water for too long.

Marseh placed himself elsewhere within the space station. Rounding a corner, he approached the doors to Arak's private hangar. They didn't open. He walked through them.

In the hangar stood two paladin, Ishka and Lután. The latter crouched over a small spot of spittle and green blood on the floor.

Ishka snapped to attention. Lután rose and made an identical salute.

Marseh waved away their shows of fealty. "Leave us, please, Ishka."

He turned to Lután. "I have a mission for you."

"Yes?"

"Take Shaula, assemble teams of your most trusted men, and bring Commander Hastings to me."

FOURTEEN

DEROVIAS EMERGED FROM the *Filomena*'s wreckage shaking his head.

"They are not here, sire," he reported. "There are three corpses, all human. Two burned beyond recognition but, judging from their builds, likely male. Doubtful anyone of note. No tracks, due to the rain, but Orchard City is the only conceivable place they could have gone."

Arak said nothing.

"Shall we pursue?" Derovias prodded.

"No," Arak replied. "I reckon they'll be forced our way before long. Get back on the ship."

Derovias bowed. He walked as quickly to the ship as the mud would allow.

Arak stood alone upon the soggy ground, considering the wrecked hulk of the stolen cutter. It took him barely a moment to deduce that the Allies had not come upon a Confederation ship without aid. Marseh surely provided it to them, just as he somehow guaranteed that its occupants would survive.

Arak ignored the inconsequential human casualties. Ray and Daedalus were alive. That human woman, Anjali Hastings, the Allied admiral's daughter, must also have survived, since her body was not among the wreckage. He knew that Ray was sentimental, but not stupid enough to carry a corpse for miles.

Most important, the tube stolen from the Overground lab was empty.

Not knowing who or what had been inside the container, Arak still assumed it part of some obscure plot cooked up by Marseh. It angered the Butcher to be so ignorant, to be left to guess at what had transpired, in secret, right under his nose.

He turned in a circle. The mud squelched with each of his steps. He gazed at the leering, collapsing old barn and at the empty western plain that ended at the foothills of the Southern Fangs. Then he looked at the highway and the buildings of Holst's Hollow in the eastern distance. A strong breeze blew across the barren bogland, buffeting his braids.

Derovias waited at the top of the ramp to the ship. He watched the man, whom he'd served so faithfully, try to reason through recent events. Arak completed his circle. He looked up at Derovias, who cast his own eyes groundward. A practiced gesture. Unhurried, Arak walked to and up the ramp. As he passed, Derovias fell into lockstep in another display of servile obedience.

Arak entered the bridge of his ship. He looked at his helmsman, Tolon Intiri, who awaited instruction with a guileless face, but Arak wasn't sure whom he could trust anymore.

"Destroy the cutter," Arak ordered, "and depart for Blackwing."

FIFTEEN

DAEDALUS PUSHED SARGAS toward the trapdoor and watched him climb down.

"Someone has to stay up here and close this thing," said Edmund in a rueful tone, not even flinching as an explosion erupted from the storefront.

Bjorn hurried back to the storeroom.

"You climb," said Daedalus to Edmund. "I'll pull it down on top of us."

"Bjorn, go," Edmund ordered.

Daedalus grabbed Rozhenko's plasma cannon with both hands and hauled it along the floor until it rested near the hatch.

"Go, old man. We wanna be far away when this shit blows."

Daedalus set the cannon's power cells to overload and dragged the tarpaulin to cover the trap.

Edmund scurried down the ladder followed by Daedalus. He wedged himself in the shaftway. With both hands, he pulled the trick door welded to the heavy fridge. It was a struggle, but he gritted his teeth and hauled the entire apparatus down atop the hole.

"Back here!" a voice yelled as the fridge clattered flush to the floor. The Confederates unleashed a hail of gunfire at the contraption.

Daedalus cranked the hatch, hoping none of the blasts would pierce it, nor set off the cannon prematurely.

"Slide down!" Edmund implored, nimbly putting his feet upon the outside of the ladder. He vanished into the darkness below, through which even Daedalus could not see. He followed. It felt like forever before touching down. Sargas and the old man were already retreating down the tunnel. Daedalus didn't hesitate to follow.

"Move, move," said Edmund, grabbing Daedalus around the wrist, pushing Sargas with the other hand. "Hurry."

Daedalus heard clear shouts rain down from above.

"They're through the hatch—" Edmund began but was cut off by the deafening explosion of the plasma cannon.

The tunnel's oppressive darkness retreated for a moment from the brilliant green flash. Bits of bricks and mortar fell all around. A thick cloud of dust enveloped them.

"Well, I should think that's taken care of them," Edmund quipped with a cough.

"Surely there are others," Daedalus replied, unwilling to congratulate himself. "And other ways into these tunnels."

"You're keen, but fret not. We've covered every point of entry. No one's ever made it through without an invitation."

Daedalus slowed his pace while he pondered the warren's security.

"Don't dawdle, now, dammit," Edmund said, pulling him.

They came to a door, which Edmund pulled aside. He directed Sargas and Daedalus to enter a brickwork arcade. Small candle lamps hung from the arched ceiling. The damp walls sweated with humidity. Rushing water droned nearby. In the arcade stood the humans from the store above, including the silver-haired woman and Bjorn and his mouth.

"You're dead!" the woman blurted, agape at Sargas.

He looked down at his chest and touched his finger to one of the holes in his jump suit. He pushed against his skin, which was smooth and unmarred.

"This is crazy, Edmund. Bjorn killed him . . . it . . . what is this?"

Edmund again held up his hand and she quieted.

"Be glad he didn't, and let it be." He turned to his group. "Give them your cloaks."

Without protest, seven of the humans doffed their cloaks. They relinquished them to each of the Allies. The silver-haired woman was one of the donors, revealing her buxom hourglass figure. Her armor seemed impractical, as if purely for show, to sate some puerile adolescent fantasy. It offered little protection except to her internal organs. And, thus, it left little to the imagination.

She handed her cloak to Anjali, who slipped into it. Anjali fixed upon the woman's smooth, light-brown skin. A scar crossed her face from above her right eye, across her nose, and down her left cheek. The loaned garment hid Anjali's pleasant, albeit slight, figure. The other woman's voluptuous form was wide open to perusal. Her breasts would not have fit in even Ray's large hands. Anjali couldn't help but feel inadequate next to such feminine abundance. All the men except Edmund eyed the zaftig woman with lascivious intent. As did Ada. But the woman ignored them all. She enjoyed taunting them with what she'd never deign to share.

Ray approached Edmund. "Will you tell us who you are?"

Edmund smiled a tight, thin-lipped grin, visible only by the slight upward movement of his beard. "No questions from you, either, I'm afraid. We have to keep moving."

Faint recognition continued to tug at Ray's memory. They walked on in silence. After some time, the silence gave way to new sounds. Bustle echoed off the walls. Light grew in the distance.

"Cover your heads—"ordered the silver-haired woman.

Daedalus removed his helmet. He and Ray pulled their hoods over their heads.

"Keep your eyes on the floor."

SIXTEEN

EDMUND LEAD THE Allies through an old service door. They climbed a short switchback staircase and emerged through another door into the enormous, vaulted mezzanine of an abandoned train station. The ceiling loomed high enough to hint at the dozens of meters they had descended to get there.

The expansive area brimmed with tents. Set into rows, they created lanes like at a bazaar. Most denizens wore earth-toned cloaks like those loaned to Ray and his charges. An intricate network of catwalks and platforms loomed above the throng. They made use of the high ceiling, creating a tiered community. The latticework connected balconies and other, smaller mezzanines. People seemed to occupy nearly every cubic meter, a tally of tens of thousands.

"So many humans . . ." Daedalus said. The sheer numbers disquieted him. If anyone heard, no one replied.

Edmund approached Ray.

"Your human friends are free to move about, so long as they leave their helmets behind. Should they cause any trouble, know that the community will exact swift justice. You and your corren charge will stay with me."

Ray replied with a short shake of his head.

Edmund shook his head in reply. "No. We already draw more attention than I care to explain. I would like that you trust me—and your own charges—enough to let them disperse. Because I doubt you want to deal with the ire of all of these people," he gestured at the mass of humanity, "whom your race alone will inflame."

Ray protested. "But you brought us here."

With patience, Edmund continued. "I can stem that ire if you and the other corren stick with me. A crop of fresh human faces in the company of two distrusted aliens will make everything unpleasant for all of us."

Ray turned to Anjali. He pointed at her and indicated the others. With both hands, he made scattering motions.

She opened her mouth to protest.

He cut the air with his hand. "It's an order. Just follow it."

She shoved her helmet into his hands.

Edmund piped up, loud enough for his voice to carry to the group. "That man there could use medical attention," he said, pointing to Patrick. "Why don't you join us, son?"

The relief on Patrick's face was plain and he followed Ray, Daedalus, and Edmund into the tent. The silver-haired woman and Bjorn took up guard outside.

"Could I have some water, please?" Ada requested.

One of Edmund's acolytes dipped into the tent and returned with a metal cup. He handed it to Ada. She tried not to be greedy, but it was as if she'd never tasted anything so delicious.

Anjali caught her eye. Ada arched an eyebrow and offered the cup to her superior. Anjali took a sip. Then another. She handed the cup back.

"It's best if we don't stick together," she said. "Regroup here in thirty mikes."

Ada replied with a big smile. She dragged Sargas into the crowd.

"And you?" Anjali asked Rozhenko.

"I will be finding something to do," he replied.

She nodded and headed down the lane perpendicular to Ada's.

SEVENTEEN

THE NURSE TENDING to Patrick finished her work and moved to depart. As she reached for the flap, Edmund pulled it aside and stepped in. She bowed and nodded and curtsied at him, falling over herself in deference. She then nearly collided with Anjali, who deftly stepped aside and winced in pain.

Anjali entered the tent and stood to the side, alone. Ray looked at her.

"We're assembled," she reported. "Eager to depart."

"Then let's get out of here," Ray replied. He looked at Patrick. "On your feet, kid."

They exited into the lane where Anjali, Daedalus, Patrick, Ada, Sargas, and Rozhenko waited, armed again with their confiscated weapons and armor. Manon and a human adolescent stood near the tent flap. The boy was sulking and filthy.

"A'arilon Ray," said Edmund, prefacing an introduction. "This is my granddaughter, Manon. And this," he put his hand on the boy's shoulder, "is my grandson Adnan."

Manon smiled knowingly at Ray and left without a word. The boy glowered from beneath his black eyebrows.

"Adnan is your guide," Edmund continued. "He has provisions for you. I expect it's been long since you've eaten."

Wary, Ray looked at Adnan, who still glared through his greasy mane of thick black hair.

"Edmund, I think—" Ray began.

"This is nonnegotiable. You need a guide. Adnan is your guide. I bid you the fondest of farewells." Edmund blended so well into the surroundings that he vanished before their eyes.

"He doesn't like you," Daedalus whispered in Ray's ear, casting a sidelong glance at Adnan. The boy seemed to have no other look in his arsenal beside the baleful stare.

"I doubt he likes you, either," Ray replied in a low tone. He assumed the boy an orphan by corren hands. "Nobody does."

Smiling, Daedalus turned back to Adnan. "Lead the way, kiddo."

Without a word, the boy led them to the subway tracks. He jumped down into the trackbed and skirted the length of the platform, heading east. With uncanny agility, he scrambled over a huge garbage pile and into the tunnel. One by one they filed after him. The guards on the platform above looked pleased to see Edmund's guests depart.

Ada tried to cover her nose and mouth against the hot stench of rotting refuse. She kept her visor up because having it down trapped the noisome stink. Thanks to the counterfeit respirator in her helmet, there was no escape. Breathing through her mouth proved no alternative to her nose. The detritus was as palpable as it was rank. She retched and retched again. She paused and tried to master herself. She swallowed down the hot bile. It burned the back of her throat.

"Not much in the way of municipal services, hey, kid?" Daedalus jibed. "Where do you guys put your shit?"

Adnan continued to ignore him.

Anjali trod through the muck with neither visible nor audible complaint. Her brown eyes burned with determination bordering on anger. Ray caught her as she careened down the other side of the trash pile. Once everyone had surmounted the obstacle, they continued after Adnan. He showed no care for whether they kept up or not. The light from the station succumbed to the darkness. Adnan withdrew a beacon. They walked until they encountered another station and passed through it.

Ray walked up to him. "How much farther?"

The boy continued walking without reply. The group followed in silence. They passed through a third station and, in the next stretch of tunnel, Adnan stopped next to a service exit and cocked his head at it.

"I know you can talk," said Ray.

Adnan's bruise-ringed, tired eyes gleamed with malevolence. His lips curled. "This way."

The group came to a stairwell, littered with broken concrete and dust where parts of the ceiling had collapsed. Adnan darted easily over every obstacle without hesitation, familiar with every cranny of the sprawling underworld. He proceeded without heed for his followers, made no effort to see if they kept pace. After surmounting a particularly large rubble pile, he halted before a heavy steel door. The soldiers' boots scuffed atop the steps, scratching against the particulate.

Ray joined him first.

"I can't open this," said the boy. "I'm done. I'm going." He turned to leave.

Ray grabbed him by the collar. "Just hold on a minute."

"Fuck off me!" Adnan barked.

Rozhenko blocked the way at the bottom of the stairs.

Ray relinquished his hold, turned to the exit, and grasped the handle. It came free in his hand. The door didn't budge. He dropped the handle and it clanged upon the floor, ringing through the claustrophobic stairwell.

"Reggie, I need your help . . ."

Daedalus came up to stand next to Ray on the cramped landing. Adnan fell back by a few stairs.

"Will you *stop* with the fucking 'Reggie,' for fuck's sake . . ."

"It pisses you off, huh?" said Ray. "Good. I need you good and mad, Reggie. Reginald. You obnoxious sack of shit. I need you to hit m—"

Daedalus head-butted Ray in the nose. He drove his right fist into Ray's abdomen, caving in the thin armor. Face alight with glee, he landed a thundering left hook against Ray's temple.

Ray growled, deep and animal.

Adnan, Patrick, and Ada shrank backward in terror.

Ray, still in control, albeit barely, pushed Daedalus away. Green blood streamed from one of Ray's nostrils. His face contorted in anger. The bones on his face grew more prominent. His talons jutted from his fingers and he brayed. Daedalus didn't flinch. He grabbed Ray by the collar and the belt, thrust him at the door, and stepped back.

Ray bellowed again.

In Adnan's mind, the sound evoked fables of monsters that came in the night to steal and eat little children, but he didn't need old wives' tales to inspire such fear. His experiences with Ingili, Allies, and Confederates provided scars enough. He huddled against the wall, hands atop his head, face in the crooks of his arms. Hot tears streaked his cheeks, but he mastered his bowels and bladder. He refused to give monsters the satisfaction of him mewling in his own shit and piss.

Ada wanted to go to him, comfort him, but large, unmovable Daedalus stood in the way. He reveled in his handiwork. Ray transformed into a berserker and attacked the offending doorway. He jammed both hands into the metal, near the top hinge, piercing it like wet paper. He hauled it toward the floor. The rending steel emitted a banshee keen.

Adnan clamped his hands over his ears and screamed. Daedalus shifted his weight onto one leg. Ada forced past him. She enveloped the terrified boy.

"It's okay," she said in his ear. "I won't let anyone hurt you."

Ray exhausted his rage. He took a step back.

"There . . ." he panted. "It's open."

His features receded, returning to normal. His talons retracted.

In the sudden quiet, Adnan returned to his senses. He shoved Ada away. "Get off me, you stupid bitch!"

Surprised by the outburst, she shot to her feet and staggered against the wall. She folded her arms across her chest. Daedalus stared at her. She refused to meet his gaze.

Ray wiped the back of his hand across his mouth. His broken nose began to mend.

"Let's keep it moving," he said, catching his breath.

Adnan got to his feet. His tears left streaks in the grime on his face. Without a word, he flitted between Patrick, Anjali, and Sargas down the stairs to where Rozhenko stood sentry.

"Get out of my way, asshole!" Adnan shrieked.

"Let him go, Roz," said Ray.

The big man turned sideways, which left scant more room than before, but Adnan squeezed past and retreated.

The Allies clambered over the rent metal door. They filed into the corridor, walking until they came to a ladder. Ray grasped the rail and a head-high rung. He put his foot on the bottom rung. The ladder wrenched free from the mortar, showering him with rust and brick dust. A bolt bounced off the top of his head. He staggered to his feet and unhanded the ladder in disgust.

"Come on. There has to be another one."

They walked farther until they came to the next ladder. Ray regarded it and pulled, cautious but firm. It held.

"Reggie. You first."

Daedalus shouldered past Ray.

"Last time, Raymond," he said quietly, so only Ray could hear. "Last time. Or you don't recover from the next beating."

"Strong words," said Ray, unimpressed.

"I chose my name. Call me by it." Daedalus climbed.

Sargas followed.

Ray beckoned Anjali to the ladder, then ushered Ada upward. Patrick approached next.

"Can you climb?"

"Not much choice," Patrick replied.

Ray shrugged and watched him struggle until he was out of sight. Only Ray and Rozhenko remained.

"You first, boss; I am too heavy. I am not wanting to be stranding you."

"I'll claw my way up if I have to. Go ahead," Ray replied.

Rozhenko clumsily scaled the ladder. It whined in protest. Dust, mortar, and bits of brick rained down on Ray. The bolts strained in the wall. Quietly, he hoped the ladder would hold.

"I am not fitting," Rozhenko's called from above. "I must be coming back."

"Fuck," Ray said to himself.

The big man touched bottom, bereft. "The hole is not for man of my size."

"Goddamnit."

"I am not wanting to keep you from mission success. Please to be leaving me."

"I can't do that, Sergeant."

"Commander," Rozhenko nodded toward the surface, "you have all of them. I am already once dead man. I am not much of man now. If I am to be dying again, so what? Two is more lives than are having most men."

Ray looked at him in confusion.

"You look at me and I seem . . . cyborg, yes? How many like me are you knowing, hmm? How many are they living?"

"None."

"Because it should not be. Men like me . . . big men . . . we are dying, and they never letting us rest. They are rebuilding us and making us sentry. Better to be dying here than somewhere I am being found."

"Roz . . ."

"*Nyet.* You say they are expecting not that we surviving. Perhaps I am not surviving. You cannot fight me. You cannot . . . be forcing me through too small hole. You must be going. Stop wasting time."

Ray couldn't argue.

"Go, now," Rozhenko urged.

Ray mounted the ladder. He climbed, willing the weakened bolts to take his substantial weight.

Rozhenko watched him disappear into the darkness above.

EIGHTEEN

CARINA SAT AT the bar. She stared at her drink with her cheek upon her clenched right fist. She'd already drunk enough to stupor an average man but felt barely intoxicated.

Her eyes shifted from the drink to Seamus, and then to the crowd. It thrummed with nervous energy. A wave of fear and revulsion swept through the mass. It stood up the hairs on Carina's nape.

At the door, she saw three correns. They bore no Confederation insignia but were armed and armored like wealthy badlands mercenaries.

"Merciless Mother, Seamus, what the fuck are they doing here?"

He shrugged. "Ingili come in here all the time, Captain. What do you suggest I do? Throw them out?"

"Do you see any marks on their faces? Those aren't Ingili!" She decided they weren't A'arili, either; they carried themselves like Reds in active service.

He leaned close to her and whispered harshly. "What the hell am I supposed to do about it, huh?"

Her mouth twisted with rage.

"Please, don't kill anyone," he begged.

"I may have to, dammit. I am known . . ."

"Known?"

She clenched her teeth. "I kill as many of these bastards as I can. Sometimes on my own time. I am *known*. Fuck."

"You're . . . notorious?" he blinked. He stood rooted, glass and towel unmoving in his hands.

"I'm a fucking marked man," she replied.

As surreptitiously as possible, she left her seat and picked up her packs. She kept her face from view of the correns as they parsed the human throng. As they merged deeper, she headed toward the back room where she'd eaten her dinner.

One of the correns stopped and seemed to sniff the air. He registered the pulse that rippled through the crowd as Carina pushed her way through. He put his hand on the shoulder of his companion, who led their foray. She didn't need to look to feel the shift in the correns' attention. The patrons carried the transmission back to her. She shot Seamus' burly guard a look that said: *Don't try and stop me.*

He knew better. He stepped aside.

She burst through the door and bolted it, throwing down the heavy wooden beam as added security. Hasim stood with a surprised look on his face.

"Outside, Hasim! Help me get outside!"

He nodded and held out his hand, leading her into the kitchen. They wound their way through to the far wall. He pointed at the back door to the alleyway.

Carina collected herself.

She put down both of the bags, drew her Mateba from her left hip and unsheathed her knife. She held it in her right hand with the pommel facing forward. The blade pointed at her elbow, edge to the floor.

She stood placid and steadied her breathing. Her heart slowed.

At the crest of a large breath, she nodded at Hasim. He depressed the bar. She crashed through the doorway and lashed out with her knife, shooting straight ahead with her left hand. Her blade sliced through the waiting corren's neck. Blindly, she swung her shooting hand to the left, unloading her revolver at the mouth of the alleyway as she darted toward the dumpster. She somersaulted to safety. The rugged bin jolted from the impact of each pulse. They washed the alley in blue light.

"Smart bitch, Carina," a voice called, "but there's no way out. Blind alley, baby. Pretty baby."

She said nothing. She looked around for an escape. There wasn't one.

"The rest are coming," the voice continued. "Orders said dead or alive . . . Alive, I hope. I want to rape you while you can *feel* it. We'll get you in all three holes at once. How's that sound, baby? Fun, right? Don't worry, though; if it comes to it, I'll do your corpse all the same."

She fought down her rage and tried to keep a clear head. She knew he was goading her, provoking her to stupidity. Even as her bile came up and her stomach backflipped, she refused to oblige him. His voice hadn't gotten any closer. He kept his distance, waiting for reinforcements.

She reloaded her revolver.

Hasim crouched inside the kitchen, wishing he could help somehow, but the snake stood out of sight. The cook could see Carina, trapped behind the dumpster. The arm of the corren she'd felled, gun still in hand, rested atop the doorjamb. Hasim looked at it, then at Carina.

She glanced at him, followed his line of sight, and held up her hand. *Stop. Don't.*

He frowned and stayed put.

NINETEEN

WITH GREAT DIFFICULTY, Sargas squeezed himself through the too-small manhole and onto the sidewalk. He turned to help Anjali. Daedalus offered no assistance.

Blue light flashed from an alley down the street.

"Who the fuck are you?" a voice demanded of Daedalus, Anjali, and Sargas. The three correns had just emerged from the Pendragon pub.

Sargas pushed Anjali to the ground. He ran at the correns. They put aside their confusion at Sargas' Confederation jumpsuit and opened fire. The blasts dissipated around him. They arced against the invisible electromagnetic shield emitted by the nanomachines in his cells.

Daedalus didn't join Sargas nor ask after Anjali. He ran toward the alleyway.

The correns in the street stood agape at the onrushing Sargas. Unarmored, unarmed, and unharmed. They dropped their guns and reached for their blades.

Ada climbed from the hole into a crouch. She crept over to Anjali. "What's going on?"

Anjali shook her head.

Sargas barreled into the nearest corren. He grabbed the Confederate's exposed head with both hands and wrenched it violently, twisting as he threw the man to the ground. The corren's vertebrae snapped like firecrackers. His body went slack. A wet sound answered his head smacking the pavement.

Another of the correns jabbed his knife at Sargas' back. The blade pierced the bodysuit but skidded off his skin like it were metal or stone. The nanoscopic machinery within Sargas responded to signals from his nervous system. In the presence of danger, they increased his skin's yield strength to a threshold stronger than steel. He turned to his assailant, wrapped both hands around the man's throat, and squeezed until the airway collapsed and the arteries ruptured.

Patrick emerged from underground.

The last corren standing threw down his knife and retrieved his blaster. He fired point-blank at Sargas, vaporizing the jumpsuit's back. The blast threw him to the ground. It should have obliterated the entire point of contact, blown a hole straight through, but Sargas remained whole. Whole, but unconscious. Charred black, bloody blisters marred his flesh.

The corren turned toward the Allies.

Patrick clenched his teeth and forced his left arm into position. He fired his pulse rifle. His right eye didn't fail him. He landed three consecutive shots in the same location, piercing the corren's armor and the heart beneath. The man staggered, fell to the street, and lay still.

***

Weapon drawn, Daedalus came around the corner of the alley. Stealthy as his boots would allow, but not quietly enough. The other corren turned on him, pistol aimed.

Daedalus took one hand off his weapon and raised his opaque visor.

"Do I know you, brother?" asked the Confederate. His face indicated he felt he should.

"Humans ambushed us," said Daedalus. He held his gun at his hip, finger light upon the trigger.

"We fight to the death—" the man objected.

The sound of Carina's revolver boomed off the walls. Daedalus threw himself to the ground as she pumped all six shots into her hunter's back. The Confederate pitched forward, landing on his face.

"That's *six* holes for you, motherfucker," Carina spat. She grabbed a speed loader and popped open the cylinder.

Daedalus sprang to his feet. He leveled his pistol at her.

"Move and you die!" he shouted. "Raise your weapon, you die!"

Carina looked up. A sickened expression overtook her face, part defiance, part nausea.

"If you're gonna kill me," she said, "just do it."

***

Ray peeked over the lip of the manhole and saw Anjali and Ada frozen in rapt attention. He climbed out all the way.

"Report!" he hissed. The sound of his voice broke Anjali's reverie.

"Three correns," she said. "All dead. Sargas . . . dead, too. Daedalus . . ." she pointed at the alleyway.

Ray cursed to himself and ran to Sargas. His body was unmarked; the charred flesh had completely healed, but the hole in his jumpsuit evinced he'd been shot. Crouching down, Ray put his fingers on the man's neck.

Sargas rolled over. He snatched Ray's arm and pulled him down into a crushing bear hug. Patrick kicked Sargas hard in the side of the head. The grip relaxed just enough for Ray to deliver a head butt and skitter off. Sargas lashed at Patrick's leg and hauled him down by the ankle. He began reeling in the smaller man.

"Sargas!" Ray shouted.

Sargas halted. Turning his enraged face toward Ray, recognition glinted in his eyes. He let go of Patrick, who scuttled away in a lame crab walk.

"Stand down," Ray said. "For fuck's sake." He winced, putting his hand to his back. "What the hell happened?"

***

Anjali approached Daedalus. He kept his weapon trained on Carina. She held the speed loader in her right hand and, by one finger, the open revolver in her left.

"She doesn't believe me," said Daedalus without looking at Anjali. He knew her by the sound of her footfalls. "Why don't you try?"

"What are you doing with him?" Carina demanded, surprised at the sight of a human woman.

Anjali held up both her empty hands. "Allies."

"Bullshit," Carina replied.

"He saved you, didn't he?"

"I shot the snake," said Carina.

"Watch your mouth," Daedalus warned.

"Fuck you." Carina looked him right in the eyes. She turned her gaze to Anjali. "Are you here to kill me?"

"Of course not."

Carina loaded the bullets and snapped shut the cylinder.

"Don't you raise that at me," Daedalus warned.

She holstered the gun, then picked up her knife from the ground. She frowned at the green blood. Hasim was dazed, still crouched at the door. He hovered over Carina's packs. She knelt down in front of him and cupped his cheek in her hand, caressing his weather-beaten skin with her thumb.

"You," she nodded, "are a sweet man, Hasim. A good man. There should be more like you."

His black eyes glittered. The corners of his mouth rose, just barely straightening his mustache. He closed his eyes and exhaled through his nose.

She wiped her knife against the inside of the dead corren's elbow and sheathed it. Prying the gun from the corpse's hand, she jammed it into one of her bags. Donning both packs, she stepped over the corren into whom she'd pumped six holes. With her hands at her sides—palms down, fingers outstretched—she approached Daedalus and Anjali.

"I'm leaving."

She walked past them, turning as she did. She backpedaled to keep them in sight.

"Don't follow me."

Content with the distance between them, Carina turned and ran, catching a glimpse of the others as she went.

***

Daedalus and Anjali returned to the others, who knelt or stood around the three corren corpses made by Sargas and Patrick.

"We need to double-time it to Dorance," Daedalus said. "I think we just met an Allied soldier who's gonna report us as hostiles. I wanna at least get to the door before she can open her mouth to anyone who could marshal a strike. Nobody who meets us on the street is gonna let us talk it out."

Ray got to his feet. "Agreed. We're all reasonably whole; let's move."

"Wait," said Ada. "Where's Rozhenko?"

"Put him out of your mind," said Ray.

Ada didn't want to put him out of her mind; she liked him. There was a decency and sweetness to him that she rarely encountered in men, but she held her tongue.

She fell in line.

TWENTY

CARINA GAVE THE food to Sergeant Liggan and ordered her to leave it with Al-Farid in the galley. She left Liggan to it and hurried to Van Sinderen's office.

"Come," he said in response to the door chime.

The door slid open with a mechanical groan and closed behind her. Looking up from his desk, he raised his eyebrows at the harried, frenzied look on Carina's face. "Captain?"

"I requisitioned the supplies. We have food. Real food."

"Very good. And you?"

"I encountered a death squad. They were after me, specifically."

"I trust, since you are here and whole, that you dispatched them?"

Carina tilted her head slightly to the left. Her nostrils flared, albeit barely. She pressed her lips together and clenched her jaw.

She exhaled through her nose. She inhaled.

"Yes, sir. A corren and a human came to my aid."

Van Sinderen blinked, uncomprehending. "A corren . . . and a *human*?"

"Yes. The corren was especially ugly, scars on his face, but not Ingili. The human, a woman . . . she was pretty."

The colonel dismissed the aesthetic observation with a wave of his hand. "Aside from pretty, describe her to me."

"Thin. Indian. Big, dark eyes. Nice lips?" she struggled. "Honestly, aside from that she's pretty, I don't know what to say."

"The corren," said Van Sinderen. "Describe him further."

"Large, even for a snake. Thicker than usual. Bulky. More muscular."

"And the scars," he traced them with his thumb. "One across the lips, one across the nose?"

"Yes." She cocked her head to the right, wondering how he knew.

"And you didn't see anyone else?"

"I saw four others, three male, one female. The woman who came to my aid said they were Allies. But they wore Confederate uniforms. They wanted to follow me back. I shook them."

"Very good, Captain. Thank you. Dismissed."

Carina clenched her fist. She inhaled through her nose and dropped her eyelids.

"Something else?" he asked.

She slowly opened her smoldering eyes and looked right at him.

"No, sir."

She went straight to the infirmary dressed in her civilian clothes, stained with corren blood, armed with two pistols and her knife. She realized she'd left the Confederate weapon in one of the bags she sent to Al-Farid and made a mental note to retrieve it. As she walked into the med bay, Tuah looked up. She thought to say something, but Carina shook her head.

TWENTY-ONE

SARGAS AND THE five Allied soldiers approached the Dorance Building. Two sentries blocked their path. "Declare yourself," one sentry demanded in his hollow, mechanized voice. The other leveled his plasma cannon at the group.

"A'arilon Raymond, lieutenant commander. Third Fleet, Venus."

The sentry queried the network and confirmed Ray's existence, rank, and posting.

"You are far afield, Lieutenant Commander A'arilon Raymond. We have no record of orders for your presence here. You are considered a deserter. Surrender to our custody. Your companions must also surrender."

Anjali interjected. "We're here on orders from Major General Alton Heston, of the Maxwell Montes cloud base on Venus. It is imperative that we secure, here, cargo taken from Confederation forces."

"Identify yourself."

"Hastings, Anjali, lieutenant commander. First Fleet, Venus."

"You, too, must surrender," the sentry ordered. "Resist, and be terminated. Turn around and present hands for detention."

Ray turned around and put both hands behind his back. The sentry bound him.

"Order your charges to submit or they will be terminated."

"Do it," Ray said.

One by one, they submitted to restraint. Only Sargas remained. He made no movement, neither menacing nor complicit.

"Comply, or be dispatched," dictated the sentry.

"Sargas, please," said Ray. "This is just protocol. Trust me."

"They cannot harm me," Sargas replied. He couldn't feel the nanomachines at work, but he sensed them the way anyone could sense their body adapting to stress.

"Fire on my command," said the sentry, his dead voice devoid of human consciousness, bereft of subjectivity and emotion. The other sentry's plasma cannon whirred as it charged.

"Belay that," Ray stated.

"You are in no position to give orders, Lieutenant Commander A'arilon Raymond," the sentry replied.

Ray looked at Sargas. "Maybe they can't hurt you but, please . . . submit quietly like the rest of us. We've been through enough today."

"I will not be restrained," Sargas balked.

"Lieutenant Commander A'arilon Raymond, this is your final warning. If your charge will not submit, he will be terminated. He persists only through your complicity and his own passive posture. Order him to submit. Should he refuse, he will be terminated."

"*Please*, Sargas," Ray implored. "We've come this far. It's a formality. If we comply, we protect ourselves. These sentries are dead men—machines—programmed machines. They don't think; they don't have reason. All they have are the orders they can access, and our mission might as well not exist. Use your reason, Sargas. *Please.* Submit to them. I give you my word that nothing bad will come of this."

Sargas breathed deep and exhaled through his nose. He turned his back to the sentry with his hands behind him.

"Thank you for your compliance," said the sentry, binding him.

Another sentry came to retrieve Ray and his cohort. It ushered them inside where two more sentries guided them to the lifts.

The Allies descended deep below the Dorance Building, to where Lieutenant Andersen, Sergeant Liggan, and a contingent of armed MPs waited. At the fore of the welcoming party was a gnarled, stocky, dark-skinned human with a colonel's crown and two pips on his collar.

"Take them to holding for debriefing," the colonel ordered, shaking his head. "You two," he added to the sentries, "go back to your godforsaken posts."

They obeyed without remark.

As the MPs marched the group down the corridor, the force fields responded to the chips embedded in their hands, allowing passage.

Daedalus emitted a gentle snort and shook his head. "Force fields . . ."

"You object to our defenses, mister?" asked Van Sinderen.

"Quite pathetic, Colonel. Any idiot with half a brain can outwit a force field with a phase modulator . . . this is the best you've got?"

"Our defenses are not your concern."

"With all due respect, sir, they are my concern because I'm here, now, and the quality of your aegis affects me. You must know there are only two of us. And although we all look the same to you, I bet you know which one I am."

"You *must* be A'arilon Daedalus. Because I doubt Lieutenant Commander Raymond would ever be so insolent."

"Such a good little soldier, Raymond," Daedalus mocked.

Ray clenched his jaw and his fists behind his back.

"Where are we going?" Sargas asked.

"Don't you listen?" Daedalus sniped. "They're throwing us in a cell while they diddle themselves . . ."

"Prison," Sargas replied dully.

"He's a sharp one, everybody," said Daedalus.

"It's temporary," Ray insisted.

"Endless Gray!" Van Sinderen cursed. "Cut the chatter! Or I'll have you all muzzled—" He stopped short at the sound of Sargas' restraints breaking. Van Sinderen turned to his armed escorts. "Shoot him!"

Lance Corporal Mahoney and Private Vanier managed to pop off a few rounds of blaster fire before Ray shouted them down.

"No! Belay that!" Ray screamed. "Hold your goddamned fire! He's not to be harmed!"

Mahoney and Vanier stopped shooting. Sargas was unharmed. He attacked, launching Mahoney from his feet with a push to the chest. Sargas grabbed Vanier by the collar and flung him like a toy. The private planted his hands and rolled like a gymnast, mitigating the impact as he hit the floor.

"I give the orders here!" Van Sinderen postured.

"We have orders from higher than you!" Ray bared his teeth. "General Heston demands he be delivered *alive* . . . no matter *who* has to die. Did you even read today's orders, or are you such a hack they didn't even bother to tell you?"

It was a hedge. Ray suspected their mission was totally black and there would be no mention of it in the general orders, but it was his only card to play.

Van Sinderen fumed at the insult. "Shooting him did fuck all anyway," he muttered. "Restrain him!"

The remaining men had already engaged Sargas.

Mahoney and Vanier rejoined the fray. The soldiers bum-rushed. Sargas beat them back with a combination of martial arts and brute force. Mahoney tried to trip him, applying pressure to his chest to create a fulcrum, but Sargas just shoved again. He sent the lithe human tumbling backward, end over end.

Vanier kicked out Sargas' knee from behind. The big man clattered to a kneel. He kicked like a donkey, breaking Vanier's nose. Stars exploded across the soldier's vision. His head swam as he fell back, clutching his hands to his face.

"Fuck!" he yelled through his hands. Blood gushed from his nose.

"Restrain him, dammit!" Van Sinderen yelled, panicked. "He's one man!"

Ray strained against his cuffs and they broke with a high-pitched *plink*. Another dulcet chime signaled Daedalus breaking free. At the sight of the two correns freed from their shackles, Van Sinderen unleashed a litany of curses in progressively darker shades of blue.

Ray said nothing. Daedalus needed no direction. Ray slammed his shoulder into Sargas' back, flattening him prone. Daedalus throttled him with a headlock. Mahoney, Vanier, and the rest of the human soldiers piled on top of Daedalus. He panicked. His focus shifted from restraining Sargas to getting free of the humans.

"Get the fuck off of me!" he howled, letting go of Sargas.

Daedalus threw Mahoney, Vanier, and the petite female private, Burke, from his back. He rounded on them. Rational thought began to recede, replaced by bloodlust. His bony features grew more prominent as berserker rage started taking him over.

Ray climbed flat on top of Sargas. Lieutenant Andersen threw himself over Ray's back. Daedalus bellowed at Mahoney, Vanier, and Burke, each defenseless in their cloth uniforms. He fought back the urge to kill them. He put his head into his hands and forced his instinct for battle back into its cage.

Ada caught Van Sinderen's eye. "Let me go," she demanded.

"Pfft," he replied. "What the hell are *you* gonna do?"

"If I'm no threat, let me go, and I'll *show* you."

He nodded at Sergeant Liggan. She removed Ada's restraints.

Ada ran to Sargas and got down on the floor in front of him. Taking his enraged face in her hands, she forced him to look in her eyes.

"Shh. Sargas! It's okay. Just relent."

Daedalus turned away from the three terrified humans. He walked over to the pile of bodies and sat upon Sargas' legs, still cradling his own head in his hands. Mahoney, Vanier, and Burke lent their bodies anew to the pile, careful to avoid contact with Daedalus.

"Please, you need to be calm," said Ada. "You need to trust us. I know you have every reason not to."

A tall, thin human in full armor with an opaque, mirrored visor walked up behind Ada. He removed one of his gloves and placed his bare hand on the back of her head. She felt her power amplify. Her will to put Sargas to sleep smashed through his defenses and he lost consciousness.

The man removed his hand from Ada's head and she, too, knocked out. The soldiers piled off of the neutralized threat.

"Get him to the highest containment you have. Now," Ray demanded. "If you've got anything that can actually hold a corren, you'll need more."

The colonel's eyes bugged out with indignation. "I don't take orders from you."

"This isn't a pissing match, Colonel. Did you see that? We're only alive because he let us live. You don't know what he is and what he can do. He won't be out for long."

"Take him to the psionic holding cell, right now," ordered the slender, armored man as he put his glove back on.

Ray looked at the man's nameplate. Gardiner. He had a major's crown on his collar.

Andersen ordered Mahoney and Vanier to pick up Ada and to ferry the correns, Anjali, and Patrick to the holding cell. The remaining MPs tried to pick up Sargas' body but could barely get him off the floor.

"Dammit, pick him up!" yelled the colonel.

"Sir, he's too heavy," Private Burke objected.

"Daedalus," Ray said, picking up Sargas' feet.

Daedalus grabbed him under the arms. "Urrgh. He does weigh a fucking ton. And I thought the tube was heavy."

Andersen and Burke each lent their arms under Sargas' midsection.

"Lead the way," Ray said to Gardiner.

Van Sinderen thought to protest the correns walking free, but he needed someone to handle Sargas, and no one else could. They carried the dense, seven-foot-long body through the complex to a holding cell designed to detain telepaths.

"Take off his clothes," Gardiner ordered.

"Really, sir?" Andersen balked.

Gardiner stared at Andersen and said nothing. The lieutenant could see only his reflection in the major's visor.

"Okay . . ." the lieutenant relented. He looked at Burke for help. "Private."

She shrugged and unzipped the bodysuit. They peeled it off while Ray and Daedalus held him up.

"Whoa," Burke exclaimed.

"I should show you mine sometime," Andersen replied.

"Yeah right," she replied.

Andersen's face faltered.

"Hang him up," Gardiner ordered. His face remained hidden.

"I think he's already hung enough, Major," Andersen joked, wanting to deflect attention from Burke's outright rejection.

No one laughed.

He and Burke helped Ray and Daedalus secure Sargas into the arm and leg restraints, which pulled him cruciform. Spittle drooled down his chin, pattering onto the floor.

"God, it's pathetic to see him like this," Daedalus said quietly.

"Come on, before he wakes up," Ray said, pulling Daedalus from the room.

Outside, the colonel stood with his arms crossed over his chest. Reproach lined his scarred face.

"What?" Daedalus snapped.

"You two will still be detained for debriefing."

"Detained?" Ray balked. "After that? What else could we do to prove that we're on your side?"

"I assume you're A'arilon Ray . . . but I won't stake my reputation on it."

"What reputation?" Daedalus yawned.

"Throw him in the brig," Van Sinderen ordered.

"Try me," Daedalus challenged.

"If he resists, kill him."

Andersen walked up to Daedalus. "Just give me an excuse. I'll blow your ugly ass away."

"How about you just blow me?" Daedalus replied.

"Funny, snake. March." Andersen indicated the direction with his rifle.

"Fucking idiot human," Daedalus retorted. "We're not even reptiles."

"Shut up," said Andersen as he led Daedalus away, accompanied by Burke.

Lance Corporal Curwen and Private Berkey led Ray to a separate holding cell, away from Daedalus.

When they arrived at the holding cell, Curwen tried pushing Ray through the door but he wouldn't budge. Berkey added her effort to the cause.

"Please, Commander," Curwen implored, "with all respect . . . get in the cell."

Ray allowed himself to be pushed inside, but only after multiple shoves from both Curwen and Berkey. He derived childish satisfaction from showing them how weak they were. The door closed behind him and he closed his eyes. He breathed deeply to stem the rage that boiled just beneath the surface of his control. When he opened his eyes again, he saw Anjali sitting against the wall. Pain wracked her face. He went to her.

"What is it?"

"Ugh, my stomach . . ." she replied. "Something's wrong, Ray. Really *wrong*."

He looked around the room.

Ada dozed with her chin to her chest, still under Major Gardiner's spell. Patrick sat in the corner, head against the wall, arms tight around his midsection. Daedalus was in the brig. Sargas, in containment. And Rozhenko was missing in action, wandering the tunnels under the city.

Anjali doubled over. She vomited on herself and on the floor. As she leaned forward, Ray saw the blood on the bench. He put his hand upon the inside of her thigh. His fingers came away red.

"Hey!" He ran to the door and banged it with his fist. "Hey, dammit! We need a doctor in here!"

Ada startled awake. The door groaned open. Andersen stuck a plasma rifle right in Ray's face.

"What the fuck is your goddamned probl—?"

Ray snatched the rifle out of Andersen's hands and threw it into the cell.

Andersen gawped at Ray.

Ada and Patrick dodged the gun as it clattered on the floor. It slid beneath the bench. Curwen's hand shook as he aimed his pistol at Ray. The lance corporal steadied it with his other hand.

Andersen recovered himself and sneered up into Ray's face.

"Commander Hastings is sick," Ray barked. "She's *bleeding*. We have to get her to the doctor."

"Our doctor isn't in," the lieutenant replied, crossing his arms over his chest. "Besides, even if she was, she's useless."

Ray grabbed Andersen by the collar. Curwen waved his gun uselessly, unwilling to shoot an officer. He holstered the weapon and grasped at one of Ray's arms, to no avail. Ignoring the grunt, Ray bared his teeth at Andersen.

"Listen to me, you piece of shit. If she dies, you die. I will stop at nothing to kill you."

"You'd throw away your career for little ole me?" Andersen goaded.

Ray shook him hard. Andersen's head bobbled.

"We are all members of the same fucking military!" Ray shouted, punctuating his speech by shaking the lieutenant. "You're gonna let one of your own bleed out just to *fuck* with me?"

"Um . . . sir," said Curwen to his commanding officer, "perhaps we *should* take her to the infirmary."

"Get the captain and fucking bring her here," Andersen growled. He looked at Ray. "Let. Me. Go."

"Commander!" Ada cried, cradling Anjali's head in her lap. "She's fainted."

Ray's rage bubbled over. He hoisted Andersen from his feet and hurled him across the hall. The lieutenant slammed into the bulkhead and fell, unconscious, to the floor. Ray punched the thick metal wall. The bones in his hand audibly broke. He howled, grimacing as the pain washed the rage away.

"Get the doctor!" he shouted at Curwen. "Get the goddamned medic!"

The lance corporal ran to the medical bay.

Ray awaited the warm feeling that coursed through his body while it repaired itself. He could not open his broken fist. He lurked in the open door, looking at Andersen's unconscious body, regretting his lack of control. Moments passed that felt like an eternity.

Just as he was able to open his hand and test his fingers, Carina burst past him into the cell. Mahoney followed, pushing a hover-gurney. Tuah trailed them both.

Carina wore her dirty street clothes and was fully armed. Ray looked at her guns and her knife, at her shirt stained with corren blood. The sight of her filled him with unease. Manon sprung to mind.

Tuah checked on Andersen, feeling for his pulse. She eased him onto his back. She entered the cell and joined Carina at Anjali's side. They put Anjali's limp body atop the gurney and rushed her to the infirmary.

Ray tried to follow but Curwen held up his hand. "Please, sir . . . Please. Stay here. I don't want to lose my posting. Let's not make this personal."

"Any more personal than he already made it?" Patrick piped up, pointing at Andersen. "You see this?" He pointed at his charred shoulder. "I could use real medical attention. You're treating us like prisoners!"

"We don't even know who you are!" Curwen retorted, exasperated. "You come here, dressed in Confederate uniforms, claiming to be Allied soldiers on a mission nobody knows about! You've raised hell since you got here! You may have killed my CO!"

He made an emphatic gesture at Andersen's limp form.

Ray scoffed.

"Just, please," Curwen implored, "for fuck's sake, sit tight while we sort this out. The doc'll care for her as best she can."

The door slid closed. Ray pounded it once with the meaty part of his unbroken fist. He put his forehead against the door and emitted a faint groan.

TWENTY-TWO

THE LIGHTS OF Blackwing spaceport glittered below.

Intiri initiated the landing sequence and the ship descended vertically. The sleek, black craft touched down upon the tarmac. The stabilizing thrusters hissed, and the landing struts flexed to absorb the shock.

Arak strode down the gangway behind Alesh and Derovias, the latter of whom pushed Kir in front of him. Kir stood with his chin up and shoulders back, refusing to show weakness. A fierce wind blew into the hangar through the open roof, tossing Arak's black, vermilion-lined cape to and fro. Inishi and Irva'a stood behind their master, boxing him in.

Intiri stood alone.

Members of the Red Guard arrived in welcome. Their armor was the color of dried blood, leafed with black enamel. Maroon fabric lined their short black cloaks. The half shields of their helmets left their mouths and chins exposed. The guardsmen snapped to attention and saluted.

Arak dismissed them with a gesture. As the four members of the guard began to move away, he pointed to the captain and beckoned him to stay.

"Pongsrion Klahan," Arak said.

"Yes, Lord?"

"There will be no communication to or from this installation—nor from any part of this city—without my consent."

"Of course, master," Klahan replied.

"Assemble the rogues to the Great Hall; it's time to stop . . . pampering them and put them to work. Dismissed."

Klahan nodded, bowed, and hurried off.

Arak and his centurions ignored the teleportation window. While the dimensional jump was instantaneous, the walk to the manor took much longer. But Arak refused to put his life in the hands of a technology that could instantly end his life at random.

Once Arak and his men arrived at the manor, two Red Guardsmen—one corren, one human—approached.

"Hello, Falco," said Arak to the human guardsman. "Pick for me . . . a woman from the stable . . . and bring her to my chambers."

"Yes, Lord." Falco bowed. He departed with his corren partner, Asharan Ji'ilaad.

Arak turned to Derovias and Kir.

"Kir . . . tend to the dungeon. Familiarize yourself with it; you may find yourself living there. Remain until summoned. I expect you to remember . . . how to behave."

Kir bowed and disappeared behind the grand staircase.

Arak held up his hand, indicating that all but Derovias should keep their distance. He drew his lieutenant to his side. They stepped away from the others.

"Marseh is making a power grab," said Arak. "The cargo stolen from Overground needs to be intercepted and destroyed. Clearly, it is a creature . . . and it is coming either straight here, of its own volition, or—"

He paused.

Derovias arched an eye ridge in response.

Arak cocked his head to the side and abandoned his previous thought. "Marseh will surely try and flush them out of Orchard City. He can't want his weapon idling there. What would be the point?"

"Do you mean to say that all this is by his design?" Derovias asked.

"I don't know his mind. He's long since kept me from his plans. From the moment he decided we were better at odds than as allies. But . . . if I understand him, this is a scheme and whatever its purpose . . . he will want his pawns in motion, not hunkered down in some strategic bywater. He'll flush them out . . . surely. And, then, where would they go?"

Derovias recognized the prompt. Arak had made his conclusion and he wanted to see if his pet could draw the same one.

"Before they head here?"

The Butcher nodded.

"They'll have to pass through Coventry first. But what of the cargo? Why would it come here?"

"It is most certainly a weapon, that organism. And I doubt . . . that Marseh intends it to kill the very Allies he enlisted to steal it in the first place. No. I think . . . he intends it for me."

Derovias stood in still silence, presenting an air of perfect obedience.

"Manage the assembly," Arak ordered. "I'll join you when I'm done."

"But, Lord. What shall I say to them?"

"Keep them busy." Arak stroked his chin in thought. "I will want to send my best men, but . . . I will need at least a few loyal men to stay here with me. Whom shall I keep, Derovias?"

Derovias felt the lump in his throat. He waited a moment and the tension subsided. "I would recommend that you keep Irva'a and Intiri."

Arak nodded.

"And what of Kir?" asked Derovias.

"I fear that, by favoring him, I've emboldened him to confront me as an equal. Have I made the same mistake with you?"

"Of course not, Lord," the corren replied, neither rushed nor hesitant. "I would never presume to be your equal."

"Tell me, Derovias, have I undermined myself in your eyes, and in the eyes of your brothers, by not killing him? Have I encouraged you all to challenge me?"

Derovias forced himself to hold Arak's gaze. "No, master. Your compassion is no weakness in its proper measure. Kir is valuable. He has always been dependable. To delete him over what was, yes, an inexcusable breach of decorum . . . I would consider it too extreme. I reckon the others would agree. Kir is our brother. We love him. We appreciate your mercy. We do not believe you weak."

Arak said nothing. He clenched and opened his fists.

Derovias waited through the long silence. It felt as though eternity had transpired.

"Retrieve him when the meeting convenes," said Matar. "He needn't be briefed; he need only follow your orders. Go, hold court while they await me. I have my own work to do."

Derovias bowed and headed to the Great Hall.

Arak scaled the staircase to the upper levels of the manor. Alesh and Inishi obediently followed his every movement. They took their places outside Arak's chambers, to either side of the massive oaken door. The Butcher retired within.

Falco, with a buxom human woman in tow, knocked upon the door.

"Enter," bade Arak.

The heavy door swung open without a sound, guided by Falco's hand. He ferried the slave woman into the room. The visible portion of Falco's face belied no emotion. But every time he did this job, he thought of Carina being presented to the prefect of Tripas in the same way. It felt as though his heart pumped poison instead of blood. It spread to his every extremity. When the woman was fully within the room, he retreated to the hallway and closed the door. He rejoined Ji'ilaad. Together, they stood vigil opposite Alesh and Inishi.

Mirrored shields hid the centurions' faces. Falco could not read them. He set his jaw and clenched his teeth. He steeled himself against the sounds he knew would soon resonate through the door.

The sound of a mighty retch carried out into the hallway from behind the closed chamber door. Falco's mouth ticked.

"If this displeases you, Falco, consider yourself relieved," Alesh stated.

Falco looked at his own reflection in Alesh's mirror shield. He wondered if the corren was smiling. Despite the suggestion to leave, Falco remained still, corrected his face, and kept his post. He tried to meditate through the screams and groans permeating the door. At certain moments, he recognized sounds of unambiguous enjoyment emanating from the girl, and it wrenched his guts. Worse yet, he enjoyed to hear it. Inwardly, he cursed his arousal. He castigated his prurient depravity. His face burned with shame.

Eventually, the noises within Arak's chambers died down. Moments of silence followed until the door swung open, revealing the Butcher, naked but for the helm covering his face. Blood and other bodily fluids mottled his penis, which hung nearly half the length of his thick, muscular thighs. He hurled the woman toward Falco, who reflexively put up his arms to catch her.

"Put her in the rookery," Arak croaked. He slammed the door.

Falco's stomach twisted. He choked down the bile that seared the back of his throat. He tried to dispel the sheer enormity of Arak's phallus from his mind's eye, but he fixated on it like a scab and felt childishly insecure for doing so.

"That tiny little body," said Inishi.

Alesh chuckled.

The woman said nothing, holding on to Falco tighter than was necessary. Her head rested against his breastplate. He tensed and thought to confront the correns but bit it back. His entire career in the corren-dominated military consisted of slights toward his species and reminders of his physical inferiority. Falco hoisted the woman into his arms and carried her toward the rookery. Ji'ilaad followed two steps behind.

"Mind your human, brother," Inishi called after Ji'ilaad. "Such a liability requires added vigilance."

Falco ground his teeth at the insult but kept moving. He brought the woman to a new berth in the rookery. She stirred in his arms and panicked, struggling to free herself from his grip.

"Relax," he said, trying in vain to find a soothing tone and consoling words. "I'm not going to hurt you."

He brought her to an empty bunk and set her down. She sat there, fully nude, and hung her head. Not knowing what else to do, Falco pulled off his glove and put his hand to her crown. He stroked her hair with his thumb and looked at the other women. There were at least fifty of them, all in different stages of pregnancy. He regularly consorted with some of them. He wondered what happened to the children, when they came to term. Little did he nor any of his fellow guardsmen know that all the babies would be corren.

Arak's latest unwilling incubator startled at the touch. She looked up, eyes level with Falco's waist. His pistol hung from his hip and she grabbed at it. He swatted her hand away and slapped her hard across the face. The sound of it filled the rookery. He stood upright and glared at the woman. She sat mute with her hand upon her cheek and a faraway look in her eyes. As a nurse came over to tend to her, Falco turned on his heel and stormed out.

Ji'ilaad kept pace. He said something and received no reply, so he jerked Falco by the collar.

"Dammit, I said, 'Are you listening?'"

"I hear you, dammit," Falco replied. "I fucking hear you."

Ji'ilaad let him go and eyed him, wary. "You need to be harder than this."

Falco turned and slammed his gauntleted fist against the stone wall.

As he reeled his fist back to punch it again, Ji'ilaad grabbed Falco's arm and twisted it behind his back. He pushed him face-first against the cool stone, gently enough to avoid harm.

"Stop," Ji'ilaad said. He administered enough resistance to still Falco without injury but refused to let him budge. "Stop. Or I *will* break your arm."

Falco ceased to struggle. Ji'ilaad let him go. The human turned, leaned against the wall, and regarded his corren counterpart with a mixture of disdain, resentment, and desperation.

"Do not . . . be a damned fool," Ji'ilaad warned. "Don't think that this moment of indignation somehow redeems you for all of the wrong you've done at His behest. You are a *murderer*, my boy. Just like Arak Matar. Just like me. We all have blood on our hands . . . and those of us capable of guilt have bodies on our conscience. But you have no right to follow this . . . nascent streak of righteous outrage over evil *you* have wrought. Remember your place. You are not righteous. You are not innocent . . . and neither is anyone else."

"That woman did *not* deserve what she got," Falco complained. "None of them did!"

"Better to live well here than be a whore out in the world. You heard her enjoy it. Don't throw your life away over a human slave whore."

Falco's eyes widened in anger.

"Grow up, child," Ji'ilaad chided. "Find me a woman who hasn't fucked for food or sucked dick for a blanket. Hell, find a man who hasn't done the same out in the badlands. It's a cold truth, dearest boy: people are whores of circumstance."

"Fuck you, Ji'ilaad. Fuck your 'cold truths.' You use 'human' like an insult. *I'm* human. *I* was a fucking slave. *I* am a 'whore of circumstance.' And, after a lifetime of nothing but you snakes for company, I'm at the end of my *rope*."

Ji'ilaad spat on the floor and frowned. "Have you forgotten that I was *there*? Did you forget why you're even *here*, and not still a slave? Or *dead*?"

"You had no choice but to sponsor me," Falco replied, "because of what I had on you."

"How dare you throw that in my face!" Ji'ilaad growled. "After what I *risked* for you! You had nothing on me until I helped those girls. Damn my soft heart."

"That's not what I meant," Falco offered.

Ji'ilaad bared his teeth. "Then what did you mean?"

"Amazing. You've hijacked my pity party—" Falco stopped short at the steady clomp of boots upon the stone floor.

Alesh, clad in black, could barely be discerned from the shadows.

"Come with me," he beckoned, making clear his displeasure at having had to hunt them down.

TWENTY-THREE

FALCO AND JI'ILAAD followed Alesh to the Great Hall, which Arak had converted into his war room. There convened a crowd of centurions and a handful of rogues whom Falco recognized as mercenaries.

He wondered if Alesh had overheard the treasonous conversation and worried they'd been marked for recrimination. As no one paid Falco any mind, his fears abated. He evaluated the talent. Two of the human hires stood out. An exceptionally tall bald man and a woman at least six feet in height. She had thick, unnaturally blond curls with reddish-brown roots. Her hair radiated from her scalp like a corona. Two crude, purple streaks upon each medium-brown cheek complemented her smoky green eyes.

She looked so much like Carina.

While the female mercenary showed no flesh beside her exposed face, her outfit left little to the imagination. Her skin tone didn't match Falco's memory, but her eyes conjured the indelible image of him on his back, looking up at Carina. Recollection transported him back to the mid-Atlantic archipelago, *Las Tres Islas de la Paz*—derisively called "Tripas"—where he cried, bereft, as Ji'ilaad stowed Carina, Michèle, and Agnès onto the cargo ship to Isla Sangrante. To their demise.

A fresh tear welled in Falco's eye, jarring him back to reality. He blinked it away. The mercenary woman was too young to be Carina. The faces didn't match up in his mind, even accounting for sixteen years, but he felt in his guts that he beheld either Agnès or Michèle. It meant at least one of them had survived. And, maybe, so had Carina. His heart leapt into his throat. He took a breath, lest he be swept away by adolescent memories.

A tense, palpable air of anxiety and animosity polluted the room. The centurions kept significant distance from Carina's sister. She wore two swords, strapped in an X across her back. Vicious, serrated metal branches protected the hilts. Greenish-brown tassels hung from the pommels. The issue dawned on Falco. The tassels were corren hair. The coppery grips were leather made from corren skin. She was a bone and scalp hunter. It's what the face paint signified. He looked at Ji'ilaad, who returned the glance with a wry smile.

"My boy," he said, so only Falco could hear. "Should our master persist to outrage me like this, I may join you in the fool's errand of killing him."

"My Lord!" Intiri finally erupted. "What is the meaning of bringing this human bitch into our midst, if not to kill her for the mere *insult* of her existence?"

Arak Matar rose from his seat to stand at his full imposing height. He cast his gaze about the room. "Mind your tongue, if you wish to keep it. This 'human bitch,' vile as she may be, is a formidable asset . . . and she may well be more of a man than any of you."

Falco watched her eyes smolder at the insult, but the corner of her mouth ticked up at the backhanded compliment.

"Derovias has briefed you fully," Arak continued. "I expect to be very pleased by your results."

He and Derovias moved through the room, talking in private to the groups of centurions, guardsmen, and mercenaries. Arak's regal bearing and slow gait emphasized his already daunting mien. His cape flitted about with apparent life of its own. Its every move accented the Butcher's graceful motion. Arak passed from group to group. The crowd dwindled until only Ji'ilaad and Falco, the tall, bald man, the female scalp hunter, Alesh, Inishi, Derovias, and Kir remained.

Falco, his eyes hidden behind his visor, looked upon Derovias with distrust. The corren caught the look and sneered, showing his sharp eyeteeth. Kir appeared sullen and defeated, unlike his normal, haughty self. Falco wondered why.

Arak came to them, drawing their attention. "The eight of you are to find the Aktali—you know their names—and bring them all to me. The insult of their adopted surname is infuriating enough, but make no mistake, they have forsaken *us*. It is not the other way around . . . You," he said directly to Ji'ilaad, who tensed, "may once have shared a name with *Daedalus*, but he has discarded Asharan for A'arilon. He has forsaken *you* and your brothers, and you *will not* be thwarted by sentimentality."

"No, my Lord," Ji'ilaad replied. "I will not."

Arak looked over the three humans and five correns.

"A'arilon Ray must be brought to me alive. Put your differences aside, or you will understand my displeasure. My centurions and you guardsmen, your rewards will be immeasurable prestige and privilege." He turned to the woman. "As for you, Ceres . . . you and your companion will know significant riches . . . and conditional immunity."

"I can live with both," the tall, bald human replied.

"No one asked you, Andrei," remonstrated Ceres.

Arak smiled beneath his mask. "Your prey are well-trained Allied soldiers, and better-trained Confederate defectors, so take heed. They will not be alone, and there will surely be collateral damage in the attempt to apprehend them."

"I'm not concerned with bystanders," said Ceres. "We have our objective. We'll carry it out."

Arak inclined his head in approval and left the room.

Derovias' helmet sat atop the lavish wooden table. He pulled his long hair, such a dark green that it seemed black, into a ponytail. He smiled again at Falco, who suppressed a shudder and forced a smile. He removed his own helmet and Ji'ilaad did the same.

"Interesting company we keep these days," Ji'ilaad said to Derovias.

"I couldn't think of better company than yours, Asharan Ji'ilaad. I'm honored."

"I've heard worse lies," Ji'ilaad laughed.

Falco could tell it was forced from their years of partnership, but Ji'ilaad did well to conceal it.

Derovias insisted on his sincerity. "You and Lután are the only two of your batch who haven't yet died, defected, or deserted. It is something to be proud of, brother."

"I accept your praise with all humility," said Ji'ilaad. He and Derovias conferred while Kir stood silently by. They all seemed to derive comfort from their likeness.

Apart from the other correns, Alesh and Inishi stood together, as always. They cast hard looks at Ceres and Andrei.

Falco stood alone between the brooding centurions and human mercenaries, stranded in a crossfire of icy glances. He felt the need to play peacemaker.

"I'm Falco Sotillo," he said to the humans.

"Andrei Balan," the man said, offering his hand.

Falco took it. He looked at the woman.

"Ceres," she said, crossing her arms.

He shrugged at the strange name, wanting to press for her real one, to ask if she knew Carina, but it wasn't the time to play detective. He rued that he'd never met her younger sisters and, so, remained a stranger to them.

"Have you met Asharan Ji'ilaad?" Falco asked. "And these men are Kurgan Derovias and Kurgan Kir."

A glimmer of recognition flitted across Ceres' face as she looked at Ji'ilaad. She mastered it. Shaking her head, she told herself: *They all look the same.* No such recognition occurred for Ji'ilaad; the ten-year-old girl he'd rescued bore little resemblance to the woman she'd become.

Falco looked at Alesh and Inishi and realized he didn't know their batch names. He wondered if his service in Blackwing had insulated him too much, or if he were slipping somehow, because nearly everyone knew Arak's core centurions. They were the closest thing to celebrities that existed in the Confederation, along with Marseh's core paladins.

Derovias, catching Falco's hesitation, picked up the slack.

"Ceres and Andrei, meet Ishtafan Alesh and Tolon Inishi."

The humans offered perfunctory nods. Alesh and Inishi offered nothing.

Falco sighed through his nose and gave his head an imperceptible shake.

"Shouldn't we proceed?" Ji'ilaad asked, hoping to dispel the tension.

"Indeed," Derovias replied. "Ray and Daedalus are believed to have been part of an Allied team who raided Overground."

Ceres narrowed her eyes. "They raided Overground? Interesting."

Derovias reduced his own eyes to slits in response to the interruption. "I should say they *attempted* a raid. The emperor shot down their ship. That should stand as proof of their futility."

"And what would you call their continued survival?" Ceres asked.

"Miraculous," Derovias smiled, baring his fangs. "They crash-landed here, on Nova Spes. We discovered three casualties amid the wreckage. Three humans of no consequence. The rest are certain to have survived. Three of them are the Aktali, whom you know, and a female lieutenant commander from the Allied Navy. Anjali Hastings. The daughter of Fleet Admiral Alistair Hastings. She is a high-value target that we would like to capture. As our Lord has stated, the survivors would surely attempt to reach the local Allied base."

"Perhaps we should depart for Orchard City before their trail gets any colder," offered Falco.

"A fine idea, but no," Derovias replied. "We will go to Coventry."

The hair on the back of Falco's neck prickled.

"Coventry?" said Ceres. "If they're in Orchard, we'll be too far north."

"Don't worry yourself with the details, my dear. Have faith that there is a plan."

"Little choice," she conceded.

Derovias smiled at her again. "Gather what weapons, armor, and resources you need. Meet me in the statuary in one half hour. Dismissed."

Falco and Ji'ilaad took their leave through the doors by which they entered. Derovias, Kir, Alesh, and Inishi used the opposite doors.

Andrei and Ceres waited for the room to clear.

He looked down at her. "This is fucked up."

"Shut up," she replied. "The spoils are too good to pass up."

"I've got a bad feeling about this," he replied.

"Sort it out, then, 'cause I'm tired of your unease. If you're suddenly too old, or too soft, or you lack the stomach to do this . . . walk away, Drei."

"Yeah, no," he yawned. "But I still think you're nuts; this borders on crazy. No, it's beyond that. Working for these monsters . . . working with them."

She pushed him in the chest.

"We have no *choice* since you blew the last bounty on whores, and weapons we couldn't transport, or cache. We had to sell them at a loss. You've put it on me to take care of your increasingly useless ass and I am full fucking fed up."

Andrei started to say something.

"Shut up," Ceres ordered, pointing her finger at his chest. "You're only here 'cause of my charity. You better recall the talents that made you worth the investment in the first place. From now on, you do as I say when I say. Don't presume to talk to me like we're equals. And don't even think about asking after my pussy 'til you've done something to earn it."

She resumed walking.

Andrei lagged for a few moments, chewing on her words before falling in behind her.

TWENTY-FOUR

MANON AND JACK walked through the same tunnels Adnan had used to guide Ray and the Allies to the surface.

She and her android companion diverted northward, away from the Orchard City chaos toward a different brand of bedlam in Coventry, the badlands city amok with Ingili and vagabond humans.

Jack opened his mouth to speak, just like any human. He perfectly emulated the behavior.

"That corren in which you've taken such an interest has my nose. It's unsettling to look at his face . . . and see traces of me. The face that I had."

His voice was a very human low tenor, with just a trace of tin.

"And that large human. Not the cyborg, the flesh one. Obviously a genetic experiment. He has my whole face, Manon. Does that make him my child? How is this possible?"

"How are you possible, Jack?"

She couldn't bring herself to pronounce his name without the French inflection. She preferred the first language of both her parents. It frustrated her that Jack rarely spoke to her in it, despite being perfectly capable. But she also spoke English perfectly well. It was essential, since few on Nova Spes spoke anything else.

"I'd like to be angry," he said, "but I'm not allowed by my programming. And I'm reminded that I am not," he looked at her, "a 'real man.'"

"Tu es mieux que n'importe quel 'vrai' homme, Jacques," she said. *You're better than any* "real" *man, Jack.*

"Who is making copies of me? Of whom I was."

"You know who's making copies of you," she replied.

Jack looked down at her and frowned. "So, Marseh looted my corpse. I *wish* I could get angry."

"What do you want to do about it?" she asked, exasperated, getting close to him.

"There's someone here," he said, gently pushing her away. He listened to the sound, still dozens of meters away. "Large, mechanical. But . . . organic. It's the cyborg from the camp."

Manon drew her sword with one hand and her pistol with the other.

"Yes, I know," said Rozhenko in his thick accent, "my approach is not mystery. I am not drawing weapon. I am being at your mercy."

He came into view after a few hundred paces and continued toward them, his hands away from his sides, palms outward.

"Why are you back?" asked Manon.

"The way up is too small for me."

Manon looked at Jack.

"For him, too, yes?" Rozhenko followed.

"There are other ways out," said Manon. "You're welcome to find one."

"So, I am returning to your camp? They are welcoming me? Or I am going alone, somewhere? Trying the odds?"

"That's up to you."

"But I am thinking they will not be taking me. Yes?"

Manon's flat expression answered his question.

Rozhenko regarded Jack, who stood quietly, apparently dormant.

"Does he move or speak?" The cyborg took a few steps closer to them.

"Don't get too close," Manon warned.

"We are not friends?" Rozhenko asked.

"I am not Edmund," she replied. "We are *not* friends."

"But I am wishing to be your friend."

She cleared her throat. "Look, that is very . . . touching. But you," she said to Rozhenko, "aren't built for stealth, and obviously not for speed. And I'm not interested in slowing down for you." She turned to Jack. "*We* need to go. And he needs to stay."

"And he is 'built for stealth'?" Rozhenko indicated Jack. "Such big machine?"

"He's speedier than you, I bet. And he holds his own in a fight."

"Ah. Me, too. Hard to kill. Strong, too."

"*Putain de merde! J'ai pas le temps pour ces conneries! Non!* The answer is 'no.' I travel with him, and only him. Not with you. Not with anybody else."

"I am needing place to go," Rozhenko said. His despair grew with her relentless refusal, but he remained collected. "I . . . am not knowing what to say. I am not knowing how to be changing your mind, but I am wishing it to change."

"You won't change my mind," she said, walking away.

Jack followed.

After a few paces, she stopped. She bit down on her lower lip and drew her teeth across it. She turned around, shaking her head.

"I'll probably regret this but . . . if you can get to Coventry, and you can find us, you can tag along from there."

Rozhenko's face brightened. "Thank you—"

"But. If I catch you on my tail in less than an hour, your second chance at life is over. We'll both make sure of that," she said, gesturing at Jack.

"I am accepting your terms," Rozhenko said, smiling and nodding.

"What do I call you?" she asked.

"Vasily Rozhenko," he replied.

Manon shrugged and turned her back on him. He watched her and Jack disappear into the shadows.

He waited.

TWENTY-FIVE

NEARLY AN HOUR had transpired. Rozhenko waited still. He sat against the wall, slapping his hand against the packed dirt floor to scare away the rats.

Out of human earshot, but audible to his cybernetic right ear, the sound of light footfalls approached. He rose to his feet and remained alert, listening to the nearing steps. It was either a woman or a light man. He scanned his memories of the camp. He remembered the surly, irascible boy. A likely candidate to be skulking the tunnels alone.

Rozhenko stepped into the middle of the tunnel and made himself conspicuous. "I am hearing you, there."

The footfalls stopped.

"I will not be harming you," Rozhenko assured.

"You're the big robot from that group," Adnan replied, coming into view.

"I am man. Part man."

"Yeah?" Adnan sneered. "Doubtful where it counts. Olga said the big one had no dick. Spread like wildfire through the camp."

Rozhenko blushed. He wondered why they even preserved any of his flesh and organs. Why not just build robots? Why cyborgs? Why resurrect men who had died, as husked puppets? And, his most burning question: Why had *his* consciousness survived the resurrection? Unlike any other sentry, he was forced to live completely aware of what he lacked. It made him sad. And that made him angry.

And now the boy was mocking him. He thought of killing Adnan for the slight, but only for a moment. That was not the man Rozhenko wanted to be. He walked away.

"Hey!" Adnan called, running after him. "Hey! Where are you going? *Hey*!"

Rozhenko said nothing. He followed Manon and Jack's trail, determined to ignore Adnan and make the journey to Coventry alone.

Adnan caught up to him. "*Bismillah,* what? Are you mad? Fuck. I'm sorry, okay? *W'allah.*"

"You apologize like shit," said Rozhenko.

"Dude . . . calm down."

Rozhenko turned so quickly, it belied his size and girth. He placed his big right hand atop Adnan's chest and shoved with such force that the boy flopped heels over head before landing ten feet away on his seat. Before he could cry out, Rozhenko was on top of him with blinding speed, the benefit of his mechanized parts.

He grabbed the boy by the lapels and hoisted him into the air.

"You think I am joke? I am *stupid* joke? I am *not*! Who are you?" He shook Adnan like a rag doll. "Who are *you*?"

Adnan's eyes opened so wide that Rozhenko could see the whites all the way around. He knew the look. He had seen it on those who knew they were about to die. Disgusted, he threw Adnan to the ground. The boy landed with a thud and a whimper.

Rozhenko turned. He continued toward the rendezvous with Manon and her android.

Adnan chased him. "Look, I'm sorry! Really!"

Rozhenko ignored the boy and continued walking. They emerged from the tunnels into an open-cut, abandoned railroad bed.

"Hey!" said Adnan. "Do you even know where you're going?"

"To Coventry."

"And how do you get there?"

Rozhenko stopped and looked at the boy. "I go north."

"That's it, huh? Look. I don't know how many times I can apologize, but I know how to get there. Take me with you."

Rozhenko exhaled in exasperation. "You are just leaving home? No parents are missing you?"

"Nobody gives a hot dump about me, man. There is just as good as here. Maybe better. Why the fuck do *you* care where I go?"

Rozhenko shook his head at him and turned his back. He resumed walking.

"So, is that a 'yes'?"

"I am feeling that you will not be leaving me alone, yes?"

Adnan shrugged. Rozhenko regarded the boy like something stuck to his mechanical foot.

"We better get moving," said Adnan. "It's going to take us, like, days, on foot. Whoa—!" he exclaimed as Rozhenko scooped him into his arms. "What are you doing?"

Without saying anything, the cyborg jumped over three meters high and ten meters forward. He landed and took a short hop before vaulting again, even higher and farther.

"Holy shit!" Adnan blurted.

The more Rozhenko jumped, the higher and farther he went. He chewed the distance faster than walking would allow. He passed the first kilometer in eighty-eight seconds. The next kilometer took half that time.

***

As Jack and Manon arrived in Coventry, he set her down and again reconfigured his legs to a more human facsimile from one suited for speed and distance.

"We've got maybe an hour until the Russian gets here . . . if he's even coming," said Manon. "I never set a rally point. *Comme c'est stupide.*"

"So, now you recognize his value?"

"I can see how he might be useful, yeah, since you explained what he can do. But it doesn't matter. If he finds us, he finds us. We still need to worry about us."

"We still don't have any money." He looked at the fresh, bloody scalp hanging from her belt, spoils of a detour along the way. "And I don't think anyone's going to want that."

She frowned at him. "We'll see about that. Someone wants to get to Whiton's Heath from here; it's a dangerous road. They don't want the scalp, we'll offer protection in exchange for a ride."

TWENTY-SIX

RAY PACED THE holding cell. He had no idea what was wrong with Anjali; no one had come to tell him. Knowing that she was bleeding out from inside, he maddened himself with guesses. Being captive further infuriated him. He grew angrier with each step.

Ada watched him pace, shocked at how his face altered and reverted. The bones around his eyes grew and receded while he wrestled with rage and calm. As an empath, she felt his fury. She couldn't resist it. She felt herself crumbling beneath his grief.

The cell opened. The occupants turned their attention to the figure standing in the doorway. It was neither Andersen nor Curwen, but Gardiner, the major who defused Sargas. He looked at Ada from behind his opaque, mirrored shield. She immediately felt placid. Ray's emotions fell away from her.

Gardiner looked at Ray. "You need to come with me."

"Where?" he snarled.

"Come with me, Commander," the major ordered.

Telepaths could often sense each other, yet Ada was only an empath. Relative to Gardiner, her abilities were weak and proved unreliable for sniffing out those more powerful. Psychic Allied soldiers were required to identify themselves, so those without enhanced abilities would know their minds were exposed. While it was futile to think differently or shield thoughts, the courtesy of knowing one's own exposure was a token gesture. Gardiner flouted the regulation.

He exerted his influence over Ray. The corren's temperament evened. His face reverted to a rested state. Gardiner couldn't read corren thoughts but could sense their feelings. He absorbed Ray's negativity like a sponge. Without a word to Ada and Patrick, Ray followed the major from the room.

As the door closed, Patrick rose to his feet. "How do you like that?"

***

As Gardiner marched Ray down the corridor, Ray felt his mood improving by the second. Simultaneously, behind his opaque visor, Gardiner's expression soured into borderline rage. They paused outside the infirmary. Two soldiers stood guard.

"Take him inside," Gardiner snapped. "Inform me when he's done here."

Ray looked over his shoulder at Gardiner and smiled.

The major sneered back. All Ray could see was his own face reflected in the mirror sheen. When he turned away, Gardiner placed both hands on the corren's broad back. The hatred and anger flooded back into Ray. He cried out, collapsing to his knees as if struck. He vented the sudden influx of emotion like a steam valve. Crumbling to his side, he wept.

"Pick him up and get him inside," Gardiner barked.

The soldiers tried to pick up Ray, but he was too heavy. They tugged on his arms. "Sir. Commander, sir. Up, please."

Ray grew quiet and slowly rose to his feet. He looked again at Gardiner. "What did you do to me?"

"Your charge, Lieutenant Commander Hastings, is inside. She requires your presence," Gardiner replied. "Good day."

The soldiers prodded the still-befuddled corren into the infirmary.

Gardiner headed to his quarters with a singular goal. After an emotionally draining telepathic encounter, he felt tainted. Like garbage. It inspired him to be treated as such. He reached out with his mind. He planted an urge in Pablo Sotillo's consciousness. The lieutenant experienced the intrusion as a natural thought. Feeling desire, he followed it to Gardiner's quarters.

***

Each bed in the medical ward held a body. Some patients looked well, mending from minor injuries. Others were far worse for the wear.

Ray's eyes dashed over a double amputee who stared at the ceiling. Under better circumstances, the man would have been airlifted to London and fitted with a pair of cybernetic limbs. Or, if he were a noncom, he'd have been given robotic replacements he could use solely during active service. The heavy Confederation blockade along Nova Spes' eastern shores made Britain difficult to reach. Only the most imperative issues inspired circumvention. The present injuries didn't rate.

Following the man's gaze to a fault in the bulkhead, Ray then glanced at another patient. He had gauze all around his head, including half his face. Fresh blood seeped through the bandage over his eye.

Ray looked away.

Tuah, dressed in civilian scrubs devoid of military insignia, walked up to him.

"You're Lieutenant Commander A'arilon?"

He nodded.

"I'm Tuah Bell, the head nurse . . . please, follow me."

Ray followed her to the doors of a private observation room.

***

As Sotillo approached Gardiner's door, it opened automatically.

"Thought I might find you here."

"Did you?" Gardiner replied, face still hidden behind the visor he rarely removed. He leaned against the edge of his desk, facing Sotillo.

"Take it off," Sotillo demanded.

"You want to see my face?" Gardiner asked, surprised.

"No. Why the fuck would I want to look at *your* face? Turn around. *Then* take it off. Bend over the desk."

***

"Are you and Commander Hastings a legal couple, sir?" Tuah asked.

The automatic doors to the observation room opened for her.

"No," Ray answered quietly.

"Please step inside, sir. Our chief medical officer, Captain Duvais, is with Commander Hastings. You should speak with her."

Ray walked through the doorway. Tuah cast a sidelong glance at Carina, who smiled in reply. Tuah stepped away, allowing the doors to close.

***

Sotillo forcibly pulled down the major's pants, bent him over the desk, and penetrated him. With a sneer, he pressed Gardiner's pale head against the desk.

***

Anjali lay sleeping. Carina leaned against the counter with her arms crossed.

Ray looked at the caustic doctor, his face stoic.

Carina shrugged. She looked at Anjali. "You two are an item."

Ray pulled his face together into an annoyed grimace.

"Look," said Carina. "I don't care about fraternization. Maybe it's okay in the navy. It's not like it doesn't happen here."

"Yes, we're a couple—"

"Miscegenation's a different story, though. You think she really likes you, or is it just some weird fetish?"

"Watch your mouth." Ray bristled.

"Did you know she was pregnant?"

Ray looked at Anjali, then at Carina. He blinked.

Carina nodded and pursed her mouth. "So, no. Okay . . ."

"Pregnant?" Ray said, incredulous.

Carina looked at the nails on her right hand. "Yeah. Fetus was terminated by a significant trauma. I'm surprised she didn't reject it sooner."

"She was pregnant . . ."

"Commander, please. Pull it together. I need you to shore up some inconsistencies." She picked up a tablet from the counter.

"Inconsistencies?" He composed himself. "Do you think I care . . . about your report?"

"Fine. Fuck the report," Carina threw the tablet back onto the counter. She crossed her arms again. "Before you lose your shit, though, consider this: She's alive. You're alive. The fetus was eight weeks old. You can make another one."

She put her hand to her stomach.

"Not that the world needs another half-breed variant child."

***

"I'm gonna come so deep in your asshole you're gonna choke on my load," Sotillo boasted.

Gardiner moaned. His orgasm spurred Sotillo to climax. The lieutenant released while buried to his testicles in Gardiner's rectum. Lingering for a moment before pulling out and zipping up, Sotillo then left without another word.

Gardiner lay still, his torso prone atop the desk, palms flat on the surface. He let his eyes lose focus. Slowly, he slid to a kneel and covered his face with his hands.

***

Ray looked at Carina, unsure whether to be appalled or enraged. His face twitched.

"You know they have it pretty tough in this world," she continued. "This could all be for the best."

She looked down at the hand over her belly. Frowning at herself, she dropped it to her side.

"What the hell kind of doctor are you?" Ray finally emitted.

"You didn't know she was pregnant."

"So what?"

"She was knocked up long enough to know."

"So *what*," Ray said through clenched teeth.

"Why do you think she didn't tell you? You think, maybe, she wasn't sure she wanted it?"

"Watch your fucking mouth."

"Or maybe she wasn't sure you did?"

"I said—" Ray stepped toward her.

He stopped short at the sight of the .44-caliber revolver she pulled from nowhere.

"Give me a reason to shoot you dead; you're already unpopular around here. Probably everywhere, with that face. Van Sinderen would commend me right off this rock for bagging you. I'll make major barely two weeks after captain."

Ray sputtered in shock.

"But I don't want to kill you, Commander. Unless . . . you want me to."

"Why would I *want* that?"

She slipped the Mateba back into the holster on her left thigh. It hid beneath her white coat. "I read your file."

"You . . . read my file."

"I needed some background on the baby's daddy, to break the news in the best possible way."

Ray thought to reply but caught the sardonic note.

"You know," she said, "there's barely anything in there besides your picture, your rank, and your posting. Just about everything about you is classified. Except something about a human woman you used to fuck, and your other variant child, both of whom are dead now. It was in the bit about your defection."

Ray made up his mind not to engage her. He entertained responding to her abuse with physical violence. She could shoot him, but he'd likely succeed in killing her anyway. Even if he died in the process. If he survived, he had no desire to face the consequences. As much as she angered him, he knew that to murder her for the slight would only validate the humans' belief in his monstrosity.

For a long moment they stood in silence. They stared at each other.

Ray studied her face. The shape of her eyes, the texture of her hair, and the tone of her skin again reminded him of Manon. He broke his gaze away to look instead at Anjali. She stirred.

"You two, have a moment," Carina said walking toward the door.

Ray grabbed her by the left wrist.

"Let go of me," she growled through clenched teeth.

"You remind me of someone," he said.

She shook free of his grasp. "So what?" Shaking her head in disgust, she left.

Ray put his hands over his face, rubbing them up and down. He strode to the bedside and sat. Anjali remained unconscious. Her expression changed from placid to pained, with him near. He tried to pinpoint the aching in his gut and realized it was guilt. He was glad she miscarried. His relief disgusted him.

She had been his one positive token. But now, on top of his doubts of her role in the mission that marooned them, he wrestled with new misgivings planted by Carina. He wondered why Anjali had kept the pregnancy from him. If she'd known he didn't want the child, he wondered how; they never talked about children, about making a family.

Her fingers on his arm roused him from his thoughts.

"Ray . . ."

"Hey, baby."
"I'm sorry . . ."
"Shh. It's okay."
She contorted her face. Her eyes watered. "I'm sorry I didn't tell you."
"It doesn't matter . . ." he said, looking away.

TWENTY-SEVEN

GARDINER OPENED THE door to the holding cell and walked inside.

"If you'd please come with me."

"Now what?" Ada asked.

"I've secured your release. You're free to go about as you would, but I recommend you come with me. I'll acquaint you with the facility and show you to your quarters."

"Don't you have grunts to do grunt work?" Ada inquired.

"We have a staff of about twenty fit to serve at the moment. I have privates and corporals doing work integral to improving our defenses, rather than wasting them on this."

"Twenty?" Patrick blurted. "This base holds at least four hundred."

"I'm aware of that, Corporal. Thank you."

They followed Gardiner out of the cell.

"So . . . why are you only twenty, then?" asked Patrick. "Sir."

"Fifteen attacks in the last two months and no reinforcements delivered. Before all this began, we had 350 men."

"So, we're on the verge of losing—" Patrick started.

Gardiner whirled around and put his forefinger to his mirrored shield where his lips would be.

"Save it," he admonished Patrick. "You know it. I know it. Hell, even Van Sinderen knows it. But he's not going to admit it. He'd rather see us all die than retreat. And I'd rather die on my feet than live forever in the brig . . . so let's keep the dissent to ourselves, hmm?"

"Are you the XO?" Ada asked.

"Yes."

"How many other officers are there?"

"Excepting the colonel and myself, there are three uninjured commissioned officers. Captain Duvais, our doctor. The head of Military Police, Lieutenant Andersen, whom you've met. And Lieutenant Sotillo, our communications officer. The rest of our uninjured staff comprise Andersen's MPs, and other noncoms, almost all of them privates. We have a few noncommissioned officers who are not MPs and are not in the medical bay."

"Do you have an engineer?" asked Patrick.

"No. Sergeant Duquesne and Lieutenant Sotillo have overseen our engineering projects, along with Corporal Macaluso, who has a mechanical acumen . . ."

"The corren in your brig is an engineer," said Ada.

Gardiner paused for a moment. He looked around and spotted a red-haired, bearded private walking toward them. Ada perked up at the sight of him and flashed him a smile.

"Private Gray, show the lieutenant and the corporal to quarters," Gardiner ordered and then took off. He stormed into Van Sinderen's office unbidden, using telekinesis to open the locked door.

"We have to release the corren," Gardiner demanded.

The colonel hastily withdrew both hands from his lap and slapped them atop the desk. His dark complexion camouflaged his embarrassment.

"Blackened fucking Earth, Gardiner . . . don't barge in on me!" Van Sinderen exclaimed as the flush of blood slowly drained from his face. "You're *so* damned lucky there's no one fit for your post and I can't bust you down . . . because I would. I would bust you down so far you'd be coming out of your mother's cunt."

"Sir, you could spare yourself embarrassment if you'd reserve that behavior for your private quarters."

"Just shut up, dammit . . . fucking hell." He zipped his trousers.

"The corren you have in the brig, we need to release him."

"The hell I will."

"We can't withstand another attack with the feeble security Duquesne put in place. He, Sotillo, and Macaluso are out of their depth and you know it."

"And what's the snake going to do for us?"

"Did you read his goddamned jacket? The 'snake' is a mechanical genius."

"Funny how his reputation doesn't precede him."

"Doesn't it? He was good enough to be stationed on Venus while we languish here."

"Shut your mouth. I'm here because it's an important tactical asset. This assignment is an honor and a testament to my service."

"Of course, sir. I apologize. Shall I help you to sign the release?" Gardiner made no motion but Van Sinderen's right arm lifted, poised as if it held a stylus.

The colonel struggled to manipulate his own appendage.

"What the fuck?" His eyes flashed. "You fucking cocksucker!"

Gardiner pantomimed writing with Van Sinderen's hand, held in thrall.

"Major . . ." Van Sinderen growled.

"Do you understand me, Colonel?"

"Let me go, Major."

"Shall we be releasing the brothers A'arilon?" He forced the colonel's hand to dance as if he were signing the release.

Through clenched teeth, Van Sinderen's face flushed with anger and exertion. He agreed. Gardiner let the colonel's hand flop to the desk.

"I should throw you in the brig," said the colonel.

"Don't threaten me, sir; you know that's foolish. We should work together."

Van Sinderen signed the releases. He submitted them to the base computer. "The snakes are free. Are you pleased?"

Gardiner smiled, though his face remained hidden from view.

"Very."

***

Carina walked the corridors with no destination in mind, until inspiration struck.

"Computer, name and rank of the female officers who arrived today."

"Hastings, Anjali. Lieutenant commander. Bennett, Ada. Second lieutenant."

"Where is Lieutenant Bennett?"

"Lieutenant Bennett is in the mess hall."

Inside the mess hall, Carina found it as bare as she had expected. Private Milner sat alone at a table near the corner, his bright orange curls springing out in every direction. He sulked as he choked down his bland fare. Patrick and Ada ate together. Carina recognized their builds from the stolen glance outside the Pendragon pub. They both looked considerably fresher, having showered, received treatment, and changed out of the enemy uniforms.

Carina grabbed a tray and went to the counter. "Cook me up some of that chow I brought in."

"Sergeant Liggan brought me that food, Captain," Al-Farid replied.

"And I gave it to her, to bring to you. Don't fuck with me, Ibrahim."

"You have your ration card, Captain?" Al-Farid asked. His look was one of perpetual boredom.

She cast him a cold glare. It spoke volumes about the violence she would do to him if he didn't do as she pleased.

He frowned, but acquiesced. "Yes, sir. Comin' up."

She waited for her meal, watching Ada and Patrick poke at their ration. It had not been made from the meats, fruit, and vegetables she brought back from the Pendragon. On their trays sat recycled, sterilized fecal-matter protein. They drank purified urine. Milner ate and drank the same. After a few minutes, Al-Farid doled out a small piece of steak, half a white potato, and a few broccoli florets.

"There was a gun in the bag Liggan brought you," Carina said.

The cook closed his eyes and sighed. He disappeared for a moment and then returned, placing the firearm on the counter. Carina clicked on the safety. She put the weapon on her tray.

"Shukran, habibi," she said. *Thank you, darling.*

She took her chow and approached the new arrivals. "May I join you?"

"Um, sure . . ." Patrick said, his mouth full. He half stood up as Carina took a seat next to him.

Ada felt the hairs stand up on the back of Patrick's neck and hers followed suit. She got goose bumps. She realized he was turned on. Carina's assertive, smoldering intensity lapped at Ada. Patrick tried to take in as much of Carina's hourglass figure as he could from his vantage. He couldn't help himself. He was greedy for the sight of a such a woman, but she scared him. She was taller than he. Her physical power was obvious. Even without Ada's empathic abilities, he could sense Carina's animosity toward him.

She cast him a sidelong glance.

"Um . . . I'm gonna . . . I'm gonna take off," he said, standing suddenly. "I'll catch up with you later, Lieutenant. Captain."

"Corporal," Carina replied. She watched him from her periphery. A satisfied smile played over her lips. She fixed her intense gaze on Ada, who sat upright and flashed a nervous smile.

"You're the hot ticket," Carina said, sitting back.

Ada eyed the tray, unable to ignore the gun. "Sir, I'm not certain what you mean—"

Carina turned the weapon so that the barrel pointed away from Ada, then pushed the tray toward her. "You want some real food? Go ahead. Eat it."

Milner looked up, jealousy plain on his face. He glanced again at his own meal. It looked doubly bad. Ada cast a leery gaze at Carina but picked up the knife and fork. She tucked into the meat, grateful for real food.

"Has anyone shown you around yet?"

"A private . . . um . . . I don't remember his name . . . showed us our quarters and then left us here; we were hungry."

"So, there's more for you to see. But eat your food."

"My food? But . . ." Ada had skewered a piece of meat and held it just above the tray.

"Is that for me?" Carina smiled.

Ada offered the fork. Carina took Ada's hand in both of hers. She turned the tines forward, eating the bite while peering into Ada's eyes.

Ada blushed.

"Eat," Carina ordered. She picked up her own fork and stabbed a broccoli floret. "I didn't order this for me."

Carina noticed Milner staring. She cast him a forbidding glare. The private averted his eyes. When Ada had finished eating, Carina rose to her feet. She tucked the Confederate pistol into her waistband and held out her hand.

"Come with me."

Ada took it. They walked through the halls without speaking. Ada began to wonder what there was to see or to learn. Every corridor looked the same. The doors were labeled. Nearest the mess, general purpose rooms abounded. As they walked farther, the rooms gave way to officers' quarters. She had an inkling earlier, but now knew for certain. Desire rolled off Carina as clearly as it did from the men.

"I think my room is around here somewhere," Ada offered. She asked herself why she should go through with it, but then countered with an immediate, *Why not?*

"Oh?" Carina said, looking down with half a smirk. "Show me."

"Here," Ada said as they arrived.

They stopped. She stood with her back to the wall. Carina loomed. Ada looked left and then right, unsure whether she was scouting for help or hoping none would arrive. A small misgiving still nagged at her.

Carina stepped closer, leaving nearly no room between them. Ada flattened herself against the wall as much as she could. Carina put one hand, palm flat, upon the wall aside Ada's head, and then added the other hand on the opposite side.

Ada squirmed but didn't try in earnest to get free.

"Lieutenant . . . are you uncomfortable? Or don't you like girls?"

"Sir, I don't know if we should be doing—"

"Of course we should," Carina replied.

She leaned in, stopping just before Ada's face. She hesitated for a moment, offering one last moment for refusal. Ada closed her eyes and pursed her lips. Carina closed the distance. She brushed her lips against Ada's, which acquiesced. Carina flicked her tongue against the underside of Ada's top lip.

"Open the door," Carina ordered.

Ada stepped in front of the door and it slid aside. She grabbed Carina by the belt and pulled her in.

TWENTY-EIGHT

VAN SINDEREN HAILED Gardiner. They approached the cell holding Sargas. The guards stepped aside.

"You sent Duquesne to release the other snake?" asked the colonel as they walked into the room.

Gardiner nodded, his face still hidden behind his visor. Within the cell, Sargas hung from his restraints on the wall.

"Where is A'arilon Ray?" Sargas asked. "He broke his promise to me."

Van Sinderen waved the comment aside. "I don't know anything about that. What I want to know is who and what you are."

"I am nothing. No one. Where is A'arilon Ray? He broke his promise to me."

"Alleviate yourself of your fixation," Van Sinderen replied. "The corren doesn't matter. His promises are flaccid. If you want this to work out in your favor—in any way—you need to listen to *me*."

"You have nothing of interest to say," Sargas replied. He fixed his gaze on Major Gardiner.

"Fuck me," Van Sinderen uttered. He put his meaty fists on his soft hips and looked at Gardiner. "Major, do you believe this asshole?"

Gardiner didn't acknowledge the remark. The shield of his battle helmet obscured his face, but he sensed that Sargas could see right through it. Sargas did not give off a typical psionic signature, but there were hallmarks of extrasensory power, similar to what Ray exhibited. What they both exuded was artificial, not intrinsic. It seemed mechanical, though Gardiner couldn't pinpoint its origin. But he knew in his bones that Sargas was dangerous.

"Gardiner!" Van Sinderen snapped.

"Sir," Gardiner replied calmly, not removing his gaze from Sargas, who kept his own fixed stare on the major.

"Dig into this insolent motherfucker," ordered the colonel.

Gardiner exhaled through his nose. He attempted to delve into Sargas' mind. He met immediate resistance. Sargas didn't flinch. Gardiner could not find purchase in his adversary's consciousness. The major's abilities were hampered by the intentional interference in the cell, intended to impede the prisoner. He had to move close enough to touch Sargas, though no contact was made.

I mean you no harm, Gardiner offered. He planted the words quietly at the threshold of his subject's awareness. *I bear you no grudge and I do this with great displeasure.*

Placid, silent calm was Sargas' response. The resistance from his conscious mind did not relent. The door remained barred. As Gardiner pressed, he forced it open a crack. He caught glimmers of immediate memory, senses deprived by stasis, pulses of fear and adrenaline. It all bubbled up into Sargas' consciousness. Images of wreckage, carnage, and death followed. A wave of arousal swelled up with the memory of Anjali's body pressing against him.

Gardiner experienced Sargas' mind like two projections upon the same screen. The major retained his own thoughts and feelings. He simultaneously felt and *recollected* Sargas' experiences. As if he were Sargas, Gardiner experienced his host's heterosexual urge for Anjali. He felt Sargas' penis bulge at the memory. And, since the man was naked, Gardiner also witnessed the arousal. He fixated with his own lust upon the organ. Blood flowed into his own genitalia. The sensation diverted his attention.

Sargas lay in wait for such an opportunity.

From the instant Gardiner had foisted his way in, Sargas read him like a menu. He served up exactly the imagery and sensations most likely to enthrall the intruder. When the distraction succeeded, Sargas struck back.

"Shit," Gardiner said dully, realizing too late his mistake.

If Gardiner's foray into Sargas' mind had been a live wire, Sargas surged back more voltage than Gardiner's brain could process. The major screamed. He clutched at the sides of his head. Van Sinderen looked on in slack-jawed horror. Gardiner tore his helmet from his head and spiked it on the floor, revealing the burn scars that marred half of his face. He grabbed at his hair, but it was too short to pull. He slapped his skull with both hands, in concert. His screams pierced the air.

"Geeeeaaarrrgggh! Out! Out! Get . . . out!"

He began to hyperventilate and threw himself against the wall. He slammed his back and shoulders against it, again and again. The doors opened and the guards ran in.

"Sound the fucking alarm!" ordered the colonel.

The computer responded with a klaxon.

Gardiner screamed once more and stumbled backward. He collapsed against the wall and slid to the floor in a sitting position. His arms flopped at his sides. His heterochromatic pink and blue eyes gazed vacantly. Spittle dripped from his chin.

The guards froze.

Van Sinderen looked dumbly at Sargas, still hanging from the wall. Sargas smiled. The shackle around his right leg clicked and fell open, followed by the left. He had culled from Gardiner's mind the locking mechanism. Sargas envisioned how the parts moved and undid the fetters with telekineses. He was no natural telepath nor telekinetist, as Gardiner had correctly deduced. The nanomachines interacted with the electromagnetic fields of nearby matter, repelling its molecules, creating force enough to move it. The method differed, but the result was the same. The manacles binding his hands released. Sargas dropped to his feet. He took one step toward Van Sinderen.

"Shoot," the colonel whispered hoarsely at the stupefied guards. "Shoot . . ."

He found more volume.

"SHOOOOOT!"

The guards recovered from their stupefaction. They opened fire, but the barrage of bright green energy pulses failed to reach Sargas. They arced harmlessly away along the invisible EM shield that surrounded his body.

"Shoot him, dammit!" the colonel yelled again.

The guards opened fire again. Sargas turned to face them. The energy crackled up Sargas' arms and dissipated. The Allied soldiers lowered their weapons and despaired.

Van Sinderen's mouth hung open.

Sargas shoved the guards out of his way without touching them. They toppled like bowling pins. He stepped into the hall. An immediate energy salvo rained down on him from both sides. Just as before, the energy crackled around him and vanished into the air, leaving him unharmed. The guards charged, wielding their weapons like clubs. Sargas braced to meet them. His invisible shield provided no cover from the bodily assault, but his steel-hard skin did. Six soldiers rained down on him in a hail of rifle butts and fists.

Though he could absorb the blows with minimal damage, Sargas' rage swelled. He had an objective. These misdirected fools were thwarting it with their needless, futile displays of force. He bunched his fists and tensed. With a hum, white electricity burgeoned. It arced and snapped along his extremities. The energy grew. With a mighty bellow, he swung his arms outward and rose to his feet. He discharged a pulse of brilliant light that sent his six assailants sailing through the air. They fell to the ground in heaps. Their armor smoked from the heat.

Sargas scowled at their agony and pleas for help.

"Oh, God!" Private Milner cried. "I'm on fire!"

He fumbled to discard his melting armor.

Reinforcements rounded the corners and blocked each exit. Sargas bent his knees and roared in one direction, and then the next. The guards hesitated for a second, but then charged.

Van Sinderen watched from the cell doorway, dumbstruck.

Sargas roared again. In the midst of the howl, the tenor changed from distinctly human to something alien, deeper and more resonant than any man could emit.

The guards stopped in their tracks. They looked at each other, hesitant with doubt.

White electricity again arced around Sargas. He brayed a fourth time, deeper, more alien and more unsettling than before.

A blinding flash forced Van Sinderen to shield his eyes. When the light died away, he hazarded a glance. Instead of his prisoner, the colonel saw something he'd only seen depicted in art: the Confederation emperor, Darek Marseh.

Gone were the human, masculine good looks of the stolen Confederation cargo dubbed "Sargas." In his place stood a hulking, naked, impossibly muscular hominid beast. Bony plates protruded upward from his forehead and sharpened to razor points. He had empty white eyes like a bust of Plato. Horns protruded from his chin like the pincers of an earwig. He had no nipples, nor a penis, just a hairless slit between his legs.

Van Sinderen felt a hot trickle of urine cascade down his leg.

Sargas turned to the colonel and howled again, revealing a mouth of big, sharp teeth. Again, Sargas began to glow white.

The trickle of urine turned into a stream.

As the energy around Sargas grew, Van Sinderen anticipated death. His bowels cramped in fear. He quietly swore to hold on to his excrement while his heart still beat. He closed his eyes against the intense light and said a hasty prayer to no specific god.

The light faded.

Slowly, the colonel opened his eyes. He saw nothing but the corridor walls. Stepping fully out of the cell, he looked left and right. The ragtag reinforcements—a few privates along with Corporal Macaluso, Lance Corporal Curwen, and Lieutenant Andersen—looked around, equally dumbfounded. Satisfied for the moment that the beast had disappeared, Van Sinderen took charge.

"Get these men to the infirmary!" he barked, indicating the fallen, smoldering soldiers.

As the men carried their compatriots away, Van Sinderen looked back into the cell at Gardiner. He remained sitting like a doll, eyes wide open and staring at nothing. Only drool and the slow rise and fall of his chest betrayed his humanity.

"What the fuck just happened?" Van Sinderen asked.

There was no one to reply.

TWENTY-NINE

DAEDALUS WALKED OUT of his cell and the alarm sounded. The faltering lights of C-level flickered overhead as the strips of lighting along the floor changed from white to red.

"What now?" he asked.

René shrugged. "Could be anything. Another Red raid or . . . the colonel misplaced his shit-steak sandwich." He walked over to the nearest communications port. "Looks like a prisoner escape on B-level."

Opening the nearest munitions locker, René tossed Daedalus a plasma rifle.

"Uh, Sergeant, this . . ." Daedalus poked his big finger at the trigger guard. "My finger doesn't fit."

"Putain," René cursed.

"You confiscated a pistol of mine when I got here."

"It's upstairs," René replied. He jammed a little button on the underside of the barrel and the trigger guard popped off. "Trigger's still bound to be a little small, but . . ."

Daedalus fired a blast down the deserted hallway at a bulkhead wall. He made an insincerely sheepish face at the black scorch mark it left behind.

René raised his eyebrows. "Seems fine." He removed two sidearms from the locker for himself. "Let's go hunting."

Daedalus licked his lips and smiled.

***

Ray detained a short, portly soldier running down the hallway.

"What's going on, Private?" he asked, reading the placket on the soldier's breast.

"General alarm, sir," Lindner replied. "All hands. Come with me, please."

Ray followed Lindner down a series of corridors. An animal wail rumbled through the complex. At the oncoming junction stood a cadre of guards. The sound of crackling electricity filled the air. A bright white light swelled from the perpendicular hall. Ray turned his face away from the bright flash. He noticed the guards relax and then advance.

He and the private followed.

***

Van Sinderen canceled the general alarm.

Carina and Ada approached behind Ray and Lindner.

"Captain, attend to Major Gardiner," the colonel ordered Carina.

"Where is he?" she asked.

Van Sinderen jerked his thumb at the open cell door. Carina looked inside and inhaled sharply. She hurried toward Gardiner but slipped upon the colonel's urine. Ray steadied her.

"Why is the floor wet?" she demanded, but no one answered.

She went to Gardiner and checked his pulse. It was steady, but his eyes remained fixed at nothing.

"*Putain*, he's a fucking vegetable," she muttered. "Major . . ."

He didn't respond.

"Gardiner." She shook him. "Maks!" she shouted, slapping him hard across the face.

No reaction.

"Is that medical protocol?" Ray asked from the doorway.

"Fuck medical protocol," Carina snapped back, anguished. "And fuck you!"

Ray felt a twinge of guilt at the extremity of her grief.

"Help me get him to the infirmary," Carina ordered.

"Does it matter how delicate I am?" Ray asked.

"I doubt it matters to him," she said bitterly.

Ray shrugged and picked him up.

***

Daedalus and René arrived in time to see Carina duck into the cell.

"Colonel?" asked René.

"You," said Van Sinderen. "Take him," he pointed at Daedalus, "and all the muscle you can wrangle to find our escapee."

"Who are we looking for?" René inquired. "Or what, based on that sound?"

"If you find anyone lurking these halls who shouldn't be . . . do your damned job, okay?"

René rapped his knuckles on Daedalus' breastplate. They headed off on their orders.

"We'll stage from here," René said at the B-level security office. "We can sweep each level and see if anything abnormal turns up."

The doors slid open and the two men stepped inside. René went to a console and ran his fingers over the keypad.

"All security personnel, this is Sergeant Duquesne. I need two teams of two for a sweep of each level. Report to your designated post. Any unauthorized persons are to be detained. Do not use deadly force. Over."

Confirmations came in over the comm.

"Now, let's get to our scans."

René moved to another console. He ran his hands blindly over the controls with accuracy borne of countless repetition.

"So, I hear you're an engineer."

Daedalus shrugged.

"We definitely need someone like you," René added.

"It seems like you need a lot of things here."

"Mince alors." René screwed up his mouth. "I don't even know what I'm looking for here. And I wouldn't trust this shit to find it for me, anyway."

He punched up the surveillance from the corridor where Sargas escaped his cell.

"Look at this," he called to Daedalus, who brought his attention to the scene of Sargas stepping out of the cell and being bombarded by weapons' fire.

"Wow," Daedalus remarked. He watched the energy blasts fail to cause any damage. "What do you suppose that is?"

"Looks like some kind of force field . . . some disparate energy that negates our weapons. But there's no tech on him . . . I mean, he's naked. Unless it's up his ass. Some kind of massive kinetic discharge is all I can guess. A contrary force. EM interference. I don't know. Magic."

"Psh . . . Magic," Daedalus scoffed.

"What's the difference, really?" René asked. "Like telepathy is easy to get your head around? It's all magic; it's all incomprehensible shit that defies explanation. The word's just a catch-all for 'I don't know how the fuck—'

"*Putain de merde!* Look!" René pointed at the screen as Sargas metamorphosed into the fierce, naked alien creature.

"How do you suppose he did *that*?" asked Daedalus.

René shrugged. "*Pas de putain d'indice.* Maybe some kind of camouflage that lets him project different appearances."

The secreted nanomachines transmitted a holographic image of whatever Sargas desired to project.

"Do you know who that is?" Daedalus asked.

"Same guy as before," René replied, "just . . . different."

"No. That . . . whatever it is . . . looks just like Darek Marseh."

"The Red Emperor . . ." René said, unconvinced. "You think he's, uh, masquerading as a well-hung human male?"

Daedalus frowned. "All I know is that thing looks like every representation of Marseh I've ever seen or heard of. The drawings, the word-of-mouth accounts."

René sighed and got up from the console.

"So, now what?" Daedalus asked.

"Let's go find His Royal Highness."

"Wait," Daedalus said, watching Sargas wink out of view. "No one just disappears from view without a d-jump and, like you said, he's got no tech on him."

"So?" René replied.

"So, sit back down and scan through the invisible frequencies. It's got to be some kind of cloaking."

René blinked at Daedalus.

"What?" the corren asked, not understanding the sergeant's blank expression.

"We can't do that," René told him. "No infrared, no UV. All we've got is visual. And we don't even have that on each level."

Daedalus closed his eyes and rubbed his forehead. "Fine. Let's do it the old-fashioned way . . . but I want my pistol."

A loud boom reverberated through the complex, shaking the floor. René listened to the report coming over his comm while Daedalus tapped his foot in anticipation.

"D-level," René said. "He must have triggered one of my mines. Come on."

***

Ray stopped as the alarm sounded anew and the lights again shifted to red.

Carina turned to him. "No point in stopping, we need to get him to the med bay, either way."

She walked into the infirmary with Ray behind her, the major in his arms.

"Find an empty bed and put him there," she ordered.

"Aye, Captain," Ray replied, walking over to a recently vacated bed onto which Tuah had just put fresh sheets.

He sloughed Gardiner onto the bed. He and Tuah arranged him into a comfortable position. Carina went into her office and the door closed behind her.

"Is she always so pleasant?" Ray asked Tuah.

"I enjoy her company," she replied without looking at him.

Ray made a dubious face, unsure whether Tuah's dull tone of voice and her sour expression were for him, but kept his mouth shut.

"We'll take it from here, sir. Thank you."

Realizing he'd been dismissed, he left. The lights remained at red alert, but the alarm ceased to ring.

Tuah looked over her shoulder at Carina's closed office door. She walked over to it and requested entry. She knew the override, but she was trying to reign in her emotions. She knew that barging in wouldn't help.

The door opened at Carina's permission. She leaned against the counter, drying her hands with a towel.

"What can I do for you, love?"

Tuah looked at Carina and said nothing. She knew her lover's swagger. She knew how Carina acted when she had killed or had fucked, and she was acting like that now.

"Who was it?"

"Who else would it be?" Carina replied.

"Was it good, at least?" asked Tuah. Her voice was even, her tone flat.

"What do you want to hear?"

Tuah tilted and shook her head. "Why even bother to wash the pussy off your face?"

"Would you rather I kiss you with a mouthful of strange?" Carina replied.

"You would think to kiss me . . . like everything's just fine."

"Everything is fine, Tuah," Carina said, moving toward the door.

Tuah moved away from the wall. She blocked Carina's path with her small body. "No, Carina. Everything is not fine."

Carina snaked her arms across her chest. Her face hardened.

"Why?" asked Tuah.

"Why?" replied Carina. "Why *not*?"

Tuah said nothing, but stood firm.

"Please," said Carina. "Now isn't the time."

"Tell me you only fuck me because nobody else is around."

"Someone else *is* around and I'd gladly have you right now. And tonight, and tomorrow."

Tuah just looked at her.

"What do you want, Tuah?" Carina's inflection flattened. It was hardly a question.

Tuah bit her lip and looked away. "I want you to love me." She felt foolish to be so emotional in the face of someone who seemed so devoid.

Carina's face faltered. She winced and then stepped in, enveloping Tuah in an embrace. "I do love you, baby."

Tuah didn't fight. She melted into Carina, nuzzling her breasts. "Then how could you do it?"

"You can do whatever you want to whomever you want, Tuah. You know that. I've never demanded monogamy from you."

Tuah shook her head and looked at the floor.

"I know you'd fuck around on me if you had the chance—"

"I haven't fucked *anyone* else!" Tuah blurted, pushing Carina away.

"There's no one else to fuck!" Carina retorted.

"You think I've never fucked a man?" Tuah replied. "You think I wouldn't? Andersen's after my ass like his life depends on it."

Carina's nostrils flared and her eyes flashed. "I fucking warned him," she said through clenched teeth.

"Oh?" Tuah replied. "So, you're allowed to spread it around, but I'm not?"

"I'm not fucking *men*, Tuah!"

"Neither am I!" she erupted. She looked Carina in the eye. "But Andersen's fit, he's good-looking. And he *wants* me. It's right there for the taking . . ."

Carina moved her lower jaw from side to side, glowering at the wall.

"I haven't done it because I've only wanted you," said Tuah.

"Bull*shit* . . ."

"It's not bullshit! I *love* you! Are you too *stupid* to realize that? What is *wrong* with you?"

Carina said nothing. She crossed her arms, grit her teeth, and looked away from Tuah's probing gaze. The chimes on her office door rang.

"Come," she said.

Tuah cast an angry glance at her.

Deputy Head Nurse Agrait stood in the doorway. "Chief," he said to Carina, "we really need you out here."

"Fine, we're coming . . ."

Agrait nodded and stepped away from the door. It slid closed.

Carina's face relaxed into a sad expression. She looked at Tuah, forlorn. "I'm sorry, Tuah."

"Sorry? Sorry for what? That I love you?"

"Yes," Carina said, walking past. "Sorry you love me. Sorry for you."

Tuah closed her eyes. She opened her mouth and clenched her lower jaw, sighing bitterly as she shook her head. She followed Carina from the office.

***

Daedalus and René climbed down to D-level and stopped at the base of the ladder.

"I rigged this floor with mines," René said. "He must have set one off. If he isn't kibble, maybe he's still here."

"Yeah, okay. But you saw him vanish, on the monitor. He could be standing right next to us—"

Sargas appeared on cue, right between them. He swatted Daedalus' pistol from his hand and pushed him backward. The corren tumbled over. Sargas ducked beneath the barrel of René's rifle. He punched him in the stomach with his right hand and disarmed him with his left. Sargas then struck René in the solar plexus with the rifle butt. Daedalus scrambled for his pistol. He snatched it up and leveled it at Sargas, who presented René as a shield.

For once, Daedalus didn't know what to say. He held his tongue. He lowered his weapon and let it hang at his side.

Sargas looked him in the eye and cocked his head toward the floor.

Daedalus dropped the gun. "Why all this, Asshole? Why not just leave?"

"Because I can't," Sargas replied.

"All of your fancy magic, and you can't thwart a couple force fields and march out of here?"

"I have some powers, but I'm not omnipotent. And I'm not indestructible."

"Could have fooled me," Daedalus replied. "Especially with all the shit you talk."

Sargas glowered at him.

"So, you need a ticket out of here," said Daedalus. "You really think we went through all the trouble to get you, just to let you go?"

"Would you prefer that I kill this man?"

"I wouldn't advise it; he's the one who set up the defenses down here. He's your passport. What the hell do I know?"

Sargas aimed René's rifle at Daedalus.

"So," he said to René, "shall I kill *him*, then?"

"You think you can hit him from here with a rifle, with one hand, be my guest," René replied.

"You're both so tough," Sargas said, mockingly. "I *will* find a way out of here, with your help or without. Would you rather I kill everyone I encounter between here and the lift to the surface, or that I kill no one and walk out through the breach?"

"I'd rather you weren't such a pain in my balls," Daedalus replied.

"You're the disobedient one," said Sargas. "You bristle at taking orders . . . at order itself. You prefer chaos. You want to be free to act according to your own whims."

"You've got me all figured out," said Daedalus, yawning.

"Why do you serve, then? A man like you could survive easily out in the world."

Daedalus tilted his head and looked at Sargas with a bored expression.

"Why do you serve?" Sargas repeated.

"Because I *like* being disobedient. If there's no order, what would I resist?"

Sargas smiled. "But aren't you *bored*?"

"Not lately. The past day has been a real adventure."

"Surely. But, now, here you are, back on base, back to the ho-hum day-to-day. I overheard this one," he jostled René, "say that you're an engineer. Will you be satisfied to patch up this decrepit facility, or would you rather another adventure?"

"Are you making me an offer?"

"Lieutenant . . ." said René, but Sargas pressed the rifle against the side of his head.

"I won't miss from here, human."

Sargas turned his attention back to Daedalus.

"Yes, I am making you an offer. Come with me and end the war."

It piqued Daedalus' curiosity.

"You want me to go AWOL on an adventure with you to end the war. How grand," Daedalus said, the sarcasm plain in his voice. "And what's your scheme, Sargas? How do you, one man, plan to stop a conflict that's been raging for a century? Or more."

"I'm going to kill Arak Matar."

"Vous êtes si plein de merde," said René.

"He thinks you're full of shit," said Daedalus.

"I know what he said," Sargas replied.

"Then it sounds, to me, like he's the one who needs convincing."

"Then convince him," Sargas demanded.

Daedalus smiled. "How about it, René? Sounds fun, right?"

"I won't abandon my post, sir."

Sargas frowned.

Daedalus shrugged. "He's a good soldier, Sargas. What can I say?"

Sargas threw the rifle to the floor, spun René around, and grabbed him by the jacket. He bared his teeth and shook the much smaller man.

"Stupid, narrow-minded, myopic little fool. Whom do you owe such loyalty?"

"I took an oath!" René protested. "They took me in! Do you know the difference in my life? Have you ever lived among rapists, murderers, and cannibals? The world is a cesspool. Anyone too kind, too gentle, is easy prey to men without conscience. Do you know the *hell* of living when the only choices are to be victim or abuser?"

Sargas let go, unconcerned with protecting himself from either man.

"Do you realize that this cocoon into which you've escaped is responsible for that cesspool? The privation you felt as a civilian is because of the bounty hoarded by this Allied war machine! Those at the top live large while the majority suffer, starve, and die!"

"Then why don't you go kill Fleet Admiral Hastings or Field Marshal Courtois?" René asked.

"In due time," Sargas replied. "But they are merely symptoms. I'm interested in the cause."

"Why just Arak and not Marseh?" Daedalus asked.

"Marseh is not my concern," Sargas hedged.

"You mean he's your master," said Daedalus.

"All men have masters," Sargas retorted.

"If we end the war, what then?" Daedalus asked. "No more chaos? I cringe at all the boredom I'll feel."

"There will be other adventures, corren," said Sargas, "should you survive this one. And there will be plenty of chaos when we kill Arak Matar. It will not be tidy."

Daedalus looked at René. He knew that Daedalus had made up his mind, but the Frenchman wrestled with his own conflict. He didn't want to abandon his post, but he couldn't deny Sargas' logic.

"I don't know what to do," René admitted.

"I think you do," said Daedalus. "Be your own man. If we succeed, we'll be heroes. If we fail, we'll be dead. You want to live out the rest of your life knowing you passed on a chance to kill the Butcher?"

René looked at Daedalus with a mixture of helplessness and intrigue. Daedalus smiled; he knew René was in.

"We need to clothe this naked schmuck," Daedalus said.

"I don't require garments," Sargas protested.

"Yes, you do," Daedalus retorted, "'cause I don't want to behold your bare ass."

"Wait here," said René. "I'll grab his jumpsuit from the security office."

"Make it snappy," Daedalus ordered.

***

Colonel Van Sinderen ordered Lieutenant Andersen and Lance Corporal Mahoney to his office.

"Computer," said the colonel, "where is Sergeant Duquesne?"

"Master Sergeant Duquesne is not on base," the computer replied.

Andersen raised an eyebrow. Mahoney looked at him.

"Computer," the colonel repeated. "Where is A'arilon Daedalus?"

"First Lieutenant A'arilon Daedalus is not on base."

"Not on base," he said to Andersen and Mahoney, "neither of them. So, where in green hell are they?"

"Do you think that creature took them off premises?" Andersen asked.

"He's one man! What do you suppose he did, picked them up under his arms and carried them out like children?"

"From what I witnessed," said Mahoney, "I wouldn't put it past him, sir."

"Just go look for them. The explosion came from D-level. Start there. Once you've got an inkling of a clue, cancel this red alert. This light's giving me a headache."

Andersen paused on the way out as his fingers fell upon the data stick in his pocket.

"Sir?" Andersen said, turning back to the colonel.

Van Sinderen looked up from his desk as Andersen placed the data stick upon it. It was stamped with Confederation insignia.

"I took this off the snake when I threw him in the brig."

"What's on it?" Van Sinderen asked.

"I didn't look," Andersen replied.

"Very good, Lieutenant," said the colonel, taking the stick and putting it in his desk. "Thank you. Dismissed."

THIRTY

AS CARINA, TUAH, and Agrait saw to the recent injuries sustained during Sargas' escape, Ada walked in. She stood to the side, absorbing the scene. Tuah looked up and tensed. Her jealousy and bitter anger washed over Ada, whose breath caught in her throat.

Fuck, she thought.

Carina noticed Tuah's baleful gaze and followed it to Ada.

"Tuah, I need you and Aggie to manage the floor while I talk to the lieutenant."

Tuah grabbed Carina's wrist as she walked away. Carina stopped. She looked at Tuah but said nothing. She didn't glare or scowl. Tuah said nothing but spoke volumes with her eyes. She let go.

Carina approached and Ada cast her eyes at the floor.

"Don't be like that."

Ada looked up. "Like what?"

"I'm no counselor," Carina replied, "but I know shame."

"Please," said Ada, looking at Tuah, "not here. And not now."

Carina plastered her face with a fraudulently bright smile. "What's up, then?"

"The colonel said I should come to you for a space . . . that I could use for work . . . to counsel the ranks."

"You can use my office; I barely do." She led Ada into the office.

Ada scanned the small room, noting its desk. In front of it were two chairs, and one chair behind. "Okay . . ." she said with a shrug.

"You going to advertise?"

They stepped inside and the doors closed, isolating them from the rest of the infirmary. Tuah balled her fists.

Agrait stopped next to her. "You okay, Tuah?"

Carina walked around her desk and sat down. Ada remained standing.

"Van Sinderen suggested I take who you've got here now," said Ada. "That they're the neediest cases."

"I got a needy case for you," Carina said, leaning back in her chair with a sly smile.

"Captain, please . . ."

"Oh, so we're formal, now? Lieutenant?"

Ada's nostrils flared. She strengthened her stance. "Do you want to talk right now, with me, about what happened? Have this be your session? Because this could be therapeutic for us both."

"About 'what happened'?" Carina replied. "We fucked."

"Yes, we did."

"And you regret it now . . . already."

"Carina . . ."

"Why." It was more demand than question.

"What are you trying to accomplish?" Ada asked.

"I want you to tell me why you regret it, barely an hour later. After there's barely been time for it to sink in that I had you moaning my name."

Ada opened her mouth to speak. She inhaled, but no words came out. She fixed her jaw and cocked her head to the side. Her jaw shifted from left to right. She put up her hands before slapping them down against her thighs.

"What, then?" Carina goaded.

"I didn't know you were taken," Ada replied.

Carina screwed up her face with indignation. "Taken? I'm not some betrothed maiden. I'm no one's property. And that's bullshit, anyway; you didn't give a damn about Tuah until you saw her just now. I didn't hear you asking if I was spoken for before we got to it."

Carina rose from her chair. "No. I know what it is."

"You know what *what* is?" Ada asked.

"I know what's got you so twisted up inside."

"Sure you do," said Ada.

"You like dick," Carina said as she approached. "And you don't know what got into you. But I'll tell you what happened. *I* happened." She put her mouth right near Ada's ear. "And you couldn't resist."

Carina flitted her tongue into the orifice and Ada flinched away, glaring in reproach. Carina smiled. She grabbed Ada by the hair, placed a hand between her breasts and pressed her against the wall. The air left Ada's lungs in a gasp, but she didn't fight back. Carina kissed her. It was rough, aggressive, and Ada relented completely. Coming up for air with her eyes closed, Carina slowly raised her lids and looked at Ada. She gazed back, helpless and wanting.

"Yeah . . ." Carina said, smiling. She looked down with hooded eyes. "I feel it, too."

She walked out of the office to find Sotillo standing just inside the infirmary doors. Though barely taller than she, he seemed much more so. He was lean and muscular, with short black hair, black eyes, and medium-brown skin. His angular jaw jutted forward with a confident, defiant air. The deep scar down the side of his face, from his scalp to his chin, made him look both tough and, somehow, more handsome. Again Carina was reminded of how she imagined Falco might look as an adult. Her stomach churned.

"Fuck," Sotillo said as she walked up to him.

"He's over here," she said, leading him to Gardiner's bedside.

"What the . . . what's *wrong* with him?"

"We don't know. His vitals are good, brain waves are steady, but he's just . . . not there. Fixated on nowhere. We've had to apply wetting drops and blink his eyes for him so they don't dry out."

Sotillo looked at Gardiner. "Even with the scars he's still pretty handsome, huh?"

Carina didn't reply. She looked at Gardiner's marred face and tried to imagine him whole.

"He can hear me?" Sotillo asked.

"By all indications, yeah," Carina answered.

Sotillo put his mouth next to Gardiner's ear and whispered. "Wake up, bitch."

Carina watched the major's readouts for any reaction. Ada walked over to them. Her breath caught in her throat at the malevolence that poured from Sotillo.

"You know you can't get laid lying on your back, right?" he said to Gardiner, his voice low. "Not unless I throw your legs over my shoulders, anyway."

Sotillo looked at Carina and winked. Carina frowned, disgusted.

"I'll tell you what," he continued, speaking into Gardiner's burn-mangled right ear. "I'll give it to you *real* good if you'll just get up and walk . . . right onto my dick."

Carina noticed a brief spike in Gardiner's brain activity. His pants bulged at the crotch.

"I guess that meant something to him," she said.

Ada tugged at Carina's sleeve.

"Yes, Lieutenant?"

She motioned for a quiet conference and Carina lent her ear.

"He doesn't like him," Ada said, trying to rein in her panic. "It's not . . . I think you should keep this guy away from the major."

"What do you mean?" Carina asked, appraising Ada dubiously.

Sotillo stepped toward them. Ada tensed and took a half step back.

"I'm not going to bite," Sotillo said. "Unless you want me to."

Carina made a barricade of herself. "Give us a minute, please, Lieutenant," she said to Sotillo. Her face expressed that she would tolerate no dissent.

Sotillo adopted a low tone of voice. "Can you put him somewhere private? Maybe I could . . ." he looked around, "do some shit that . . . you know . . . requires privacy? Help bring him around."

"No, Lieutenant," Carina answered. "Okay? Go take a lap."

Sotillo scowled but skulked off.

Carina turned her attention back to Ada and tacitly bid her to expound.

"There's something really awful going on between them," said Ada.

"They fuck."

"No . . . it's not that simple. It hurts him."

"I bet it does," Carina said. "Ever been fucked up the ass?"

"Fuck, Carina, that's not what I mean. Be an adult. Be serious, right now."

"Okay. Go on."

"I want to take him somewhere else. Somewhere private."

"That's funny. Sotillo just said the same thing."

"Well, I'm not Sotillo."

"We can put him in my office."

"No," Ada refused. "Even that's too public. I want to take him to my quarters."

Carina looked wary. "Why?"

"It may seem crazy to you, but I need you to trust me. Whatever you need to do to allow it, come with me. Monitor me. Make it an official medical experiment."

"I can't just let you take a patient to your room, Ada."

"Better that he be a vegetable here? Just lying here, with no one knowing what to do? I think I can help him, Carina. Let me help him."

"What is it with you?" Carina asked, crossing her arms.

"I feel things. More acutely than you, or anyone else."

Carina exhaled so that her lips fluttered. "You haven't met Tuah."

"Captain, be serious, dammit. Please. I'm an empath. I can't read thoughts, but I can sense what people actually feel. It's like one big bullshit detector and it's horrible."

"I bet."

"And what's especially horrible is that man, Sotillo. I've met a lot of malignant souls, people almost irredeemable, but most had *some kind* of positive quality. All he wants to do is hurt people. You. Me. Him," she tilted her head at Gardiner. "I've never encountered feelings so black."

"You grew up on Venus, didn't you?" Carina replied.

"Yeah, so what?"

"Welcome to Earth."

Ada realized her best tactic with Carina was to say nothing and just look at her.

Carina mulled the proposal. There was nothing to do for Gardiner but put drops in his eyes and blink his lids for him. She had no idea what was wrong with him, nor how to fix it. Of all the people on the base, Tuah, René, Private Gray, and Gardiner were the only ones she liked. She believed that Gardiner was the one man who didn't want her. Therefore, he was safe. She felt that it earned him a shot at recovery.

"Fine."

Ada blinked. Surprised. "Really?"

"Yes," Carina replied. "Tuah!"

Tuah looked up at Carina's call and cast a wounded glare, but she came as bidden. Her anger hit Ada like hammer blows. She did her best to steel herself to Tuah's reproach.

"The counselor believes she can help Major Gardiner, with her . . . abilities," said Carina, "but she needs privacy to do it. More than even my office will allow. We're going to take him to her quarters."

"Abilities," said Tuah in a salty tone. "Right. And what should I do while you're gone, Chief? Just tend to things here, as usual, while you *come* and go as you please?"

Carina jerked her head to the side, beckoning Tuah to join her for a private conference.

"I'm sorry that I hurt you."

"Then don't go with her to *her* room."

"Why don't you come with us? Aggie can tend to the ward."

"I don't want to come with you," Tuah replied. "I don't want to be around her."

"She didn't do anything. I did. I was the aggressor . . . as I'm sure you can imagine. I want you to come with us."

"Are you ordering me?"

"No, Tuah. I am asking you . . . to, please, come with us."

Tuah rubbed her face with her hands. She sighed. "Fine."

The red alert was canceled, and the lighting returned to normal. Tuah went over to Agrait and informed him that he would be in charge of the ward. He was happy for the responsibility. She unmoored Gardiner's bed and hovered it toward the door. Ada and Carina followed.

Tuah looked over her shoulder at Ada.

"You lead the way, honey; I don't know where you live."

***

"Colonel, there's no sign of them. They're just gone," Andersen reported.

"Go," said Van Sinderen. "Dismissed."

Once Andersen and Mahoney had left his office, the colonel slammed the desk with his fist.

"God*damn* it!"

***

In Ada's quarters, they placed Gardiner on the bed.

"So, what's your plan, Lieutenant?" Tuah asked, bite in her words.

"I feel a little foolish, relaying all of this, but . . . he wants to be loved."

"Excuse me?" Tuah scoffed. "You gonna fuck him, too? Is that your cure for everything, just throw some pussy at it?"

Ada closed her eyes and exhaled through her nose. She opened her eyes and looked directly at Tuah.

"Everyone carries pain, Tuah, and I've encountered a lot of it from a lot of people. But, while most people lash out or become hard or brutal, he's . . ."

"Gentle," said Carina.

"Yeah," said Ada. "How did you know?"

"'Cause I know him," Carina replied. "He could probably kill us all with so little effort and he's never used his power on any of us . . . at least that I know. Not even against Sotillo. That relationship, I don't understand. Why he lets that piece of shit handle him so rough when he has so much power at his fingertips."

"He doesn't want the power," said Ada. "It frightens him." She started to disrobe.

"What are you doing?" Tuah and Carina asked in unison.

Tuah blushed at the coincidence, angry at herself for being happy to be of a mind with Carina.

"I'm going to mother him," said Ada.

"What the fuck, Ada?" Carina replied. "How many mothers climb into bed, naked, with their grown-ass children?"

Ada stood with her jumpsuit halfway off and unfastened her bra. She felt inclined to cover her breasts in front of Tuah but decided it was a ridiculous impulse.

"In his mind, he's not grown. And let's face it, I'm not his mother. There's nothing perverse about this, unless you start projecting."

"He's comatose and you're getting in bed with him, naked," said Tuah. "He likes men. He doesn't want you like that, Lieutenant . . . I'd say that's perverse."

"I'm not sure he actually likes men," said Ada. "But I'm not trying to fuck him." She looked at Tuah and then turned to Carina. "Was this really a good idea?"

"I want her here," Carina replied. "Deal with it."

Tuah angered to be glad of Carina's defense.

"Fine," Ada replied. "But I need you two to get on board. This isn't for me; it's for him. I can't have you interfering. He needs to be touched in a loving way—not sexually," she said, cutting them off, "per se. Can I finish taking this off without you two piling on?"

"You sure you don't want us to pile on?" Carina teased. "The three of us would be fun, I think."

Both Ada and Tuah shot Carina a discouraging look.

"There's no wrong moment for a come-on from you, I see," said Ada.

Carina wanted what was best for Gardiner, but she also wanted to sate her own desires. She had doubted either woman would go for it but would have kicked herself if she hadn't tried. Besides, she reasoned, Gardiner was in no immediate physical danger. Aside from needing his eyes lubricated. She figured whatever Ada proposed, to cure him, could keep for another short while.

"Help me lift him," said the counselor.

Obviously, she was having none of Carina's plan. As much as Ada enjoyed sex, it didn't pervade her thoughts when something else required serious attention.

"We need to undress him," she stated.

Tuah came to Ada's aid.

Once Gardiner was naked, Ada asked Tuah to help put him on his side, with his back to them. They tucked his legs into a fetal position. Ada climbed into the bed with him. She put her right arm around his torso and pressed her breasts against his back. She bent her legs so they followed his, maximizing skin-to-skin contact. Then she brought her left arm up so her head lay atop her bicep. She rubbed his nearly shaven head and rested her right palm flat on his chest, above his heart. Slowly, she rubbed circles in his chest hair with her fingertips.

"His name is 'Maksim,'" Carina offered, unbidden. "Maks."

"Hi, Maks," Ada said softly, her mouth near his ear. "You're safe here. You don't have to be afraid."

Tuah unconsciously drifted closer to Carina, who watched Ada with rapt attention.

"I'm sorry for what happened to you," Ada said. "No one deserves to be treated that way."

She kissed the back of his head and went with her gut. He was paralyzed by the psychological prison into which Sargas had cast him. While she didn't know exactly what Gardiner had experienced in his life, she understood the feelings that radiated from him. Shame. Guilt. Fear. Rage. Sadness. Helplessness. She recognized the emotional wake of abuse and trauma.

Knowing what she did about his relationship with Sotillo, she assumed the abuse had been sexual. She sensed his age at its genesis. She knew she dealt, in part, with a child who had never really grown up, despite that his body had matured to manhood and he'd learned to emulate adult behavior. His morality and integrity flew in the face of the monster his experience could have made him.

What the major emitted was weak, like a stream almost fully dammed. Ada tried to visualize breaking the dam, certain that it caused his catatonic state.

"You deserve to be loved, Maks; you've grown into such a beautiful man."

She heard him sniffle before she felt him stir in her arms. The trickling stream she envisioned began to flow more freely, beginning to break through. She brought her right hand to his cheek and felt the moisture of his tears.

Tuah gently curled her hand around Carina's.

Gardiner shifted his weight and turned around. He looked into Ada's light brown eyes and said nothing. His mouth pursed. She kissed him.

He scooted down the bed and rested his head on her chest. She embraced his head with both arms and he sobbed.

Carina tugged at Tuah's hand. They looked at each other. Carina jerked her head toward the door and Tuah nodded. They left.

"I don't even know who you are," Gardiner said.

"I'm your friend, Maks. I'm Ada."

"I don't know . . . how to feel about this." He tried to parse the experience, tried to understand why this strange woman aroused him. "I want . . ."

He trailed off, but she understood him.

"It's okay," she replied. "Don't be ashamed. We can, if you want to."

"I've never done it before."

"You don't have to worry about that. Whatever you want to do, I want you to do it. And we won't do anything you don't want to."

"I don't know if I can . . ."

"I think you can." She reached down and wrapped her hand around his erection. "Does that feel good?" He nodded, but she could both see and sense his ambivalence. She worked his foreskin up and down in a slow rhythm. "Do you want me to stop?"

"I don't know," he replied.

She stopped.

"No," he said.

She resumed her slow, steady stroke. She kissed his ear. "You're a sweet man, Maks. You know that, don't you?"

He shook his head. One hard, sharp shake. He refused to meet her eyes.

The realization set in that she skirted dangerous territory. His feelings about himself were so pejorative. She had no power to contradict that, in an instant. She was already on difficult ground, engaging with him sexually. She didn't do it out of lust; she derived joy from giving joy and—more than for any other man she'd met—she wanted fervently to introduce at least a semblance of it into Gardiner's life.

She couldn't think of anyone who deserved it more. From her vantage, sex could be the most cathartic, unsullied, blissful interaction, oft-ruined by the baggage of its participants, their inability to be honest with themselves and their partners. Sotillo believed Gardiner got what he wanted from their liaison. But then Ada reasoned that Sotillo couldn't care less about his partner at all. In fact, he enjoyed Gardiner's suffering.

Ada wanted, somehow, to allay some of it.

"You can touch me, too," she offered.

He obliged. He ran his left hand along the contour of her body from her jaw, just below her ear, down her neck. He brushed her skin with his fingertips. He traced her nipple with his forefinger. Then he ran his fingers slowly, one by one in a repeating pattern along her belly. It was the most loving touch she'd felt in a while.

"You're in charge, Maks, but, if you want, I'll guide you."

He nodded.

"Here, let me get on my back."

She slid onto her back and gently pulled him on top of her. She spread her legs and rubbed her left foot down the back of his right leg.

"Come here."

She wrapped her arms around him. He dug his arms underneath her. His chest pressed against hers and he penetrated her.

"Oh, my god," he whispered.

He didn't want to move. He'd never felt anything like it. Had never penetrated another person, male or female. Had never been touched in a wholesome, loving way by anyone. Nor had his genitalia ever been stimulated but in the most perfunctory way by men who'd used his body for recreation.

"You don't have to hold back," she said. "Let go. Do what feels good."

Gardiner moved to and fro, slowly at first, but he picked up the pace.

"Oh, my god . . ." he repeated. And again, adding her name.

He nuzzled his face into the crook of her neck. He kissed her there and it sent a tingle down her spine. She got goose bumps.

She ran her fingers down his back. It arched in spasm as he came. She opened up her mind to his emotions and let his ecstasy wash over her. It was the best gift of her otherwise burdensome extrasensory perception, to experience her partner's orgasm in tandem. It brought her immediately to climax.

They lay together, him still inside her, still erect despite his orgasm. The slightest movement overwhelmed him. When he laid the full weight of his body atop her, she bore him easily. After a long while, he slid from within and rested his head upon her chest. She kissed the top of his head and held him there, with his cheek on her breast and his eyes closed.

She closed her eyes. They both fell asleep.

THIRTY-ONE

DEROVIAS AND HIS small band of centurions, guardsmen, and human mercenaries parked their four jet-bikes. Each vehicle towed a cylinder big enough for each of the group's targets, once captured. They stopped outside the Coventry limits in a derelict industrial slum.

Kir let go of Derovias and climbed down.

Once Derovias touched ground, he ordered the others to electrify the bikes to prevent theft. They then hid the vehicles with spectral camouflage.

"We travel from here on foot. Ceres, you're with me. Kir, you and Andrei. Ji'ilaad, you travel with Inishi."

Falco looked at Alesh, whose face did nothing to belie his displeasure at the pairing.

"I trust, human, that I needn't worry about you objecting to my behavior?"

"No, sir," Falco replied. He wondered if Alesh would test him.

"Our rendezvous point is the Integration monument at the city center," said Derovias. "We're looking for information that will lead to the capture of our targets."

***

Daedalus, Sargas, and René ran out of the tunnels beneath Orchard City and, as the ceiling gave way to the gray skies, they skidded to a halt and assessed their position.

"We need to move quickly," Sargas insisted, dressed again in the ill-fitting Confederate jumpsuit with a giant hole in its back and bullet holes in its chest. "There is a road to the east and there are regular transports between the free section of this city and Coventry."

"Yes, I know," said Daedalus. "But how do *you* know?"

Sargas ignored him. "At least one of the routes is run by an A'arilon. With luck, we'll encounter him, hitch a ride, and be to Coventry within the hour."

"Sure," said Daedalus, realizing that pressing Sargas would yield no answers. "Fuck it. Lead the way, chief."

They climbed out of the open-cut railroad and crossed acres of derelict warehouses. The humans they passed looked up in curiosity at the two large men dressed in Confederation uniforms and their smaller companion in Allied military gear, but no one dared to interfere. When the three men reached the road, they looked for shelter that would allow them to see oncoming traffic, but hide them from it.

"How do we make out if a convoy is A'arili or Ingili? Ingili won't deal with me, you must know that," said Daedalus.

"The Ingili here are not nearly as proud as the American varieties," said Sargas. "They'll deal with you, if you have money."

"And we have no money," said René.

"Then we should hope for an A'arili convoy, then, hmm?" answered Sargas.

René sighed. "C'était une idée stupide."

"Well, we're here," Daedalus replied, "So deal with it. We can't go back and say: 'Hiii, we deserted but we realized it's a *real* bummer. Okay if we come back and pretend nothing happened? Thaaanks.'"

"Quiet, both of you," said Sargas. "You, A'arilon, go flag down this convoy."

"Dressed in this fucking uniform?" Daedalus balked.

"I'll join you," said René. "Seeing both sides' colors together ought to give them pause enough not to just shoot you."

"Oh, yeah, that's a real relief," said Daedalus, frowning. "They can shoot both of us instead."

He and René stepped out into the road. The convoy came to a halt. They were greeted by weapons in the hands of every crewmember. A voice barked orders in corren to watch all avenues for signs of ambush. An aged corren, shorter than Daedalus and dressed in a long, heavy trench coat, jumped down from the middle transport. He approached with another, much younger corren and a human, both heavily armed.

"Do I know you, brother?" asked the convoy's representative.

The question seemed benign to untrained ears. To a fellow A'arili, it was a mutually understood greeting.

"You do," Daedalus replied. "And I know you."

The corren smiled, but his eyes were cold. "You know the words, A'arilon Daedalus, but you don't know me."

"But you obviously know me," Daedalus replied.

"We *all* know the defectors."

The armed corren behind the representative muttered to his leader in their shared language about traitors and rewards. The representative held up his hand to silence his charge.

"Yes, a reward . . ." Daedalus replied, in English, with an affected air of boredom. "I'm sure if you go ring the ole guv's doorbell, someone at Blackwing will just hand you a big chestful of money."

The representative smiled without showing any teeth. "Your reputation for having a smart mouth is well-earned."

"Since when do A'arili do business with the Reds?" asked Daedalus.

"Since when does A'arilon Daedalus wear the uniform of the government he betrayed?"

"That's a long story . . ." said Daedalus.

"We were beset by Confederates," Sargas interjected. "Our armor took a lot of damage, but we prevailed. We took the clothes from two of our kills. As you can see, mine don't really fit."

The representative looked at René. "And this one? Unarmored and unscathed. And wearing a skirt. I suppose you picked him up along the way, hmm? Or he's just very lucky."

"It's a kilt . . ." said René.

"We're deserters," said Sargas.

The representative laughed heartily. He allowed his attention to be diverted from René. "Oh, Daedalus," said the old corren. "Neither side was good enough for you?"

"Afraid not," said Daedalus.

"I like this," the representative replied. "I want to know more, but we need to be moving. Relinquish your arms and join me on board."

"And your name, brother?" asked Daedalus, frowning as he allowed himself and René to be disarmed by the representative's younger corren companion and the human.

"Call me Asimov," the representative replied.

***

"Ceres is a strange name for a hunter," said Derovias.

"What do you know about it?" she replied, without looking at him. Her tone made it clear she didn't want a response. Derovias didn't care.

"My knowledge of human gods is far from complete," he replied, "but I've been to the belt and to Ceres herself. I like to know things . . . so I educated myself about her namesake. A poor choice, in my opinion; she's an inhospitable chunk of rock just big and round enough to be planetary, but just as lifeless as the rest of the debris. Might that be why you took the name?" He smiled.

Ceres scowled askance at him.

"Are you making a statement about how cold and dead your heart is?" he prodded.

She stopped and turned to him. "Must you make this experience more unpleasant than it already is?"

He smiled, showing her his fangs. "You don't enjoy chitchat?"

Ceres rolled her eyes.

Derovias put his smile away. "Well, if the goddess of fertilizer doesn't want to play, then let's get down to brass tacks. It's no accident you're here, alone, with me."

"Is that a threat?" She took a step back, creating distance to draw and use her swords.

"No, Ceres. It's not a threat . . . I need your help."

***

Elsewhere in the city, Kir bent Andrei's ear.

"Alesh and Inishi need to be eliminated," said Kir.

Andrei ran his hand over his cleanly shaven head. "This is a con."

"I assure you, human, it is not a con. I compromise myself, just having this conversation with you. Why would I enlist you to help me kill my own kin?"

"So you'll have a reason to put me down," Andrei replied.

"If I wanted you dead," said Kir, "you'd be dead."

Andrei expanded his chest. He tried to use his height advantage to intimidate the corren.

Kir ignored the display. "Derovias is having the same conversation with your partner. When we all convene at the monument, you can confirm this with her . . . discreetly."

"And you could be setting us both up," said Andrei.

Kir sighed. "I understand you're wary. You'd be a fool not to be. It's the way of this world that we distrust everyone . . . with good reason, hmm? Here I am, colluding with a human to murder my brothers."

***

Manon froze. She watched her sister walk with Kurgan Derovias. Regathering herself, she ushered Jack backward so they remained out of view.

"She is well, at least," Jack said in a hushed tone.

"Well?" Manon exclaimed. "In the company of that monster? I'd hardly call that 'well,' Jack."

"She appears unharmed. She's unfettered and it seems she's here of her own volition. I think, love, we couldn't hope for better."

"No. I can hope that she would come to her senses and keep better company. Fuck this. I'm taking him out. Come with me."

Jack followed her command, knowing he could do nothing to dissuade her.

They barely made a sound, but Derovias heard them. He whirled around, drawing his gun. Ceres turned to see Manon, bearing down on them with a blade in one hand and a pistol in the other.

"Non, Manon!" Ceres cried out. "Non! Pas maintenant!" *Not now!*

Derovias fired, but Jack anticipated it and shoved Manon to the ground. The corren's blast shot harmlessly over her. Jack was on top of Derovias before he could fire again. The robot drove Derovias to the ground. His pistol clattered away.

Manon got back on her feet, blade still in hand. She retrieved her gun.

"You know this woman?" Derovias growled at Ceres, pinned to the street. He twisted his neck to look at Manon. "Yes . . . I suppose you must. I see a resemblance."

"Fuck you, snake," Manon said, raising her pistol to fire.

"Would you really murder someone like this?" Derovias asked, helpless beneath Jack's considerable weight. Were Manon's android not supporting himself, he would have crushed the corren.

"Arrête, Manon!" Ceres implored. *Stop!*

Manon looked at Ceres and hesitated to fire.

"Dammit!" Derovias chided. "Listen to the woman! Don't meddle where you don't belong."

"Listen to my sister . . ." Manon replied, turning her attention from Ceres, jabbing her pistol toward Derovias, "who's taken leave of her senses, palling around with you?"

Ceres took advantage of Manon's distraction. She struck the gun from her hand. In a continuous movement, Ceres grabbed her sister's other wrist, placed a hand on her elbow, and twisted until she dropped the blade. Manon, surprised, tried to fight back. But Ceres twisted her kin's arm behind her back and drove her to the pavement.

"I'm sorry, Manon, but you need to calm the fuck down," Ceres remonstrated in French.

Cursing back in French, Manon let Ceres know exactly how insane she seemed.

"Don't be blinded by your hatred of them," Ceres replied. *"You can't meddle in every affair."*

Derovias smiled, still pinned by Jack. "Does this mean I have your trust, Ceres?"

"You tried to kill my sister. I am . . . deeply conflicted."

"I did no such thing," Derovias replied. "It was set to stun."

Manon blinked at him. She didn't believe it.

"Go ahead. Retrieve the pistol, if you doubt me. See for yourself."

"I would, if she'd let me go," Manon said in a tart tone.

Ceres let her up and backed away, expecting Manon to lash out. She did no such thing. Manon picked up Derovias' pistol and saw the truth for herself. She rubbed the top of her forehead, tousling her curls in thoughtful consternation.

"Let him up," Manon said, finally. Jack obeyed without question.

Derovias rose to his feet and brushed himself off. "Ceres has volunteered to be part of something monumental, Manon."

Ceres' face tensed. She had agreed to nothing, aloud, but was too intent on what Derovias had proposed to back out. Apparently, he knew as much.

"Yeah? And what's that?" Manon asked.

"I wish I could tell you," Derovias smiled, "but I can't give away the goose just yet."

Manon looked at Ceres. "You know I think you're nuts, right?"

Ceres shrugged. "I'm not the lost little girl you took in."

"Yes, you are, *cher*," Manon replied. "And you always will be. God is bullshit but, somehow . . . despite the odds, we found each other. Think about that. It seems divine . . . to me, anyway. Miraculously improbable.

I haven't experienced much divinity in my life. Have you? I don't want to lose you, now, because you misplace your trust."

"I don't trust him, Manon."

Derovias made an expression of feigned hurt.

"But," Ceres continued, "if he's not completely full of shit . . . I need to see this through."

"I wish you'd tell me what it is," Manon implored.

Ceres opened her mouth to speak, feeling she owed no loyalty nor silence to Derovias. *"You know ... "*

He interrupted her. "Anything you tell anyone—even her—compromises us, Ceres. I know you have less than no love for me, but I beg you to put your faith in what I've said. You can kill me yourself, if I don't deliver. I won't resist."

Both Ceres and Manon looked at Derovias in disbelief. Neither woman had experienced much of what could be called "conversation" with correns. The sisters were used to being targets for rape and murder. Much of their verbal dealings with their alien opponents arose from such conflicts. Manon and Ceres both had shared brief dialogue with Ingili and A'arili, but no exchange had included anything close to humility. Especially not the outright forfeiture of one's life as payment for a broken promise.

Naturally, both women assumed the offer was disingenuous.

"I know you don't believe me," Derovias said, "but I'm ready to die either fulfilling this mission or failing at it. It's that important." He looked at Ceres. "And you know it."

Ceres closed her eyes and took a deep breath. She shook her head and exhaled. Opening her eyes, she turned to Manon.

"I'm going with him."

Manon reached for Ceres' arm. She pulled back but, noticing the soft look on her sister's face, she allowed Manon to pull her into an embrace.

"Je t'aime, chérie," Manon said, kissing Ceres' forehead.

Ceres gave Manon a gentle squeeze. "Au revoir, mon cœur. À bientôt."

Manon appreciated the sentiment but doubted she'd see her sister again, let alone soon. She and Jack watched Ceres and Derovias walk off until they were out of sight.

THIRTY-TWO

DAEDALUS WONDERED WHO A'arilon Asimov might once have been.

It was one of the chief problems with A'arili. Since they all adopted the same batch name and often chose new forenames, the history of their original batch and birth names remained hidden. Yet everyone knew that A'arilon Daedalus was Asharan Antal. The Asharan batch were one of the best-known batches of natural-born correns. It had yielded more A'arili than any single batch that came before.

Asimov was visibly older than Daedalus. It gave some clues to his provenance. Most tube-born correns didn't live long enough to yellow near the temples. Asimov showed hallmarks of natural-born senescence.

"I can hear your wheels turning," said Asimov. "There's no harm in asking questions. I won't promise to answer all of them, however."

"What's your real name?" Daedalus asked Asimov.

"My name?" He paused a moment, pondering what to divulge. After a while, he replied. "I was once Aldebaran Hi'ifto."

"Aldebaran Hi'ifto," said Daedalus, shocked. "You're . . . kind of famous. The first to leave. That makes you . . ."

"One hundred and fifty-three," Asimov replied.

"You have to be the only one left," said Daedalus of the other Aldebari.

"To my knowledge."

"How do you know whether someone is trustworthy?" asked Sargas, unbidden.

Everyone looked at him.

"How do you?" Asimov asked.

"I don't," Sargas replied. "I elect to trust whom I must, to the furthest extent that I can, without endangering myself. I accept that I could be betrayed by anyone, and I'm prepared to deal with it."

"Then you and I are of a mind . . ." said Asimov. "I didn't catch your name."

"Sargas."

"That sounds like a star . . . to someone named for one," said Asimov of his original batch name. He looked at his young corren companion.

"Scorpius," replied the young man.

"Urso is our resident astronomer," Asimov explained. "Although only in books, since we can't see the sky." He looked at Sargas. "Any credence to your namesake?"

"Aren't we all equipped to fight with the full use of our natural gifts?" Sargas retorted.

"Fair . . . but did you choose your own name?"

"I did."

Asimov smiled, again without levity. "I named myself after an author whose books opened my mind to a future rich with possibility and who awakened me to the lies of our existence. And you, after a vicious, poisonous insect."

"No," said Sargas. "I named myself after a star in the same constellation from which the name of my companion was derived."

At the revelation, Daedalus' eye ridges crept up his forehead.

Asimov settled back into his seat. This time, his smile conveyed some warmth.

"Ah, a romantic. I feel so much more at ease."

***

Ji'ilaad and Inishi walked through the city. They conveyed a sense of authority and impunity. It proved highly effective against some humans but was useless against the rest, and especially the Ingili.

"Do you think we might tailor our approach to our audience?" Ji'ilaad suggested.

Inishi spat on the ground. "For what? The Ingili would never cooperate with us. And I refuse to defer to these humans."

"And where has it gotten us?"

"Nowhere. But not because it wasn't effective. You can't tell me some of those humans were not sincerely terrified. They'd have offered up Old Nan if we'd demanded it."

Ji'ilaad couldn't refute that.

"They simply aren't here," said Inishi.

***

Rozhenko and Adnan wandered through Coventry with the overly curious air of two outsiders. It took barely fifteen minutes for the news to circulate that a sentry and a young boy had arrived, out of place and aimless. Ripe for the picking.

The hairs on the back of Adnan's neck pricked up. He sensed eyes on them, everywhere. "Do you have a plan? I don't like this."

"We are needing to find that woman and robot," Rozhenko replied.

"How do you suppose we do that?"

"We will be asking questions?" Rozhenko proposed, with little confidence.

Adnan sensed sudden movement and whirled around to face it. He was struck across the face by a truncheon. Stars burst before his eyes. He fell to the cobbles with a groan. Rozhenko couldn't react before another man jammed a tasing club into his side, under the arm, beneath the breastplate. The teeth of the club punctured Rozhenko's body armor. The crippling jolt of electricity rendered him inoperable. His lumbering cybernetic body crashed to the street. His head struck the cobbles with a dull, metallic *thunk*.

"Get the cart," Adnan heard a male voice say. "Get the big one to Petrovias."

"And the boy?" another man asked.

"He's pretty enough," said the first man. "We can sell him at the next auction."

"We won't get as much since you fucked up his face."

"I didn't know he was pretty before he turned around."

***

Asimov's convoy rumbled into Coventry. They came to a halt outside a large warehouse that teemed with humans and correns. The scars branded onto the Ingili faces distinguished them from the A'arili.

"You deal with Ingili?" Daedalus asked. He could see it with his own eyes but had to voice his disbelief.

"It's impossible not to," Asimov replied. "Up here, you do business with anyone who can offer you something. In my experience, it's better to do business than to make enemies."

"That seems wise," said Daedalus. "It's not how I do things, but it seems wise."

"You've never been in the badlands," said Asimov. It was not a question.

Neither was it true, but Daedalus didn't protest.

"You may fancy yourself a badass," said Asimov, "because you piss off uniformed humans who value you too much—who are too afraid of you to ever really discipline you—but that's over now. Every free corren you meet out here has either defied our masters or been discarded by them. You are not special. And none of us are impressed."

Sargas approached and spoke to Daedalus. "We need to go."

"Not so fast," said Asimov. "I may be generous, but that ride wasn't free."

Sargas frowned.

"Where are your manners, Sargas?" asked Daedalus, making a mock-incredulous face at the big man.

Asimov turned to Daedalus. "I need you three to help unload the food."

Sargas turned on his heel and immediately set to work, hoping to dispense with the task as soon as possible. Urso handed him a box and gave him directions.

"I'd ask you to serve it, too," said Asimov to Daedalus, "but I expect you'd push back."

"Actually, that's fair," Daedalus replied, "but we don't have forever to dawdle. Sargas has an aim, and our fate is tied to his. We're not exactly his prisoners . . . but we go where and when he goes."

Asimov shrugged his shoulders and took a box of food from the convoy. Daedalus did the same and followed him into the warehouse.

"How do you maintain order?" asked Daedalus.

"It pretty much maintains itself," Asimov replied. "Everyone gets the same dispensation, though I always account for a little extra. People who want more can work for more, or they can go try and find it elsewhere, but I don't play favorites. It takes some prep, but we take roll, we know our inventory. We do the math, and everyone gets the same base amount. It's fair and so no one acts out. Well, sometimes there's a greedy fool, but we dispense with them as a community."

"How do you pay for this shit? It must cost a fortune . . ."

"All kinds of ways, some more savory than others. For one, we pull shifts protecting the indoor farms in Free Orchard City. I'm sure you can imagine they're beset by thieves and raiders who want to take by force and give nothing back . . . so we kill those pests. As much as I abhor violence, it's necessary because other people employ it. Try and passively resist someone who will kill you for fun—rape you either before or afterward—and you just wind up dead and raped. And they still take what you had. Violence is the lingua franca out here and it's all some people understand. I'm sure you know you have to speak to people in their own language."

Asimov looked over his shoulder at Daedalus.

"And, well . . . I think there's something in us that desires to kill."

"Just us, or the humans, too?" Daedalus asked.

"I don't know about the humans," Asimov replied. "And I guess I don't know about us, either. Do we want to kill because we were raised to be killers? Because we were trained to be weapons? Or is it innate?"

"I've never met a corren raised in the wild," said Daedalus, "free of Red influence."

"There can be no experiment because there exists no control," Asimov stated. He handed his box to a human. One link in a long chain of people who would serve the contents of each parcel they'd been handed.

"Come down here with that," Asimov said to Daedalus, directing him to an empty-handed Ingilon who silently accepted the box.

The man's two burn scars ran parallel down his face from above his eyes to the corners of his mouth. He would not look at Daedalus.

"But this is an experiment of a different sort," said Daedalus to Asimov.

"Is it?" asked Asimov as they walked back to the convoy.

"I didn't think any civilization existed in the badlands."

"Is that what you'd call this? Civilization?"

"It's civil, anyway."

"Yes, in the generic . . . but civilization is subjective. The walled cities throw out the benchmark, up to which nothing in the badlands could ever measure. In those places, you have access to clean water at will, quality food, well-balanced meals, physical safety . . . reliable shelter from the elements. If we encounter any of those things out here, it's either miraculous or the result of great effort."

"How *do* you get water?" asked Daedalus as they each retrieved another box.

"We boil groundwater, river water, any source like that, catch the evaporate and direct the condensation elsewhere. But only the correns can drink it; it's full of heavy metals, and even we'll get sick after a while.

It requires too much energy for little yield. It's hugely inefficient and the majority of our . . . civilization is human, so it helps very little."

"You could just drink the dirty water," said Daedalus. "Why even evaporate it?"

"Because it's filthy . . . but, yes, I could drink it dirty. It still doesn't solve the human problem. They drink it anyway, though. Poison water is preferable to dying of thirst."

"I find that humans themselves are the problem," Daedalus said without even the care to lower his voice.

Asimov frowned. "If I adopted that stance, I'd have few allies and a much smaller community. Sure, water is our biggest expenditure, but we have many humans and their numbers give us strength. Sometimes we can truck the liquid in from Whiton's Heath and the eastern coast because the pollution there is low enough for the distillate to be less immediately lethal to the humans . . .

"Sometimes we get purification tablets, which spares us the boiling, but . . . if only we could get a hold of machinery . . . or build it. We have no way to process urine so it's clean enough to drink, and that's the biggest waste of liquid out here. But, even then, if we imbibe poison, we output poison. The metals are our biggest problem. Everyone gets sick, eventually. Even those who escape murder die far younger than they should."

Daedalus didn't reply. He didn't know offhand how to build a purification system, but knew he had the skills. He could do it if provided proper information and resources.

"Did I lose you with my talk of piss?" asked Asimov.

"What? Ha. No," Daedalus answered as René approached. "It's just that we've got to move on. I'll get the boys to each grab another box, but we can't stay."

"Not even to eat?" Asimov asked.

"Are we eating?" René asked, hopeful.

"You certainly could," Asimov replied.

THIRTY-THREE

AT THE INTEGRATION statue—a grotesque monument to the forceful commingling of humanity and their corren invaders, defaced and vandalized, but still standing and intact—the eight members of Derovias' party congregated.

"Can I talk to you?" Andrei whispered to Ceres.

She beckoned him away from the rest with a jerk of her head.

"Go ahead," she said.

"The snake I got paired with . . . Kir. He . . ."

"Spit it out, Drei."

"He said we have to kill the other two . . . the centurions. I forgot their names. But not that snake with the human. He . . . Kir . . . said he'd create a diversion and that we should cut their throats."

Ceres' mouth bloomed into an incredulous smile. "So it's true."

"He said the same thing to you? You didn't believe him, either?"

"I still don't believe him," said Ceres. "It feels like we're being played. Correns don't murder their own. I don't know what this is, and I don't like it. But . . . I do like the chance of taking two of them out. Just stay frosty."

While they spoke in private, a human man approached Derovias. The two men conferred for a moment. Derovias pressed something into the human's hand and the man departed.

"Would you mind joining the rest of us?" Derovias called to Ceres and Andrei. "Conspiring humans make a corren nervous."

He smiled, showing his fangs.

Ceres knew that the former was not a request and the latter was a threat. She wondered if he was putting on a show for Alesh and Inishi, to make the two men feel as though everything were normal. She and Andrei rejoined the group.

"I've been informed that our quarry has arrived," Derovias stated.

***

Manon saw the men pulling the cart before they saw her and Jack.

She could see by their gaits that they were armed. It was nothing exceptional; anyone who wandered the badlands without a weapon was either a fool or an unfortunate. The dirty, yellow kaffiyeh wrapped around their heads raised her hackles. The scarf was the emblem of a clan that made no secret of its human trafficking. In fact, they used the gaudy marker to instill fear and to intimidate. They called themselves the Golden Horde, though the rank-and-file members were ignorant of the namesake.

Manon drew her light short sword and quickly advanced on the men. Jack matched her pace. The two horde members looked up to see her and the large android bearing down. The men dropped the cart to fumble for weapons, but too late. Manon preferred intimate combat. Unless someone drew a gun on her, she wouldn't shoot. But she was happy to strike first with a blade while close enough to be touched.

The man she chose was the slighter of the two, tall and dressed in rags. His greasy black hair peeked through the eyehole in the scarf that swaddled his head. She let him draw a makeshift mace from his belt but cleaved his hand from his wrist before he could attack. He clutched at the severed stump and screamed in hysterical shock. She flipped her sword in her hand so the pommel faced forward. She punched him, sword still in hand, in the ramus of his jaw. He collapsed to the street in an unconscious heap. She stabbed him through the back of the neck.

Jack took the burlier man and made short work of him. In two swift movements, Jack broke the man's sword arm at the elbow and destroyed his pivot leg with a merciless kick through the knee. The man whimpered against the cobblestones. Both his arm and leg were bent at sickening angles. He lay moaning in the street.

"Shut him up, please," said Manon.

Jack stomped the man's skull, crushing it like a bug. The yellow headscarf became a sackful of brains, bone, and organic pulp. It turned brown as it soaked up the blood.

"Let's see what we've got," said Manon, walking around to the back of the cart. She threw back the moldy blankets to reveal Rozhenko's unconscious body. "Oh, *putain*."

Jack examined Rozhenko. He placed one hand on the burly cyborg's metallic skull. "He's been shorted. He might be dead."

Manon looked at the big man and frowned. She pulled off her glove and put her fingers under his nose. She felt very faint breathing.

"No, he's alive. Somehow . . . I guess he's more organic than he seems."

"He could be braindead, however," Jack suggested.

"He wasn't sharp to begin with," she said. "Revive him. Let's see."

The tips of the index and middle fingers on Jack's right hand flipped backward, revealing two plugs: one positive and one negative. He gently pressed his left thumb against the base of Rozhenko's skull to open a small panel into which the plugs could be inserted.

"You made all of this?" Manon asked in wonderment.

"Don't be so impressed. At this point, it's two-hundred-year-old technology. Probably older. Back before the Blight, I was just the facilitator. I had capital. I had ideas. Sure, I contributed something to the designs, but I didn't have all of the science. I used to joke that I knew just enough to be dangerous. I had people working for me who were truly brilliant, who realized a lot of the innovations—like Petrovias," Jack frowned to mention the name. "He made my ideas into finished products. This, though," he wiggled his fingers, "this is just fundamental physics. A jump start."

He jolted Rozhenko with electricity and the big man's eyes fluttered open. He looked around from his vantage, lying on his back. He blinked as Manon and Jack came into focus.

"What has happened to me?" Rozhenko asked.

"We were going to ask you that question," said Manon.

"Where is boy?" he asked, panicked. He sat up and bounded from the cart, landing unsteady on his feet. Jack righted him.

"What boy?" Manon asked.

"Adnan," said Rozhenko. "They take Adnan."

"If the Golden Horde had you, they have him," Manon said.

"But why separate us?" Rozhenko asked.

"They were taking you to Petrovias, I'd guess," Jack suggested.

Rozhenko made a face; the name meant nothing to him.

"I'm not the only one who couldn't let go," Jack replied.

"Let go of what?" Rozhenko was truly confused.

"Forget it," said Jack. "Pietro deals in all kinds of illicit mechanical trade, especially robotics. Sentries and other cyborgs are especially interesting to him because, unlike me, he has organic parts. He didn't want to give up his humanity . . ."

"Ironic," Manon interrupted, "since I hear he's now occupying a corren body that he heavily modified. It's a snake torso atop some kind of machine with six legs. He's, like, a mechanical spider."

"The only consistent thing about him is malignancy," Jack replied.

"And a flair for the dramatic," said Manon in a mocking tone. "What the fuck is a 'Petrovias,' anyway?"

Rozhenko remained confused but realized that neither Manon nor the robot would explain it away.

"So, where are they taking boy?"

"Is the boy handsome?" Jack asked.

Rozhenko shrugged.

"Yes," said Manon. "Have you never met Adnan? Delicate. Pleasant face. As most of Edmund's descendants have, obviously." She dipped in a mock curtsy, framing her own visage. "There are a lot of men who would pay for a boy like that."

Rozhenko frowned.

"Before they put him on the market, they'll probably take him back to camp and pass him around," she added, frowning in distaste.

"Oh, *pizdyets*," Rozhenko lamented. "We must be rescuing him."

"How do you propose we do that?" asked Manon. "Three of us against hundreds, if not thousands?"

"We cannot be leaving him to being raped in ass by hundreds, if not thousands!" Rozhenko protested.

"As much as I hate to leave my own defenseless cousin at the mercy of disgusting savages, I can't forfeit my life for a futile cause," Manon replied.

"He is family and you are just leaving him?"

"There's nothing noble in throwing your life away, Vasily," she replied. "No matter who it's for."

Rozhenko looked at Jack, pleading with his eyes.

"From personal experience," said Jack, "I have to agree."

"Then I get him myself," Rozhenko replied. "Tell me where I go."

"Don't be stupid—" Manon admonished.

"Look," Jack interrupted. "We need to pass through the Horde to leave the city, anyway; they occupy the road to Whiton's Heath. Perhaps we can inquire into purchasing the boy."

"After he is raped many thousand times?" Rozhenko raged.

"Truth is," said Manon, "he's probably being raped right now."

Rozhenko growled. "Goddamn it! You . . ." he sputtered. "How are you being so calm? How you talk like this is fucking weather? You are sick woman."

Manon looked at Rozhenko with a mixture of mild pity and chagrin.

"Maybe things are different wherever you came from, but rape happens every day out here. So does murder. Often hand in hand. As a desirable object, they likely won't kill him."

"He is not object! He is boy! Better if he lives? What kind of life he has? What is *wrong* with you?"

"Go get him, then, if you want," said Manon. "Go on. Get captured and given to Petrovias, and nothing will have changed. You'll go where you were headed when we found you, and Adnan'll still get raped and sold and raped again. Or . . . you can calm down and accept the unpleasant reality. Accept that we've offered to help you save him. You may not like the terms, but it's the only way that *any* of us come out ahead."

Rozhenko opened his mouth as if to speak, but said nothing. He looked away and closed his mouth, sighing through his nose. His shoulders slumped. He nodded.

***

A commotion erupted by the main entrance to the vast warehouse where A'arilon Asimov's community congregated for their meals.

A blue pulse struck the ceiling. It dissipated along the steel skeleton of the edifice. Screams burst from the panicked crowd. Some people darted for the other exits but found them blocked.

Asimov headed toward the fray. Daedalus grabbed him.

"Confederates? Don't you have a fucking perimeter?"

"Of course we have a perimeter," Asimov barked.

"Fat lot of fucking good it did." Daedalus reached for his pistol.

"No! Don't you dare."

"What, then?" asked Daedalus.

"No one here is armed except me, Urso, and a handful of others."

Daedalus shook his head in disbelief.

"These are civilians!" Asimov hissed. "We have a no-weapons policy. You want to eat, you leave your gun at home, or you put it in our locker. I don't need people shooting each other over food. We gave you a pass 'cause we thought you'd be useful against a rival faction. I didn't expect Reds."

"You need me," Daedalus insisted.

"No. I don't want you taking them on. Don't make this a battleground in your bullshit war. This is time for diplomacy."

"Fuck," said Daedalus. "You're gonna let these people mill about like sheep for the wolves."

Derovias' voice filled the warehouse. "Dearest people of the Free City, we wish you no harm. But it has come to our attention that you harbor fugitives, whom we have come to collect. Let us have them, and we'll leave you in peace. Resist . . . and be left in pieces."

Asimov waded through the crowd of tense and anxious people to where Derovias stood with Alesh. The crowd parted for their leader.

"Oh, my," Derovias said, holding his fingers to his collarbone. "A celebrity."

Asimov ignored the remark. He knew Derovias was to be feared, but he refused to take an obsequious or weak stance before him.

"What do you want, Derovias?"

"Oh, he knows who I am!" said Derovias in mock excitement. "Alesh, did you hear that?"

Alesh, his face invisible behind his opaque visor, ignored Derovias.

Asimov tensed at the mention of Ishtafan Alesh. He knew it almost certainly meant that Tolon Inishi was there, too, blocking one of the other exits. Three of the most brutal centurions known to lore were on Asimov's doorstep. Even at 153 years of age, having seen and done all the things that he had, that knowledge gave him pause. The aged deserter realized he was afraid, not for himself—he had lived the fullest, longest life of any corren beside Arak Matar—but for the people for whom he'd become a shepherd.

Derovias looked at Asimov. The mirth in the centurion's eyes gave way to one of the coldest looks Asimov had ever seen. "I want what you have, Hi'ifto."

"You'll have to be more spe—"

"Don't fuck with me, old man," said Derovias. He bared his fangs with a sneer. "We all know you're a legend, but heroes die. Don't make me kill you. Give me what I came for."

Asimov thought for a second to further protest his ignorance, but knew it was a stupid risk. To force Derovias to repeat himself once was foolish enough; there was no room for confusion. There was no escape for Daedalus and his companions. It was time to stop pretending.

"And I have your word that you won't harm any of my people?"

"Does my word really mean anything to you, *Aktalon*?"

"It does," Asimov replied. "You call me a traitor, but I've lived an honorable life. I've tried always to make the decision that felt right at the time. Honor is one of the things they taught us, Derovias. When you come up against something that feels wrong to you . . . I wonder how different you and I will really be."

Derovias almost dropped the mask, the fear-inducing expression on his face that had been so carefully cultivated and, for so long, had been genuine and proudly brandished. He wanted to tell Asimov that it was all an act, that he had reached precisely that crossroads and found himself unable to do things that rang false to his honor. It had changed unbidden and became dissonant to the orders he'd been made to follow.

"I trust that you are an honorable man," Asimov continued. "And I accept your word as bond."

"Then you have it," said Derovias, staying in character. "As long as your guests don't misbehave, I shan't kill a soul."

Asimov led Derovias into the warehouse.

Alesh and Kir stayed by the main doors.

Inishi, Ji'ilaad, Falco, Ceres, and Andrei all guarded the other points of access. No one could come or go without going through any of them.

When Asimov emerged from the crowd with Derovias in tow, Daedalus drew his pistol.

"What the fuck is this?"

Asimov held up his hands. Derovias made no move for a weapon.

"I'd put away that gun if I were you, Antal," said Derovias.

"And why the fuck would I do that?" Daedalus replied.

"Because you don't want all these nice people to die," Derovias stated.

"What makes you think I care about these humans?"

Derovias shook his head. "The funny thing about you, Daedalus, is that everyone but you knows you're full of shit. Now, either shoot me, or holster your gun. I'll even let you keep it and walk out of here like a man. Or I'll have you dragged out like a bitch in front of all these lowly little humans. Which would you prefer?"

"I prefer the scenario where you die and I go nowhere," Daedalus replied.

"Then you'll be very disappointed, because I don't even need you alive."

With a movement so deft it could have passed for sleight-of-hand, Derovias procured his gun and trained it on René.

"Nor this human," Derovias added. "Whom I'm guessing you care about. Like all the humans. Just like our friend Hi'ifto here," he nodded at Asimov, "because why else would you defect to defend them . . . from me, and from our Lord. And from the rest of your brothers whom you've so utterly forsaken?" His voice dripped with scorn.

Sargas looked Derovias in the eye, then put his hand on Daedalus' shoulder.

"Let us go peacefully," Sargas said.

Daedalus closed his eyes. He looked inclined to vomit. He holstered his weapon.

"Red Two through Five, hold your positions," said Derovias into his comm. "Six through Eight, come to me."

Ji'ilaad, Inishi, and Ceres emerged from the throng that surrounded Derovias, Asimov, Daedalus, René, and Sargas.

"I've agreed to let them walk out of here like men," said Derovias. "Mind that they allow that arrangement to proceed without incident."

"They're still armed," said Ceres.

"Yes," replied Derovias. "That's what I mean. They get to keep their surrogate penises, so be extra vigilant. I trust you're quite quick enough to kill them before they pull."

Ceres smiled at Derovias, but it never reached her eyes. She took her place behind Daedalus.

"You take your orders from him?" Daedalus said to Ceres with disdain. "You'd sell out your own people like that?"

"Such irony, coming from you," said Derovias. "Go. Take them away."

Ceres pushed Daedalus in the back. He bristled, but he marched. Sargas and René acquiesced without protest. As they passed, Derovias bowed to Asimov but did not take his eyes off the man.

Asimov crossed his arms and made no other gesture of reply.

THIRTY-FOUR

ANJALI TURNED THE corner to find Ray standing in the abandoned corridor, silently considering an open door.

"There you are," she said. "I've been looking all over for you."

He turned his head for a moment and then returned his attention to the opening. "You're all right to be up and about?"

"The doctor checked me out. Discharged me."

"I'm not sure she's qualified."

She shook her head and changed the subject. "What are you doing out here all alone?"

He rubbed his face with one hand. "Thinking."

"We need to talk, Ray."

He tilted his head back. "Then talk, Angie. I'm listening."

"Cut the shit," she pressed, responding to his standoffish posture. "We've all got it rough here, remember? Our baby is dead. My back is fucked. I could recite the whole list, but you know it all. Tell me what you really want."

"I want him dead."

"Arak Matar."

"Yes. And Marseh . . . if I could have it. But I want to kill Arak myself. He's the visible one, in the way of anything ever changing. The hand guiding the violence, marshaling the armies. Marseh . . . is the idea. Arak is the execution."

"You're not the only one who wants him dead."

"I know that. But he's careful. Hard to pin down."

"Does it matter to you how he dies? Or is it enough that he does?"

Ray looked at her. "You know something."

"We're not the only ones who want him dead."

Ray narrowed his eyes.

"Marseh wants it, too," she said.

Putting his head in his hands, he thought to ask her how she knew, but he knew. He opened his mouth to speak, then closed it. He opened it again. And closed it. He looked right through her. Closing his eyes, he shook his head and then breathed deep. With a heavy sigh, he laid his eyes on her once more.

"Why you?"

"Heston knew I disagreed with my father. General Bennett struck up a dialogue with Marseh's top paladin, behind the field marshal's back. Bennett told Heston to find someone outside daddy's reach, someone motivated to defy him. I was on Venus. Far, far from Berlin and the great Alastair Hastings. When they proposed the mission . . . it surprised me how willing I was to betray him."

"And me," said Ray.

Anjali frowned. "I haven't betrayed you, Ray."

"You lied to me. You lied about the baby, and you lied about this! How am I supposed to trust you, Anjali? Obviously you don't trust me!"

Anjali looked around. "Keep your voice down!"

Ray looked at the door, grabbed Anjali by the arm, and flung her inside the storage bay.

"Hey!" she protested, stumbling. She regained her footing and turned around, adopting a defensive posture.

Ray stepped inside and pulled the door shut. "No one can hear me shout in here."

"I need you to calm down," she said, holding up her hands. For the first time in their relationship, she feared for her safety. "I need you to remember who I am."

"Who are you, Angie? Do I even know?"

"I love you, Ray."

"Spare me the treacle."

His admonition angered her, and her anger subsumed her fear. "How would you have reacted if I'd told you? Your bullshit honor would have gotten in the way. You would've pissed and moaned just like this, no matter when you found out. You didn't get in on the ground floor because everybody knew how you'd respond. And, frankly, they *still* don't trust your motives for defecting. But *I* trust you. *I* believe in you. I suggested you as an asset. I wanted you to be a part of this. I wanted . . ." she choked on the words.

"What?" He bared his teeth at her. "What did you want?"

"I wanted you with me."

Ray threw back his head and sighed. He ran his hands through his hair.

"It was easy to show why you'd be a tactical asset," said Anjali. "I convinced them I could manage you . . . but my motives weren't just practical. I needed you there."

"Manage me . . ." he scoffed. "It's more important that I die with you than live without, is that it?"

"It sounds bad when you put it like that."

"You manipulated me, Angie. Used me like a pawn. Put me in harm's way so *you* could have what *you* wanted. That's selfish, love. *Selfish*."

"Were you happy there? Floating on a fucking cloud? Doing nothing, waiting for Arak to crush what's left of us? He has an enormous army of loyal correns. It's why Marseh can't just denounce and overthrow him. It would risk civil war.

"Marseh can't even covertly supply us with weapons and manpower we'd need to adequately fight back, 'cause Arak's men are so entrenched. It's everything Marseh can do just to keep Venus peaceful. Even some of the paladins admire the Butcher. They could be swayed to retaliate . . . against their own emperor."

Ray folded his arms across his chest and rolled his eyes.

"What?" she replied.

"I can't believe you," he said. "I can't believe you kept this from me."

"Stop it! I *had* to keep it a secret. So much was riding on its success, and it wasn't fucking easy, Ray. That cutter that we used to raid Overground? Do you know how much subterfuge that took? How *long* that con was? We *tried* to plan it all out. We were *all* supposed to survive. Marseh even ordered Arak to let us live . . . to make it hard on us, but he let us escape. Made him believe we were stealing a Trojan horse, so he'd let us go. And he *did* make it hard on us, huh? He shot me, remember? Maybe not to kill . . . but you know what we lost."

Ray swallowed hard at the thought of the unborn child. His uncertainty had waned. Sentimentality rushed in to replace it. He wanted to share life with Anjali, to make life, and have a peaceful future in which to live it out, but it never seemed possible. He was angry at her but, listening to her faith in the plot, he wondered if there was room to hope for their mutual happiness.

He shoved the thoughts aside. "What about Adams? And Smythe and Norris? Were *they* supposed to live?"

"Yes. I don't know why they didn't make it to their pods."

"Did *they* know what was up? Or was I your only stooge?"

His words hurt her.

"No one knew but me," she replied.

"Well, thank heaven for that. I'd feel like an even bigger asshole if Daedalus were in on it while I twisted in the wind."

"We all want what you want," she insisted.

"Cloak and fucking dagger," he retorted, ignoring the attempt to find common ground.

And she ignored his attempt to undermine.

"Admiral Hastings isn't the only one who thinks Confederate annihilation's the only acceptable outcome," she continued. "Howe's another. There are too many people in our High Command who refuse to treat with Marseh. Courtois pulls the strings and he doesn't want peace. The fucking field marshal, Ray! Daddy's his right-hand man and has lost all perspective. They all have. Sure, there's Bennett, and Heston, and a handful of others who want it over without any more blood, without any more cities destroyed, but ole Allie and Maurice . . . their little cabal . . . they hold the real power. They make the policy.

"They sued for peace, got a treaty, and look what's happening here, and at the frontiers . . . Arak refuses to honor the agreement. He flouts it with impunity, and Marseh looks ineffectual, or apathetic."

"Little do they know he's impotent," said Ray.

Anjali ignored the remark.

"Daddy doesn't know Marseh isn't complicit and, of course, doesn't care. He just wants them all dead. He wants utter Confederate capitulation, and he'd gladly lose you and Daedalus in the process."

"Of course. Because we're all bad. Such horrible creatures. Of course."

"Obviously I don't believe that. So what if he does? Once we've assassinated Arak . . . Hastings is done. Everyone will turn on him, on Howe, on Courtois. The war machine will lose its teeth. Bennett, or maybe Adeola—one of the reasonable leaders—will come to power. Marseh will rein in Arak's men . . . eventually . . . and there won't be any fighting left to be had."

"How could Marseh do that?" Ray sneered. "Rein them in? Derovias will step up. There's a whole host of loyalists ready to step up."

"Derovias won't step up. And neither will Kir."

Ray cocked his head, suddenly interested. "Oh no?"

"Somewhere along the way," said Anjali, "they lost their taste for it. Marseh turned them."

Ray rubbed his hand over his mouth. He refused to be convinced. "Even still, they're not the only ones. Tolon Inishi, Ishtafan Alesh. Pick anyone. Uron Absalom. Soleron Besucher! The list is endless, Anjali! The rest of the Centurion Guard will not. Just. Quit."

"Yes. You're right. There'll be more fighting but—with Sargas as the assassin, someone rogue and unknown—instead of an inferno, there'll only be flares, and they'll be put out. Without the head, the body falls. Derovias and Kir'll eliminate anyone who knows the plot but can't be trusted. There won't be any evidence pointing to Marseh. There won't be a civil war."

"Listen to yourself," Ray scoffed. "I never thought you, of all people, could be so naïve."

Anjali's mouth dropped open and her brows converged.

"You think it's really gonna be so tidy?" Ray scoffed. "Do you know how many hundreds of thousands of Confederation military commanders there are? How many wield power of political office, like Arak? When . . . if . . . he dies, there'll be a power vacuum and it's not just going to go away. Someone's going to fill it, babe. Marseh can't just step in and say: 'Oh, some rogue assassin killed my right-hand man, let's just let it be and sue for peace.'

"He has to pin it on someone . . . and he won't pin it on himself. He can't put it on some *rogue* organism. He has to put it on *us*. There's no peace coming here; there's nothing pending except our annihilation at the hands of a newly motivated, bloodthirsty enemy. And you've delivered it."

"How dare you . . ."

"How dare *I*? How could *you* let yourself be so played? Marseh doesn't want to eliminate Arak so that we can all hold hands and sing folk songs together! He wants to create a martyr who'll turn the tide, once and for all, in *his* favor!"

"I don't believe that," she replied.

"Will you listen to yourself!" He raised his voice in disbelief. He put his hands to his head and threw them back to his thighs. "You've been sold a bill of goods by the man who, for two hundred years, has presided over the near extinction of *your* species and their continual elimination through orchestrated acts of violence . . . and you *trust* him? Have you lost your fucking mind?"

"Shut. *Up!*" she shouted, struggling to rein in her anger at Ray. She refused to let it overwhelm her. "*Shut up*! Just listen to me, dammit!"

Ray crossed his arms over his chest and slowly exhaled. "Arak isn't the leader, baby. Marseh is. He's the one responsible for all of our woe."

"You're wrong," she said, shaking her head.

"You forget I served them both. I spent thirteen years in the Confederation. The latter three here as a centurion under Arak's command. But the other ten? I was a paladin. I did Marseh's bidding. And I didn't dispense peace and love."

"You're blinded by your prejudice," said Anjali.

"I'm informed by my experience," Ray replied.

"You won't even hear me," Anjali said, rubbing her forehead with her fingers.

"I hear you—"

"But you won't listen!" she snapped.

"No, Angie. I've listened to you. You just want me to agree . . . and I don't. And you're angry I don't."

Anjali looked away. "Then I guess there's no point in talking about this, is there?"

Ray didn't reply.

She looked him in the eye. "What are you going to do?"

"What? You worried I'm gonna turn you in?"

She said nothing.

"I'm not," he said.

She looked away again and nodded.

"I just wish you'd trusted me," he said.

She forced herself to look at him. "How could I have trusted you with this? After the conversation we just had . . . telling you would have ruined *everything*. Whether you believe in this or not, Arak's days are numbered . . . I say it's a better world without him, no matter what happens."

"I wish I shared your enthusiasm but, in my experience, when you make that vacuum, the results are never good. It needs to be filled."

She gritted her teeth and sulked to the door, but it wouldn't open. She tried the control panel, but it didn't respond.

"How do I get out of here?"

Scowling, Ray pulled the door open.

She lingered for a moment but said nothing. She left. He slammed the door behind her.

THIRTY-FIVE

GARDINER SAT AT the edge of the bed, rubbing his face.

Ada could feel his disgust with himself. He was conflicted, confused. Ambivalent.

She sat up and touched his shoulder. He flinched away as if burned and jumped to his feet. Suddenly conscious of his nudity, he grabbed his pants from the floor and stumbled in his haste to pull them on.

"Maks . . ."

"Don't call me that. No one calls me that. You don't know me."

"I know you're confused. I know you're scared."

"You don't know me." He picked up his undershirt and pulled it over his head.

"No. But I'd like to."

He paused.

"If you don't believe me . . . see for yourself. I know I can't stop you from reading my thoughts. I'm surprised you haven't."

"You think I want to be in your head? In anyone's? Do you know how much energy it takes to shut everyone out? It's like being trapped in a tiny little box and everyone's right outside, beating on all sides, demanding my attention, trying to get in. I hate it. My life is hell. I don't want to hear your thoughts."

"Do you know what I am?" she asked.

"You're the woman who fucked me. You're the only woman who's *deigned* to fuck me."

"That's not what I mean."

"Don't talk to me like you know me."

"Whether you like it or not," she said. "We know each other now. And I know you're frightened . . . that you feel vulnerable . . . and I'm sorry that was a consequence of what I did to bring you back . . ."

"You don't know me, Ada!" he shouted. He muted her and pinned her to the bed, using only his mind for the assault.

She tried to move but couldn't. Only her eyes were allowed to wander. She tried to speak, but no words came out. Gardiner could feel her distress and her fear. He hated himself for lashing out. He let her go.

She felt her body come back to her own power. She clenched the sheet and pulled it up to her chin. Tucking into a ball, she rested her head against her knees.

Gardiner sighed. "I'm sorry . . . I'm sorry I did that."

"Will you let me speak without hurting me?" Ada asked without looking at him.

He rubbed his forehead with his hand. "I'm not a monster."

She picked up her head and looked at him. "*I* know you're not a monster . . . but I don't think *you* do."

"I don't want to have this conversation. I don't want to talk about this!"

His anger frightened her, but she believed the impression of him that she felt most strongly, that his life had left him deeply wounded but he was good-natured at his core.

"I'm the fourth man you've fucked in the last three days," he said, disgusted.

"I thought you weren't going to pry into my mind," Ada replied.

"And you and the captain? Just today."

"I've had sex with three people in the past twelve hours, Maks, if you want to get down to the fine grain. Why does that matter? I've been sterilized, and they're all military. Well . . . just about. But none of them were civilians. So, no diseases. No risk of pregnancy. What does it matter?"

"Don't you ever feel . . . unsafe? Vulnerable?"

She put her hand on her knee and her cheek on her hand. "I *like* to feel vulnerable. I like being overwhelmed. Powerless, yet . . . willful . . . powerful. I don't know how to explain it."

"Don't you ever wonder what they think about you?"

"Why would I care about that?"

"You don't care if they respect you? You don't care if they don't deserve to be with you? You just let them in?"

"I'm not looking for respect, Maks. I'm looking for ecstasy. I'm not some precious resource. I can't get used up if I let 'too many' men come in me. I'm getting something out of the arrangement. If they're just taking, it's fine, because I'm just taking from them . . . But it's barely ever like that. I mean, yeah, some guys are assholes. Like the corren, Daedalus."

The thought of her with a corren repulsed him.

Ada ignored his expression. "And even he has tenderness in him . . . but, honestly, most of my partners have been respectful. In fact, the only time Daedalus was *ever* respectful was in bed. I've been treated really well, all told."

"Well, how lucky for you," Gardiner replied bitterly.

Ada understood what he felt, but she didn't know what to say. "Will you come here?" she asked after a brief moment of silence.

He crossed his arms.

She patted the bed.

He made his way to her and sat down.

"You're disgusted right now," she said.

"I wish you wouldn't read me," he replied.

"I don't need to be inside your head to see that, Maks. I don't want you to feel disgusted with yourself. You don't need to feel that way."

He sat next to her and stared up at the ceiling. "Yeah, but I do. I feel repellent."

"I find you not at all repellent."

He turned suddenly, displaying his burn-scarred face to her. "No? Do you not *see* me, Ada? Does this look *good* to you?"

She didn't flinch away from his disfigured appearance. "I see you." She touched him gently.

He didn't expect the gesture. He flinched as if struck.

"Oh . . ." she cooed, heartbroken that his expectation was of violence, rather than tenderness. "Please, come here."

She held open her arms. He allowed her to envelop him in an embrace. Again, he rested his head atop her breasts. She stroked the short hair on his scalp and kissed the top of his head.

"I don't understand how you can give yourself up to someone and still feel safe," he said.

Ada shrugged. "I've never thought about it. I've never felt threatened. Never had any reason to . . . no one took anything from me I wasn't willing to give. I've always felt like I had control, even when they took pleasure from my body . . . because it pleased me, too. Because I wanted it."

"I've never had control," Gardiner admitted.

"What about with me?"

"I don't know. I don't know how to feel about that."

Ada sensed his confusion. After a lifetime of being a bottom for other men, for Gardiner to have his first heterosexual experience so late in his life—to have his first ever sexual experience where he gave, rather than received—she knew it was a lot to parse.

"Don't you ever want to have kids?" he asked.

Ada cocked her head to the side. "Why would you ask that?"

"I don't know. You said you were sterilized. It's elective, right?"

"Yes. I chose to be."

"How could you be sure you never want kids?" He looked up at her.

She shifted in the bed, sitting up so that they could look at each other. "Why would anyone want to have children in this world?"

"Why would *you* think that, though? What was your childhood like? General's daughter. Well-to-do. What horror did you go through?"

She lowered her eyelids and sighed through her nose. She looked at him, her light brown eyes intent on his blue and pink ones.

"Yes, I've had a charmed life. But did you?"

He shot her a look that spoke volumes.

"How many people do?" she posited. "Very few. I'm a freak, Maks. But I'm not blind. I'm not insulated and shuttered from reality. I know the world is a horrible place and I don't want to bring a child into it. Isn't that enough?"

He shrugged.

"The military has my eggs," she said. "They took them when they sterilized me. If they want to use them to make a person . . . I signed the contract. I gave them the right. Hell, they probably already have. But I don't want to raise them. I don't want to be a willful parent and risk losing my kid, whom I've loved, to the millions of cruel fates that await them out there."

"But you don't mind if they're grown in a lab, without a mother and a father. Raised by the war machine and sent off to die once ripe?"

"Of course I mind," she answered. The question made her testy. She prided herself on keeping her cool, but Gardiner had struck a nerve. She set her jaw and looked away. "I just don't have a choice. I gave it up when I signed up."

Gardiner said nothing.

Ada tucked her knees up against her chest.

They lingered in silence for a long moment before Gardiner got up from the bed.

"I need to be on duty," he said. "I have to go."

He donned the rest of his uniform and hurried from the room. In the hallway, he nearly ran into Carina.

"Oh!" she exclaimed. "I was just coming to check on you . . ."

"I'm fine," he said, not looking her in the eye. He tried turning the burn-scarred half of his face away from her. "Thank you."

He walked off.

"You're . . . welcome," Carina said to his back.

She pressed the chimes on Ada's door. It opened and Carina went inside.

"No, Carina," Ada said, seeing who it was. "I'm exhausted."

"I'm not here for a piece of you, Lieutenant."

"Then what for?"

"I just wanted to check in on you both and see if everything was okay."

"Everything's okay."

Carina shook her head. "Then why does Maks seem . . . weird."

"He's blinking his own eyes and walking around, isn't he?" Ada retorted.

Carina frowned.

"What do you expect him to be like?" Ada asked. "He just lost his virginity."

"So you fucked him."

"Yes, Carina, I *fucked* him. Let's just call it the basest thing we can think of and suck all the value out of it. You know, not all sex is fucking. Not all sex is some kind of power struggle."

"I wouldn't know anything about that."

Ada blinked at her and, sensing hurt, she changed her tactic. "I'm sorry. I didn't know." She patted the bed, inviting Carina to sit, but she refused.

"No," Carina said adamantly. She began pacing. "No, I don't want to sit. I don't want you to touch me."

The admission surprised Ada. "That's sweet," she said, sarcastically.

"Tuah is pissed at me," said Carina.

"Well, you hurt her," Ada replied. "I think she has every right to be upset with you."

"You participated! Why do you have to take her side?"

Ada closed her eyes before she rolled them, and quietly cursed herself. She was still put off by the abrupt end to her time with Gardiner. It took a concerted effort to revert to counselor mode.

"I'm not taking her side, Carina. You did something that hurt her. That's a fact. If you care about her, you should acknowledge that."

"All she wants to do is control me. Lock me up and keep me to herself. I don't want to be locked up . . . by anybody."

"She loves you," Ada replied. "It's not tantamount to prison."

"What the hell would you know about prison?" Carina snapped. "You and your silver spoon. You've never wanted for anything! I grew up in a slave colony!"

Ada wasn't sure how many more surprises were in store, but she knew that trying to encourage empathy for Tuah was not the right tactic anymore. It was time to be a vessel and collect whatever Carina was going to throw her way.

"I didn't know that. What was that like for you?"

"What was it like?" Carina blurted, incredulous at the banal inquiry. "What was it *like*? I was raped *every day*, multiple times a day, for *months*! Do you have any idea how fucking *repulsive* that was? Do you have any idea how big a corren's dick is? He *hurt* me, Ada. He hurt my body . . . and he fucked up my head . . . He got me *pregnant*. The fucking prefect of Tripas! And I stabbed myself in the guts rather than have the fucking thing."

Her eyes were crazed as she recounted her experience. Anger, bitterness, and resentment contorted her pleasant features into a fearsome, withering expression.

Ada blanched at the intensity.

"Every day," Carina continued, agitated, "I have every. *Fucking*. Man trying to put his *dick* in me, and just I want to cut them all off. I want to geld *all of them*. I want to beat them to death with my bare hands."

She clenched her fists. Her hands were large enough for the sight of them, ready to deliver a blow, to be frightening.

"I *hate* it," Carina continued. "I hate it. I fucking *hate* the attention. Why won't they leave me alone? I just want to be left *alone* . . . can't you *understand* that?"

Ada nodded, wide-eyed.

"But then Tuah is there, and she wants my time, and then I'm not supposed to want you. I'm not allowed to want to feel *good*."

Carina jammed both of her hands into her short curls.

"It's such *bullshit*! Sometimes, I need an escape from my life. I spend all of my time caring for people. Fixing them. Catering to their needs. Sometimes I need to do what *I* want to do. When the hell do I get to look after *myself* without someone *chastising* me for it?"

"What are you sad about, Carina?" Ada asked. Her voice was soft and muted.

"Sad?" Carina bristled. She stood up straight to her full, imposing height. "I'm not sad, Ada. Are you listening? Do I look *sad* to you? I'm *angry*. Are you *stupid*?"

Ada allowed the insult to roll off. "Anger doesn't exist by itself. It's an aggressive response to something we fear or that saddens or disappoints us."

She got up and retrieved her panties from the floor.

Carina drank up Ada's naked body with her eyes. She felt warm between her legs as Ada bent over, revealing her pudenda without a hint of self-consciousness.

"I can't believe you fucked him," Carina said. "How do you even *do* that? How do you let them *touch* you?"

"Are you jealous, Carina?" Ada asked, looking over her shoulder as she pulled her underwear up over her buttocks.

"Jealous?" Carina bristled. "Why the fuck would I be jealous? I'm disgusted."

"Jealous because I fucked a man," said Ada. She turned, exposing her breasts.

"I'm not jealous, Ada. I'm *sick* because you're full of his cum right now."

Ada ignored the remark. "And yet you're attracted to Lieutenant Sotillo." She crossed her arms. "You want to be just as full of his cum as I am of Gardiner's."

"Shut your mouth," Carina warned through clenched teeth.

Ada cocked her head to the side and looked thoughtfully at Carina. "Or maybe it's not him, specifically . . . but that he looks like someone you care about. It's an old feeling."

Carina's eyes flashed and her nostrils flared. "Get out of my head, Ada."

"But still, you *do* want him. Sotillo. It's not just confusion with an old memory. Your desire's both latent and current. The lieutenant *actually* excites you."

She was treading dangerously and she knew it. But Carina was being a bully and Ada refused to be intimidated.

"Shut up, Ada!" Carina shouted, balling her fists.

Ada flinched imperceptibly but held her ground. She stuck out her chin. "Are you gonna hurt me, Carina?"

Carina unclenched her hands and frowned. She looked ill.

"For all your hatred of men," Ada said, "you're blind to that you're just like them."

"I am not. Like them."

"Aggressive. Violent. Emotionally distant. Sexually dominating. Averse to commitment."

"Ha! Coming from the woman who fucks *everyone* she meets."

"We're not talking about me right now," Ada replied. "Refute any of the things I just said."

"This is bullshit," Carina replied. "I didn't come here for this."

"What did you come here for?" Ada pressed. "To fuck me? You don't have a standing invitation, you know."

"I already told you I wasn't here to fuck you! And I sure as hell didn't come here for this."

"I know you're lonely," Ada said.

Carina closed her eyes and shook her head. She flared her nostrils.

"That's not fair." She looked Ada in the eye. "You can't just go into people's heads and see what they're hiding."

"I can, though," Ada retorted. "So why don't we dispense with the bullshit and just get down to it. You can't hide your feelings from me. You can present whatever you want to anyone else, but I see you, Carina. All of you."

"That's not fair . . ."

Ada shrugged. She walked over to the bed and sat down. She patted the mattress.

Carina stayed where she was. She pouted. She crossed her arms high upon her chest.

Ada patted the bed again.

With a sigh, Carina walked over and sat down.

Ada slid one arm across Carina's midsection and caressed the far side of her head with her other hand. Ada guided Carina's head to her chest and cradled it in her arms.

"You don't need to be tough here. You don't have to impress me, or try to influence my perception of you . . . I see you, Carina. The real you. And I accept you."

BOOK II

ONE

ASHARAN LUTÁN STOOD on the bridge of the Confederation gunship. His chief lieutenant, Miro, guided the craft onto the makeshift spaceport in Holst's Hollow.

As the automatic landing sequence took control, Lutián turned to Shaula.

"We'll take the most direct route to the Dorance Building and go in through the front door. You and me, with Miro, Skal, and Ishka. The others will d-jump from street level and the access tunnels."

"I know the plan," she replied.

"I want you to remember that we're on foot for you. It's too dangerous for you to jump with the baby, and we need to be extra sharp to ensure you don't get shot."

Shaula frowned. "Marseh said the armor is impenetrable to projectiles and can absorb an energy blast."

"The armor's a prototype," Lutián replied. "We tested it on men and they had significant bruising and, under heavy fire, internal hemorrhaging and even organ failure. Yes, they lived, and you may live, but would your child? Do you really want to stake your pregnancy on it?"

Shaula frowned again and said nothing.

Lutián considered the foolish stupidity of her even being present. It struck him as some pigheaded display of gender equality at a moment when all things were not equal and egalitarianism should not apply. It was not some everyday task where Shaula's pregnancy was a moot issue; it was a tactical operation with the threat of physical violence. But Marseh, for some reason, insisted she come.

In no position to refuse his master, Lutián still couldn't comprehend the woman's desire to risk the life of her own child for the near-zero chance of seeing its father. Marseh had stated that Shaula had earned the opportunity to roam free and to prove herself. Prove what, Lután didn't know. To him, she seemed only to be proving her own recklessness, at best. Abject idiocy, at worst. However, it wasn't his business to care. He had wasted too much time thinking about it already.

"Remember our formations and you'll be fine," he said.

Shaula nodded. She looked down at her boots, designed to tether her to Earth's gravity. Her homeworld and the environment Marseh had created on Overground for her and her fellows exerted greater pull than Earth. Without ballast, her greater adaptive strength would allow her to bound across the surface.

At will, she could deactivate the boots, allowing full access to her heavy-G leg strength. Even with them activated, she had a significant upper-body advantage over both correns and Earth-bound humans. She picked up a large, heavy cylinder from the cargo hold. It felt lighter to her than it would to the men. She strapped it across her back.

"Let's move," said Lután.

Excepting the detachment left behind to guard the ship, and the core group of five, the Confederation soldiers left the vessel in twenty teams of four. Lután, Miro, Skal, and Ishka created a box around Shaula. They made their way to their assigned checkpoint. The five wore similar black armor but, while the correns' bodysuits were trimmed with red, Shaula's bore a rich, royal blue. When they arrived at the checkpoint, they approached like any routine detail. Their weapons remained holstered. On the Confederation side of the checkpoint, four armored guardsmen stood vigilant. A corren soldier came out to greet them.

Lután handed him a data stick.

"We're here on official diplomatic business, Corporal. Please convey these orders to your Allied counterpart."

The soldier nodded. He carried the documents to his counterpart, a human woman wearing standard Allied fatigues with three chevrons. Four armored and heavily armed Allied soldiers guarded their side of the checkpoint. The sergeant went to her terminal. She consulted the documents furnished by the Confederate corporal. Her face curdled, but the orders seemed to check out. Not content with appearances, she contacted Van Sinderen.

The colonel couldn't hide his disbelief. He told her to wait. He tried for immediate connection to London, which had at all previous junctures been refused. This occasion was no different. Van Sinderen demanded her to double-check the credentials. When she did, and they checked out, he sputtered that she should still not let them pass.

The sergeant looked dubiously at Lután and Shaula and the three other correns.

"Sergeant Card," said Lután, reading the placket upon her left breast as he responded to her indecision. "I would prefer that we not come to violence. As you can see, the papers we have are official and check out with your own ordinances. I admire your loyalty to your CO, but he is making a bad decision for which I'd rather you not pay."

The woman said nothing.

"There are ten of us and five of you," he said, including the Confederates stationed at the checkpoint. "Eight of us are corren. Do you like those odds?"

Sergeant Card shook her head.

"May we pass?" Lután asked.

She nodded.

As they walked away, Skal and Ishka kept an eye on Sergeant Card and the four Allied guards, in case of an ambush. Lután wondered if any of the other parties would encounter checkpoint resistance. He imagined they would. He also knew it was of little consequence. The Confederates would rout the small Allied contingents if they resisted. The Allies stationed guards to keep civilian rabble from entering the perimeter around the Dorance Building—not to face well-armed soldiers they never expected to see.

Lután, Shaula, and the others continued deeper into Allied territory. They passed the Pendragon pub. There, they found a small pack of wild dogs gnawing the bodies of three correns that lay in the street. The dogs retreated from their meal as the unit approached. Huge flies swarmed. Giant cockroaches skittered over the corpses.

"Stack them up and burn them," Lután ordered.

Miro, Skal, and Ishka threw the bodies over one another. The dogs lingered nearby, their gaunt bodies trembling. They leered at their food and bared their teeth, but kept their distance. Miro pulled the pin on an incendiary grenade and threw it at the pile, setting the corpses, and the roaches, ablaze. The dogs bolted in fright. The flies careened from the growing heat.

"Who did this?" Miro asked Lután.

"Do you want blood for blood?"

"Blood for blood is our way of life, brother," Miro replied.

"I thought we were not killing anyone, if we can help it," said Shaula.

Lután looked at her and at Miro. "Maybe we won't be able to help it."

They pressed on in silence.

Shaula hoped they could avoid killing anyone. The thought of dealing death repulsed her. She believed it better to make friends than enemies. Long after she had acclimated to Overground, she had grown restless, shunned by the members of her own species that Marseh had also saved. Petting her big cat had ceased to be an adequate source of comfort. Marseh had taught her how to use weapons, and she played the dutiful student, thankful for a new distraction, but she relished only the novelty. She had craved human consolation more than anything else. She thought she'd go mad with frustration, until Marseh introduced her to Sargas.

She believed every move her strange savior made was plotted. But she was not immune to lust. Especially after waiting years for a suitable partner. Sargas was well-made, as was she. She'd been starved for physical release. Neither she nor Sargas had cared why they had met, just that they had. Thinking of him excited her, both sexually and emotionally. While Marseh told her that finding her lover was unlikely, Shaula still hoped to find him. It was the only reason she'd come.

Perhaps he was waylaid, she thought. *Perhaps I can see him, even briefly.*

She felt their child in her belly. It reminded her that she had abandoned all reason. Marseh knew, too, that she was being emotional, irrational, but he humored her. Maybe he knew that seeing Sargas for one moment would mollify her. Maybe he was testing her mettle as a solider. She couldn't know for sure. All she knew was that she was as tantalizingly close to Sargas as she had been in months. She was ravenous just to see him with her own eyes.

The five Confederates approached the outer perimeter of sentries. The outer cordon, which guarded the Allied base beneath the Dorance Building.

"Power down your weapons and gear," ordered Lután. "We need to be analog for this."

The others did as commanded. They initiated their weapons' safeguards to inoculate the armaments against electromagnetic interference. Shaula shrugged the big, heavy cylinder from her back and hefted it in her left hand as if it weighed nothing. Lután admired her strength. He didn't want to be on the receiving end of one of her punches.

"Halt," the lead sentry called. "State your business."

"Please consult your general orders," replied Lután.

He hoped General Bennett had made good on his promise to remove all roadblocks. The setback at the checkpoint with Sergeant Card did not bolster his faith.

"I am here on a diplomatic mission," Lután continued, "and I present this device as a gesture of good will."

He indicated the electromagnetic pulse generator in Shaula's grasp. He hoped the sentries were not sophisticated enough to recognize the device as a weapon.

"State your name," the sentry demanded. It showed no signs of suspicion, no reasoning, whether deductive or algorithmic.

"Asharan Lután, colonel, Confederation Elite Imperial Guard."

The sentry queried the network and retrieved General Bennett's second order, for admission to the facility. It hid in plain sight on the Allied network, noticeable only to a sentry. If a human had tried to sniff it out, the computer would have filtered the results and shown them nothing.

The sentry was just a computer. Unlike Sergeant Card, whose sapience afforded her skepticism, the resurrected cyborg had no suspicion beyond the bounds of its programming. It saw the data, confirmed General Lawton Bennett's credentials, and the Boolean resolved to "true."

"You may proceed," said the braindead cyborg.

Shaula, Lután, Miro, Skal, and Ishka continued toward the Dorance Building. The sentries outside the edifice allowed them entry without interference.

"How is this possible?" Miro asked.

"Diplomacy, Miro," Lután replied.

"Then why do we fight at all?"

"Because continued violence is what certain parties desire."

"But—" Miro continued.

Lután silenced him with a gesture.

Shaula put the EMPG on the floor in the lobby and pressed the button atop it. It emitted a pulse for five hundred meters along every axis. The sentries fell where they stood, the lights went out.

"Weapons hot," Lután ordered.

The group reactivated their gear.

"Set them to stun. We've got maybe twenty mikes, in and out. Once the aux lights come on, we've overstayed. Whoever finds Hastings jumps out with her, and onward to the rendezvous. The rest will make their own way."

"And Sargas?" asked Shaula.

"Use your head, Shaula," Lután replied. "Not your heart. Don't put us at risk. Don't put yourself at risk."

He looked at her stomach.

Her face hardened. She had known him longer than Sargas and, while Lután was not her lover, she respected and admired him. He was the one person besides Marseh with whom she interacted. She suspected he thought she was either insane or merely stupid, and she resolved to disabuse him. She was determined not to compromise him, nor the men about whom he obviously cared.

Lután and Miro hurried to the elevator bank. They forced open the doors of the sole lift with subbasement access. Each of the men grabbed a line in their armored hands. They slid down the cables, leaving wakes of wispy smoke. Ishka followed, then Shaula.

A few beats after Skal landed atop the elevator car, a barrage ripped through the carriage. The correns danced out of the way, but there was no escape from the fusillade. Lután pressed Shaula, belly-first, to the farthest corner of the shaft. He shielded her with his body. The bullets unrelentingly penetrated the compromised steel.

Lután gritted his teeth at the hundreds of rounds pelting his legs and his back. He knew, despite the pain, that his armor would hold. Inwardly, he cursed Shaula for forcing him to provide her special care.

Inside the lift, Private Berkey and LC Curwen fed long belts of ammunition into the heavy weapons wielded by Sergeant Liggan and Lieutenant Andersen. Every electronic device active during the electromagnetic pulse had been knocked out, leaving analog weapons the main recourse.

Miro switched off his night vision, anticipating the addling effects of muzzle flashes in the darkness. He pulled open the hatch door and braced himself against the backward momentum. Ignoring the .308-caliber bullets that pinged off his visor and dented his plate armor, he threw an analog concussion grenade into the lift.

With a loud *phoom!* it detonated, washing the darkness in blinding white light. The shooting stopped.

Miro jumped down, wincing against the bruises and welts that riddled his body. He kicked the unconscious Liggan in the face. Stepping out of view from the vantage of the hatch, he purposefully walked atop Liggan's and Andersen's limp forms. He took a moment to stomp hard upon Andersen's torso and then stepped, too, on the unconscious bodies of Curwen and Berkey, grinding his heels into them both and kicking them each, repeatedly, for good measure.

Lután dropped through the hatch, followed by Shaula.

When Skal and Ishka were down, they took point and entered the corridor in formation. The correns boxed in Shaula who, despite their protection, held her rifle at the ready against her left shoulder. A small detachment of Allies in night-vision-equipped helmets attacked from behind crates and detritus. The soldiers fired their analog projectile weapons at the advancing Confederates.

While Shaula, Lután, and the others were practically invulnerable to mortal harm, they were not immune to bruises and, in extreme cases, broken bones. Skal and Ishka absorbed the brunt of the bullets. The impacts hurt but still could not penetrate the plate. Yet the armor was not without its chinks. Skal winced as a bullet glanced his ribcage. The bodysuit held, but the shot would leave a bruised lesion.

The five Confederates methodically stunned their Allied targets, leaving a trail of unconscious bodies. Lután and Miro were the rear guard, picking off anyone who lay in wait.

Elsewhere in the complex, the other Reds were jumping in.

TWO

ANJALI HAD JUST entered the medical bay when the electromagnetic pulse knocked out all power. The door didn't close behind her. The auxiliary lighting did not come on. Everyone was thrust into utter darkness.

"Seriously?" she said, annoyed.

Carina felt her way to the emergency supply kit and fished out a beacon. She handed another to Tuah. They swept the lights around the room. Carina's light fell upon Anjali.

"What are you doing here, Commander?"

"I was never assigned quarters. I don't have anywhere else to go."

"I don't know what you think you'll do here," Carina said. "But, by all means, stay."

She handed Anjali her beacon and moved toward the door.

"Wait!" called Tuah after Carina. "Where are you going?"

"This isn't a power failure, honey," Carina replied. "I'm getting my armor, and a big gun."

"Don't go," Tuah protested. "Please?"

Carina gave her a kiss on the forehead. "I'm not waiting for trouble to find us, love; I'm gonna find *it*."

Tuah pointed her beacon at the floor. Her aggrieved expression was lost in the dark.

Carina heard weapons' fire as she dashed down the corridors to her quarters. She couldn't see anything in the pitch but had the route memorized. Tripping twice on debris, she didn't fall. She felt along the wall, counting the doors until hers, then flipped the panel and fished for the manual release. The door opened enough for her to get her fingers through the gap. She forced it the rest of the way.

Inside, she stumbled around her messy quarters and groped for her helmet. She kicked it and cursed. Feeling around in the direction it might have gone, she found it and put it on. The night vision kicked in. She strapped her armor over her street clothes, replaced her gun belts, then grabbed as much ammunition as she could find. She stuffed it into a bag, along with the steel she'd set aside. Wondering where the Confederate pistol had gone, she realized she'd left it in Ada's room. She cursed herself and snatched up her pulse rifle.

Looking up, she saw her open door and ran to pull it closed. She didn't know where the raiders were and didn't want them happening upon her in a confined space, door wide open in welcome.

***

The instant the lights went out, Gardiner went looking for Ray. He found him in the empty cargo bay.

"It's a raid. Come with me."

Ray followed the major's order without a word.

"You can see?"

"Yes," Ray answered. "Darkness doesn't handicap us the same way it does you."

"Yes, but a blast to the head without armor probably handicaps you the same way it does me. There's a weapons cache up this way. Perhaps we can find you a helmet. We can at least arm you."

The mechanisms to the doors had been disabled by the pulse, but Gardiner didn't need electricity nor a manual override. When they reached the cache, he forced the door open via telekinesis.

"That's a neat trick," said Ray.

Gardiner handed Ray a pistol and then a rifle. Ray holstered the former and slung the latter over his shoulder. Gardiner handed him a knife and Ray clipped it to his belt.

A blue flash lit up the corridor and blasted Ray backward. He crashed to the floor with a grunt. Gardiner spun around. He fired his pistol without looking, diving for cover behind one of the obstructions meant to thwart the dimensional jumpers. He knew his best bet wasn't to blindly shoot with an inaccurate weapon, but to use the debris. The bits of metal and garbage rose from the floor like marionettes. He envisioned them swirling madly through the air and they responded, creating a flying assault of sharp and blunt objects. He pushed the mass down the corridor. Exciting the detritus, it picked up more and more speed.

"Fall back!" Miro yelled from the direction of the blast that had felled Ray.

"*What the fuck is this?*" Skal exclaimed.

Gardiner didn't know where the assailants were, but he hurled the swarm in the hope of hitting a target. Ray sat up with his hand over his chest. Gardiner dashed over to tend to him. Free of telekinetic attention, the junk clattered to the floor.

"You okay?" the major asked.

"Stunner," Ray gasped. "I guess it's set for you . . . or I'd be out cold."

"A blast that knocks you out would kill me," said Gardiner. "They want us alive, then. That works to our advantage."

Ray grabbed his arm. "We don't know how many there are."

"What are you saying?" asked Gardiner.

"The base is compromised. We don't know how many intruders. They want to *capture* us . . . we're better off escaping. We have to get out of here."

Gardiner didn't like Ray's point, but he couldn't argue with it. "And what about our people? Just leave them to the mercy of the Reds?"

"How do we get out?" asked Ray, ignoring the question.

"The only way, beside the lift, is the D-level breach."

"Then we make our way there. Pick up anyone we meet on the way. Can't risk getting caught trying to collect all hands."

"Even if that means leaving your woman behind?" Gardiner asked pointedly.

"Yes," said Ray, without hesitation. "But I defer to you, as ranking officer."

Gardiner thought for a moment. He looked within the cache and withdrew a large helmet, shoving it into Ray's hands.

"Let's go," the major replied.

***

Miro dodged the flying debris by ducking down the adjoining corridor, separating him from the others.

He turned to rejoin them but was pushed back by a concussion grenade. Sotillo came running out of the smoke. He attacked Miro, knocking the corren's rifle from his hands. Miro swatted away Sotillo's subsequent blows. He grabbed the smaller human by the breastplate and slammed him against the bulkhead once, twice, before throwing him to the floor.

Miro retrieved his rifle and aimed it point-blank at Sotillo's face.

Lután emerged from the dissipating smoke. "You'll kill him at that range."

"Would that really be such a bother?" Miro replied.

Lután shot Sotillo from a safe distance, stunning him into unconsciousness.

"No killing unless we have to, remember?"

Miro frowned. He fell into formation around Shaula. Skal and Ishka brought up the rear for respite from the barrage.

"Where do we find this woman?" Shaula asked Lután.

She wanted to ask if he thought Sargas would be with her but realized she sounded like a lovelorn little girl. The realization set in that her motives for tagging along were not only selfish and foolish, but futile.

"She was shot on Overground," Lután replied. "Presumably, she's wounded."

"So, the infirmary," Shaula inferred.

They reached the medical bay and found the door open. Lután gestured that they proceed with caution. Miro pulled a concussion grenade from his bandolier, but Lután grabbed him by the wrist.

"It's a sick bay, Miro . . . that could kill someone already in distress."

Miro rolled his eyes behind his opaque visor. He holstered the grenade. "Fucking delicate humans," he complained.

Lután stepped into the room. A quick sweep revealed no threats. A few of the patients were well enough to have propped themselves up in attempts to better assuage their bewilderment, but no ambush awaited.

"Check the beds. If anyone gives you trouble, incapacitate them—gently—with your hands. No weapons in here."

Lután made his way through the ward, glancing at some of the beds and finding almost all of the occupants to be male. Ishka had to fight with one of them but suppressed the man with as delicate a chokehold as possible. The only place left to check was the Chief Medical Officer's private office. Just as Carina had uncovered the manual override for the door to her quarters, Lután did the same. The Confederation had occupied the base for years before it fell into Allied hands. It harbored no secrets.

"She's not in any of the beds," said Miro, coming up behind Lután.

The door to the office released when Lután pulled the lever. He forced it open.

"Stay back!" Tuah warned from within.

Lután saw Anjali and Tuah pressed against the back wall, armed with scalpels. They had decided that to stay in the dark was a better defense than to advertise their positions with the beacons. But the correns could see them, whether with night vision or without.

"Lieutenant Commander Hastings," he said. "I am Colonel Asharan Lután of the Confederation Elite Imperial Guard. I need you to come with me."

"What the hell is this?" asked Tuah.

Anjali looked in Tuah's direction, but the darkness was complete. Tuah felt Anjali move away from the wall. She dropped her scalpel and took small, tentative steps through the sheer black.

"Commander?" asked Tuah. She took a step.

"My little lady nurse," said Lután. "For your own sake, please, don't move."

"What are you doing with Commander Hastings?" Tuah demanded. "Commander?"

Anjali didn't reply. Once within reach, Lután guided her toward them. He ferried her into Miro's arms.

"I want to know who killed the correns in the Allied quarter," Miro said.

"What do you mean?" Anjali replied, surprised.

"We found three dead—"

"Now isn't the time, Miro!" Lután barked.

"But you said . . ."

"You can find out from her at any point later. We are *not* meting out revenge today."

"You said that I could—"

"I said you may question her," Lután stated sharply. "Not here. Not now. We'll meet you at the rendezvous. Jump, Miro. Now."

A bright blue flash lit up the entire medical bay.

Tuah and the others threw up their hands to shield their eyes. When the flash subsided, she could see the afterimage, an outline in blue of two bodies in an embrace.

Shaula turned to her. "Have you seen a big human man? Tall, handsome . . . has anyone like that been h—?"

"Dammit, Shaula," said Lután. He grabbed her arm and pulled her from the office.

Shaula thought to protest but mastered herself. She resigned herself to that, if she were to see Sargas again, it would not be here. They retreated through the medical bay and back into the corridor. Over the comm link, Lután administered his orders.

"Black leader to all teams. Continue your assault. Jump out in five."

Shaula, Skal, and Ishka followed Lután as he traced their steps back to the lift.

"If the auxiliary lights come on," said Lután, "the sentries are rebooting. By that point, we're too late. Move, move!"

"What happens if they reboot?" asked Shaula.

"We had one pulse. We can't knock them out again. It means we have to fight them . . . and we'll lose."

***

Gardiner came across Sotillo's unconscious form. He picked him up with telekinetic aid, wielding the larger man as if he weighed almost nothing.

"You're stronger than you look," Ray remarked.

"It's not mere strength. I can move things with my mind, assist my physical strength, make matter nearly weightless." Gardiner jerked his head. "D-level is this way. Take point."

Ray held his rifle at the ready. They passed the dismembered torso of a Confederate. "What did this?"

"His legs materialized inside the box. It cut him in half. Thank Sergeant Duquesne; it's the most brilliant defense I've ever seen. I'm amazed nobody came up with it before."

"Sir!" a voice called from down the corridor. "Don't shoot!"

Gardiner looked past Ray to see Privates Gray and Milner carrying Lance Corporal Mahoney.

Gardiner and Ray hurried to them.

A knife protruded from Mahoney's left thigh. His entire leg was soaked with blood, leaving a trail of it behind them. The flap of skin between the thumb and forefinger of his left hand had been sliced through to the bone. His biofeedback chip was gone, cleaved from its hiding place.

"Report," said Gardiner.

"We took out five of them with grenades; our guns were useless," Mahoney said, wincing. "I thought they were all down, but one was playing dead. He slashed at me . . . I blocked it with my hand." He waved the bleeding appendage at the major. "And then he stabbed me in the fucking leg!"

"Did neither of you fools think to cauterize him?" Gardiner barked at Milner and Gray.

"Respectfully, Major," Milner replied, "it's his goddamned artery. We take out the knife, he's gonna shoot blood for a mile. We can't just seal him up so he bleeds to death internally, either. And we didn't want to fuck up his hand for life."

"It doesn't matter," said Mahoney. "I'm a fucking goner."

"Stow it, Corporal," Gardiner ordered.

"No, fuck it," he grimaced. "No bullshit, sir. Good thoughts won't get me through this. It's my fault. I should have made sure the motherfucker was dead. Goddamn it."

His normally ruddy face had drained of all color and his floppy auburn curls stuck with sweat to his forehead.

"I heard them on their comms. They're here for Commander Hastings."

Ray's ears perked up and he looked at Gardiner.

"Don't even think about it," the major replied. "You said it yourself: we're not going back for anybody. We're bugging out."

Ray gritted his teeth. Now he wanted to find her. He wanted to know if she was being kidnapped or going willingly.

"Put him down," Gardiner ordered. "Gray, cover the west end. A'arilon, take the east. Milner, gimme some light."

The major set Sotillo down against the wall, and the lieutenant stirred like a napping child.

Milner shined his beacon on Mahoney's leg.

Gardiner ignored Ray's and Gray's weapons' fire; he would know when the position was compromised. He withdrew his own knife and cut the trouser leg from Mahoney's pant, just above the knee.

"Not many men are fond of pants, Corporal," said Gardiner. "But they make a good tourniquet."

"I guess I'm lucky I didn't let the ole balls swing today, sir."

Gardiner cut the pant leg into strips.

"Just hold on; we'll fix you up."

***

Carina looked through her medical bag and was surprised at its contents. She hadn't touched it in months. It was stocked to handle a decent amount of triage. She flung it over her shoulder and left her quarters, laden like a pack mule.

D-level was the only viable option for escape. She wasn't waiting for the order to evacuate. She just needed to retrieve Tuah and they'd make a break for it. Peeking around the corner, she saw the Confederate raiders. She hugged her packs to her body and bounded across the intersection in two steps. She drew fire but escaped harm.

The path to the med bay was impassable.

It twisted her stomach into knots, but Tuah would have to fend for herself. Carina retreated toward the ladder to D-level with deep regret. She knew Tuah would believe she'd been abandoned.

"Hey!" called an unfamiliar voice.

Carina whirled toward it with her rifle at the ready.

"Whoa! Don't shoot!" Patrick exclaimed, hands up in surrender.

She flipped up her visor. "Who the fuck are you?" she demanded.

"Corporal Patrick, First Battalion, Ishtar Terra. I'm one of Commander A'arilon's charges. You . . . uh . . . intimidated me out of the officer's mess earlier. Sir."

Carina scowled. "You're walking in front of me, Corporal. Step out of line and I'll shoot you."

Patrick nodded and led the way. At the next intersection, Carina ordered him to sneak a glance around the corner. He saw Ray, rifle trained right at him. He pulled his head back to safety.

"Friendlies!" he yelled. "Corporal Patrick and Captain, uh . . ." he didn't know her name and she didn't tell him. He settled upon: "The pretty and mean one. Don't shoot!"

He offered Carina a shrug and an apologetic glance. She scowled and shook her head. When he looked away, she smiled.

"Come on then, Corporal," Ray replied.

Patrick and Carina darted around the corner and took cover behind Ray.

Gardiner had applied the tourniquet above Mahoney's wound, but Carina could tell he'd lost a lot of blood.

"Out of the way, Major," she said.

She opened her medical bag and pulled out a canister of coagulating disinfectant and a small gun with a narrow cone on its end.

"Private," she said to Milner, "I need you to withdraw the knife, pull up the pant leg, and open the wound. But be careful because the blood is going to shoot out of there."

She looked at Gardiner.

"Major, shine light in there; I need to see the artery."

Milner took off Mahoney's unruined glove, folded it both ways and put it in the lance corporal's mouth.

"Sir, you're gonna want to bite on this."

"No fucking anesthesia?" Mahoney mumbled around the glove.

"Do I look like a full-service med bay?" Carina snapped.

Mahoney clamped down on the glove. Milner withdrew the knife. Blood spurted, but the tourniquet limited the flow.

Milner gritted his teeth and pushed apart the flesh of Mahoney's thigh. The corporal growled and clenched down on the glove.

Gardiner shined light on the opening.

Carina sprayed the disinfecting coagulant into the wound and Mahoney growled anew at the burning sensation. She crimped his femoral artery above the knife wound.

"Major, please, put your finger in there, underneath the artery, and present it to me. Gently."

Gardiner removed his gloves. "My hands are dirty."

"Rubbing alcohol in my bag. Find it."

He found the bottle and doused his hands. He gingerly slid his finger under the artery and curled his digit to bring the blood vessel toward her. Carina aimed the small gun at the wound and sealed the gash. Gardiner withdrew his finger, allowing the blood vessel to return to its place.

"Push the thigh wound closed, both of you."

Milner and Gardiner worked in concert to press the rent flesh together and Carina sealed it with the cauterizer. She shook her head at the smell of cooking flesh, but said nothing.

"What about his hand?" Gray asked, waving Mahoney's mangled appendage at Carina. She shook her head and sprayed it with the coagulant. Mahoney growled again at the burn and Carina wrapped his hand with gauze.

Sotillo revived. He moved his legs, getting a feel for them, and helped himself to his feet. "I feel hungover."

"How do *you* feel?" said Carina to Mahoney.

"Like I'm not going to make it." He'd grown pale as moonlight.

"Are you quitting on us?" Carina asked in jest. She untied the tourniquet.

He gave her a weak smile and shook his head. "I'm too stubborn to quit."

"We have to move," Gardiner ordered. "Sotillo, take point. A'arilon is the rear guard."

Mahoney motioned for help in getting up. Gray and Milner each took one of his arms over their shoulders. They limped toward escape.

At the ladder to D-level, Mahoney agonized, dropping to each subsequent rung on his good leg and good hand until the bottom. As Gray and Milner helped him sit down, an explosion ripped through the adjoining corridor.

"Oh, shit!" exclaimed the squat private, Lindner. "Booth just fragged himself!"

Corporal Macaluso presided over the crowd of noncoms that had been first to arrive at the logical point of escape.

"Guess that was a bad idea," Macaluso deadpanned.

The noncoms despaired at the treacherous stretch, littered with René's mines.

In immediate response to the explosion, six blue flashes occurred almost simultaneously. Confederates d-jumped from the level above; one of them materialized in the same space as Private Berkey. She couldn't even scream. The blue flash collapsed on itself and both she and the Confederate ceased to exist.

It took a split second for the remaining Reds to materialize, coalescing from nothing into fully formed corporeal beings. The delay bought the Allies precious time to prepare.

Gardiner and Sotillo, Carina and Ray, and Milner and Gray were each armed and ready, as were Lindner and a few of the other grunts. Privates Burke and Nergaard drew their weapons. Grim determination overtook Burke's face.

In his weak hand, Nergaard backed up his gun with his knife, ready for close combat. Even Mahoney, sitting against the bulkhead, drew his pistol. His wounded leg began to tingle as sensation returned.

Macaluso licked his lips at the advantage presented by the materialization delay. When it came to killing people, guns were his last choice. Too impersonal. Knives were better, but hands were best. He was a big, powerful human—tall and broad, on the hefty side—and always ready to fight. Bedecked in an exo-suit with armored mitts, they increased the power of his punches by a factor of ten.

He tackled the first Confederate to materialize, wrenching the man's helmet from his head. With one punch, Macaluso collapsed the corren's face. The second punch cracked the corren's skull and ruptured his scalp. His brains oozed onto the floor like porridge from a broken bowl.

A rifle blast struck Lindner in the chest, blasting him backward. The private's unconscious body fell over the top of Macaluso. He sloughed off the smaller man and then charged at the closest corren intruder. The raider shot Macaluso, but the blast dissipated across the exo-suit. The corporal tackled the corren and wrapped both mitts around his neck, squeezing until the satisfying snap.

The Allied noncoms fired their pistols but were no match for the corren soldiers in a firefight. Macaluso's exo-suit and Ray's superior physiology were the only useful weapons and defenses. The other Allies had no recourse against the stun rifles, and little means by which to fight back.

Ray followed Macaluso's lead and engaged the raiders hand to hand.

The Confederates shot down Burke and Nergaard.

Gardiner held one of the corren's in telekinetic thrall. Carina slashed at the soldier's neck with her knife. The Confederate body armor wouldn't relent to her blade. She felt a twinge of guilt. Usually, she dealt death quickly, without time for a second guess. With the corren paralyzed by Gardiner, Carina was able to remove his helmet and unzip the collar. She looked the helpless man in the eye, then jammed her blade through his esophagus.

Nausea swelled in her guts. The wave forced its way up her throat.

She tore off her helmet and spat bile. While she vomited, another Confederate slammed the butt of his rifle between her shoulder blades, sending her to the floor. Light burst before her eyes. She knew she had a concussion.

Ray grabbed Carina's assailant and snapped his neck.

Every corren had been born within the Confederation. Raised to value each others' lives. Forbidden to kill one another. It was ingrained in them that they were all brothers and their bond was to be honored, valued, cherished.

Ray had been born from a tube. The sole member of his batch, raised in isolation. He didn't know he was the result of Marseh's experiments, spliced DNA from more than two parents. The emperor unilaterally tinkered with the formula. Messed with what made a corren a corren. Ray knew only that he was different, estranged from his so-called brothers. He'd lost count of how many of his kin he'd killed.

Sotillo and Gardiner teamed up to eliminate one of the two remaining adversaries. Unlike Carina, Sotillo had no problem killing in cold blood. He enjoyed it. The telekinetic paralysis allowed him to calmly remove the corren's helmet. With a delighted smile, he slowly jammed his knife through the man's eye.

Milner and Gray teamed with Macaluso to eliminate the final threat.

Carina rolled onto her back, holding her neck. Trying to rest, she stayed on the floor. She knew better than most the side effects of an untreated concussion. She rued that she'd have little time to recover.

Lindner, Burke, and Nergaard regained consciousness.

"I feel gross," said Lindner. "Ugh. Like I've been drinking."

"Yeah, it sucks, huh?" said Sotillo. He wiped the green blood from his knife onto his kilt. At the sound of boots on the ladder he drew his pistol. He aimed it upward until he noticed the Allied uniforms.

Sergeant Liggan touched down first, followed by Lieutenant Andersen. Liggan had a black eye from Miro kicking her in the face.

"Good of you to join us," said Sotillo. "What about the colonel?"

"When we woke up, we tried to reach command," Liggan said, "but our weapons are useless against their armor. I don't know what they did, but they've solved the projectile weapon problem."

"We unloaded at least a thousand .308-cal rounds at them and it didn't do shit," said Andersen. "Now we're totally powerless. All we could do was retreat."

"We can't stay here," Gardiner insisted. "We need to get out somehow."

"Sir, we can't get through to the breach," said Nergaard. "Private Booth wouldn't wait. He just went for it and . . . well . . ." he shrugged, made a face, and looked in the direction of the gore and body parts spattered on the walls, ceiling, and floor near the junction.

"'Private Booth.' Ha," Sotillo blurted. "You'd think, with a name like that, you wouldn't enlist. Or you'd join the navy. 'Ensign Booth' makes so much more sense. 'Uh, excuse me? Private Booth, party of two.'" He laughed again.

Private Nergaard looked at Sotillo in mild shock. He wanted to admonish the lieutenant for speaking ill of the dead but knew better than to confront his superior.

"Shut your mouth, Lieutenant," said Gardiner. "No one else is amused." He walked to the mined corridor. "Clear!"

With a telekinetic command, he disrupted the debris atop the mines, causing them to detonate. The blast blew him backward. He slammed into the bulkhead. It knocked the air from his lungs. As he slid from the wall to the floor, he smeared the chum of Booth's corpse.

Macaluso helped the major to his feet. "Sir, I think that was unwise."

"Yes, Corporal, I'd agree with you. But now we can leave."

THREE

LUTÁN GRABBED SHAULA'S arm. He pulled her onto the lobby floor from the elevator cable.

Once Skal and Ishka both had their feet firmly on the floor, the quartet ran at full speed for the street. They cleared the lobby. Shaula saw the sentries begin to stir.

"Run! Run! Faster!" Lután implored.

Shaula turned off her gravity boots, untethering herself from the surface. She bounded away, leaving Lután, Skal, and Ishka to chase her. As the sentries rose to their feet, the three correns turned the corner. Though outside the radius of the zombie-soldiers' protectorate, they kept running.

Shaula shortened her jumps. She landed and reactivated her tether right outside the checkpoint, where the Allied guards trained their weapons upon her. She shot them down before they could fire, then turned on the unarmored Sergeant Card.

Card put up her hands. Shaula shot her anyway, stunning the young woman into unconsciousness.

"Easier this way," Shaula said to Card's crumpled body. "Sorry."

Lután, Skal, and Ishka caught up with her.

"No point in stopping, now," said Lután. "Get to the ship."

As they crossed through the checkpoint, the Confederation corporal came out to address them.

"Do you know how much harder this makes my job, Colonel?"

"You didn't do it, we did," Lután replied. "Tell them that when they wake up."

"You really think that's going to work, sir?" the corporal complained.

"Pick them up," Lután suggested. "Sit them somewhere, make sure they're uninjured. When they come to and they find they've not been neglected, that will surely help your cause. Things are changing, Corporal. I recommend using this as an opportunity for détente."

"We had a pretty good relationship before your girl shot them," the corporal replied.

Shaula rolled her eyes.

"Then leverage that, too, when they come around," Lután replied.

***

Throughout the raid, Ada sat in complete darkness hearing shouts, screams, and weapons' fire. She had not been paralyzed by fear, but by pragmatism. An unseasoned combatant, unable to see, she would have been useless in the total blackness.

She hadn't fired a weapon since her last mandatory trip to the shooting range on Venus, days before the mission to Overground, and had never fired her weapon in combat. Her hand-to-hand fighting skills were untested, though she'd learned everything she was taught. She acquitted herself well during training and practice. But she was never intended to be in the field doing battle. She was a medical professional meant to serve, on base, the needs of those who saw battle and needed to talk about the consequences. Or about any issue that arose over the course of their service. So she sat, feeling useless as the fighting raged.

The sounds of combat subsided. An eerie, utter silence took their place. The auxiliary lights came on. She rose from her bed and checked her appearance in the mirror. The dim red light offered little aid. Trying the door, it opened automatically. She peeked outside, looking one way and then the other.

"Computer, report," she asked.

"Principal systems offline. Operating under auxiliary power. Restoring essential systems."

"Computer, locate Captain Duvais."

"Captain Duvais is not on base," the computer replied.

Ada bit her lip. If Carina were dead but on base, her biofeedback chip would still transmit, indicating she was present, but deceased.

"Computer, list available personnel."

The computer obliged. Everyone Ada knew was gone. She headed to the colonel's office and rang the chime. Van Sinderen bid her to enter and she walked inside.

"Lieutenant, you're XO. I've put in a dispatch to London. I don't see how they can ignore us now. I'm waiting on a reply—"

He looked down at his desk as it beeped, letting him know the reply had come.

"They're sending a transport for us. I need you to work with Nurses Bell and Agrait to prepare our sick and wounded for the trip."

"Yes, sir," Ada replied, and she left to carry out her orders.

FOUR

GARDINER LED HIS contingent of Allied soldiers from the confines of the tunnels beneath Orchard City. They ascended from the open-cut railroad onto the main road. Near the city limits, they bet on being a big and well-armed enough force to avoid predatory attention. But they ran the risk of encountering a Coventry-bound convoy big enough to overwhelm them.

"Major, aren't we a little exposed?" Liggan asked.

"Yes, Sergeant, but that's the point," Gardiner answered. "If we're going to make Coventry quickly, we need a ride."

"But, sir," she protested, "who's gonna pick us up? We're just as unpopular in the badlands as the Reds!"

"Less," said Andersen.

Gardiner waved away the remarks. "Your concern is duly noted, Sergeant, but if I need your counsel, I'll request it."

Liggan fell back into formation, into lockstep with Macaluso.

"He's as bad as the fucking corren," she muttered.

Macaluso nodded.

Carina opened a private comm to Gardiner. "Nicely done, Major. I never expected everyone to be this mouthy. You handled that well. But I'm just as curious about your plan. You do have a plan, right?"

"Yes, Captain," Gardiner replied. His voice was weary. "The next convoy, if it has a reasonable complement of humans and one of them holds particular sway, I'll enthrall him into allowing us to join them."

Down the road, they could see a convoy approaching.

"Get off the road!" Gardiner warned. "Move, move!"

"Move! Take cover!" Carina shepherded the ragtag crew off the main drag to the cover of an alleyway.

The major had no time to explain. He gleaned the convoy's makeup from one of its human passengers. It comprised mostly Ingili. The trucks rumbled by. The Allies held their breath. After all the trucks had passed, Gardiner waited until he was certain it was safe. The convoy didn't stop.

The Allies continued northward, keeping to the sidewalks. Derelict buildings once used for offices and manufacturing flanked the wide avenue. Storefronts that long ago purveyed retail goods stood empty of wares. The spaces were occupied, but rarely settled. People used them for shelter until an aggressive party either killed or rousted them. In some places, though, communities had taken root and maintained their claims.

The civilians allowed the well-armed soldiers to go unmolested, so long as the soldiers also paid them no mind. Both Gardiner and Carina were glad to avoid additional hassle, especially with the Allies so despised. It was enough of an undertaking to get himself, Carina, and their twelve charges from one city to another. Mahoney's wounded leg hindered their progress. They needed another convoy—a human one—to come.

They heard the sound of trucks a few miles behind.

"Do you believe in a higher power, Captain?" Gardiner asked Carina over their private comm link.

"I believe in myself, Major," she replied.

"Well, I'm not sure it's your doing, but our prayers have been answered. This convoy has a good share of humans. A lot of Ingili, too, but it's a partnership . . . and there's one human who'll suit our aim very nicely."

"It's scary what you can do, Maks. You know that, right?"

"Would you rather be out here without me?" he replied.

"No. Absolutely not. But it's still hard to get my head around that you can sense a person miles away and . . . know him. It's not even the least of what you can do, is it?"

"I know it unsettled you to kill that helpless corren, back on base."

"I don't want to talk about that," she objected.

"It surprised you, didn't it? Your feelings."

"Why should I even answer? You know what I felt. Don't poke around my head, eavesdropping on my feelings."

"I'm merely making conversation," Gardiner said. "But our ride is here. Time to be seen."

He stepped into the road. Carina directed the group to follow.

Ray approached her and asked what was going on. She told him.

"I don't like being so out of the loop," he admitted.

"Not used to being third link in the chain, huh?" she replied.

"No, I am. Having charge of one mission didn't make me forget my place. I'd just rather be privy to command conversations."

"The major and I aren't keeping you out of the loop. You'll get any info we think you need."

"I appreciate that," he replied.

The convoy stopped. A crew of humans and Ingili trained their weapons on Gardiner and the others. Mounted on the lead truck was a nasty-looking cannon that could lay waste to them all.

"Get out of the way, fools!" a bald Ingilon admonished from behind the human gunner. "You want a fight, we'll cut you down."

The Ingilon had a long face. The two burn scars, where he had been branded, made his visage more fearsome. His cleanly shaven head, an aberration among correns, made him outright terrifying.

"Why are you bald?" Macaluso blurted like a child. His wonder at seeing a corren without hair overtook him.

"What fucking use do I have for hair?" the Ingilon replied. "There's no sun! Why don't you fuck off instead of asking stupid questions?"

"Not looking for a fight," Gardiner replied. "We seek transport."

Unbeknownst to the gunner, Gardiner had paralyzed the man's hands.

The bald Ingilon laughed. "We look like a fucking taxi, human?"

"What's goin' on here?" a human man called out, stepping down from one of the middle trucks. He was armed with a rifle and backed up by a quartet of armed guards: two Ingili and two humans.

He was shorter than all of the Allied troops except Lindner. Dearth of height wasn't uncommon in the badlands. Human civilians didn't often receive care or nourishment enough to grow as tall and toned as wards of the state. The man had short black hair and a long beard. Despite the rifle in his hands, his face seemed almost congenial.

Gardiner worked on the man's mind, breaking it in, preparing it to produce the chemical reaction to a remembered friend. The major took off his helmet.

"Billy Saps," Gardiner said. He smiled. His scarred face ensured that it always looked like a snarl.

"Maks?" Saps replied. "Holy shit."

"Saps, you know this ugly fuck?" asked the Ingilon behind the gunner.

"Yeah. Stand down," Saps ordered.

"That big one's wearing Confederation armor!" the Ingilon added, pointing at Ray.

Saps looked up at the corren. "Just fuckin' relax, Abdoh. If they try somethin', you can blow 'em away, but calm down for a second. Bloody hell."

The short, bearded human turned back to Gardiner.

"What the hell're you doin' out here?"

"It's a long story," Gardiner replied. "And probably better relayed on the move than standing around here like a bunch of assholes."

"Yeah," said Saps. "You're right. But you're gonna have to satisfy our curiosity first. Nice as it is to see you, we're not just takin' all of you on when I don't know . . ."

Gardiner planted a memory of Carina in Saps' mind.

"Billy, you remember Carina Duvais, don't you?"

He gestured for Carina to remove her helmet. She revealed her face, and Abdoh let out a wolf whistle.

Saps looked like Cupid had shot him between the eyes. "How could I forget that face?"

"Look," said Gardiner, "I know it's been a while, but we're the same people you've always known. These are our charges. The big one is corren. He's one of us."

"Oh, yeah, Allies got lots of love for us!" Abdoh exclaimed. "They keep you as a pet, boy?" he yelled to Ray.

Ray took off his helmet and looked at Abdoh. The smile sagged right off the Ingilon's face. He recognized Ray. All correns did, with that bare nose. Any human well-traveled or associated with other correns knew of him, too.

"A'arilon Ray," said Saps. "Okay. I can dig it. I don't know what the fuck's goin' on, but we'll take you . . . we'll take your weapons, too . . . but we'll take you."

"Saps, come on," Carina protested.

"We'll give 'em back, Carina. But if you wanna ride, cough up the pieces."

Abdoh called to another corren. He ordered him to stand behind the gunner, then jumped down to join Saps in the middle truck. Excluding Ray, Carina, Gardiner, and Patrick, Saps directed the Allies into two groups. He sent one to the truck in front of his and the other to the truck behind. In each case, the soldiers surrendered their weapons.

When they demanded that Macaluso turn over his exo-suit, he refused.

"Saps, the man is paralyzed," Gardiner said. "The suit lets him walk."

"Let him be, then . . . but take those mitts," Saps ordered. "He can have his legs, but he's not puttin' his fists through my men."

Carina looked at Mahoney, who was ashen and damp with sweat.

"He needs to ride with me," she said. "He needs medical attention."

"Of course," Saps acquiesced.

***

The convoy rolled quietly along.

Carina tended to Mahoney. "How are you feeling?"

"Not good, Cap," he replied. His normally booming baritone voice was weak and labored.

She knew the answer to her own question. He needed blood. She didn't even know what type he was. With his chip cut from his hand, his personnel and medical files were missing. She couldn't trust him to know. Neither could she guess whether—if she, Patrick, Lindner or Gardiner weren't—any other humans in the convoy were matches. But, if she didn't try something, he would die within the next few hours.

"What blood type are you, Corporal?" she asked.

"I don't know," he replied. "Red?"

"That's not the answer I need, Mahoney." She looked at Saps. "Billy, is there anywhere in Coventry like a hospital or a triage center?"

He opened one eye and looked at her with it. He waited a long while before replying. "Have you ever been to Coventry, Carina?"

Her heart sank. The closest facility she could think of was the Allied base in Klippeborg. To get there, they needed to traverse the misnamed region where combustible gas emanated from the Hugtaender i Nord mountains. It was not a plain and the gas was not plasma, but "Plasma Fields" had entered the lexicon and everyone knew it as such.

The Allies had no transport beyond Coventry. It put Klippeborg well over two days away on foot. Mahoney would die before they arrived. He would probably die hours upon making Coventry.

Saps closed his eye. "Though I'd guess the armory has a medical bay," he added, referencing the abandoned Allied facility near the center of Coventry.

Carina looked at Gardiner. "We have to get in there, then."

"Good luck with that," said Abdoh. "Everyone in the city's been trying to get in since the Allies withdrew. Including us. You know there's a stalemate, right? Every bit of muscle in town guards it against every other. Nobody's gettin' in there without a lot of bloodshed."

"I can live with that," Carina said.

Saps opened both his eyes. "He means *a lot* of bloodshed, Carina. Like, hundreds of people. Your man's life worth hundreds of others?"

"Personally? Yeah," Carina replied without hesitation. "I don't know any of these fools. I know him. He's my comrade. His life means more to me than theirs."

Abdoh shook his head. "We got people guarding that armory. *Our* comrades. You think we're just gonna let you slaughter them so this asshole can live?"

"How about a deal?" Gardiner interjected.

Saps arched an eyebrow at the major.

"Help us get in and we'll arm you . . ." Gardiner proposed.

"Now, wait a minute, Major," Ray objected. "We can't go tipping the balance of power where we have no jurisdiction."

"Objection noted, Commander," Gardiner replied, "but it's the badlands. I'm not going to let the corporal die just because we don't have *jurisdiction*. Besides, what better reason to disrupt this supposed balance than empowering old friends?"

Gardiner looked at Saps and grimaced. It was the closest thing to a genuine smile his disfigurement would allow.

FIVE

GARDINER, CARINA, AND Ray climbed down from the convoy. Saps' and Abdoh's encampment was a courtyard enclosed by a series of tenements. Thousands of humans and hundreds of Ingili milled within.

Abdoh and Ray deposited Mahoney atop a makeshift pallet.

"He's got, maybe, an hour or two before I can't help him anymore," Carina told Gardiner.

He didn't acknowledge her. He looked as though he were listening to something far away.

"Maks?"

Gardiner turned to look at her with a craze in his eyes. "What?" he snapped.

Carina bristled. "Don't snap at me, Major. I'm talking about what to do with our dying man. This should be important to you."

It was obvious that something nagged at Gardiner's attention. He forced himself to focus. "What is it?"

"He needs blood! He doesn't have much time. If we're going to hit this armory, we need to do it now!"

He put up his hand to silence her. He walked away.

"What the *fuck*, Maks?" She followed.

Gardiner ignored her. He looked around the camp as if following a distant sound, trying to determine its source.

Saps followed her. "What is he doing?"

"I don't know," Carina replied.

They kept after Gardiner, leaving a little bit of distance.

He stopped in the middle of the courtyard, looking at the rear windows of the tenements. The street-facing doors of the buildings had been sealed. The encampment had only two heavily guarded entrances. Armed guards manned the roofs, directing their vigilance toward the outside world. Residents occupied the buildings to the point of overcrowding. Traffic flowed in and out, milling among the courtyard's tents.

Gardiner donned his helmet.

Carina did the same, hoping he'd communicate with her over the comm. "Talk to me, Maks. What the hell are you doing? You're weirding out our hosts. This isn't cool."

Gardiner ignored her.

"Maks!" she insisted, but she couldn't reach him.

He heard the thoughts of every human in the compound. Initially, all the minds together sounded like a cafeteria din. With a little focus, he could home in on a single "voice." He could pick out any one of those voices among the hundreds he saw and the thousands more he didn't. The innermost workings of the residents' minds writhed and slithered over one another like snakes in a pit. Most were mundane concerns: hunger, worry, petty grievances, scheming, lust. But the latter feeling put him on the trail of worse, predatory urges.

Gardiner instantly recognized the hallmarks. Once uncovered, they blared out at him louder than any other thought or feeling that radiated from the mass. The base sensations so acutely evoked his own trauma. The camp was full of rapists. Rapists of all stripes. Men who victimized adult and adolescent women and/or other men, women who preyed upon other women. But, among the predators were the worst criminals of all: men and women who preyed upon children.

"You," Gardiner said to a man tending to ropes supporting a tent.

The man turned around and looked at his own reflection in the mirror shield of Gardiner's helmet.

"Who the fuck are you?" the man replied.

"Maks," said Saps, coming up behind the major.

"Saps, do you know that this man rapes children?" Gardiner asked as calmly as if he wanted to know his ersatz friend's favorite color.

"What?" Saps replied.

The man in front of the tent looked dead-eyed at Gardiner.

"No denial," Gardiner said to the man.

"I'm no child rapist, you wacko," he replied, finding his tongue.

"Maks, really, what the fuck is this?" Saps insisted.

Gardiner silenced Saps with a thought and rounded on the man he accused.

"Your name is Aemonn Rindfleischer. You're twenty-nine years old. You have genital herpes, syphilis, and gonorrhea. You have a small dick. You feel humiliated by your inability to sexually interact with adult women. It renders you impotent, and you want to feel powerful. So you rape little girls."

Aemonn just blinked at Gardiner. All of it was true.

Without waiting for a reply, Gardiner killed him without moving a muscle. The man's corpse flopped to the ground.

The major turned toward Saps, unmuting him.

"Your camp is full of them," Gardiner warned.

"Full of who?" Saps exclaimed. "Child rapists? How can you know that?" He knelt to check Aemonn's pulse. "He's dead, Maks! What the hell?"

"How can you *not* know?" Gardiner shouted, ignoring the diagnosis. He took off his helmet and shouted to the sky. "All of you, pay attention!"

Every human in the camp was bidden by Gardiner's will to turn their focus to him. The Ingili did so of their own volition, simply for the spectacle and to sate their own curiosity.

"Who among you has ever forced yourself upon a child? Who among you has *raped* a child? *Raise your hand*!"

One hand went up. Then another. And another. Horrified and bemused looks plastered the men's and women's faces. It was obvious that the hands did not go up of their owners' volition. From some of the buildings, people came trickling out with one hand raised in the air.

Gardiner burned with rage. He looked at Saps, who blanched before the fury, but still found his voice.

"I don't know what you're doing, Maks, but you need to stop."

"I think you can spare a few dozen pedophiles," Gardiner replied acidly.

Saps nodded at Abdoh, who ordered the correns to train their weapons on the major.

Gardiner turned to face Abdoh. Without so much as a gesture, the firearms flew from the correns' hands to the ground. Unable to penetrate the correns' minds, Gardiner opted to manipulate inert matter. As his rage grew, his focus faltered and his influence increased. Tent spikes shot out of the ground and halted in midair.

A gentle wind whipped around the open space. It grew in intensity as his self-control waned.

Kill, he thought. It was a command. The humans with their hands raised turned on each other.

Gardiner returned control of both hands to the rapists and pedophiles. The group attacked one another with their bare fists and whatever they could use as a weapon. A melee erupted. A large man grabbed a woman by her hair and jammed his thumb into her eye socket. He pulled back and popped the orb from her head. She screamed. Her eye dangled down her cheek. The screams stopped when he bashed her mouth against his knee. He drove her to the ground and smashed her skull against jagged concrete until only pulp remained.

As he tried to rise, Gardiner telekinetically hurled a tent spike at him. It pierced his skull and emerged from the other side.

The carnage lasted five minutes. Throughout it, every bystander stood rapt. The correns didn't try to retrieve their weapons. Gardiner released from his thrall the humans not involved in the fray, but they remained rooted to their spots.

"We're going, *now!*" Gardiner shouted, looking at Saps, Carina, and Ray. He ordered Gray and Milner to pick up Mahoney.

Carina looked at Ray, who shook his head at her. There was nothing they could do but fall in line. Gardiner had instilled fear and awe in everyone.

The sole survivor killed the runner-up.

With one last look at the bloody, corpse-littered courtyard, the major saw the last man standing. Blood dripped from the dazed man's hands. Gardiner hurled a tent spike through the man's head and he dropped dead. Every pederast in the camp had been killed, but the major's anger still burned. He marched toward the courtyard's western exit. His cohort fell into formation behind him.

"I need my mitts," Macaluso said to no one in particular. He lumbered to a teenage boy who had climbed down from one of the transports. "Get me my mitts."

The boy looked at him, unsure whether to mouth off or not.

"Don't fuck with me, kid, or I'll sic that skinny psycho on you. He'll pull your head out through your asshole and I'll punt it back on your shoulders for good measure."

The boy's eyes widened. He scrambled back into the truck, procuring Macaluso's mitts.

"Thanks," said the corporal. "Good choice."

The rest of the Allies retrieved their weapons from the convoy.

"Stay here," Saps told Abdoh while scurrying after Gardiner and the Allies. "Get this shit under control. Black motherfucking Skies."

The camp was in hysterics. Abdoh's harsh, bony face contorted in rue. The task was enormous. He thought to protest, but Saps was already gone.

"How could we have such a weapon and be losing this war?" Ray asked Carina.

"I don't think anyone knew what he could really do," she replied. "I didn't know. I thought he was gifted . . . I didn't know he was godlike."

"He's dangerous, Captain. His actions aren't sober. They're not tactical."

"I'd agree he's acting a bit . . . irrational"

"Irrational? He's fucking lost it! Calling it irrational is kind; it's fucking lunacy!"

"Shut *up*!" Carina hissed. "You want his wrath on you? I don't. Don't bring his attention to me."

They made their way to the armory on foot, guarded by the awesome power of Gardiner's fury. As they approached the moat, the camps sprang to life and rallied to guard the spoils.

Gardiner halted. Carina, Ray, Saps, and the rest stopped behind him.

A motley band of opposing hordes united to oppose the new, common enemy. Behind the human and Ingili mercenaries, a lone bridge led to the armory's interior doors.

"Who's in charge, here?" Gardiner asked.

"Who the fuck wants to know?" asked a large Ingilon wielding a long length of heavy pipe with a homemade mace.

Gardiner said nothing. His mouth twitched. Disdain crept across his face. He telekinetically tore the corren's right arm from his body. For pure theater, he accompanied the feat with a sweeping gesture. It shocked the onlookers.

The Ingilon's limb, club still in hand, lay on the ground. He crumbled to his knees as if to retrieve his appendage. He looked up at Gardiner, incredulous.

"Who else wants to lose an arm?" shouted the major.

They responded by raising and aiming their weapons. The humans were easily thwarted. With minimal visible effort from Gardiner, each found the muzzles of their own weapons under their chins. Planting the suggestion was the easy part, keeping them in the pose took greater effort.

"Or more?" Gardiner added.

He lifted his left hand and swatted the air, palm toward the ground. The Ingili dropped their guns as if driven from their hands.

"Is this not enough for you?" he yelled.

The Ingilon whose arm Gardiner had torn off recovered his wits. "You fucking punk bitch. Take me man-to-man, you pussy. I don't need two arms to beat you to death."

Gardiner stepped on the corren's severed arm and pried free the club. He brought it down against the Ingilon's head with a loud crack. The man tried to stand. Gardiner struck him again and again until the Ingilon fell to the ground. His green blood looked black as it pooled beneath his broken skull.

"Who else wants to die?" bellowed the major.

Carina had never seen such hard men look so afraid. So defeated. The humans remained with their weapons pressed under their chins. The Ingili made no attempt to retrieve their guns.

One of the humans noticed Billy Saps.

"Saps, what the fuck is this? What are you doing with this psycho?"

"Maks," said Saps to Gardiner. "Some of these men are our people. I need you to spare them."

"Point them out to me," Gardiner replied through clenched teeth.

"The blue and white ones are mine," Saps told Gardiner, pointing at the banners and bandannas.

Gardiner cringed. It was not easy to hold so many men in thrall. It was even harder to discriminate. The amount of energy it took exhausted him, but he knew he could do it. Only doubt limited his power. He visualized the blue and white banners and associated them with those men he held in thrall. He released them. A palpable wave of relief went through the men.

"We're going inside," Gardiner stated. "Make way."

"You trust this asshole, Saps?" said someone in the crowd.

Saps looked weary. "You wanna say 'no' to this guy?"

The freed men forced the horde to part, pushing the others into the moat. The men thrashed with their one free hand. Some of them drowned. The rest slapped and paddled their way onto the bank, muzzles still pressed to their jaws.

Gardiner and his group crossed the bridge. The Allies held formation as they crossed. They refused to be lulled into complacency by Gardiner's omnipotent display. Vehement anger colored the enthralled men's faces. If the major's concentration broke, it would spell death for his entire party.

At the armory doors, he beckoned to Carina. She joined him at the access panel.

"They've managed to breach the outer doors, obviously. But not the inner ones."

"There is no way we get in without advanced clearance," she said.

"Let's not worry until we have something to worry about," Gardiner replied.

The panel for the interior doors required the credentials of two officers for entry. In its days of normal operation, anyone posted could access the building. Like any other compound. It made no sense to force two officers to chaperone every charge. But, since the withdrawal, the facility required more stringent safeguards.

Gardiner submitted his credentials. The panel requested a second set. Carina waved her right hand at it. The system then demanded a secondary credential from each of them.

"Fuck!" Gardiner spat. "What the hell is this?"

Ray joined them, sensing the trouble. "We need to get inside quickly, Major—"

"You think I don't know that?" Gardiner snapped.

He felt his attention to the horde waver. He regathered himself but knew he couldn't hold them off for long. It was physically and mentally exhausting to exert influence over so many minds. It was emotionally debilitating.

"Unless you're sure you can keep our new enemies at bay, indefinitely, the urgency needs voice," Ray continued.

"I can't keep this up," Gardiner admitted. "So, yes, we need to get in now. If we don't, I'll falter. And they'll be free to kill us."

"Patrick, to me," Ray ordered.

The corporal joined him, Carina, and Gardiner at the door.

"Get us access," Ray demanded.

Patrick looked at the screen. "It's two-times-two-factor authentication. It doesn't just require two credentials, they each have to submit an additional, random code that refreshes at a regular interval."

Gardiner stepped close enough to Patrick to kiss him.

"I don't care how it works. Make it work for *us*."

"I need a terminal!" Patrick protested. "I need some kind of device I can use to network with the panel. We don't have anything like that! Did you think to bring it?"

"Don't get mouthy with me, Corporal," Gardiner warned.

"Mac!" yelled Carina. "Move your big ass. Come here! Hurry!"

Macaluso pushed his way through the throng of his wary Allied cohort, as bidden.

"I need your computer," she said. "Give it to Patrick."

He closed his eyes and gritted his teeth. Exhaling through his nose, he tamped down the annoyance of handicapping himself. He opened his eyes and sat down. Removing the exo-suit computer would deactivate it, rendering useless his paralyzed legs. The angry mob lingered across the bridge with vengeance on its mind, and he hated to feel vulnerable.

Patrick seized the handheld apparatus and activated it for external use. He connected via wireless to the closed armory network. It was self-contained to the building. The network allowed a close-range device with Allied credentials to join as a guest. Still, it gave him difficulty. He didn't have authorization at the root level. It inhibited his access to essential directories, files, and processes. The well-engineered system aimed to prevent hacking by anyone spoofing proper authentication.

Any enterprising, intelligent brigand could lift Allied apparati from dead soldiers and attempt cyberespionage. And they had, to varying—but never catastrophic—levels of success. It was how they had breached the armory's outer doors.

"Well?" Gardiner pressed.

"It's gonna take some time, Major. I need a few minutes. I need, like, fifteen. At least."

"We don't have fifteen!" Gardiner exclaimed.

He didn't want to kill all of the humans he held in his thrall, but that thrall was wavering. Once it collapsed, he'd be unable to influence them at all. He had already exhausted his ability to manipulate matter. He felt dead on his feet, as if he might fall asleep just by blinking his eyes. He leaned his back against the wall of the alcove and slid down until he sat upon the floor.

"Be ready to fight. Carina … you're in charge."

"What?" she replied with a hint of panic. "Major?"

She had never commanded more than her medical staff. As a lieutenant, she had meted out her captain's and major's orders. In her short time as a captain, the only time she'd used her rank was to pull it on Lieutenants Andersen and Sotillo. To thwart their sexual advances.

Gardiner fought to keep his eyes open. He focused upon keeping the humans enthralled.

Patrick looked for an exploit. Nearly all programmers left a back door that allowed them emergency access. While it left the system vulnerable to hackers, the gambit was to defend it well enough to prevent cracking without insider knowledge. As a trained Allied system operations engineer, Patrick had—if not explicit knowledge of the exploit—better familiarity than some rogue badlands tech-head.

He affixed the computer to a metallic portion of the alcove wall. He tried every trick he could muster to gain root access. After examining the hidden directories, he pored over the hidden files in the visible directories. There, he found a simple "README" file disguised as a system file.

Gardiner knew he would fall asleep the next moment he closed his eyes. It was over. He had two options: kill all the humans and better his own group's chance for survival or spare those humans and surely die.

Nearly one hundred weapons fired all at once and the human mercenaries fell dead.

"Holy shit!" Sotillo exclaimed.

Gardiner lost consciousness.

"I need my computer, meat!" Macaluso demanded of Patrick. "I am not dyin' on my fuckin' ass!"

"Just hold up!" Patrick retorted, exasperated.

The Ingili began milling about, retrieving their weapons.

"Form up!" Carina shouted. "We have to hold the bridge. If they set foot on it, open fire."

"Oh, fuck. Oh, fuck. Oh, fuck." Patrick spoke it like a mantra. He turned away from Macaluso's computer and directed his attention at the armory's access panel.

"Commander, sir, can I please have my fucking legs back?" Macaluso pleaded angrily at Ray. "This fucking chump doesn't know shit about anything."

"Will you shut the fuck up?" Patrick shouted. He hooked his arms under Gardiner's armpits and hauled the major's unconscious body over to the panel, getting his chip within range. The panel recognized Gardiner and requested another army officer.

"Captain! I need you here."

Carina wrenched her attention from the marshaling Ingili. They conferred, wary of mounting a full-on attack.

"What?" she snapped.

"I need your chip, sir. I need your authorization!"

Carina waved her hand at the panel and immediately turned back toward the bridge.

The panel accepted her credentials. It then prompted for both the major's and captain's second factor. Patrick didn't have it. But, as he'd surmised, an emergency menu presented itself. He opened it and saw that he could seal the alcove's outer door, even if he couldn't open the interior one.

"Get everyone inside here!" Patrick demanded.

Carina looked over her shoulder at him and then looked at the size of the group.

"No way we all fit in there!"

"Then someone's got to hold the line!" Patrick insisted.

"We can fit, dammit," Ray said.

He dragged Macaluso into the alcove with one hand. The corporal crossed his arms, wearing an expression of pure annoyance. Already infantilized by his paralysis, being dragged like a giant sack of potatoes only heightened his displeasure.

Ray then drew Mahoney's pallet into the space. The two incapacitated men took up a lot of the available space. Ray, Patrick, Gardiner, and Carina left about half of the alcove available to fit the rest. Saps, Andersen, Sotillo, Liggan, Lindner, Nergaard, Burke, Milner, and Gray piled in. Carina was right, it was too many people for such a small space. But she refused to leave anyone at the mercy of the Ingili, because they knew no mercy. The Allies would have to find a way to cram together.

"Fall back to the alcove," she ordered. "Now!"

The line backed into the space. They jammed themselves into every square inch surrounding Mahoney's prostrate form.

Billy Saps' humans and Ingili realized that the opposing factions were mounting an attack on their leader. They raised their weapons and began shouting down the opposition at point-blank range. A close-quarters gunfight erupted on the banks of the moat.

"Everybody in?" Patrick yelled. Bodies pressed against him as he crouched at the panel.

"Clear!" Carina yelled.

Patrick activated the outer door. It began to slide down. The opposing Ingili opened fire with projectile weapons. A bullet tore through Nergaard's side, puncturing his left lung. The payload lodged in Sergeant Liggan's armor. Another bullet pinged off Macaluso's exo-suit. It grazed Private Burke's forehead before lodging in the masonry. She touched her hand to her head. Observing the blood on her fingers, she looked at Macaluso. They shared an incredulous smile.

Saps' men and the opposition massacred each other on the banks of the moat.

The door came down hard and crushed the front half of Private Lindner's left foot. He screamed out in pain and kept screaming.

"Shut him up!" Carina demanded.

Lieutenant Andersen put the private in a chokehold to render him unconscious. Lindner's body had no room to fall. It slumped against Andersen, Saps, and Sotillo.

Patrick rose to his feet. "Commander, sir, please hand me the computer."

Ray released Macaluso's computer from the inner armory door and pushed toward the alcove terminal. Patrick took the device and affixed it anew to the armory's inner door, near to him. The computer's screen and the alcove access panel were the only sources of light in the cramped space. They did little to assuage the darkness.

Patrick worked diligently and the chatter died down. Together with Ray and Sotillo, he decoded the disguised "README" file, which contained an old-fashioned cryptograph. It gave him command-line instructions for downloading permissions to create a super-user account. He felt giddy.

"I'm in. I'm root. Holy shit."

He assigned Carina and Gardiner regularly refreshing secondary keys to act as their second-factor authentication.

"Can I have my goddamned computer, please?" Macaluso asked.

Patrick ignored the gripe. He grabbed Gardiner's limp wrist and waved the major's hand at the panel, then input the major's secondary key.

"Captain?"

Carina waved her hand over the panel. Patrick put in her secondary key and the armory's inner door rumbled open.

SIX

WITHIN THE ARMORY a pair of sentries awaited the haggard Allies.

"Halt!" one of the sentries ordered.

"Stand down," Carina barked, flipping up her visor. "I'm in no mood for your shit."

The sentry's expressionless face betrayed no confusion, but its silence spoke volumes. Too far away to read her chip, it analyzed Carina's face and physical dimensions. It pulled her file from the Armory database, which was out of date by close to a year. A firewall protected the internal network from the operating system of the exterior access panel, preventing the sentry from interfacing with it.

"Lieutenant Karin Duvais," the sentry stated.

"*Captain*," she corrected, walking up to and waving her right hand at the sentry. "Read my chip."

It linked up with her chip and confirmed her promotion.

"Apologies, Captain," he replied.

"An apology!" she exclaimed. "Never expected to hear that from one of you. Look, like I said, don't bother me with old protocols. I'm the CO of this party, and you will follow my orders."

The sentry looked at her with vacant, robotic eyes. "Yes, sir."

"Is there a triage bot in the medical bay?" Carina asked the sentry.

"Yes, sir."

"Take Major Gardiner and LC Mahoney to the medical bay," she demanded, pointing at the two men. "Have the bot type Mahoney's blood and prep for a transfusion. He'll need a new chip and his hand repaired, too, if you can manage that."

"Yes, sir."

Carina turned to Nergaard and Liggan, who stood behind the private still applying pressure to his exit wound.

"You two, follow them. I'll be right there to patch him up," she added, nodding at Nergaard.

***

Macaluso waited for Carina to finish putting Private Nergaard back together. But the brawny corporal's face betrayed his desperation. He'd already sat through Mahoney's blood transfusion and Private Lindner's grisly foot surgery. He didn't want to wait a moment longer.

When Carina snipped the final suture, he intercepted her.

"Captain . . ." He hesitated. His face flushed with embarrassment.

Carina recognized his discomfiture and steered him to a more private corner of the medical bay. "What is it?"

"Sir . . . I . . ." He closed his eyes and stuck out his lower jaw, inhaling as he weathered the insult to his pride. "I need your help. It's . . . well . . . it's my time."

Carina wanted to say, *You're having your period?* but she mustered her tact and summoned her compassion as a physician. She realized, due to his paralysis, that he must have a regimented schedule for his bowel movements. At the Dorance base, managing that task was left to the nurses, whom Tuah had supervised.

"Come on," Carina said. "There's a private washroom right over here."

She grabbed a wheelchair and ordered Macaluso to sit in it. He shut down his exo-suit, rendering him immobile from the waist down. Carina set about removing the apparatus.

"Please hurry, sir," Macaluso said, a slight panic in his voice. "I'd do this myself, but I can't take the time to do it right, or I'll . . ." he looked her straight in the eye. "I'll shit myself."

"Shh, Mac. No matter what happens, there's nothing to be ashamed of."

He frowned and shook his head but kept his mouth shut. Divested of his cybernetic enhancement, Carina wheeled him into the washroom and closed the door.

"Okay, now it's time to lose those pants," she said.

Macaluso hemmed, but only for a moment. He swallowed his pride, knowing that to dally would only cause him greater shame. After undoing his belt, he worked his trousers and underwear down. He cleared his genitalia, his penis covered by the condom catheter that prevented him from urinating upon himself. Carina picked up the slack. She pulled his garments down to his ankles.

"I can't carry you," Carina said. "Can you help me?"

Macaluso nodded, doing everything he could to avoid looking her in the eye. He grabbed the bars on either side of the toilet, using his significant upper-body strength to lift himself. Carina helped him turn, and he sat, putting his face in his hands.

"I'll give you some privacy. If you need me, call me. I'll be right outside."

The corporal's evacuation transpired without incident. He struggled through dressing himself, washed his hands, and wheeled out of the lavatory. Carina, leaning against the wall, looked over at him. Neither said a word as they retrieved his exo-suit. When Macaluso was again mobile, she patted him once on the leg. She returned to survey Mahoney and Nergaard.

Private Burke dozed in a chair, a bandage upon her head wound. Major Gardiner slept atop one of the beds. Satisfied that all of her charges were well, Carina threw herself into a chair with a heavy sigh. She took a sip from her flask, followed by another, and then a third. Closing the container, she cast it into her lap and slid down in the seat.

Exhaustion overtook her.

***

Gardiner awoke and squinted against the bright lights of the medical bay. Everything around him was stark, white, and antiseptic. It was the cleanest room he'd seen since he left the London Academy.

Carina slept nearby. Her left hand rested on the grip of the energy pistol in her shoulder holster.

The major swung his legs around so that he sat on the edge of the bed, then stood. He moved like a cat, but Carina's head jerked up. In the same instant, she drew her gun. The flask fell from her lap and rang out upon the floor.

"Easy, Captain. It's just me," said Gardiner with his hands up. "You're a light sleeper."

She slid the blaster back into its holster and retrieved the flask. She unscrewed the cap and took a swig.

"I don't really sleep, Major. I just close my eyes sometimes."

"Report," he ordered.

"We typed Mahoney. Lucky for us, he's AB. Greedy fuck. There was blood in the fridge already, so I didn't have to sap anyone to replenish him. We're lucky the bags were still viable. Hooray for cryogenic storage," she said without enthusiasm.

She took another pull from the flask and Gardiner frowned at her.

"I patched up Nergaard, but he's hobbled for weeks," Carina said. "The bullet went through his lung.

"Lindner's foot . . . fuck. That was the ugliest. It's a club now. The best I could do was remove what was left of his metatarsals and graft some skin over the cuneiforms and cuboid. He's gonna need a replacement . . . probably from the ankle. I can't do a cybernetic graft and, besides, even if I could, there aren't any parts here. He's knocked out right now."

"You know he doesn't qualify for cybernetics, right?" Gardiner asked. "He's a noncom."

She shrugged and considered having another drink. Instead, she screwed shut the flask and dropped it back into her lap.

"We've got no outside communication," she said. "So we can't even airlift anyone to Klippeborg or London. We have to leave them all behind."

"What's the food situation?" Gardiner asked.

"I had Milner and Gray check the pantry. It's full. Nothing real, but there's enough rations to feed, probably, ten people for a couple months. The reclamators work, too, so if your protein intake is high enough, you could further stretch it by eating shit-steaks every few days. The same ten bodies could persist maybe six months that way."

"So, Mahoney, Lindner, and Nergaard have to stay behind, at least. And you, too."

"Excuse me?" She wanted to wring his scrawny neck for the thought alone of leaving her behind.

"You're a doctor. We have wounded men. They're your responsibility," Gardiner replied.

"I'm a *doctor*, not a fucking nurse. The three of them are stable. They just need a babysitter now. I'm not a fucking babysitter, Maks."

"Carina . . ."

"*No*. You are *not* ditching me here. Leave Andersen behind. Leave Burke; she's a field medic. There's a triage bot. *And* the sentries . . . they're all programmed with rudimentary wound care . . . uh . . . *qu'est-ce que c'est le mot*. . . knowledge. I am *not* needed here. What happens if something goes down after you leave? Would you rather have me there to tend to you, or somebody else? A couple of fuckwit privates who only know how to apply dressings and sew ugly stitches for nasty scars? At best?"

"You don't seem to have a lot of faith in them," Gardiner retorted. "What if something happens to our wounded here?"

"Nobody's gonna spring a leak, Maks. Nergaard's the biggest risk, because he's young and ballsy and stubborn and, aside from the extra holes in him, he's fit . . . but he's not stupid, and I confined him to a bed. He's sewn up. If he doesn't start doing cartwheels, he's gonna stay sewn. Just put a sentry on him, prescribe an activity regimen, and he won't be able to blink without permission from the big, dead nanny watching his every move."

"Fine," Gardiner replied. "I'm convinced. You can come along. But we do need to thin the herd before we move out. Greater numbers are a liability at this point."

He walked out of the medical bay and almost collided with Billy Saps, who stood lurking outside the door.

Ray stood a few paces away, minding Saps from a distance.

"I don't know you," said Saps, who had been released from Gardiner's thrall when the major lost consciousness.

"That's right," Gardiner replied.

"Who the fuck are you, then?"

"That really doesn't matter at this point," said Gardiner. "We had a deal, and I'll uphold it. Join me in the armory and you can have your pick of the lot, within reason. Take it back to your camp and thank your lucky stars."

Saps blinked. "My lucky stars? You . . ." he struggled to find the words.

He wanted to dig into the major, dress him down for murdering or facilitating the deaths of more people than Saps had ever witnessed in one day. Dozens in his camp and scores outside the armory. He couldn't muster the indignation. He knew his settlement had been rife with unsavory characters. He hadn't known how many were pederasts, but pederasty was as common in the badlands as breathing. It wasn't something he excused, nor condoned, but to try and fight it was to try and kill every cockroach. It was almost impossible by ordinary human means. He'd become inured to the depravity just to survive the stress of daily exposure.

Saps looked again at Gardiner, who stood more than half a head taller. The major was lean, elegant, and graceful, but his face was a brutal melange of delicate beauty and grotesque disfigurement. The shorter man blinked with realization. Gardiner had actually done him a favor by exterminating the cockroaches, killing scads of opposition mercenaries who'd guarded the armory, and cowing the Ingili allied with them.

The major inhaled through his nose. He exhaled the same way. He fixed his one blue eye and his one pink eye upon Saps, waiting for the retort.

"Yes," Saps said at last. "Thank you. The sooner I can requisition those arms, the better. I'd like to return to my camp."

***

The Allies raided the munitions depot for both light and heavy armaments.

Macaluso and Patrick perused the wares like kids in a candy store. Gray and Milner stuck together and did the same. Sotillo started calling them the Ginger Twins.

Carina found a light exo-suit that conformed to her body, along with thrust boots and mitts similar to Macaluso's. She tested the mitts on a suit of armor she first made sure no one else wanted. She caved in the breastplate until it touched its back.

"Comme c'est merveilleux," she said, satisfied. *Marvelous.*

Ray gladly relinquished his Confederation uniform for Allied threads. He found both a bodysuit and plate mail that fit him.

Two sentries vaguely followed the group's every move like oversized butlers. They waited to be called upon but otherwise stayed out of the way.

Gardiner scoured the shelves for lightweight armor. He was overexposed in his cloth uniform. He desired greater protection that wouldn't bog him down. He found a suit of body armor. He unbuttoned his jacket, removed it, and dropped it to the floor. He peeled off his undershirt and paused with it over his head at the sound of a low wolf whistle.

Sotillo sauntered over, wearing fresh body armor and gleaming black and hunter-green plate. Gardiner knew it was him without having to look, without having to sense Sotillo's mind. He knew him by the tone of the whistle and by the sound of his footfalls. The major pulled the shirt the rest of the way over his head and dropped it atop his jacket. He didn't look at Sotillo.

"Have I ever told you that you have a beautiful body?" Sotillo asked. "It's lithe, like a woman's, but so incredibly muscular. Powerful. Sculpted, like an anatomy model."

He placed his left hand on Gardiner's hip. Sotillo's long fingers brushed the bulge between the major's legs. It was the first time Sotillo had ever deigned to touch Gardiner's penis.

"Hi, there," the lieutenant said with a predatory smile.

Gardiner stepped back, bucking his hips to emphatically reject the touch.

"What's your problem?" spat Sotillo. "For once, I touch your dick and that's what I get?"

"Decorum, Lieutenant. This is neither the time nor place."

"You don't refuse me."

Gardiner looked balefully at Sotillo and took a few more steps back. "I *am* refusing you."

Sotillo's nostrils flared. He took an aggressive step. Gardiner retreated no farther. Ambivalence flashed in his eyes. Sotillo took another step. He reached for Gardiner's neck and cuffed him around the nape.

"If I say I'm gonna have you, I'm gonna have you." Sotillo applied pressure to Gardiner's shoulders.

The major resisted. "No."

"'No' is just an encouragement," Sotillo replied. "If I have to force you, I will."

"No," Gardiner replied. "You won't."

Sotillo was physically stronger and bigger, but Gardiner was more powerful. His telepathic and -kinetic abilities tipped the balance. He realized that Sotillo truly believed his physical superiority made him the stronger party. The major grabbed Sotillo's hand, interlocked their thumbs, and, with scant effort, twisted Sotillo's wrist. Without even the aid of telekinesis, Gardiner used the fulcrum to force Sotillo to his knees. The pressure on his elbow and shoulder left little choice but for the body to follow. He gasped in surprise and winced in pain. Shock prevented him from lashing out.

Gardiner let go and stepped back.

Sotillo's shock subsided. Anger crawled across his features. Before he could retaliate, Gardiner kicked him hard in the chest. Sotillo fell backward but kipped to his feet.

"Brute strength isn't going to help you here, Pablo," said Gardiner calmly.

"I'm gonna *kill* you," Sotillo promised. He put his hand on his pistol.

Gardiner allowed him to draw the weapon free of its holster but then cast it from his hand with a telekinetic command. The gun skittered away on the smooth concrete floor.

"You're an *idiot*." Gardiner shook his head with a mixture of sadness and disappointment. "Did you *see* what I did today? How many people did I kill? You want to be one of them?"

Sotillo's mouth twitched. His eyes narrowed. The muscles in his face contorted into a mask of malignant hatred. He scoffed.

"Imagine the hell I could rain down on you," Gardiner continued, "just through normal channels. You just assaulted a superior officer. Threatened me with violence. Threatened to *kill* me. Are you that *stupid* you don't realize my word is all it takes to get you court martialed and executed? Do you value your life that little . . . or are you just so contemptuous that you don't care?"

"Why should I *care*?" Sotillo blurted. "We're off the reservation. We've lost the war. What good will your rank be when the Allied military's just a memory?"

Gardiner shook his head, dismayed. "Every logical part of me says I should take you out."

"You seem to forget you're my *bitch*," Sotillo replied, ignoring the earnest look. "That it's been *my* dick in *your* ass for *months*."

"You really are the most myopic, hateful fool I've ever met."

Sotillo's lips curled back in disgust, baring his teeth. "Fuck you." He held the "F" and spat the word.

"Listen to me," said Gardiner. "Very carefully. There's nothing you've ever done to me . . . I didn't allow you to do."

Sotillo rolled his eyes.

"Let today be a free lesson about who's in charge," Gardiner added. "About who's always been in charge."

Sotillo looked away and set his jaw. He turned on his heel and walked away. Stopping for a moment, he got down on all fours and fished his pistol from beneath the shelves. He holstered it. He didn't look back.

SEVEN

GARDINER JOINED HIS soldiers in the armory mess.

Carina approached him. "Sir, we should camp here for a few hours, at least."

"I'd prefer to keep moving, Captain," Gardiner replied, perusing the rations.

"We don't know what's out there, and I think it's better if we're fresh. You had a nap, they didn't."

Gardiner looked at her. He smirked. "I wouldn't call it a nap, but fair enough. We'll camp here for a spell. A few hours, no more."

Once everyone had eaten, they proceeded to the barracks.

Sotillo rose from his bunk. He walked to the far end of the room, where Carina had made her bed apart from everyone else. Gardiner took note, and so did Ray. Sotillo stopped next to the bed and stood over her.

"Why are you here?" she complained.

"I want to be near you," he replied. His voice was uncharacteristically tender.

"The feeling isn't mutual."

He sat down on the edge of the mattress. She rolled off the other side to her feet. Disgusted anger tightened her features. "You don't just sit down on someone's bed unless they invite you."

"I'd think by now, Carina, you'd know I do what I want." He rose and turned to face her with the bed between them.

"You don't know how to talk to women," she said, shaking her head.

"I'm not interested in talking."

"I'm not interested in fucking you," she replied.

"I don't think that's true."

"What you *think* is irrelevant, Pablo. I'm *telling* you. You don't get to make up my mind for me."

He looked away and exhaled sharply through his nose. "I'm not an idiot, Carina. I see the way you look at me. I know what it means."

"Right. You know me better than I know myself. Then tell me . . . tell me what I really think."

"You protest so much but then you give me those fuck-me eyes every time you look at me."

"Do you have a brother?" she asked.

Sotillo blinked in surprise. "What? Why?"

"Do you have a brother, Pablo?"

"What the hell does that matter?" He was angry and defensive, but he kept his voice low and calm.

"I don't look at *you* with 'fuck-me eyes,'" she replied. "When I look at you, I see another man. Someone I cared about. Someone I miss. It's just our bad luck you look alike."

"All the more reason for you to fuck me, then. Just pretend you're back on top of your long-lost lover."

"And you'd like that? If I rode you with another man's name on my lips? Pretending you were him? Wishing you weren't you?"

Sotillo scowled.

"I didn't think so," said Carina.

"You act like your pussy's so fucking special," he said.

"It must be; you've been trying to get in there since we met."

"I want to get into every box I meet, Carina. It's just a hole. It feels good to shove my cock in it. I like the novelty. I like learning the little ways you differ, the sounds you make. How much you can take."

"You don't get everything you want, Lieutenant."

"Oh, but I do. I *always* get what I want. Eventually."

"Go away," Carina ordered. "Go sleep somewhere far from my bunk. Before I fuck your chest with my knife."

Sotillo sneered. "You act like you're such a big deal, but all you're here for is to get stuffed. The sooner you realize what you're good for, the better off you'll be, you lousy bitch. You're *miserable*. You know it. Everyone knows it. Man-hating, cunt-eating . . . everything you do is motivated by malice."

Carina's nostrils flared, but she kept her composure. "Said the pot to the kettle. I've never met a more hateful man, and I've met a lot of hateful men. You're all so good at it. And you, fucking the major, fucking noncoms, civilian station hands. So many men . . . and yet you deride my love of women."

"'Love of women,'" Sotillo scoffed. "Because that's what it is."

"No woman's ever hurt me. Why shouldn't I love them? They've hurt you, though, haven't they? It's why you're so angry."

He scowled and rolled his eyes but said nothing.

"And the men . . . why them? Do you even enjoy them?"

He seethed at her.

She shook her head. "It's the power you like, isn't it? Domination. What's more dominating than burying your dick in another man's asshole, making him your bitch? I'm sure you feel something like it when you rape a woman, but it's just not the same, right? Because we're *just* women. And women are *weak*, yeah? And where's the fun in conquering the weak?"

"You bore me, Carina," Sotillo replied.

"Then go away. You've been boring me your whole life. You're not getting in here, you malignant prick. I'm not gonna invite you, and you're not gonna take it . . . 'cause I will rip off your balls with my bare fucking hands and feed them to you if you ever lay a finger on me."

"Ooh," mocked Sotillo. "You're *so* tough. Everybody trembles before you. One day, soon, darlin', just wait."

"Go *away*, Pablo."

"Watch your back, Carina." His tone was quiet. It might have seemed like a friendly caution if it wasn't so obviously a threat.

She watched him depart. She had betrayed no fear while they spoke but, alone again, a shiver shook her body. She clenched her fists to stop the shaking, breathing deeply through her nose to quell the nausea that threatened to rush up her esophagus.

Sotillo arrived back at his bunk and sat down. He ignored Gardiner's watchful gaze and stoked his anger at Carina to block the memories of Falco that demanded his attention. But he couldn't shut his brother out. He shot up from the bed and stalked from the barracks.

Gardiner watched him go. He'd watched Sotillo's memories like a film but derived no pleasure from witnessing the man, as a boy, give up his little brother to a slaver to feed their mother and three sisters. What the major gleaned, however, was insight.

EIGHT

LUTÁN USHERED ANJALI off the ship and onto the hangar floor. Shaula followed right behind them.

Marseh waited for them to approach.

"Leave her with me, please," he said, looking at Anjali. "And leave us. Please, return Shaula to her home."

Shaula was furious. She didn't acknowledge Marseh nor utter a word. She walked off on her own. Lutàn inclined his head and gestured for Miro, Skal, and Ishka not to follow. Miro opened his mouth but thought better of speaking after a sideways look from Marseh.

In silence, Miro trailed Skal and Ishka out of the hangar.

"Welcome," Marseh said to Anjali.

"Welcome back, you mean," she replied.

It was hard for her to believe mere days had passed since she and Ray and the others had raided the station to steal Sargas. It felt like months. She looked around at the quiet hangar, at the idle ships. A few humans moved around, tending to their duties, but the scene was so tranquil and ordinary she might have believed there was no war. But there was, and Earth was the battleground. Ray was still down there, some two thousand kilometers below, somewhere on Nova Spes. The distance and her ignorance of what he faced saddened her. It was the farthest apart they had ever been since meeting.

"Is there anything you need?" Marseh asked her.

"I'm hungry," Anjali replied.

Marseh nodded and indicated she should follow him. They walked for about fifteen minutes, winding through the stark corridors of the station before reaching a private mess hall. Two Elite Imperial Guards sat before empty trays, sharing quiet conversation. Their helmets sat atop their table. They looked up to see Marseh and Anjali and, unbidden, they donned their helmets and left.

A human came out from the kitchen to bus the table.

Marseh directed Anjali to sit down, then he withdrew the other chair completely and put it aside. He fashioned his own illusion that he was sitting across from her, without having to modify his size to fit atop a too-small seat. The waiter tapped the table to bring up the menu. The surface doubled as a touchscreen.

"If nothing is to your satisfaction," Marseh said, "anything you desire can be prepared. We have significant acreage of farmland that produces food enough to feed the entire Confederation, and more."

Anjali frowned. "Such bounty . . . while billions of humans starve down below?"

"Don't exaggerate, Commander. The Allied population doesn't approach billions."

"But you see my point. You know people eat each other in the badlands. Probably in the unwalled cities, too . . . but we just don't hear about it."

"Yes, I know that cannibalism is rampant. It's the chief source of meat for the general population. Necessity has its demands."

Anjali scoffed, incredulous. "What necessity? You could feed everyone on the planet!"

"My dearest Commander Hastings, is it my obligation to feed my enemy? Were there no conflict, everyone could easily be sated."

She opened her mouth to speak but he held up his hand, silencing her retort.

"You are here as an instrument in my plan to feed *everyone*," he continued. "To dispense with the silly conflict that has created the nightmare you describe. Please refrain from browbeating me about ills of which I am thoroughly aware and that I am taking strides to remedy.

"Now, you said you were hungry. Will you order something? Or would you prefer that I do it for you?"

Anjali ordered for herself and sat quietly with a faraway look in her eyes.

"You're wounded," said Marseh.

She fixed her gaze on him.

"Your back," he added. "Those scars."

Marseh couldn't see them from his vantage, but he could sense them. His perception transcended three dimensions and lacked ocular constraint. If he directed his attention somewhere, the complete reality of that space was revealed. In human terms, he had a skill akin to X-ray vision.

Anjali thought to ask him how he knew, but let it go.

"What about them?" she asked of her scars.

"Let me take you to have them repaired, once you've finished your meal."

"No. I don't need to be *repaired*. I keep my scars."

"It is, though, rather miraculous that they should be so minor," he said, "after suffering a trauma so grave."

"How would you even know how *minor* they are?" she sneered.

"The corren who shot you was . . . thoroughly disciplined. He shot to kill, my dear. Yet you live. And I know why . . ."

"That's nice," Anjali replied, unamused and unwilling to play along.

"Would you care to know?"

"Either tell me or don't," she replied, crossing her arms and slouching.

They lapsed into silence. He felt there was little actual value in telling her that she had inherited some of Ray's nanomachines through intimate contact. Marseh sensed that she had something she wanted to say. He waited a moment to see if she would volunteer it but, when she did not, he prompted her.

"Please say what is bothering you; I'd like to address it."

"It's nothing," she replied.

"I apologize for the intrusion, but I can tell that you feel it quite acutely. To disregard it as nothing, and to refuse the invitation to speak of it, is irrational. So very human."

"Ah, there it is. I knew it wouldn't take long. Do you know how many times in my life I've heard 'human' as a slur?"

"I would imagine many. The correns know that it hurts you. It's why they say it."

"Right. Of course they do. And all of them are men. Just like Arak, and just like you. Where are the women in your Confederation? I've not encountered even one female soldier, never heard of a female governor or official. Where are your women?"

"Our military has no women," Marseh replied.

Anjali nodded her head, but not in acquiescence nor understanding; it was that her assessment had been affirmed, and she was not pleased.

"If you wish to harangue me about equality of the sexes," said Marseh, "I'll not stop you, but it will benefit neither of us."

"No?" Anjali replied. "You don't believe in the benefit of venting? You don't ever get angry about something and let somebody have it?"

"Why does it offend you so much?" Marseh asked.

"Why am I offended that your entire military is male?" She was beyond belief.

Marseh smiled his beatific smile. "I suppose you believe that women should have just as much right to kill as men? That to emulate males is the only way to be equal to them? Commander Hastings, please, I must confide something in you: we have no women in our military because we wish not to waste our women as casualties of war. Very few of even our human men serve. We don't explicitly prohibit them and, so, if they wish to serve they are permitted, but we do not press them into service nor do we encourage them. That is the purpose of correns.

"And, even still, human men are . . . and perhaps this is callous to say . . . quite replaceable—interchangeable, in the vast majority of cases—because one of them can impregnate many women. Thus, we require fewer of them. There are some men of such exceptional intelligence or physical hardiness that his genes are quite valuable, but once we've extracted those genes, we have little need of the man himself, unless we lose or corrupt his sample. And sometimes that does happen, yes, but it is rare.

"Since human men are so relatively few, they are somewhat more valuable than correns, but human women are by far our most precious commodity."

"Commodity . . ." Anjali repeated with distaste.

"We have very little need of parity in our society," Marseh continued, ignoring her displeasure at his choice of words. "Women require so much time to carry offspring, so we require many more of them than men to effectively perpetuate our Confederation and replenish the human race.

"It seems to me a waste of a perfectly good female to send her off to be killed on the field of battle because you confuse equivalence for equality. Over her lifetime, she could beget one dozen progeny, perhaps more. If she dies, she begets nothing. But, to lose a man—to lose even scores of men—is of such relatively little biological consequence that it is . . . effectively irrelevant."

Anjali looked into Marseh's blank white eyes, hunting his face for some sign of emotion, but she could find nothing. No malice, no glee. He might as well have been talking about the weather or something equally banal.

"Do you ever listen to yourself?" Anjali asked.

"I'm not burdened by crippling self-consciousness, Commander. I am having an objective discussion with you, about something in which you've expressed interest. Would it make you feel better for me to act more human toward you?"

"It always sounds like an insult."

"I don't intend it that way. However, I do find that your species prefers for everyone to behave just as you do amongst each other. You demand that your consorts mirror yourselves, and you disregard their predilections."

"Ugh. Spare me, please. I don't want to be analyzed by you. I also don't want to be simplified down to where my selfhood is irrelevant, compared to any other human. I need to believe I'm unique, okay? Individual and important. I need to believe in my own agency. Is that all right with you? Can you entertain that?"

"I can try."

Her mouth twisted with doubt.

"I appreciate the humility," she offered, though she didn't know if it were accurate to call it such. "And it pains me to admit this, but I'm . . . kind of fascinated by your . . . cold pragmatism."

She winced at the sound of her own words.

Marseh knew she had more to say but that she was ashamed to share it.

"Go on . . ."

She looked at him, a mixture of sadness and amusement in her big brown eyes. The corner of her mouth ticked down. "I can't say I view men—human men—as terribly special, either, so . . . I don't know why the way you talk about them offends me so much."

"Perhaps it is your nature to be combative," Marseh replied. "I believe that the value of the male depends upon the species. We breed corren males to fight. That is their purpose. Some of them transcend their purpose, become free-thinking, and, in those cases—if we can keep them—we incorporate them into our government, our sciences . . . into other parts of our society that are not the front lines of our military. Sadly, most correns who achieve true personhood choose to abscond to a life as A'arili . . . or Aktali, as Arak Matar would call them."

"And that surprises you?" Anjali blurted, thinking of Ray. "That you cultivate these men to be killing machines and, when they wake up to the horror of it, they don't graciously accept some less reprehensible position? I'm beginning to feel so foolish that I trusted you. Ray was right."

"And what did my erstwhile Avix Emera have to say . . . with which you now agree?"

"He said you couldn't be trusted. He said you *want* this war. If you don't, why has it persisted for so long? If one man stands in the way of your vision of peace, why rely on lowly *humans* from your enemy's army to eliminate him? You *obviously* have the power. Why inhibit it? Ray said you're setting us up to make a martyr out of the Butcher . . . to inspire—to inflame—your army of killing machines to finally wipe us out."

"And you believe him," said Marseh. It was not a question.

"I don't know what to believe."

"I admire your bravery, Anjali."

She looked at him. Until that moment, she had been unconsciously bold, overlooking the true power dynamic that existed between them. She had mistaken Marseh for an equal, but his remark—a compliment, a threat, or both—suddenly sobered her to the reality that she was sitting across a small table, alone in a room with the omnipotent architect of over two centuries of woe. Had she still felt emboldened, she would have continued speaking as before, but her voice clenched tight in her throat.

"What do you see when you look at me?" he asked.

Slowly, the muting grip on her voice relaxed. She felt that, if she wanted to answer, she could, but the question unsettled her enough that she wasn't sure she should.

"I would very much like to know," he prodded.

"I'm not sure I understand what you mean," she replied.

"Objectively. It's not a test. It's not a philosophical question. When you look at this table, I assume you see a table. It is dark gray. When you look at the bulkhead, you see a bulkhead. What do you see when you look at me?"

She threw up her hands and let them fall into her lap. A lock of hair fell across her face and she blew at it, then swept it away.

"I see a giant man. Your eyes are blank white. You appear humanoid, but there are superficial differences. You have no nose. If you have lips, they're indiscernible. Your ears are pointed. You seem to be hairless . . . which would indicate some kind of alopecia or that you're not a mammal. You have prominent bones on your face and head but, unlike a corren, yours are covered by skin. Is that enough for you, or should I go on?"

"You see a giant man," he said.

"Yes. If you want to distill all that down to one sentence, that does it."

"What if I told you that you see what you want to see?"

She blinked at him and clenched her fists.

"I am making you uncomfortable," he said.

"Yes," she replied. "By design, I imagine."

"No, Commander. I want you to feel comfortable. To feel welcome. At peace and at ease in this place that is now your home."

Her stomach clenched at the thought that she was now an exile, a traitor, a defector. She thought about her father and she wondered if he would even care.

"I wish you no harm," Marseh continued. "And I hope that you will come to accept that you've defected and that your old life is no longer available to you."

She exhaled in a sort of mirthless laugh. One sharp breath.

He stood up. "I want you to know one more thing."

She followed his movement with her eyes.

"You see a giant man who is physically imposing and characteristically fearsome because that is what commands your respect and motivates your compliance."

Her expression hardened and she glared at him.

"I'll leave you to eat in peace. Asharan Lután will retrieve you when you've finished."

With that, Marseh disappeared.

She looked around, surprised at how he vanished before her eyes. The waiter brought out her meal. She looked at him and tacitly asked if he had witnessed Marseh disappear. The man gave back a weak smile and said nothing as he set down the food.

Though her appetite had gone, she forced herself to eat.

***

Marseh appeared mere feet from where Shaula stood. Instinctively aware of his presence, she whirled around in fury.

"You're angry," said Marseh.

Shaula curled her upper lip. She was still dressed in her uniform from the raid, a translation collar sewn into the neck of her bodysuit.

"Yes, Darek. I am angry. I am *pissed*."

"And why?" he asked in the steady, benign tone with which he almost always spoke.

"Because Sargas was nowhere to be found! Because he was not there!"

"I believe you knew that would be likely. You knew that his mission demanded he move on."

"Then why even let me go! Why waste my time?"

"Was it a waste of time?"

"I could have been hurt! I could have lost the baby!"

"I believe that I and Lután both mentioned those risks to you, in advance of the mission, and yet you still demanded that you be allowed to participate."

"That does not matter!" She spiked her helmet on the ground of the artificially sustained paradise that was as much her prison as her home.

"Shaula. Your emotions have overridden your good judgment. I understand that you are angry, but I will not humor it. I'll leave you to calm yourself and, when you are ready, I'll return."

Before she could speak again, he was gone. She screamed in frustration. She stalked about before sitting down against the trunk of a tree. Her big gray cat loped over and lay down next to her. She put her hand on its head. It purred, eyes closed in contentment, passing that calm through Shaula's hand and spreading it throughout her body.

She thought of seeking out the other survivors from her homeworld but abstained. The mutual distrust predicated by millennia of conflict between the humans and the other sentient, anthropomorphic species could not be undone by ten years of relative peace on Overground. Distrust persisted even among the other humans Marseh had rescued from Lambda Scorpii. Variations in skin tone, eye and hair color, and their tribal affiliations had again become the paramount factors in socialization. Eons of progress, gone.

Shaula wanted détente. She believed that the other species did, too. Aside from the handful of humans—who might well prefer to die before breeding across ethnic lines—only the kangaroos and elephants had partners with whom to copulate. The other species were the lasts of their kinds. They resented Shaula for her pregnancy. They wouldn't deign to make the first move.

She looked at her cat. When he died, his species would be extinct.

Putting her hand on her belly, she thanked the stars for her baby. And for Sargas, wherever he was.

***

Marseh appeared in Lután's quarters. The corren gave no outward sign of being surprised, but it jarred him nonetheless.

The emperor's shows of power made Lután feel insignificant, which, surely, was the purpose. Each exhibition chipped away at his willingness to suffer the intrusions in silence.

"I apologize for intruding," Marseh said, reading Lután's annoyance. "I owe you more courtesy than that."

"I appreciate the apology, Lord, but I am your servant."

"An able servant," said Marseh. "Exceptional. And proud."

Lután looked at him.

"Pride can be a weakness," said Marseh.

Lután said nothing. He returned his attention to his notes.

Marseh walked over to the other side of the table and looked down at the touch-based surface.

"I'm composing the debriefing for the mission to retrieve Commander Hastings," Lután explained. "It was a spectacular success. The metrics recorded by our armor indicate we withstood well over a thousand rounds of projectile ammunition. The pulse-resistant armor suffered damage from the projectiles, but the body armor withstood every assault. If we can mass manufacture this, it's unlikely we'll lose another soldier in ground combat. Without significant heavy weaponry, the Allies could not defeat such armor."

"I believe you've proven that," Marseh replied.

"By my reckoning, we killed no one in retrieving the Commander."

"Delightful news. I need you to make a suit of our new armor, plate and a bodysuit, for Ms. Hastings. I want her fully protected. And armed."

Lután nodded but kept his eyes on Marseh.

"Yes, Lután?"

"What happens now, my Lord?"

"We will produce this armor for as many men as we have the resources and continue to improve it. But, soon, the Allies and our own homegrown nuisance will be of no consequence. Once Arak is out of the way, and we have tidied up the mess he leaves in his wake, we must focus our attention outward."

"Outward, Lord?"

"Yes, Lután," Marseh replied. "Our biggest threat is among the stars."

NINE

DEROVIAS AND THE others returned to their encampment on the fringes of Coventry. One crispy human corpse littered the ground where they had parked their jet-bikes.

The vehicles remained camouflaged, but the cloaking technology was not perfect; it bent light, allowing the shape of the object to be discovered by a keen eye. The charred remains were evidence of attempted theft. There had likely been multiple bandits, but the lone body meant he had touched the electrified vehicle first. His accomplices had scrambled.

Derovias held up his fist. The others halted. Alesh and Inishi were already alert, looking for any hint of an ambush even before they discovered the would-be thief. Kir, Ji'ilaad, Falco, Ceres, and Andrei all drew their weapons and took defensive stances.

Derovias held up one finger and made a circular motion. Alesh, Inishi, and Kir disbanded. They searched the immediate area for anyone lying in wait. Ji'ilaad, Falco, Ceres, and Andrei guarded Daedalus, Sargas, and René.

Moments later, the three correns returned.

"All clear," said Inishi.

"Well, that's a relief," Derovias replied. He smiled at his captives, showing his fangs. "We'll camp here. Tether the prisoners so they can't escape."

Ceres and Andrei set to tethering Daedalus, Sargas, and René.

As she tied Daedalus' legs and fixed him to the ground with a spiked eyelet, he sneered at her.

"Does it make you proud to do the Reds' dirty work, baby?"

"I bet your scalp would look a lot better hanging from my belt," she replied. "Keep talking and I'll cut off every part of you I can sell."

"Why don't you suck the best part of me?" he taunted.

Without another word, Ceres drew her knife and started slicing it across Daedalus' forehead, just below the hairline. Kir grabbed her hand and pulled her away. So stunned, Daedalus didn't cry out, nor even speak. He exhaled like a Lamaze student as he willed his thoughts away from the searing pain.

René looked at Daedalus and shook his head in disbelief.

"We want them intact," Kir warned Ceres.

"Then I suggest you tell him to shut his mouth," she replied, breaking free of Kir's grasp. She moved to Sargas and tethered him.

Blood oozed down Daedalus' forehead as he took note of Sargas' complicity. "You lose your shit in Orchard City but you're a little lamb here?"

Sargas shot him a bored expression.

At the same moment, Alesh took issue with the orders. "Camp?" he protested to Derovias. "It's barely three hours to Blackwing!"

Derovias looked Alesh in the eye. "Who's in charge of this mission?"

"What if I told you our Lord gave us different orders?" Alesh challenged.

"Then I'd say you're full of shit," Derovias replied.

"What if He told us that you couldn't be trusted?" Inishi added.

"What the fuck is this?" Derovias replied, secretly relishing the discord. He looked at Kir.

"Don't look at him," said Inishi. "He shouldn't even be alive, let alone in the field."

"Except that our Lord saw fit to let him live," said Derovias, "and to accompany us. Are you questioning His judgment?"

Inishi said nothing.

"Perhaps He questions His own judgment, and told us as much," said Alesh.

"Perhaps you both need to sit down before someone gets hurt," Derovias replied, sneering.

Alesh took a step toward Derovias, whose hand twitched over his holster.

"Will you be the one, brother?" Alesh taunted. "To kill one of his own?"

"Should I leave the honor to you instead?" Derovias jabbed. "How else should I take this dissent? Would you like a hug?"

Alesh smiled without humor and shook his head.

Ceres drew one of her swords and Andrei his pistol. They slowly circled behind Alesh and Inishi, the latter of whom stood a few paces back of his partner.

Falco inched toward Ji'ilaad. "What the hell are we supposed to do?"

Inishi turned so he and Alesh were back to back, the better to see Ceres and Andrei.

"Who do you suppose has the upper hand?" Derovias taunted.

"Falco," said Alesh without looking at him. "Kill this traitor."

Falco looked at Derovias, who replied with a smirk and a wink. Falco remained a statue.

"Ji'ilaad," said Alesh, "I overheard you and your human at the manor. I always thought you had a soft heart. But now I *know*. Kill these Aktali, and I shan't tell a soul about your betrayal."

Ji'ilaad drew his pistol.

Alesh smirked at Derovias. "You see, brother? You lose—!"

Ji'ilaad shot Alesh, wiping the smirk from his face. Surprise washed over his features. He staggered from the impact.

Ceres stepped toward him. Inishi lunged at her. Andrei intercepted Inishi, tackling him to the ground. Ceres stabbed Alesh through the back of the neck. She shoved the sword all the way to the hilt. He died instantly. She rued the mercy of it.

Andrei and Inishi wrestled. The human tried to slash the corren's throat, but Inishi was stronger. He rolled Andrei onto his back and turned the knife in the man's hand, forcing it downward into his chest. Andrei howled as the knife point pierced his skin. He resisted with all of his might, halting the blade, but not for long.

Kir grabbed the side of Inishi's helmet through the open visor and sliced his throat. Blood vomited from the gash, spattering Andrei's face. He cried out in disgust, clenching his eyes as he spit the coppery gore. Kir threw Inishi's lifeless body to the ground, walked a few paces, and staggered. He dropped to his knees. His knife fell from his hand. Derovias rushed over and knelt down, putting his hands on Kir's shoulders.

Kir wouldn't look up. He stared at nothing, in shock.

Derovias sidled closer and embraced him. Kir's arms dangled loosely at his sides.

"It's okay," said Derovias. "It's okay. It had to be done."

Ji'ilaad stood in a similar state of shock. He dropped his pistol and stared without focus. Falco touched his shoulder but Ji'ilaad shrugged him off.

Ceres wiped the blood from her blade and sheathed it. She walked over to Falco, who watched Derovias trying to console Kir.

"You know what I need after a good kill?" she asked.

Falco turned his attention to her. Her beautiful face was barely a foot away. He saw Carina. He blinked. With a shrug, he shook his head.

"A good fuck," Ceres replied, stepping into him. She slid her fingers into his waistband and tugged at his breeches, pulling him to her.

"I want you in me. Up against a wall, like a fucking animal."

She took his hand. He let her lead him away from the others.

Daedalus looked around but couldn't see what had transpired behind him. "What the fuck just happened?"

Slowly, the gash in his forehead was mending.

Sargas had been facing the fray. "Two of the centurions are dead. Killed by the others."

"Who's dead?"

"Ishtafan Alesh and Tolon Inishi."

Daedalus almost whooped with delight but quickly realized that Derovias still lived. He deduced that their predicament was hardly better.

Andrei retrieved some water from one of the bikes and splashed his face. Once he'd cleaned himself to his satisfaction, he looked around. "Where's Ceres?"

Everyone ignored him.

Long moments passed before she swaggered back into the camp all aglow, a wide smile on her face. Falco followed a few steps behind her. He looked blissful but ashamed.

Andrei walked up to her. "Where the fuck were you?"

She ignored him.

He put his hand on Falco's chest. "What do you think you're doing?"

"Leave him alone, Drei," Ceres warned.

Falco locked eyes with Andrei and straightened up. He refused to be bullied by the much taller man. Ceres smacked Andrei's hand away from Falco's chest. She pushed her estranged partner with both arms.

"I said 'leave him alone.'"

"You sweet on this twerp?" Andrei asked.

"Fuck you, Drei," Ceres responded. "Grow up. It's not your pussy. It's *my* pussy. Get it through your head."

"All of a sudden you're all over this asshole?" Andrei retorted.

"He's more of a man than you are," she said.

"Yeah fucking right," he objected. "This midget?"

She grabbed him by the lapels. "Keep talking. I'll cut your fucking tongue out so I never have to hear your stupid voice again. I'll cut it out *and* I'll cut off your balls, 'cause I'm so goddamned *sick* of you thinking with them."

She unhanded him.

"Oh, my," said Daedalus. "I like her."

"What the fuck did *I* do?" Andrei protested.

"Please!" Ceres replied putting her hand to her forehead. "*Please* . . . just shut up and walk away."

Andrei opened his mouth but no words came out. He closed it. He walked away.

Ceres walked over to Alesh's body and removed his helmet. She drew her knife and dug the blade into the forehead of the corren's corpse. She made quick work of it.

Derovias looked over his shoulder at her. "What are you doing?"

"I'm taking his scalp."

Derovias hurried to his feet and snatched her hand. Alesh's scalp dangled by a mere scrap of flesh.

"No. You're not."

"Don't touch me," Ceres said through clenched teeth. Her green eyes flashed with anger.

Derovias refused to relinquish her hand. "Drop the knife, Ceres." His voice was calm. His gaze didn't waver.

Indignant, she jutted her chin but dropped the knife.

Derovias unhanded her.

"You wanted him dead but won't let me take a prize," said Ceres.

"I didn't *want* him dead," said Derovias. "He *had to* die. There is a difference."

"Right. Tell yourself that. That absolves you," she replied.

"I don't expect you to see the nuance."

"Nor do you expect me to to be compensated, it seems," she said.

"You're on retainer *and* getting paid on delivery! You don't get to desecrate our brothers as a bonus!"

"Listen to yourself," said Ceres. "You enlisted us to kill your 'brothers' and you're wringing your hands about what we do to their husks."

"I don't expect you to understand."

"How could I? Nothing about you snakes makes any fucking sense."

TEN

MANON, JACK, AND Rozhenko approached the Coventry Flesh Market and were barred at one of the side entrances by two members of the Golden Horde. Each man wore a grubby yellow headscarf.

"Not happenin', missus," one of the guards said.

"My money spends just as well as anyone's," Manon objected.

"Maybe so, but you're trouble. Too famous for your own good. There's no gettin' in here for you, Manon. Not your big beasts, neither."

The other guard tensely gripped his electric pike. Only his eyes were visible, but they were wide and nervous in the hulking presences of Jack and Rozhenko.

"Okay," Manon conceded, holding up her hands.

The guards relaxed and she grabbed the nearest one by the top of his headscarf, pulling it down over his eyes and pulling his head down toward her knee. She drove her knee up into his jaw. His mandible shattered into countless pieces and his teeth cascaded from his mouth like pebbles.

Jack struck at the first glimmer of movement from Manon. He clapped his giant hands together around the other guard's head, crushing it.

Manon unwrapped the yellow scarf from her victim's head. His teeth plinked upon the Belgian-blocked street. She shoved her dagger into the back of his neck. Rozhenko stood stock still, surprised at the quickness and synergy of the woman and her machine. She wiped her dagger clean on the dead man's dark pants and sheathed it.

She smiled at Rozhenko. "Well, that was easy." Her tone was pleasant, almost elated.

"You might think the Horde were smart enough to have guards just inside the doors, too," said Jack. "But looks like these were it."

"Aside from us, who else are they really keeping away?" Manon replied. "Most people don't come to liberate the captives."

"And we couldn't be in the market to buy someone?" Jack mock objected.

"Our sterling reputations precede us, darling."

"Yes, yes, this is all being wonderful," Rozhenko interrupted, "but what now are we doing?"

She looked at the scarf in her hand, wet with the blood from her victim's mouth where he had bitten off part of his tongue. She shook the last couple teeth from the kaffiyeh and handed it to Rozhenko. He held it with distaste. Sloughing her swords from her back, she handed them to Jack. She stripped the mercenary of his loose-fitting tunic and put it on over her light armor.

"What are you doing?" asked Rozhenko.

"I'm going to pretend to be a man," she said.

"I am thinking you will be failing at this," said Rozhenko.

"I think I can pull it off; I've got small boobs. My armor makes me look bulky."

"But that waist . . . and," Rozhenko blushed, "your bottom. I am never confusing you for man."

Manon looked at Jack. "He's sweet. Why don't you ever talk to me like that?"

She put on the man's trousers and cinched the belt enough to keep them up. She turned her back toward Rozhenko.

"Do these pants hide my bottom, Vasily?"

Rozhenko blushed again. "Your bottom is . . . less obvious, yes. But you still have shape of woman."

"Yes, *we* know she's a woman," Jack said, his tone as close to exasperated as it would ever get. "But not all men look like you. Some are smaller, more delicate, with waists and . . . bottoms. I think she can pass, at least for a time." Jack looked at her. "Just don't be wagging that ass the way you usually do."

Manon put her hand to her collarbone and feigned offense.

"And don't open your mouth," Jack continued, "because no one is going to mistake your voice for a man's."

"People always tell me I have a deep voice," Manon replied. "Kind of husky."

"Yes. Deep, husky . . . for a woman," Jack replied. "But sexy, and feminine. Like Lauren Bacall."

"See, you *can* be sweet," said Manon.

"Who is Lauren Bacall?" Rozhenko asked.

Manon shook her head. "Don't ask that question. *Jacques est . . . très vieux.*"

Rozhenko didn't understand.

She shook her head and smiled. "He's *very* old."

She took the bloodstained yellow headscarf from Rozhenko and wrapped it around her head, hiding the blood in the folds, away from her face.

Jack picked up his victim with one hand and threw the dead man onto the roof of the building across the narrow alley. A trail of blood arced behind the body. The android then lobbed the other corpse.

"You are quite strong," Rozhenko remarked.

"I'm sure you could do the same," Jack replied.

Manon pulled the scarf down to expose her mouth. "You two are the guards now."

"And we'll be sure to kill anyone who tries to come in or out," Jack stated. "Except you, of course."

"Of course," she said, smiling.

She pulled the kaffiyeh over her mouth and went inside.

ELEVEN

THE ALLIES SURVEYED the vehicles in the armory and settled on five jet-bikes. Ray and Macaluso each got their own. They were the largest and heaviest members of the group, too heavy to ride with anyone else. Carina and Sotillo each got to drive, as the two next-biggest people in the party. Gardiner and Patrick, the two lightest soldiers, would ride behind Carina and Sotillo, respectively. Milner climbed onto the fifth bike, behind Gray.

Before the Overground raid, Patrick had never seen combat. Had never killed a man. The one corren he dropped in Orchard City hardly left an impression because he wasn't human. It made it easier. That bothered him.

Growing up in Klippeborg, as orderly a city as existed in the Allied Nations because it revolved around the stable military base, Patrick had never seen more than the occasional fistfight. Nor had he heard of more than the odd single or double homicide. It wasn't until the melee incited by Major Gardiner in the Coventry encampment that Patrick had truly witnessed death as violent, chaotic, grisly mayhem.

Of the hundreds of men who had opposed the Allies' entrance to the armory, only a handful still stood. The dead lay strewn about the bridge and the land beyond the moat, as well as in the shallow, fetid water. Many of the corpses were mangled and dismembered. In the span of a day, Patrick had seen more blood and bones, brains, and entrails than in all of his prior years. It was more than enough to last him the rest of his life.

The carnage made Patrick queasy. He tried to banish the images from his mind, but closing his eyes just brought other horrors to his mind's eye. The images flipped through his mind like an inexhaustible slideshow of death. It was almost funny, in its absurdity, and the corporal laughed. His laughter carried over the comm.

"What's so funny, shithead?" Sotillo replied.

"Cut the chatter," Gardiner ordered.

The Allies approached the foothills of the Hugtaender i Nord and slowed to a stop. They had two routes at their disposal: the coastal road along Broad's Bay or the mountain pass through the dubiously named Plasma Fields.

"What's the plan, boss?" asked Macaluso over the comm.

Gardiner was silent for a moment. "When have the Reds not guarded the coastal road?" he asked.

"Never," Ray replied. "There's no way to the Northern Base except through the Fangs."

"We can't take our bikes through there," Gardiner replied.

"I'm not sure about that," said Ray. "The gas isn't constant. We could make it all the way through and never pass through a curtain."

"There's nothing worse than constant gas," Sotillo interjected.

"Shut up, Lieutenant," Gardiner warned.

"Well, what if a curtain or a jet blows out right as we're riding over it?" Macaluso asked. He mimicked the sound of an explosion. "See ya."

"We'll have to turn off our weapons," said Patrick. "And we'll have to move real slow on the bikes to avoid . . . well, boom."

"It's still faster than we'd move on foot," said Gardiner, "and faster than going nowhere. Gray, take the lead. Sotillo, you follow. Keep at least one length behind. Then Macaluso, then Ray. The captain and I will bring up the rear. Move out."

TWELVE

ARAK STALKED THE bridge of his ship. He refused to sit.

Intiri guided the vessel out of the Blackwing spaceport and set course for Overground.

"My Lord, our flight plan has not been approved," said Irva'a. "We will not be allowed to dock . . ."

Arak put up his hand. Irva'a shut his mouth.

"When within range, emit an open broadcast," Arak ordered. "Our people man the hangars. They will receive us, even if Marseh forbids it."

"What's to stop him from shooting us out of the sky?" asked Intiri.

"Utter chaos," Arak replied.

***

Lután rushed through the corridors toward Marseh's chambers but was intercepted before he arrived. Marseh appeared and Lután came to an abrupt halt.

"My Lord, Governor Arak is requesting permission to dock. He's left the planet."

A wave of expressions crashed over Marseh's typically placid face. "Dammit! Dammit to hell and back again."

Lután had never seen Marseh be anything but calm. Even the mild outburst of dismay was unsettling.

"What are we supposed to do?" the paladin asked.

"Deny him access," Marseh replied, having gathered himself.

"We have, but he's not going to turn around. We've secured his private hangar, but he'll find a willing port manned by his loyalists." Lután tried to conquer his anxiety. He managed it well.

"Calm, my boy," said Marseh, returning to his typical soothing manner. "This was bound to happen. Block all communication to the planet. Lock down every part of the station we control."

Lután nodded. "And Arak Matar, Lord?"

Marseh looked down at him. "When a man takes up arms against you, Lután, he is not your brother anymore. Go. We waste time prattling. Shore up our position. We'll take him quietly when he lands."

Lután ran off, chattering into his comm to his commanders and lieutenants.

Marseh turned to find Reyevas standing before him.

"Exciting, no?" Reyevas taunted.

"Will my performance on this test go into your report, Reyevas?" Marseh asked tartly, walking past him.

"Oh, certainly. This is where we discern if your management skills are up to snuff. Can you weed out dissension and maintain order? Or will you be bettered by the N'horr? It would be tragic if you were. We've *never* fallen to a lesser species."

"Either make yourself useful to me or begone, you ass. I don't need you poisoning my ears."

Reyevas vanished as suddenly as he appeared.

THIRTEEN

MANON SLIPPED BACK through the door and into the alleyway. She was alone.

"Where is boy?" Rozhenko demanded.

"I can't get to him," she admitted. "Too many unfriendlies in there. I can't kill hundreds of people without attracting attention, you know."

"So, what? You give up?" Rozhenko said, distressed.

"I didn't say that. Come with me."

She headed back to the main street, unraveling the scarf from her head as she walked. She discarded it and then pulled off the tunic as she moved. She stopped to ditch the trousers and took back her swords from Jack.

"We need to separate, so we don't draw as much attention."

"What is happening to boy?" Rozhenko prodded.

"Just sold. The party that bought him wasn't large. We wait for them to leave. We stalk and ambush them and rescue him. If they're not local, the only place it makes sense to go is Whiton's Heath. Jack and I'll take the northern intersection. You watch the southern route, just in case. Signal us if they come your way."

"How I am doing this?"

Jack stood close to Rozhenko and the cyborg's built-in radio array tuned to the signal emitted by the android.

"There," said Jack. "We're linked. Just like a helmet comm. Just talk to yourself and you'll be talking to me."

Jack went ahead. The guards at the main entrance to the flesh market watched him lumber past, covered by his huge cloak. They gripped their weapons a little more tightly. Manon waited, watching the market. The men who purchased Adnan walked out with him in tow. She ducked back down the alley and parkoured to the roof, creeping along the tops of the buildings with her eyes on her quarry.

"They're coming my way, Roz, come north," Jack signaled.

As the men approached, Jack stepped into their path still swaddled in his cloak. The men halted in the street. One of them yanked Adnan's chain.

"Kill this fool," the leader ordered, jerking his head at Jack.

The man had a scar that ran from the receding hairline of his scalp down the side of his face to his chin. The left side of his visage looked slightly off. His attacker had peeled the face away from the skull. Whoever reattached it had botched the job.

Before the men could act, Manon leapt from the roof. She drove both feet into the one holding the chain. His spine broke audibly. She rode him to the ground, striking down another slaver with her sword as she went.

As the first man's body crashed upon the pavement, she sprung from his back, twisting in midair. She landed on her feet facing the man with the scar. He reached for his pistol and she sliced off both of his hands before he could draw. The sound that escaped his mouth was like someone trying to sneeze. He beheld his stumps in horror.

The remaining slaver shakily raised his gun, trying to aim it at Manon.

Rozhenko ran toward the fray. He leapt, closing the last fifty meters between him and the gunman. He crashed to the pavement, scattering the cobbles and bitumen. He shoved the man from behind with both hands. The gun flew from the slaver's hands. The man somersaulted thrice before coming to a halt.

Manon cut the scar-faced, handless man's throat. She pushed his dying body to the ground. She approached whom Rozhenko had shoved. The street had flayed him. His arm was broken in two places, his left leg bent at an impossible angle. He mewled to himself as she crouched next to him.

"How'd you guys get here?" she asked.

He continued to whimper.

She smacked him. "I'm talking to you, shitheel. Talk back and you can live. Would you like that? To live? All your friends are dead."

He made a sound as if trying to stop sniveling.

"You gonna talk to me?" she asked.

He nodded, afraid to look up.

"How did you get here?" she repeated.

"Hot rod. Corner of Grady and Christopher . . ."
"Do you have the keys?"
"No. Crash has them. He drove."
She assumed the man with the scar had been Crash. The leader. She looked back at her blubbering victim. "You let a guy named 'Crash' drive you here?" She smacked him again.

Jack walked over to Crash, who still hadn't died. He resembled a beached fish as the last squirts of blood escaped from his slit throat. He watched with desperate eyes, trying and failing to breathe as Jack patted him down and procured a set of car keys.

"Combustion engine," he remarked, returning to Manon. "Let's hope it's got enough gas to get us there."

Rozhenko broke the chains between Adnan's hands and feet.

"You are unhurt?" Rozhenko asked.

Adnan shrugged.

Manon rose to her feet and took a step away from the broken man.

"Wait," he called. He tried to crawl, vainly clutching with his one good hand at the street. "You said you'd let me live."

"I *am* letting you live," Manon replied. "What happens to you now isn't my problem."

FOURTEEN

GARDINER AND HIS party made easy progress through the winding switchback roads of the foothills until they reached the Plasma Fields frontier. They slowed to a stuttering pace, navigating around plumes of volatile gas, waiting for impassable curtains to dissipate before they could proceed.

They left the piedmont behind and continued through the mountains. Seconds passed like hours as they inched along, winding farther into the Hugtaender i Nord. After a long while, Private Gray came to a halt at the bottom of a man-made bluff in which heavy doors had been installed.

"Major, we've come upon some kind of facility," Gray reported.

"Halt there," Gardiner ordered.

He and Carina dismounted and walked to the point of their small column of soldiers. Milner and Gray awaited them outside of the impressive, obviously thick metal doorway. It was devoid of insignia.

"Fascinating as this is," Ray stated, "we don't have time to investigate. We need to reach Klippeborg, and the sooner, the better."

"He's right, sir," said Carina.

Gardiner nodded. "Mount up, then; let's keep it moving." He took note of the location's coordinates in his heads-up display. He would put it in his report.

Milner and Gray got back on their bike and the rest of the group crawled behind them. They traced the long-neglected mountain pass, skirting the bluff to its promontory, then continuing around a blind curve.

Arak Matar's centurions, Mag'err and Skru'ul, lay in wait higher up the peak. When dispatched from Blackwing, they headed directly for the mountain pass to complement coverage of the coastal road. They had waited and waited, and would have waited days more, but their patience was at last rewarded.

As Gray guided his bike around the curve, he couldn't see the curtain of gas emitting from the facility deep within the mountain, but Skru'ul saw both it and the Allies' approach.

He dropped a grenade onto the pass.

The gas curtain came into view. Gray jerked his bike to a halt, just missing the threat, but the grenade struck true. It exploded, igniting the gas, blasting Gray and Milner backward. Both men howled at an inhuman pitch. The heat melted their armor, fusing it to their molten skin.

Mag'err took aim at Macaluso and shot him square in the chest. The exo-frame defrayed the damage, but the blast knocked the big man from his bike. He fell over the lip of the bluff, hitting the ground in front of the facility doors. He rolled flush against them as his bike came crashing down, just missing him. It rolled over the lip of the path and tumbled down the mountainside.

Ray and Carina leapt from their bikes. He grabbed Gray by the cool back collar of his breastplate. She took hold of Milner. They dragged the wounded men down the path to the relative safety of the bluff.

Skru'ul lobbed another grenade. It bounced between Ray and Carina and careened down the mountain before exploding in the distance. Mag'err lined up Carina in his sights and struck her in the back. She tumbled over the precipice, still dragging the heavier Milner. He landed on his head and she landed on top of him, snapping his neck. His body went slack. Her exo-suit absorbed the blast and shielded her fall.

Macaluso sat up as they struck the ground next to him.

Ray gathered Gray into his arms and jumped over the edge of the bluff, out of Mag'err's sight line. Landing on his feet, Ray rolled, tucking Gray close, absorbing the impact of the fall. He felt the temperature of his own armor rising as the heat transferred from the private.

Gardiner and Sotillo ran down the pass. A grenade skittered in front of them and bounced off the lip opposite the bluff. It popped right in front of Sotillo's face. He grabbed it in midair and threw it back to sender. It exploded. Skru'ul and Mag'err took cover, saved only by luck.

Rock, dirt, and shrapnel rained down on Confederates and Allies alike.

"Report!" Gardiner yelled over the comm.

"Milner's dead," Carina replied.

The others checked in, except Gray, who was unconscious from shock.

"Gray's alive," Ray added. "Barely."

Gardiner stood in front of the facility doors. He tried envisioning them open, but they wouldn't budge.

Ray placed Gray on the ground.

Gardiner tried to see how the door operated and was confounded that he couldn't throw the switch. He began to panic until, through no effort of his own, the doors parted about two inches. He tried telekinetically forcing them farther but, to his frustration, found that he couldn't.

"Sotillo!" he yelled into the comm. "Duvais, Macaluso, A'arilon, get these fucking doors open or we're toast. Patrick, get in there!"

A hail of grenades came spilling over the bluff. In desperate instinct, Gardiner telekinetically swatted them away. The explosives soared back in the direction they'd come and detonated in spectacular fashion, raining metal and debris. He tried to dispel the shrapnel but couldn't thwart it all. Smaller fragments plinked off the harried Allies. Some of the larger pieces lodged into their armor.

Out of grenades, the centurions left their perch to stalk their prey down the mountain pass.

Carina, Macaluso, Sotillo, and Ray pulled on the doors. Gears whined as they forced them apart until Patrick was able to squeeze through into the dark antechamber beyond. Just inside, he found a wheel and cranked it. The doors opened yet wider. Carina dragged Gray's unconscious body into the facility. Ray, Sotillo, and Macaluso followed.

Gardiner brought up the rear. "Seal us in," he hissed.

Patrick cranked the wheel back the other way.

Through the sliver between the closing doors, Ray saw Mag'err with his rifle raised and ready.

"Get clear!" Ray yelled.

Everyone dispersed to either side of the aperture as Mag'err unleashed a barrage of blaster fire. Most of the blue flashes impotently struck the door, but a few ripped through. They struck the inner wall, leaving blackened scorch marks.

Patrick cranked the wheel one more time and the gap closed.

Skru'ul howled at the barrier. He picked up Milner's corpse and threw it from the precipice.

Inside the facility, Carina looked at Gray. The front of his armor had melted and fused with his skin. He looked like a used candle. His breaths came shallow and ragged.

"All of my medical supplies were on my bike!" she lamented.

"No way he survives," Sotillo said. "Might as well kill him now."

"We're not killing anyone," Gardiner snapped. "Whatever this place is, maybe it has a medical bay."

Patrick looked around. Etched into the wall was a logo above which it read "Artel Industries." Beneath the insignia it said: "Hugtaender Facility." Below that: "Dorance Corporation."

"Dorance. Huh," Patrick said, reading the etching. "Like our building in OC. Guy had a thing for bunkers."

"Who doesn't enjoy a nice hole?" Sotillo replied.

Silence.

The room was small and spartan, just big enough to hold them and a few more. Derelict machinery and computer terminals lined the walls perpendicular to the doorway. Patrick fiddled with the machines but couldn't bring them to life.

"Looks like the power is out."

"Which reminds me," Macaluso said, powering up his weapon.

"Wait!" Patrick blurted, but nothing happened. The air was clear.

"Relax," said Macaluso.

The others reactivated their firearms.

Opposite the doors was a lift shaft leading downward. Carina leaned over the edge of the shaftway and peered down, using her visor's night vision. She saw an unenclosed platform.

"The lift is about 150 meters down," she said. "There's a hole in it. One of the floor panels was removed. The shaft goes even deeper than that."

"So I keep trying to tell you," Sotillo said.

"For the last time, knock it off, Lieutenant," Gardiner ordered.

"If there's a med bay, it's down there," said Carina. She scooped Gray into her arms, the exo-suit made him feather-light. She jumped into the shaft.

"Wait! Carina!" Gardiner exclaimed, but too late.

She plummeted to the waiting platform, firing the thrusters in her boots to slow her descent. Landing like a mote of dust, she placed Gray upon the surface.

Above, Gardiner couldn't contain his annoyance. "Goddamn it, Carina," he said over the comm.

"I'm going to investigate, sir," she replied. "I'll relay what I find farther down."

"No, Captain. Wait there. I don't want us—" he was cut off by the alert that she had muted her comm. "Mac, get down there. Take Patrick."

Carina pulled up another panel on the lift so that she could fit the bulk of her exo-suit through the space.

"Sorry, Al," she said to Gray's unconscious form. "I'll come back for you."

Beneath the platform, she grabbed hold of the ladder that ran the height of the shaft. She slid down with her hands and feet against the rails.

Macaluso looked over the lip and saw that Carina had left Gray behind. The big man grabbed Patrick as if he were weightless and jumped down the shaft. His landing was far less graceful than Carina's, using no thrusters to avoid further burning Gray. Macaluso's exo-suit boots clanged against the corrugated steel, buckling it. He unhanded Patrick, who almost fell in the hole.

Patrick staggered against the railing, holding on for dear life. He glowered at Macaluso and waited for his stomach to drop back down from his throat.

"You could have warned me."

Macaluso ignored him.

"I almost fell down that fucking hole!" Patrick protested.

Macaluso slid up his visor and frowned. "But you didn't."

He knelt down and peeked his head through the platform. Carina was already gone from view. He stood up and looked at the hole. He couldn't fit through it but, if he pulled up any more of the floor, the others wouldn't have anywhere to stand.

Gardiner, Ray, and Sotillo were climbing down the ladder to meet the lift.

"Major, she's still on the move," Macaluso reported.

"I'll go after her," Patrick replied. "Maybe I can get the lift working, if there's an access point down there with some juice."

"So long as you don't need my legs again," said Macaluso warily.

"Go ahead, Corporal," Gardiner replied over the comm.

Patrick sat on the lip of the opening. He held out one hand to Macaluso, who took it and fed him through the hole.

Patrick grasped at the ladder. "I got it."

Macaluso let go and Patrick slid to the bottom in the same manner as Carina. When he touched down, there was only one direction to look. He saw her standing about twenty meters away. He flipped up his visor.

"Captain."

She swatted at the air, urging him to be quiet. She turned and strode over to him, flipping up her visor to reveal an annoyed scowl.

"We don't know what's down here," she said quietly. "Don't go shouting like we're in your home."

"I wasn't shouting . . ." Patrick complained, wilting at her displeasure.

"Come on," she urged. She slid down her visor and opened a private channel between them. "Close your visor and be vigilant."

With a series of ocular commands to his visor's heads-up display, Patrick kept his public channel open so his conversation with Carina would be relayed to Gardiner and the others. He set his comm to mute the mic during incoming chatter, so she wouldn't be wise to his betrayal. He didn't understand why she was going rogue, and he refused to be complicit.

"This place is completely defunct," she said, looking around.

"Carina, hold your position," Gardiner ordered, hearing her voice over his comm.

Patrick muted the private channel to Carina. "Sir, she's not on our channel. I'm relaying her to you. Over."

"Fine, I copy," Gardiner replied. "Keep an eye on her. Try and keep her from doing anything stupid. We're coming down. Over."

"Copy that," Patrick replied. "Over and out."

He and Carina walked in silence, passing doors on either side of the hallway, each of them emblazoned with the "Artel Industries" and "Dorance Corporation" standards, and a label denoting their specific purpose: "Custodial Services," "Administration," and other mundane things. The hallway ended at a set of visibly heavier metal doors, which read "Robotics Division." Immediately to their right was a less substantial doorway.

Patrick read its label aloud. "'Mechanical Closet.' If I can get in here, maybe that'll help." He looked at controls for the door. "Weird. The sensor is on the right side." He looked at all the other doors. "They all are."

"How do you plan to get in there?" Carina replied, ignoring his commentary.

Patrick flipped up his visor. "You said this place is defunct. It's not." He stood. He looked up and to the right and then left.

Carina shook her head. "What are you doing?"

"Hear that?" Patrick asked.

Carina flipped up her visor and concentrated. "I don't hear anything."

"But you can breathe. Easily. The air is cool. It should be close and stuffy, but it's not. It's circulating. This place is active, but . . . I guess just the auxiliary systems."

They heard the sound of booted footfalls upon the grated metal floor, followed by a loud thump back by the lift. Gardiner, Ray, and Sotillo materialized from the darkness. Macaluso showed up moments later, announced by the mechanized whir of his exoskeletal legs and the heavy tread of his metal boots. He carried Private Gray.

"Report," Gardiner ordered Carina. He was testy.

"What you see is what you get, Major," Carina replied.

"Don't be flippant with me, Captain. You disobeyed a direct order, and for nothing. Undermine me again, and it's your ass when we hit Klippeborg."

Carina said nothing. She flipped down her opaque visor and rolled her eyes.

"We need to stick together," he continued. "None of us know where the fuck we are. We can't be wandering. We need to be smart."

Macaluso wanted to prop Gray in a seated position against the wall, but the private's armor had cooled into a sarcophagus and he could only be placed upon the floor. Worried that the man couldn't breathe, Macaluso broke open Gray's visor, the only part of the armor that had withstood the heat. His face was unburned.

"It looks like the place is dead, but there's power," Patrick said. "I just need a terminal and . . . I think I can wake this baby up."

Gardiner made his visor transparent, rather than flipping it up. Patrick blanched slightly at the sight of the major's scarred face, even partially obscured.

"Don't get too ahead of yourself, Corporal," Gardiner replied. "We don't know what this place is. We don't want to be flipping switches."

"Flip . . . my switch," Sotillo sang out.

Gardiner shot him a look, accompanied by a telekinetic assault. Sotillo felt his airway constrict. He put his hand to his throat and fought for air. His pathetic wheezing carried over the comm.

"With respect, sir," Patrick said to Gardiner, distracting him from Sotillo. "We kind of do."

The lieutenant gasped. He flipped up his visor and sucked air. Macaluso glanced at him with a face that said, *What the fuck is your problem?* but no one offered any care or concern.

"We all came from the Dorance facility in Orchard," Patrick continued. "And a lot of our gear has components stamped with this Artel Industries logo. Our computers, our guns, the exo-suits . . . It's obviously some kind of tech outfit, probably from before the Blight."

Gardiner looked at Carina and then at Macaluso.

"Everything we use is pre-Blight tech," said Patrick. "I mean, some of it's been modified, augmented, reverse-engineered, improved upon—"

"Get to the point, Paddy," Macaluso growled.

"But everything we use is what they used 183 years ago. Or more."

"This is a dictatorship, Corporal," Gardiner said. "You don't get a vote. We need to tread with caution because we don't know what's in here. Just because the captain and Mac, here, have some brand name stamped on their asses doesn't mean we're among friends."

Macaluso dipped his hips to the left and looked under his right arm, trying to peer at his own buttocks.

Carina considered the big doors that read "Robotics Division." The sensor panel looked like those in the Dorance base, back in Orchard City. She waved her right hand at it, grateful that, for once, she didn't have to reach across her body to do so. The controls whirred to life.

"Dammit, Carina!" Gardiner barked.

Lights along the floor and ceiling of the corridor flickered on. Ray, Gardiner, Macaluso, and Sotillo drew their weapons.

The doors chimed and opened, revealing another lift.

"Hello, Karin," said a disembodied male voice.

Carina found it oddly familiar but couldn't place it.

"Please, come down," the voice urged. "Bring your friends."

She looked over her shoulder at Gardiner. He couldn't hide his confusion and distress.

"You can put away your weapons," the voice said.

Carina still couldn't place it, but it evoked memories of Manon.

"If I meant you harm," it offered, "you'd already be dead."

Reluctantly, Gardiner holstered his pistol. The rest followed suit. Carina walked into the lift and the others followed. The doors closed. The platform descended.

FIFTEEN

LUTÁN REQUESTED ENTRY to Anjali's quarters. The door opened and he stepped into the sparse room. The meager furnishings were for utility, without frill or ostentation. She stood near her bed, the impression of her seat still visible upon its surface.

He hefted three parcels, two in his right hand and one in his left.

"What's this?" she asked.

"A gift from our Lord," Lután replied.

She looked at him, dubious. "He may be your Lord, but don't try and pull me in. I'm not worshiping anybody. Does he make you call him that?"

Lutún was nonplussed. "He is our Lord."

Anjali scoffed and shook her head. "So, what's this 'gift'?"

Lután bid her to take one of the parcels from his right hand. She set it on the bed and opened it, pulling out a black bodysuit textured with a strange pattern and trimmed with yellow piping. She looked at him and he handed her the package in his left hand. Inside, she found a helmet, boots, and gloves. In the third and largest package, she withdrew pieces of plate armor.

"What is all this?" she asked.

"I believe it's self-evident," Lután replied, sliding a pulse rifle from his back. He handed it to her.

"Don't be an ass, Lután," she said, taking the rifle. "Why are you giving this to me?"

"It's superior armor. It's what we wore when we rescued you."

"Rescued me?" she said. "Kidnapped is more like it."

"Have you been treated poorly?" asked Lután.

"No," she replied.

"Then—"

"Just because you're treating me well doesn't mean I'm not your hostage."

"Lieutenant Commander, you are our guest. Please accept these gifts. I highly recommend you wear them immediately."

"Why? What's going to happen?"

Lután turned his back and walked to the door.

"Hey, answer me when I talk to you, dammit."

He turned to face her. He was not amused. "Arak Matar has returned to the station. Put on the armor, Anjali. Marseh wants you alive."

SIXTEEN

DEEP WITHIN THE hidden mountain facility, the lift stopped its descent and another set of heavy doors opened before the Allies.

"Right this way, Captain Duvais," beckoned the familiar-but-unplaceable male voice. "Follow the corridor to its end."

"Who are you?" Gardiner demanded.

"A friend," the voice replied.

Gardiner shook his head. "I don't like this one bit."

"We have nowhere else to go," Carina replied.

They followed the dogleg corridor to its end. Another set of doors opened for them, revealing a large bay full of manufacturing equipment, cables and tools, computers and monitors. Technology outfitted nearly every bit of space and, where it didn't, stark industrial piping and bulkheads showed through.

A figure stirred in the depths of the huge space, hidden in shadow. The hulking male form moved into the lane perpendicular to the doorway and the Allies froze in their tracks. As the figure walked into the light, Carina could see it was a robot.

Recognition flitted across her features. "How did you get here?"

"You know who . . . what this is—?" said Gardiner.

"I'm not the one that you know," the robot replied to Carina. "But I'm . . . similar."

"Could you please explain what the fuck is going on?" Gardiner barked, flipping up his visor. "Captain?"

The robot continued toward them, past the rows of tools and machinery, mechanical body parts in various states of repair. Gardiner tentatively reached for his pistol.

"No need for violence," the robot stated, holding up its hands in a pacifist gesture. Very slowly, it indicated with its right hand that it would like to get closer.

Gardiner's right hand twitched above his pistol, but he kept it holstered. The robot slowly reached toward the human's left hand. A flood of distasteful feelings washed over Gardiner. Frustration, confusion, fear, anger. But he mastered them. He stood still as the large android waved its hand and read the chip implanted in the major's skin.

"Gardiner, Maksim Ivanovic," the robot stated. "Major. Dorance Facility, Orchard City, Nova Spes. 1.8542 meters, 82 kilograms. Blood type A."

Gardiner curled his mangled lips into his trademark menacing sneer. "How do you know that?"

"I invented the chips you use to store your credentials," the robot replied.

"You . . . invented them," Ray repeated.

"Well," the robot allowed, "I had a hand in it. And perhaps not me, specifically. The source of my consciousness is the man responsible."

"Is anyone else sick of this shit?" Sotillo blurted. He paused, but no choke followed his outburst. "Who the fuck *are* you, man? You got a name, Mr. Robot, sir?"

"Jack Mason," the robot replied.

"You *are* Manon's robot," said Carina.

"Non, Karin. Je ne suis pas *ce* 'Jack.' Je suis un autre modele," *I am not* that *Jack.*

"If you're a different model, how do you know who I am?" she asked in French.

"The one you know is the principal," Not-Jack answered in English. "He's out in the world, living for the rest of us . . . "

"You mean there are *more* of you?" Patrick asked.

Not-Jack ignored him. "At irregular periods, Jack uploads his consciousness and we download it."

"We?" said Macaluso, looking around.

Not-Jack paid the interruption no mind. "We are . . . slightly out-of-sync copies of each other. His last upload was over a month ago. I know you as 'Duvais, Karin Marie. Lieutenant.' But when you waved your chip in front of the lift's controls, it allowed me to update and correct your rank. Congratulations on your recent promotion."

Carina shrugged.

"What the fuck is this place?" Sotillo asked.

"Cannot this one read, Captain?" Not-Jack asked Carina.

"No," she replied. "He's illiterate. An imbecile, really."

"Fuck you both very much," Sotillo replied.

"Do you have a medical facility?" Carina asked Not-Jack.

"We have . . . a Consciousness Transfer Room," Not-Jack replied. "It is the closest thing to an OR, but we deal there in relieving flesh of its life and granting immortality to the mind. We don't have much in the way of . . . recuperative miscellanea. Painkillers, perhaps. But no balms, no salves. No . . . medicine."

Carina turned to Macaluso. "Corporal . . . where's Private Gray?"

His face flickered with embarrassment. "Um . . . he's upstairs. We left him there. Sir."

Carina looked annoyed. "We?"

"I put him down and forgot about him," he admitted.

"If you hadn't gone off on your own, we wouldn't have scrambled after you," Gardiner stated. "You put everyone out of sorts. It's not like he's going to get any worse."

"He could regain consciousness," Carina retorted. "In which case, he'll be in excruciating pain."

"And what can we do about that?" Gardiner replied. "We have no way to induce unconsciousness . . . or do you suggest we physically knock out an already wounded man?"

"We can induce unconsciousness," Not-Jack interrupted.

"We need to get him now," Carina insisted. "The longer we wait, the more likely he'll wake."

"I'll send someone to retrieve him," said Not-Jack. "Shall I have him brought to the CTR?"

Carina made a face. "CTR?"

"Consciousness Transfer Room," Not-Jack clarified.

"Oh," she replied. "Yes. Please."

SEVENTEEN

NOT-JACK SET PRIVATE Gray atop the operating table.

Carina wore a lab coat over her street clothes. She had removed her exo-suit for better mobility so she could administer care. At Not-Jack's insistence, so too had she removed—very reluctantly—her shoulder holster and gun belt. She piled them atop her leather jacket on the counter. Her knife, though, remained on her belt. She refused to be completely unarmed.

The operating theater looked like any other room in which she might conduct surgery. It was clean and spare. The one oddity was a severed android head that sat in the corner with wires streaming from its neck. Unlike Jack and Not-Jack, the disembodied head had been made to look human, though it fell shy of the mark. Like the robots, the head was male.

Carina wondered if the maker, this Jack Mason, who saw fit to copy himself more than once, was willfully or unconsciously sexist. But, with her next thought, she decided there was something comforting in that he hadn't—at least, not to her knowledge—made a legion of voluptuous female sexbots.

The human-looking male android head had heavily receding brown hair mixed liberally with white. His beard was brown around the mouth but pure white on the sides, coming up past his temples. He was obviously modeled after a living person's likeness, but Carina didn't know whose. As she neared, the head's eyes opened and looked at her. The mouth opened slightly, as if to speak, but no words came forth. The synthetic skin was some form of rubber. The head reminded her of a short film she'd watched, in the Allied Academy Library. It featured a psychopathic ventriloquist's dummy. Its eyes, features, and manner had made her twenty-year-old flesh crawl.

The android's fake skin lent an additional, horror-vision grotesquerie to the severed head. It seemed to leer at her. The prosthetic brown eyeballs had no light in them, no life behind them. She moved toward the counter. The eyes tracked her. She glanced back at the head. Discomfiture crawled across her skin.

"Don't mind Phil," said Not-Jack. "You can have a conversation with him, but he doesn't really think. His 'brain' is just his own manuscripts and interview transcripts that he cross-references to devise answers. It can be amusing, but we have," he gestured at Private Gray, "more pressing matters at hand, I imagine."

Carina looked at the syringes on the cart of supplies. She picked one up, stepped in, and administered a sedative to the still-unconscious private.

"Shall we begin the process?" Not-Jack asked.

Carina shook her head. "No. Not yet. I . . . I need a minute. Just . . . give me a minute alone with him."

Not-Jack bowed his head and left her alone in the operating theater.

Carina paced and rubbed her hands together. She massaged her face, then ran her fingers through her curls. She pulled at the coils, stretching them out. They sprung back into place once she let go.

"Alex," she said. "I don't know if you can hear me. I don't even know why I'm talking to you. It's not like we're close."

She looked over her shoulder. The android head, Phil, looked at her with unnatural intensity. She grabbed a small gown from the cabinet and shrouded the head with it.

"It is suddenly quite dark," Phil said in a stilted, robotic voice. It was close to being human, but still too far to be convincing. "Hmm, well. Everything in life is just for a while."

Carina stood for a long moment, looking at the covered head, waiting for more, but it didn't speak again. She walked back to the operating table.

"God, that fucking head," she said to Gray. "If you could see this, you'd probably think it was funny, but I am so creeped out."

"Could you repeat that, please?" Phil asked. "I did not understand the question."

She looked in the head's direction and frowned, then returned her attention to Gray.

"All of this feels, just . . . so weird. That rubber head could be you, if we do this. If this crazy shit works, you'll wake up in a body that's not yours . . . I can't imagine how totally fucked that'll be.

"There's this robot, here, in charge of the lab. It's no less weird. It's a version of a man . . . who's inside *another* robot my sister hangs around with . . . which already sounds fucking crazy, I know. I mean, they're the same guy, these two robots, but different versions . . . of that guy. Do you know what I mean?

"Fuck. I'm not even sure what I mean. What am I talking about? They're not even people! And there are more of him, of this man . . . or his mind . . . in other robots. At least from what I understand, but . . . I don't understand. I don't get it at all. Why would anybody want their mind in a tin can forever? I don't even want to be in my own body. And who says they'll stop at copying you once? I mean, how many Alex Grays does the world need, right?"

She tried to smile at her own joke but it turned into a pained grimace.

"This man—Jack—the guy in the robots . . . he says he lived before the Blight. He said Marseh and Arak wanted him dead, so he backed himself up, like some file on a computer. Who would do that? I spend every day hoping to die . . . why the fuck would anyone fight that hard to live?"

She wiped a tear from the corner of her eyes. She laughed once.

"I mean, I guess I fight back every time someone tries to kill me . . . so I can't want out that bad, right?"

She laughed again, but there was no amusement behind it.

"But, really . . . I don't want to live like that. Like that robot. He doesn't eat. Doesn't drink. Can he fuck? No way I'd want to live without sex. There's no way he can feel what people, real people, feel. I mean, I feel kinda dead sometimes, like, I feel nothing, you know? But I don't feel *nothing*; I'm just . . . numb. It's just . . . whatever.

"He said he doesn't dream. He doesn't sleep." She ran her hands again over her curls. "But, then, neither do I. Oh, *putain*. Do you see how messed up I am? God. Why the fuck am I blabbering at you?"

"Could you repeat that, please?" Phil began to say.

"Ta gueule!" Carina howled in response. *Shut the fuck up!*

She put her face in her hands and took a deep breath, exhaling slowly.

"You can't hear me," she said to Gray. "This is for me . . . I know that. I know, if he doesn't dream, you won't dream. All we'll save is your consciousness. Not that your consciousness is shit, but you'll cease to be *you*. All the garbage we've got buried in the backs of our brains, the things that . . . define us under the surface, you'll lose that. You'll be . . . incomplete. And part of me thinks it's better to just . . . let you die—"

The door opened, startling her. She turned toward it, annoyed, thinking that Not-Jack had come back sooner than she wanted.

"I said, 'Give me a m—'" The word died on her lips at the sight of Sotillo standing in the doorway.

He looked at the counter and saw her guns piled there. He smiled.

"What are you doing here?" she asked. She tried to sound cool but her throat constricted and she choked out the words.

Fear and anger welled up in her. Though equidistant from her weapons, he was taller. He'd get to them before she would. She knew that. So did he.

"I wanted to see how the old boy was doing," he said, taking an advantageous step toward the counter. The door closed behind him.

"Were you two close?" Carina said in a bitter, caustic tone.

She made sure to face his intruding figure, trying to position herself to bolt toward the door. He blocked the way without making a show of it, cutting off both fight and flight.

"No," he replied. "Private Gray didn't go that way, as far as I'm aware. Or maybe he just didn't like me, specifically."

He smiled again. His handsome face lit up from the cheeks down. His dark eyes exuded no warmth.

"Small wonder, that," said Carina, turning again to keep Sotillo in view.

He walked into the space and toward the operating table, inviting Carina to go for her guns. She considered it, but he still hadn't threatened her outright. She had to turn her back on him to get them, and she feared the thought of him overtaking her.

She remembered what he'd said in the armory.

Watch your back, Carina.

It didn't get any clearer than that. But no one else had heard him. She wasn't sure, if she killed him preemptively and pleaded self-defense, that anyone would believe her.

Her head swam with doubt.

Gardiner would probably defend his lover. She'd given Ray good reason to hate her, the way she had treated him in the Dorance infirmary. Intimidating Patrick and chasing him away from Ada couldn't have won her any points. Maybe her moment of compassion with Macaluso in the armory had earned her his favor. But what influence would one salty corporal have over a major and a lieutenant commander?

Sotillo stopped within arm's reach of her and Gray. She took a step backward, farther from her guns and from escape. It was the only available direction.

"There's no need for the tart tongue, Carina." He sounded almost genuinely disheartened.

"How else should I talk to a man who can't take a hint? Who can't take 'no' for an answer?"

Sotillo took another step. Again, she backpedaled. She bumped into the cart of surgical supplies. Reflexively, she turned her attention toward it. Sotillo pounced. Carina snatched at her knife but, before she could stab him, he grabbed her left wrist and struck the blade from her hand. It rang out upon the floor. He spun her around and twisted her left arm behind her back, bending her over the cart.

He pushed his pelvis against her buttocks, driving himself, her, and the cart toward the wall until it crashed against the counter. Surgical implements went flying, but a few syringes lolled atop the cart next to Carina's face. The hypodermics blurred in the foreground as she focused desperately on her guns, but they were too far away to reach.

"Get off of me!" she screamed. She scrabbled with her right hand for anything she could use as a weapon.

Sotillo picked up a syringe from the cart. A paralytic.

"Perfect," he said and bit off the cap.

Carina grabbed a pair of scissors.

He plunged the needle into her right shoulder and pushed down the plunger. Her arm went dead. The scissors fell from her hand.

"I'd have put it in your back," he taunted, leaning over to whisper in her ear. "But I want you to feel it all."

"Get off ME!" she howled. "Mother*fucker*!"

"And it's *a lot*," he added. He worked his erect penis free with his left hand, keeping her restrained with his right.

Her pinioned arm tingled as it lost sensation.

He slapped his organ against the seat of her pants. "You're gonna love this, baby, I promise." He reached around her waist and fumbled with her belt. "You're gonna wonder why you ever fought me."

Wrenching down her pants and underwear, he rubbed his glans against her exposed pudendum. He smiled at the unmistakable sound.

"You're wet," he said, his surprise evident. "You love it, you fucking *tease*."

Carina was beyond words. Tears streamed from her eyes. She refused to be quiet, but could summon only primal, nonverbal reproach as she bucked to get away.

"You're like a wild animal," he said, his smile broadening. "I *knew* you'd be fun."

Completely oblivious to anything but her, Sotillo didn't hear the door open behind him. He rubbed the head of his penis up and down Carina's vulva, reveling at the suction. Animal rage erupted from her throat. She thrashed against the cart. She stomped her feet, bucking her hips from side to side, trying to escape.

Just as Sotillo began to penetrate her, Gardiner reached him. The major grabbed him by the throat, pulling him away from Carina. With a telekinetic assist, Gardiner lifted Sotillo from his feet and slammed him hard against the floor. His head smacked against the corrugated metal. It dazed him.

Carina fumbled, with her tingling left arm, to pull up her trousers. Her right arm hung uselessly at her side, immobilized by the paralytic. She yanked the zipper, leaving the button and belt undone.

"I'll cut his fucking dick off," she fumed, she clumsily tried to retrieve her knife.

Ray and Not-Jack came into the room.

"What the hell is going on in here?" Ray demanded.

Writhing on the floor, Sotillo stuffed his genitalia back into his jumpsuit and pulled down the two-way zipper.

"Commander," said Gardiner. "Lieutenant Sotillo has assaulted Captain Duvais."

"You shut your mouth!" Carina demanded.

Her face flushed redder than her hair. She met Ray's gaze. Her cheeks burned and she looked away.

Gardiner ignored her outburst. He drew his blaster.

"This is the latest in a pattern of unacceptable behavior from Mr. Sotillo: conduct unbecoming an officer, assault, sexual assault. Rape. I testify that he has been abusive toward me, as well. Has assaulted me. Has threatened my life. He's proven himself a threat to the safety and welfare of our party and, with you and Captain Duvais as my witnesses—"

"Fuck you, you cocksucking piece of shit," Sotillo spat, sitting up.

Gardiner pointed his gun at Sotillo's head. "I hereby sentence him to death."

Sotillo's face twisted into an ugly mask of unrepentant rage. He moved to stand. Gardiner pulled the trigger. The invective on the tip of

Sotillo's tongue died with him. The blast obliterated his head. Remnants of his skull and brains spattered the theater. His body fell backward onto the floor. Blood gushed from the top of his neck and slapped against Ray's and Not-Jack's legs.

For a long moment, neither Gardiner, Carina, Ray, nor the robot moved. They said nothing. The only sound was the blood squirting from Sotillo's headless body as it convulsed upon the floor. Soon, even those sounds stopped. Silence filled the room.

Carina leaned against the counter in a daze, her paralyzed arm like dead weight. She dropped her knife onto the cart and clamped her left hand over her right bicep, trying to massage some feeling into it. None would return until the paralytic had run its course.

Gardiner finally turned away from the corpse. Holstering his weapon, the major looked Ray in the eyes with unnerving cool.

"You could have done that cleaner," said the corren.

"Yes," Gardiner admitted. "I trust, though, Commander, that this summary execution was satisfactory?"

Ray looked into the human's heterochromatic eyes and considered the scars that marred half of Gardiner's face. He could see that the major's eyes were placid. The malevolent expression was just a side effect of his disfigurement.

Ray nodded.

"Please," Gardiner said to Not-Jack, "dispose of the body. And clean up this mess."

Not-Jack thought to object, unaccustomed to being ordered, but he recognized there was no point in dissent. He had no feelings. No pride to be wounded. He could not argue against the body being burned and the room being cleaned of the blood, the bone fragments, the organic pulp.

Gardiner looked at Carina. She felt his eyes on her and glanced up at him.

He thought of comforting her, but she didn't want it. Not from him. He didn't need to read her mind to know that. She wanted consolation, but not from any of the men, and there were no women. Gardiner left the lab.

Ray lingered for a moment, his eyes on her.

"Leave, please," she said, not looking at him.

He opened his mouth to speak but thought better of it. His face flickered through a range of emotions. He wondered why he even cared to console this woman he knew hated him for merely existing. He left her alone with the robot.

"Do you require medical attention?" Not-Jack asked. There was no concern in its voice. It was a practical inquiry.

She shook her head.

Not-Jack diverted his attention to summoning the cleaner bots that would dispose of both Sotillo and the evidence of his demise.

Carina looked at the headless corpse and quietly excoriated herself for letting things get to the point that they did.

I should have killed him after the first advance, she thought. *What else could he have wanted? How could I let him get so close? Stupid. Stupid. Stupid bitch.*

Of the fractured parts that comprised her, none was bigger than the bully that berated her for her mistakes, but another vied for her attention. It told her to be less harsh, that she was devoid of blame. The voice excused her for being thrown off-balance by a man who shared a face with Falco, toward whom she still harbored positive feelings.

That's bullshit, said the bully. *Be vigilant. Always be vigilant. See what happens when you let confusion take you over? When you get sentimental?*

Do you want to hate all men forever? asked the gentler part.

Yes, thought Carina, *what reason is there not to?*

Good girl, said the bully. *You're finally learning.*

EIGHTEEN

CARINA PUT ON her exo-suit. She hadn't spoken since the assault and didn't care to. She put on her helmet and hid behind her opaque visor.

Gardiner and Ray stood with Not-Jack.

Patrick and Macaluso awaited orders. They knew only what their superiors had told them. Neither had liked Sotillo, but his execution cast a pall.

Private Gray remained in the operating theater, alive but unconscious. Carina couldn't muster the resolve to make a decision about him. She left it up to Gardiner and Ray. They agreed to leave him in the facility and declare him killed in action. Not-Jack would take Gray's consciousness and the private's body would die. So, too, would the man; nearly everything that made him human would be lost. Only the waking version of him would persist, stripped of his emotions, his subconsciousness, his quintessence. A shadow of himself.

Carina shuddered at what seemed to her like a fate worse than death.

"You don't wish to leave the way you came, I assume," Not-Jack said to Gardiner.

Gardiner shook his head and closed his eyes in annoyance.

"Very well . . . I'm loath to give away my secrets, but I can deposit you northward. Not far from your destination."

"We would very much appreciate that," said Ray.

Not-Jack seemed to smile, but it was implied. Silently, he summoned two more robots like him. They approached the Allied soldiers.

"These models will escort you."

There was no further conversation. Gardiner and his cohort had been dismissed, and they had little time to waste. No one complained. One of the robots took the lead. The other marched behind. They led and prodded the group through another set of doors into a long corridor. They reached a platform and stepped onto it.

"Hold on," ordered one of the robots.

The platform moved horizontally, northward at great speed. Even at such velocity, the trip seemed to take forever.

The two androids simultaneously grabbed one arm of each soldier nearest to them. Carina and Gardiner; Ray and Macaluso. The four Allies jolted spasmodically and fell unconscious to the floor of the lift.

Patrick fumbled for his weapon but was too slow.

The nearest robot grabbed his wrist. The corporal's body shuddered with current and he, too, fell in a heap among his fellows.

***

Ray was the first to wake.

For once, he hadn't dreamt, and he was grateful. His eyes fluttered open. He lay on his back, looking up at the whorls of slate-, charcoal-, soot-, and heather-gray clouds.

He propped himself up and found the bodies of his companions strewn about him. He rose and checked that they were all alive. With a quiet sigh of relief, he looked around. They were atop a moor, north of the Hugtaender i Nord. The robots were nowhere in sight, nor was there any evidence of where in the mountains they had exited the facility.

Klippeborg glinted in the distance. It stood in contrast to the endless gray earth, water, and sky, and to every other city on Nova Spes. Like those other cities, it was unwalled but looked more like the walled cities of the Allied Nations than like Orchard City, Coventry, Ulterboro, or Prunty's Quay. Klippeborg had natural walls: the cliffs, the mountains, the water, its northern remoteness.

Gardiner stirred, rolling onto his side. He pushed himself up into a sitting position. Ray walked over to him and crouched down.

"Report," said Gardiner.

"We're a few klicks from the city. No sign of our escorts. No sign of how we got here, but we're all alive and accounted for."

Gardiner bent his knees up toward his chest and rested his arms atop them.

"Rouse the others. We don't have time to waste."

***

Klippeborg had few suburbs. There was little sprawl.

Before the Blight, legislation dictated that the countryside be preserved. No individual could own land on the peninsula. The city offered everything except vast open spaces. It had been a green city, replete with trees and green roofs, state-of-the-art architecture, and environmentally conscious planning. Post-Blight, Klippeborg's historic, forward-thinking approach to the challenges of an urban space had made it the bellwether of how cities could survive, and even thrive, in the aftermath of catastrophe.

The dogged Allied presence there, and their significant defense of the position, had helped. Klippeborg was the only remote outpost to which the Allies had resources enough to devote. Their tentative forays into Coventry, Orchard City, Ulterboro, and elsewhere had either already been repelled by the locals—sometimes, though rarely, with covert aid from the Confederation—or soon would be.

As Ray, Gardiner, Carina, Patrick, and Macaluso approached the very edge of the city, they were met by a contingent of Allied soldiers atop a motorized transport. The five weary, wayfaring soldiers displayed their colors. They presented the chips embedded in their weaker hands when asked for identification. The transport's quiet Maisey engine spirited them into the city.

Ray looked around. He had never been to Klippeborg. He'd barely been anywhere on Nova Spes, spending most of his time in Orchard City and Holst's Hollow. Aside from London, he had never seen a well-maintained city, and even London had been warped both by bombs during the Blight and by the ravages of rising sea levels.

Klippeborg looked like it didn't belong on Earth. Like it had been plucked from another pristine world, had its lush vegetation replaced by hardscrabble, wretched grasses and trees—which themselves were decadent displays of prosperity relative to the barren muck deserts elsewhere—and then had been deposited on a wretched, hellhole planet as some kind of sick joke.

The transport descended into a tunnel and wound its way beneath the city. The air grew cool, sheltered from the warm, humid surface. It grew colder the deeper they descended. Eventually, they came to a halt and were bidden to dismount.

Their Allied escorts exchanged no pleasantries, offered no names, and the tired quintet didn't care to ask. They followed those in front and were spurred by those behind. They passed through checkpoint after checkpoint. The display of security made the Dorance base in Orchard City look pathetic.

Beyond another set of heavy doors emblazoned with the same "Artel Industries" logo as in the facility beneath the Hugtaender i Nord, General Lawton Bennett and Commodore Rolo Gage awaited them.

"I had to see it with my own eyes," said Gage. He looked at Ray, with whom he'd served briefly in the cloud city on Venus. "Welcome to K-borg, Lieutenant Commander."

Ray looked at the wide gold band and circle on each of Gage's cuffs. "*Commodore* Gage."

It was part statement, part question. He wanted to know how Gage had jumped two ranks in only a few months, more out of jealousy than genuine interest.

Gage opened his mouth to explain that he'd received a make-good promotion from full commander to navy captain upon being relieved of his plum post on Venus. Shortly after arriving in Klippeborg, the previous commodore committed suicide. Gage had been next in the chain of command. But Bennett interrupted Gage before he could speak.

"No time for pleasantries, I'm afraid," said the general.

The commodore's mouth snapped shut.

Bennett looked at Gardiner, Carina, and Ray. "Major, Captain, Commander, accompany me and the commodore to be debriefed." He turned to the commander of the unit that had escorted the wayward Allies to base. "Captain Van Destienne will join us."

She nodded in assent.

Bennett turned to the second in command of Van Destienne's unit.

"Lieutenant Venetsky, debrief the corporals."

The lieutenant saluted. He led Patrick and Macaluso away.

Carina, Gardiner, and Ray followed Bennett and Gage to the commodore's office.

NINETEEN

ADA PACED WHILE Tuah sat atop one of the beds in their shared room. Their Buckingham Palace quarters were opulent beyond anything Tuah—and even the well-to-do Ada—had ever experienced.

The other bed was made, but not due to Ada's fastidiousness. Whether out of boredom or heartbreak—perhaps both—Tuah had invited her to bed. It had somewhat assuaged the dual despair of displacement and confinement. Though their hosts were the Allied High Command, the women felt like prisoners. They hadn't been allowed to leave the room. Elsewhere in the palace bunked Colonel Van Sinderen and the other Orchard City refugees.

The door unlocked from outside. One female and one male MP stood framed in the doorway. The woman spoke.

"Lieutenant. Miss Bell. With us, please."

Ada and Tuah walked the sumptuously decorated halls. The MPs ushered the women into an anteroom and bid them to sit and wait. Through the doors opposite the entrance, the High Command conference was ready to convene. Inside, Field Marshall Courtois presided, along with his staunch ally Fleet Admiral Alistair Hastings. Their close confidant Admiral Abdoulaye Howe rounded out the cabal.

Military commanders came from each of the Allied Nations to London to attend the conference. Major General Alton Heston represented Venus. The second planet's Allied head of state, General Adeola, had sent Heston to Earth shortly after Ray, Anjali, and the others left to raid Overground. Rather than make the trip herself, she made Heston her surrogate. He left Colonel Robinson in charge of the Maxwell Montes cloud base.

The conference waited on General Lawton Bennett. He was due to arrive at any moment from Klippeborg with Gardiner, Carina, and Ray, all unaccounted for since the siege at Orchard City.

An MP led Colonel Van Sinderen into the anteroom where Ada and Tuah waited.

"Sir," said Ada, glad to see another familiar face.

Van Sinderen turned to look at her. Relief showed on his face as well. He offered a weak smile that doubled as a pained grimace.

"Lieutenant. Nurse Bell."

"Sir," said Tuah, politely. She sat with her hands folded atop her lap.

The outer doors opened again, and General Bennett swept through like a tidal wave. He paid no attention to his daughter, to Tuah, nor to the colonel.

"General Bennett, sir," Ada called.

He stopped in his tracks, hands upon the doorhandles of the conference room. He looked over his shoulder. His face betrayed no emotion.

"Lieutenant."

Ray, Gardiner, and Carina were ushered behind the general. He threw open both inner doors in a grandiose display. He paraded the officers into the company of the men and women who ruled the martial states of the Allied Nations.

The MPs retrieved Macaluso and Patrick from the hallway, shepherding them into the anteroom. Patrick sat down next to Ada and she patted his leg.

Macaluso frowned at the little chairs and sat atop the bench instead. It creaked beneath him.

***

Field Marshal Courtois and Fleet Admiral Hastings sat atop the dais with Admiral Howe and General Bennett.

The English premier, Arabella Windsor, rounded out the council as its one civilian appointment. Both in the badlands and within the safety of the city-state of London, she was known, not affectionately, as the "Iron Bitch." Courtois often claimed she would have made a spectacular military commander.

Ray took the stand as if on trial. It felt to him as if he were.

He was the lone corren in the room. The only one in the Allied military besides Daedalus, who was missing in action. Ray remembered his year of detention at Allied hands following his defection. The torture, the tests, the endless deluge of abuse meant to expose him as an untrustworthy agent. He resented it all but had suffered every agonizing moment because he wanted the revenge he thought only the Allies could provide. The means by which to eliminate Arak Matar.

His hopes had been quickly dashed. He learned that the Allies were incapable of winning. That, barring some miracle, they would never do more than keep the Confederation at bay. They would never reclaim lost lands. Never conquer new territories. They were nothing more than the last bastion of human resistance to corren integration. Xenophobia underlaid Allied ideology. Fear of what they viewed as an invading alien army informed their ill treatment of Ray, even after they accepted him into their ranks.

His defection had been foolish, desperate, and naïve. He had known about Daedalus' own flight to the other side but knew nothing of his treatment. Ray had heard only that Daedalus had traded sides, was alive, and in the Allied service.

Ray had thought to abandon the Allies upon realizing his desire for retribution would never be sated, and the humans would never accept him. He considered living in the badlands as had other A'arili, like the legendary Aldebaran Hi'ifto. But Daedalus had encouraged him to stay on.

And then Ray had met Anjali.

Her kindness and apparent attraction to him had made him wary, but she won him over. A famous admiral's daughter with power beyond her rank, she used it to get them both transferred to Venus. There, floating atop the clouds, basking in sunlight, he'd almost forgotten his quest for revenge. He'd almost forgotten the more potent Earth-bound brand of human animosity.

The people in the cloud city were less abrasive, less closed-minded, less frazzled and battle-scarred, but to call the Venusians milder than the Terrans was to call a monsoon milder than a hurricane. Major General Heston and his cronies, Colonel Robinson and Major Pruša, had still been racist blowhards from the moment Ray arrived.

In light of recent events, Ray surmised that Heston's animosity may have been an act. He was in league with Ada's father. The coarse behavior could have been a charade to make Ray believe that the hateful status quo existed everywhere. That he was reviled. Undesirable. Discarded to die on a suicide mission, along with his miscegenating partner and the rest of the incorrigible problem cases.

"Commander," said Courtois.

The voice stirred Ray from his reverie. "Sir?"

The field marshal's face screwed up. "Shall I repeat the question, *Lieutenant* Commander?"

"Yes, sir. I apologize," Ray replied.

Courtois made obvious his displeasure. "Do try to give us your attention. I said: By your account, was the Orchard City base indefensible?"

"Yes, sir. It was. We were a force of barely more than forty—twenty of whom were injured—and I believe that the Confederates outnumbered us at least two-to-one."

"Yet," said Courtois, "it is my understanding that these Confederates did not use deadly force."

"That would appear to be correct, yes. Sir."

"To what would you attribute this . . . oddity?"

"I don't believe it's my place to speculate, sir."

"I am asking you to speculate, Commander."

Ray inclined his head deferentially. "I would speculate that they wished not to harm us."

Admiral Hastings interjected in a testy tone of voice. "Could you expound as to why not, Lieutenant Commander A'arilon?"

Ray frowned. "No, sir. I don't know why our enemies would not wish us dead. It doesn't make sense to me."

"That is all, Commander, please step down," Hastings ordered. "Would Tuah Bell please present herself?"

Tuah stood and was led by an MP to the stand. She was asked to identify herself for the record and she did so.

"Miss Bell," said General Bennett, "in your statement, you relay that Lieutenant Commander Anjali Hastings was abducted by Confederate agents from the medical bay at the Dorance facility in Orchard City."

"Yes, sir," Tuah replied.

Already diminutive, she felt even smaller in the big room, surrounded by more uniformed personnel than she had ever seen. The stern-faced men and women in fancy dress looked austere and forbidding. Her intestines teemed with anxiety.

She tried to quell her roiling guts.

"In your opinion, what was the purpose of the Confederate raid?" Bennett asked.

Tuah leaned forward. "It seemed . . ." she looked around the room. Her voice sounded small. She felt like a speck under a microscope.

"Go on, please," Bennett urged.

She made herself bigger, added more volume to her voice. "Commander Hastings seemed to be their objective, sir."

A murmur crept through the room. The gallery was agitated.

Courtois held up his hand, urging silence. "Can you elaborate, please?"

"One of the invaders addressed her by name and rank," said Tuah. She deliberated whether to share that Anjali had gone willingly. "Then they *took* her. One of the men disappeared with her in a blue flash . . ."

"Let the record state that Miss Bell is describing dimensional teleportation," Bennett interrupted.

"And then the others retreated," Tuah continued, "as if they got what they came for."

"Thank you, Miss Bell," said Bennett. "Dismissed."

Major Gardiner was called to testify.

The conference rehashed the Orchard City raid with him. Carina, Van Sinderen, and Ada were each called to the stand. Patrick and Macaluso then followed. Once the field marshal, the fleet admiral, Bennett, Howe, and Premier Windsor heard all testimony, the conference was dismissed.

TWENTY

DEROVIAS AND CERES, Falco and Ji'ilaad, and Kir and Andrei rode into the Blackwing spaceport, containers in tow. Sargas, Daedalus, and René occupied three of the tubes. The fourth remained empty; Derovias and Kir had burned the bodies of Alesh and Inishi before leaving Coventry.

Blackwing's head guardsman, Pongsrion Klahan, approached the group and removed his helmet before addressing Derovias.

"Captain?" Derovias asked, surprised by the greeting.

"The governor has left the manor, my Lord," Klahan announced. He appeared pained to deliver the news.

Derovias clenched his fists. He exhaled sharply through his nose. "And where . . . did the governor go?"

Klahan's black eyes obscured his pupils and betrayed nothing of his anxiety, but Derovias could taste it.

"He departed for Overground, my Lord," said Klahan, swallowing hard and forcing himself to look at Derovias.

Derovias closed his eyes and clenched his teeth. "Who's in charge here?"

"Um, I believe, now, that would be you, Lord."

"Leave," Derovias ordered, waving him away.

Klahan bowed and turned on his heel, heading toward the dimensional portal. He paused just out of range of it and turned to watch Derovias from afar.

On the tarmac, Derovias spun around so quickly that Kir took a step back.

"Fucking hell, Kir. Motherfucking hell to fuck and back. *Fuck!*"

"What do we do?" Kir asked. He cringed a little. He knew the question was lame.

"What do we *do*?" Derovias repeated. He ran his hand over his face. "It's fallen to utter shit. What the fuck do we *do*? What the fuck *do* we do, Kir? You tell me!"

"We have to get Sargas to Overground," Kir replied soberly.

Derovias stopped fretting for a moment. He took a deep breath, closed his eyes, and exhaled slowly. Opening his amber eyes, he walked over to the first pod and opened it.

"Get out," he said to Daedalus.

Klahan recognized Asharan Antal, the famed defector. Derovias opened the second container and then the third. Sargas and René climbed out on the tarmac. Klahan had never before seen the two men and couldn't place them. He disappeared through the dimensional portal that ferried traffic from the spaceport to the manor. When he materialized in the entrance hall, he headed straight to the communications array.

Derovias regarded Sargas. "There's very little need for ruse, now," said the corren, "but there is need for it."

Daedalus looked at Sargas, but the big man betrayed nothing.

"We need somewhere more private than this," Derovias stated.

"Do you have a place in mind?" Daedalus asked.

"In fact, I do," Derovias replied.

***

On Overground, Soleron Besucher greeted Arak Matar, Intiri, and Irva'a.

"My Lord," said Besucher. "We have, as yet, avoided violence, but the station is divided. At every point where our forces meet the emperor's, there is a standoff. No one is willing to shed first blood."

"We raised you to be averse to harming each other," Arak replied. "But back any animal into a corner and it will fight. When push comes to shove, blood will be shed."

"And shall we be the ones to push, my Lord?" Besucher asked.

"We need a tactical objective before anything of the sort," said Arak. "It does us no good to incite violence if we cannot gain control."

"How could we possibly gain control of the entire station, Sire?"

"We need access to life-support systems in areas controlled by our enemies. If we can asphyxiate them into submission, there will be no need for bloodshed."

"Master, as you know, the life-support systems are incredibly redundant. There is no central hub that can override each local command station. We need to infiltrate each section of the station we wish to subdue and affect these changes locally. That will certainly require violence. They will not allow us to march unimpeded into their spaces and turn off their air."

"Then I suppose we must devise a plan to deal with this impediment. I'd prefer to kill as few of his men as possible but, if anyone stands in our way, they leave us no choice."

"There is something else, my Lord," said Irva'a.

Arak looked down at him.

"Before we docked, we received a message from Pongsrion Klahan, in Blackwing. Derovias has returned with prisoners. Asharan Antal is among them. And a large human man Klahan could not place . . ."

Arak breathed an inward sigh at the mention of Derovias.

"Ishtafan Alesh and Tolon Inishi were not with them," Irva'a continued.

Arak closed his eyes. He waved Besucher away.

"Is anyone else missing?" he asked Irva'a.

"No, my Lord. The rest of the party returned intact." The centurion tensed, awaiting physical reprisal. None came.

Arak left the hangar and headed toward his chambers. Irva'a and Intiri followed silently behind him.

***

Condensation beaded upon the walls of the Blackwing dungeon, deep below the manor. A layer of organic slime coated the old stones and rusty iron bars.

Derovias, Ceres, and Falco guided Sargas, Daedalus, and René to an empty cell, far from the sad, moldering prisoners who'd incurred Arak Matar's cold ire. Whatever they had done to attract his attention had been enough to be detained but not killed. Instead, they faced a crueler fate, wasting away in the manor's dank bowels, ignored but once every three days when they were given dirty water and a bowl of slop.

"Klahan is not to be trusted," Derovias said, once he was sure they were out of earshot.

Falco folded his arms across his chest.

"If he contacts Arak," Derovias continued, "informs of his suspicions . . . we'll have nowhere to hide. The entire force of guardsmen and centurions in this manor will come down on us, and we'll be killed."

"I cannot be killed," Sargas boasted.

Derovias made a face. "I doubt that's true, but the rest of us certainly can be."

"Then we need to *leave*," Ceres protested. "What are we doing down here, trapped in this dungeon?"

Derovias exhaled slowly, his demeanor calm. "My dearest Ceres. Did you not see the armory through which we came? Where else would you like to make a stand than in a room full of weapons and armor? That is why I relieved the guards and posted Kir, Ji'ilaad, and your Andrei at the doors, and we continued here alone."

"He's not *my* Andrei," she replied. "You can have him."

Derovias had known it wouldn't hurt to separate Andrei from Falco and Ceres. The tall, bald mercenary had been dyspeptic the entire trip back, in a pathetic display of hurt feelings, wounded pride, and brokenheartedness. Derovias had enough to manage. He didn't need adolescent-level drama in the face of much greater concerns.

"And," he continued after flashing a toothy smile at Ceres, "should it not be our last stand, we will instead take our pick of supplies and abscond at the first opportunity."

"Abscond to where?" Falco asked.

"Overground," said Derovias.

Daedalus emitted a soft chuckle.

Derovias looked at him but said nothing.

"I finally get it," Daedalus said.

René looked at him expectantly. He had no idea what was going on and had grown tired of being dragged along and kept in the dark.

"Sargas is a weapon," Daedalus declared. "An *assassin*."

"Yes," said Derovias. "And we need to get him to where the target resides. Our quarry has flown. And so we must."

"Then why don't we just get out of here?" asked René.

"Because we can't very well commandeer . . ." Derovias paused to count the members of their party, "five ships to ferry the nine of us skyward and expect no resistance. We need a plan."

He looked right at Daedalus.

"So, let us plan."

TWENTY-ONE

IN HIS OFFICES, Field Marshal Courtois sat in private conference with General Bennett, Admirals Hastings and Howe, Major General Heston, Commodore Gage, and Colonel Van Sinderen.

Gardiner, Carina, Ray, and Ada were ushered into the room.

Courtois' secretary, Ava Vanzetti, sat apart from the rest of the group, taking notes. She wore a tight, midnight-blue dress. Her long, tight curls were pulled back and tied off into a giant puff. Carina kept stealing glances at the woman, wanting to dive into her dark brown skin and drown there, but Ava paid the captain no mind.

Carina had to console herself with having had the other woman in the room, with the very similar name albeit the complete opposite complexion. She looked at Ada, but the lieutenant ignored her, too.

"Why did they take my daughter?" Hastings bristled. He directed the question to no one in particular. "Why would they come specifically for *her*?"

"Admiral Hastings," said General Bennett. "You have my deepest sympathies, but I'd ask that you please focus on the bigger picture. We need you sober and present. However, I understand if that's impossible."

"I'm both sober *and* present, you ass," Hastings snapped. "Easy for you to talk, with your little cream puff sitting safely in this very room."

He glowered at Ada, who looked away as if she couldn't be bothered.

"That's quite enough," said Courtois, silencing the two men. The tension lingered, but the silence held. Satisfied, Courtois nodded. "I have an entire military, replete with generals, admirals, and other officers whom I trust, upon whom I rely for counsel. And yet here I am, in this room, with four minor officers I've never met, of whom I've barely heard . . . and, somehow, *you've* become my council. So, tell me," he looked at Gardiner in particular, having taken stock of who commanded the most respect, "why should I listen to you in lieu of Admiral Hastings, or any other proven man?"

"Sir," Commodore Gage interrupted, "before we go any further, you must know that, yesterday, Arak Matar departed Blackwing quite unexpectedly."

Courtois looked at Gage in annoyance but bid the commodore continue.

"We don't know exactly where he went, of course, but his trajectory indicated it was not a global journey. We surmise he was returning to Overground."

"Please, Commodore, don't waste my time. Tell me what you mean to say."

Gage took a deep breath and continued. "We've read the reports and heard the testimony of these men and women. I find it very clear that something is amiss within the Confederation. That a rift exists between Darek Marseh and Arak Matar. There have been rumblings for years that Arak's contingent is unhappy with the lack of progress in the war. They want us beaten . . . routed.

"They believe Marseh is too soft. For years, the Butcher and the emperor have not occupied the same space; Marseh on Overground and Arak on Earth . . . until the last off-world trip, weeks ago. He returned to Earth yesterday and then—after less than a day—he went back? This has *never* happened. It defies the pattern we've seen over the past decade, monitoring flights in and out of Blackwing. We believe he moves against Marseh's behest . . . so, if Arak returned to the station, it was on his own whim. Unbidden."

"I'm still not seeing your point, Commodore," said Courtois, annoyed. "And after all those words . . ."

General Bennett took up the slack. "What Commodore Gage is saying, Field Marshal, is that the Confederation is on the brink of civil war."

"How could you possibly know that?" Courtois snapped. "How does any of all that *wind* lead to *that* conclusion?"

"We speculate, yes. Of course," said Bennett. "But, in the Commodore's words—which I'd hardly call wind, sir—the evidence is there. In the behavior of the emperor and the Butcher."

"So," said Admiral Hastings warily. "Let's say it's true. Let's say Darek Marseh and Arak Matar have fallen out. What would you suggest we do?"

"That we attack Overground with everything we have," said Bennett.

Hastings blinked, dumbstruck.

Courtois ran his hand through his short, salt-and-pepper hair. He couldn't believe what he was hearing. He wanted to shout, but he refused to lose his cool.

"You want us to compromise all of our positions to attack an impregnable fortress . . . on a hunch? Lawton, I expect much more sense from you."

"Sir," Ray stated, looking at the field marshal. "Overground is not impregnable. Commander Hastings and I have been inside. We escaped with cargo from the station."

"Yes, yes, this man . . ." said Courtois, condescendingly, "this mysterious, *disappearing* man whose whereabouts you don't know. Whose purpose, whose mission you don't know. What was this mission of *yours*, anyway? Who cleared you to take the fight to them, at their stronghold?"

"I did, sir," said General Bennett.

Courtois glared at him. "You . . ." he struggled to keep his cool. "Without consulting me. A black op."

"You may recall that you gave me blanket permission to conduct operations with the intent to undermine our enemies," said Bennett. "I took advantage of that decree."

Courtois closed his eyes and inhaled deeply. "Who was part of this operation?"

"The men and women present, whom you know. And A'arilon Daedalus, who is missing in action."

"I bet he deserted," said Howe. His dark brown bald head gleamed brighter than his polished shoes. "You can't trust a corren."

Ray gritted his teeth but said nothing. Carina glanced at him and was surprised to feel herself offended on his behalf.

Courtois waved away Howe's remark and looked at Bennett.

"You spirited all of them to Venus, one by one. Hardcases and discipline problems, assembling your own little cabal. Which means that Adeola was in on this. She's always been a pain in my ass. You, too, eh, Heston?"

"Yes, sir," said Heston, unabashed.

"We have men inside the Confederate ranks," said Bennett. "That is how we penetrated the station. That is how we stole their greatest living weapon. The Reds want Arak dead. They want the radical wing of the Confederation eliminated. They want what we want."

"And what *do* we want, General Bennett?" said Courtois. "Tell me what it is *we* want."

It was Bennett's turn to blink dumbly. "Why . . . peace, sir."

Courtois nodded, almost sarcastically. It hardly seemed an agreement.

Bennett had always suspected that neither Courtois nor Hastings wanted peace. He believed them fools if they thought the Allies could ever defeat the Confederation through conventional warfare. But he knew they wanted a seminal battle. He aimed to give them one they could possibly win.

"Sir, we've never had a better opportunity to claim a real victory," Bennett insisted. "For decades upon decades, we've done nothing but keep them at bay and, even then, they glacially encroach on our lands. They chip away at us and we recede. We're weaker now than yesterday, weaker tomorrow than today. If we don't seize our opportunities . . . they will defeat us. Eventually. Soon, even."

Courtois closed his eyes and pinched the bridge of his nose. "As much as I relish this opportunity. I can't throw away the lives of our entire navy."

"Sir, I—" Bennett began but was silenced by a gesture from Hastings.

"However you penetrated Overground," said the fleet admiral. "You did so covertly. That is not an option at our disposal. Regardless of whether Marseh and Arak find themselves in a lovers' quarrel, it doesn't change that we have no way to *overtly* break the station's defenses."

Van Sinderen coughed and everyone looked at him.

"You have something to add, Colonel?" asked Courtois.

"As a matter of fact, sir," Van Sinderen replied, reaching into his pocket. "I do."

He handed the field marshal the data stick that Lieutenant Andersen had confiscated from Daedalus.

"What's this?" Courtois asked.

"An amazing stroke of good luck, I believe, sir."

Courtois frowned. "Dammit, man, don't talk to me in riddles."

"If that's what I think it is," said Ray, "it's the entire schematic for Overground."

"Black fucking Skies," Courtois exclaimed. "Do I look like an asshole to you, Commander? Colonel? Am I a fucking mirror for you fools?"

Ray struggled to control himself. He bit back the urge to respond to the field marshal with his fist.

"Sir," Ray said in a calm, even tone. "I can attest to its veracity. I was there when it was procured."

"I'm supposed to take *your* word for it," Courtois replied.

Ray threw up his hands and slapped them down on his legs. His breach of decorum took his superiors by surprise.

"Why bother to let me serve, then?" he asked, irate. "Am I a pet for you people? Am I here to be trotted out as some token example of human tolerance that doesn't fucking exist?"

"Watch your mouth, Commander!" Admiral Hastings demanded.

"No, sir," Ray replied standing up.

Courtois, Howe, and Hastings all reached for their sidearms, but when it was obvious Ray didn't intend to attack, they left their hands resting on the grips.

"I came to you because I wanted to end Arak Matar," Ray emoted. "You've treated me like shit and I have taken it. I've taken it because I know you think poorly of me. That you would gorge yourselves on satisfaction at my failure. If I prove you right about me. But I'm not your enemy. I've served well and loyally . . . to help end this ridiculous war . . . and now we can. You're holding the key . . . and you won't even turn it. What do you want, then? If you don't want to fight—if you don't even want to try—what's the point of any of this?"

Courtois made an appeasing, albeit condescending face. He gestured for Ray to sit back down.

The field marshal looked at Commodore Gage. "Return to Klippeborg and marshal your pilots . . . prepare your fleet."

He turned to Admirals Hastings and Howe.

"We haven't mounted an offensive in years. This seems as ideal a moment as we'll ever have to take the fight to them. An opportunity to breach that blasted station. We have the element of surprise."

He looked at the data stick in his hand.

"And, as our corren friend here has put it, we have the key."

Hastings' face betrayed his misgivings, but he nodded. "Howe," he said. "You'll command the fleet from the ANV *Britannia*."

Howe dipped his chin ever so slightly in acknowledgment. He eyed Ray with distrust.

Courtois turned to Bennett. "Assemble your best combatants, as well. I want to keep the fight going once we land. How much time do you need?"

"A little more than an hour to get back, at least two hours to prepare."

"We'll coordinate launches from here, and from Paris . . ." said Courtois. He looked at Admirals Hastings and Howe. "And from any port we can spare ships and manpower."

The field marshal turned to his secretary.

"Ava, call the other commanders here to my office. Heston, since you speak for Adeola, we'll need forces from Venus, too. You'll have to dispatch them. They'll be late to arrive, but that could work to our benefit."

"Sir, to transmit to Venus will give away our intent," said Heston.

"Dammit, man, I know that," Courtois frowned. "You'll have to go back personally."

"Of course, sir. I apologize. However, diverting our ships from Maxwell Montes and Beta Regio will leave us defenseless there," Heston objected.

"Leave enough ships and manpower to retaliate should the Reds attack, but they must know that any assault on our positions there will mean the destruction of their own, equally fragile holdings."

Heston nodded.

A grave countenance overtook Courtois.

"We attack Overground in five hours."

TWENTY-TWO

DEROVIAS AND HIS party scoured the armory for every useful bit of weaponry and armor they could wear and carry, and that would fit into a stinger's cockpit.

He knew they were better off taking five separate fighters than one large craft; more targets increased the likelihood that some of them would escape pursuit.

"Ceres, you're with me. Kir is the best pilot, so Sargas is with him."

"You've never seen me fly, obviously," Daedalus said.

"Frankly, I don't care," Derovias replied. "And now isn't the time. Ji'ilaad, you take Andrei. Daedalus, it's you and your human."

"His name's René, and he isn't *my* human."

"Falco," Derovias said. "You go solo."

"Why me?"

"Because you're the worst pilot and, therefore, the most expendable," Derovias replied.

"That was tactful," said Daedalus.

Falco frowned, but he accepted the order.

"Be prepared to face resistance," Derovias warned. His company steeled themselves, checking and holding their weapons at the ready. He pushed the armory doors open.

No one awaited them on the other side but their compatriots. Derovias walked slowly out and around the grand staircase into the open foyer of the great manor.

Pongsrion Klahan stood alone in front of the dimensional portal. Derovias slowly approached until they stood about two meters apart. Kir, Ceres, Andrei, Ji'ilaad, Daedalus, Sargas, Falco, and René all crept up to their leader, coming to a halt behind him. Klahan slid up the half shield of his helmet to reveal his face. He made no move for his weapons.

Derovias made his visor transparent but didn't lift it.

The others looked around the hall, keeping an eye out for an ambush, but no other soldiers presented themselves. Sargas kept his eyes on Klahan.

Derovias tilted his head in question at the Red Guard captain, who jerked his head toward the portal, slid down his visor, and turned his back. He jumped to the spaceport. Derovias looked over his shoulder at Kir, who shrugged. The portal would wrench Derovias to its terminus, leaving him momentarily disoriented and alone. An ideal setup for an ambush.

"Falco," said Derovias. "You go first. Keep your comm open."

Falco surmised what Derovias feared, that an ambush awaited. He knew he was being sacrificed. He stepped through the portal and emerged onto the tarmac, where Klahan waited. The men and women working in the spaceport paid them no mind.

"All clear," Falco reported.

Derovias and the rest of the party materialized behind him.

"I've entered a tentative manifest for your departure," said Klahan. "But I need to know, specifically, what you plan to take, so that everything jibes."

Derovias couldn't understand what was happening, but he refused to let the gift go unaccepted.

"Five stingers," he said. "The pilots are me, Kir, Falco, Ji'ilaad . . . and Asharan Antal."

Klahan looked at Daedalus and shook his head. "It has to be someone else; we can't put an Aktalon on the manifest."

"Make up a name!" Daedalus insisted. "Say I'm someone else!"

"It doesn't work like that," Klahan replied. "If I pick someone and their credentials are confirmed to still be here, the jig is up. I won't risk myself for you. You can't have five ships if you can't produce another valid pilot."

"How about I steal one and the rest of them pursue me?" Daedalus suggested.

Klahan raised his eye ridges at the thought. "You know, that's not a bad idea."

Daedalus grabbed René by the arm and dragged him toward a clutch of waiting stingers. "Come on, Pierre, let's steal a ship."

"Pierre?" René replied as Daedalus pulled him along.

Klahan forged the credentials of a crewman he'd been wanting to discard and released the stinger to the thieves.

They clambered up the ladders. Daedalus punched in the start-up sequence. It had been years since he'd flown a stinger but the knack never left him. His recent stint behind the *Filomena*'s controls had refreshed his memory of Confederation interface. The canopy closed. The vertical take-off and landing engines thrust the ship into the sky.

Deckhands came running to investigate the unauthorized launch. Klahan ran over to join them. He made a show of it. "Get up there! Get after them!" he barked at Derovias and the others.

With their faces obscured by their helmets, there was nothing odd about the scene; the leader of the Red Guard was doing his job. The four pilots attracted no special notice. The one oddity was that only three of them had a Weapon Systems Officer while the fourth climbed up alone, but none of the floor crew questioned it. Klahan and the deckhands ran for cover as the four stingers blasted straight up in pursuit of the first, rogue craft.

Projecting a terminal from his left forearm, Klahan typed up a report, indicating the theft of one craft. He validated the departures of Derovias and the others. If Daedalus and his human were killed, it mattered little; Klahan had avoided the onus of having to kill his fellow correns and had saved his own skin.

He would live to fight another day.

TWENTY-THREE

CARINA STOOD BY herself on the Heathrow tarmac. Her red curls bounced in the breeze.

The base buzzed with activity as the Allied fleet readied for battle. She took in the sights and the sounds of women and men prepping for the fight to come. To the west, the towering M25 Wall loomed, keeping the badlands rabble from invading the Allied Nations capital.

Gardiner approached. "Are you okay?" he asked.

She shrugged. "I don't really want to talk about it."

"I understand," Gardiner replied. "But you don't have to carry it alone."

She turned to him. "Are you going to carry it for me, Maks?"

He closed his eyes and sighed through his nose. He licked his lips, taking care to avoid the burn-mangled portion of his mouth, not because it hurt, but because he hated how it felt. He opened his eyes.

"Not *for* you, Carina. With you. But I am *here* for you."

"That's sweet," she said as she looked away. She meant it, though it sounded sarcastic.

"Will you carry me," Gardiner asked, "if I need you?"

She looked at him again. "Of course."

"And if you can't . . ."

"Don't, Maks."

"Or I can't go any farther . . ."

"Maks . . ."

"Promise me you'll take me out."

Carina threw her hands out from her hips. "I can't fucking promise you that."

"What's one more body?"

"You're not just one more body." She stepped close to him although no one was paying them any mind, and, amid the din, no one could overhear. "Are you really asking me to kill you?"

"If it comes to that," he replied. His face and eyes betrayed no turmoil.

"Then you've got to make me the same promise."

"You know I would."

"I don't know how that makes me feel," she said. "And I don't know how I feel going up there with you talking about this."

"I won't put anyone else at risk," Gardiner promised. "Besides, Ray's got the stick, I'm just sitting wizzo."

Carina spied Ray approaching. "Heads up. Your pilot's here."

Gardiner turned toward him.

"Shall we, Major?" Ray asked.

Gardiner nodded and they walked off. He looked back at Carina and she shook her head at him. Ray settled into the cockpit of the two-man spitfire fighter. It was the Allied analogue of the stinger-class Confederation ships, though somewhat slower and less maneuverable. Gardiner sat in the weapons system officer's chair, behind Ray. The canopy came down over their heads.

Patrick was paired with a London-based airman, Pilot Officer Jimmy Gray. They climbed into the cockpit of their spitfire and strapped in.

"Hey, mate," Patrick couldn't help but ask, "do you have a brother?"

"Yeah," Jimmy replied. "A private in the army, why?"

"Just wondering," Patrick said, settling into his WSO seat, wishing he hadn't said anything.

"I got a mother, too. Bonnie. You want the rest of my family tree?"

"No, mate, that's cool. Just curious."

Jimmy shrugged and prepped the craft for takeoff.

Macaluso watched his compatriots pair off and board their crafts. He was barred from flying because he couldn't fit in the cockpit with his exo-frame. If he took it off, his paralyzed legs disqualified him. He turned and stormed off. He took a swing at a pile of crates. His mitts protected his hands and his augmented strength dented the heavy metal, but he felt no better for it.

Ada watched his outburst. Tuah stood nearby to her, but not too close. They didn't want to advertise their connection. Carina swaggered over with a big smile on her face, helmet tucked under her arm.

"Hello, my beautiful ladies."

Tuah frowned at her.

Ada offered a gentle, closed-eyes smile.

"You know, I may not come back from this," Carina said.

"I wasn't sure I'd ever see you again, anyway," Tuah sniped, "after you abandoned me."

The playful expression slipped from Carina's face. Surprise took its place. "I didn't abandon you, Tuah."

Tuah crossed her arms. "What would you call it?"

"I tried to get back to you. I tried to get you, so you could come with me."

"You tried . . ."

"The base was swarming with snakes! Would you rather I'd died trying to reach you? Or escape and live to, maybe, see you again?"

"They didn't shoot to kill, Carina," Tuah retorted.

"How was I supposed to know that?" Carina protested.

"Tuah, she's telling you the truth," said Ada.

Tuah shot Ada a wilting glance.

"She did try to reach you," Ada insisted, unflinching.

"You're just saying that," Tuah replied. "Playing peacemaker. Should we all go back to our room and make a daisy chain?"

"I'm not bullshitting you," Ada protested. "I know when people are lying. I'm not picking her over you, I'm just telling you the truth of it. *She's* telling you the truth of it."

Tuah frowned at Ada. She looked at Carina, hurt plain in her eyes.

"I'm sorry, baby," said Carina.

Tuah put her hands together in a steeple in front of her mouth and looked away.

"I really do care about you," Carina said. She looked at Ada. "Both of you."

The swagger was gone. There was no bravado. No wall. Ada suddenly felt a wash of fear, shame, and anxiety spill from Carina, along with an impression of Lieutenant Sotillo, whose absence no one had explained. Ada wanted to ask after Carina's state of mind but knew better than to stir anything up before such a critical mission.

"I wasn't sure I'd ever see you again," Carina continued, looking at them both. "Do you know how happy I am that I have?"

Ada nodded. She smiled. "Yeah, I can kind of sense it."

Carina playfully rolled her eyes, but her face hardened.

"Seriously, I may not come back from this," she repeated, looking at Tuah. "I don't want a chance to say good-bye to go to shit because you won't forgive me. I didn't abandon you, Tuah. I *wouldn't*."

Tuah locked eyes with her and then looked away. "Goddamn it. I'm so angry at you . . ." She clenched her jaw and rubbed her forehead. "So fucking angry." She frowned and shook her head. She looked at Carina again. "But I forgive you. God knows I shouldn't. But I do."

Carina held out her arms, and Tuah allowed herself to be absorbed in an embrace. Her head came to Carina's chest and rested against her breastplate.

"I like it better when you don't wear armor," Tuah complained.

They both laughed.

Carina looked at Ada and let go of Tuah with one arm, inviting the other woman to join the embrace. Ada snaked one arm around Carina's waist and the other around Tuah's. Carina closed her arm around Ada, clutching both women, being held by them both.

"Um, Captain?" said a voice behind her.

Ada and Tuah stepped away. Carina turned to face the man. He was tall and lean with floppy brown hair that he smoothed away from his brown eyes.

"Captain Duvais?" he asked.

She nodded.

"I'm Lieutenant Anderson. Your pilot."

She frowned at the name, but he looked nothing like Per-Erik, who had ceaselessly pestered her, whom she'd been happy to leave behind at the Coventry armory. She couldn't have known by hearing the surname that it was spelled differently.

"What's your given name, Lieutenant?"

"Ivan."

"Ivan, I'm Carina."

"If it's all the same, I'd rather call you by rank."

She smiled and closed her eyes, shaking her head a little. "Ivan, would you give us another minute?"

He looked unsure. "We need to take off, Captain."

"I'll be right there, I promise."

He put on his helmet and walked to their ship.

She turned back to Tuah and Ada. "I want to kiss you both good-bye."

Neither woman objected.

Carina kissed Tuah first, then Ada. Turning back to Tuah, Carina kissed her again.

"I love you," she said, looking right into Tuah's eyes.

Tuah smiled without showing any teeth.

Turning on her heel, Carina donned her helmet and crossed the tarmac to meet Ivan.

"You're a doctor, right?" he asked over the comm.

"Yeah, so what?" Carina replied. She rued being given a navy pilot with equivalent rank; she'd grown fond of ordering men to shut up.

"Just wondering how you got in on this."

"Don't worry about it, Lieutenant. Just do your job."

She took to the ladder and climbed into the WSO chair. Ivan settled into the pilot's seat. As the canopy came down, Carina gave the women one final wave.

"I'm afraid I'll never see her again," said Tuah, waving back.

"You will," said Ada, putting her arm around the smaller woman. "She's too stubborn to die."

TWENTY-FOUR

LUTÁN AND MIRO stalked the corridors toward Marseh's chambers but the emperor, sensing their arrival, intercepted them as usual.

"My Lord," said Lutàn, coming to a sudden halt.

"Yes, Lutàn," Marseh replied. He didn't wait for the corren to share. Time was of the essence, so he read Lutàn's mind. "Arak's men refused to treat with you. I am not surprised, but we have more pressing matters."

Lutàn's mouth opened and closed without a word.

Miro kept as straight a face as he could muster, but he was awed by and afraid of Marseh's ability to reach into a man's head and extract his thoughts.

"The Allies approach," Marseh continued. "They've sent the bulk of their fleet, including two command ships. I've dispatched our own force, including two warships that will make short work of the incoming."

"But, Lord, why destroy them if we seek peace?" asked Lutàn.

"Just as Arak and his forces refuse to yield, so would a great many in the Allied Nations, if they felt they still had teeth. We have but a small handful of Allied officers who see the wisdom of our plan, while the vast majority still see fit to attack us where we live, with the full force of their armada. They will pay for that. They will lose their teeth and will weep in shock and awe at our might . . . and they will learn, once and for all, that they cannot win.

"They will learn that they cannot even resist."

***

Ceres couldn't contain her awe.

In her twenty-six years, she had never left the surface, never even flown in Earth's atmosphere. And now she was in space. She craned her neck to get a glimpse of the sun, but it hid from her on the opposite side of the planet. Instead, she took in as much as she could of the distant points of light. Stars. Other planets. The brilliant sunward sliver upon the otherwise dark mass of the moon. The moon! It existed. For all she had known, having never seen the sky beyond the Endless Gray, someone could have just made it up.

A laugh welled up in her chest and she couldn't contain it.

"Wow," she whispered. Her eyes burned with incipient tears. No one acknowledged her wonderment.

"All Father and Absent Mother," said Derovias over the comm linking their ships.

"Why are *you* praying?" Daedalus asked the erstwhile centurion.

Overground loomed, getting larger in perceived size with each second.

"Look at your rear monitor," Derovias replied.

Daedalus glanced at it. He saw the overwhelming mass of incoming ships behind them, but his attention was immediately diverted back toward Overground. His proximity alarm went off. The stick froze, locking him out from flying his craft.

"Fuck!" he exclaimed.

"What?" barked Derovias.

He looked at his monitor and it answered his question. Klahan had marked Daedalus and René as pirates.

"Shit," Derovias cursed, "Ceres, can you fly?"

"What?" she exclaimed, startled. "No! I can't fly!"

"It's easy," Derovias said, ignoring her distress. "Pull the stick toward your lap to go up, push it toward me to go down. Left is left and right is right. The lever to your left is the throttle."

"Wait a minute!" she protested, but he diverted the controls to her.

"Take the stick, Ceres!" Derovias shouted. "Just hold her steady."

In response to Daedalus' distress at his hampered ship and Derovias' attempt to unlock it, Kir relinquished the stick to Sargas.

"Just hold her level," said Kir. "I need to do something."

Sargas didn't protest; he knew how to fly.

Kir typed away at his terminal, putting up a firewall around their five-ship network so that their controls could not be easily overridden. Once satisfied they were at least marginally protected, he took back the stick.

Derovias created an uplink to override the enemy combatant flag. As he hurried to thwart the lockdown, countless ships launched from

Overground. The Confederate fleet sped toward them, and toward the mass of Allied ships beyond. Derovias kept his cool even as a cold sweat beaded on his skin and his pupils dilated in fear. He dismissed the flag as a false alarm and returned control to Daedalus.

"Take the stick, Antal, you're back in control."

Daedalus pushed forward on the yoke and jerked it to the right, maneuvering to avoid the oncoming Confederation ships. Derovias, Falco, Kir, and Ji'ilaad all took evasive action.

"Close your outgoing comms, except to our network." Derovias ordered. "Press through the fleet; getting to the station's our only aim."

They weaved their way into the sea of speeders, stingers and gunships, five battleships, and two warships. Confused pings from the other Confederate birds popped up on Derovias' comm. Their attempts to establish communication were ignored. Five pairs of stingers and speeders broke from the Confederation fleet in pursuit.

"Open incoming so we can hear what they want," Derovias ordered. "Maintain your silence."

The voice of an anonymous corren came over the comm. "Surrender immediately. Stand down to be escorted back to base. Your flight plan is invalid, and you are flagged as hostile. Surrender or be shot down. You have ten seconds to comply."

"Fuck," said Daedalus. "I get my stick back and they want to take it away again."

The voice over the comm began counting down.

"If they want to escort us back to base, we might as well let them," said Derovias.

"What?" Daedalus objected. "Surrender? Are you crazy?"

"Would you rather be shot down?" asked Kir.

"I'd rather bug out," Daedalus replied.

"There's no way we all make it," said Kir.

"Kir," said Derovias, "you have to get Sargas to Overground. If they attack us, do not engage. Get him to the Butcher."

"Copy that," Kir replied.

Derovias opened a channel to the pursuing ships. "This is Kurgan Derovias. We surrender and await your instructions."

The countdown stopped. The comm was silent. After a few seconds, the comm chirped to indicate that the channel had been closed.

"Bail! Bail! Bail!" Derovias shouted, veering starboard.

The four other dissident craft spun off in different directions as the pursuing speeders and stingers opened fire. Derovias' ship shook from the impact, but his shields absorbed the damage.

Daedalus and Kir took fire as they maneuvered to shake their pursuers.

Falco and Ji'ilaad evaded the barrage.

"Worst pilot . . ." Falco muttered. He took up after the stinger and speeder dogging Daedalus.

Ji'ilaad went after Derovias' attackers and Kir broke for Overground.

Derovias opened a channel. "Hold your fire! Hold your fire! Friendly! Friendly!"

The channel, again, was forced closed.

"They're onto us," said Ji'ilaad.

"Oh, no shit?" Daedalus replied, his craft shaking from repeated weapons' fire. "And here I was, thinking this is your typical welcome."

"Either they're Marseh's men and they think we're for the Butcher," said Falco, "or they're Arak's men and know we turned."

"You think we should ask them which and explain ourselves?" Daedalus joked.

Falco peppered the stinger on Daedalus' tail, weakening its rear shields. He launched a missile. The stinger rolled starboard at the last moment and the projectile whizzed just beyond Daedalus' shields.

"You tryin' to kill me, birdman?" he shouted.

The missile struck an oncoming speeder as it homed in on Daedalus, blasting the one-man craft to smithereens.

"Not what I was going for," said Falco. "But I'll take it."

Falco barraged the trailing stinger until it broke off pursuit of Daedalus. The enemy craft pitched downward, leaving both Falco's line of sight and his monitor.

"Get in close to the Red fleet," Derovias ordered. "They can't risk shooting at us if they'll hit their own ships."

"We need to reconfigure our transponders to transmit an Allied signal," said Ji'ilaad. "Antal, upload your credentials onto our network."

"Stop calling me that!" Daedalus protested. "Could someone, for once, call me what I want to be called? What the fuck good does it do to blare *my* credentials?"

"We can't hide from our own," Ji'ilaad replied, "there's no point in trying to be inconspicuous. We can't elude them, so why not insulate against getting attacked on *both* fronts?"

"Fine!" Daedalus shouted, uploading the information from his chip onto their now four-ship network.

"Okay," said Ji'ilaad. "Now configure an update and send it out to each ship."

"How do I do that?" Daedalus asked, unfamiliar with the networking interface. He only knew how to fly.

"Nevermind. I'll do it."

Ji'ilaad relinquished the stick to Andrei, who said a quiet prayer to an unspecified god as he took evasive action. Having listened as Derovias gave Ceres a tutorial, he thought he had the gist of it. Ji'ilaad reconfigured his transponder to broadcast a unique signature signed with Daedalus' identification. He created a signature for each craft and dispensed them across the network. He took the stick back from Andrei.

"Nice work not getting us killed."

"Yeah," Andrei replied. "My pleasure."

A stinger and speeder tandem broke off to pursue Kir, who had a big head start and a clear path to the station. He gunned the throttle, knowing he couldn't be caught. The pursuing crafts fired and he took evasive action. A missile closed on him. He released countermeasures and pitched downward to avoid the explosion. His lead decreased, but he punched the throttle anew.

TWENTY-FIVE

THE CONFEDERATION WARSHIPS loomed largest on the celestial horizon of the battle about to be met. The other craft grew in apparent size as the Allied fleet rushed to meet them.

On Ray's orders, Patrick had networked their vessels and Carina's. They shared a private comm, despite that Carina and her pilot had been assigned to a different squadron. Patrick looked out the canopy to his right to see Gardiner sitting WSO behind Ray, then looked at the back of his own pilot's helmet.

Patrick found himself wishing Jimmy were someone he knew but consoled himself that his pilot was Private Gray's kin, and that Carina, too, had been paired with a stranger.

I just hope this guy can fly is all.

"Rogue Squadron, this is Rogue Alpha, come back," said Ray over the comm channel shared by the three ships.

"Copy that," Carina replied. "This is Rogue Bravo. Over."

"Rogue Charlie," said Patrick. "I copy. Over."

"Keep the line open," Ray ordered, "and stay chatty. It's gonna turn to shit real soon so let's not lose each other. Over."

"How's it feel to be the ranking officer, Commander?" Carina asked. "Over." Her tone was pleasant and conversational, as if death weren't moments away.

"Feels good, Captain," he replied.

She could hear his smile over the comm.

"I never did like taking orders," he added. "Over."

"That makes two of us," she replied. She looked a little to her left. "Whoa, eleven o'clock."

One of the Confederation warships was charging its forward cannon. White light coursed along channels that pooled into a gleaming circle with a pure-black center. The light was so intense that the canopies of the Allied ships and the visors of their crews each darkened automatically to compensate for the glare.

Over the fleet-wide channel, Ray could hear the chatter of hundreds of Allied personnel. Admiral Howe ordered the fleet to take evasive action.

Once the cannon's black center was awash in light, a huge beam shot through the Allied fleet, vaporizing the smaller craft in its path. The discharge cut through an Allied battleship, cleaving it in half, and then bore a giant hole through the hull and out the back of the Allied command ship ANV *Victory*.

The cannon went dark, but the other warship began charging.

"Attack the warship!" came Admiral Howe's voice over the comm. "Ignore the rest of the fleet! Get that warship! Swarm the harridan bitch!"

On the bridge of the ANV *Britannia*, Howe barked orders to the bridge crew. "Get us out of its path!" On the viewscreen, he watched the *Victory* break apart.

Allied gunships, battleships, spitfires, and swifts converged on the two warships. The smaller Allied crafts swarmed the behemoth Confederate vessels, dodging them at close range, but stingers and speeders rushed to the defense. The Allied swifts and spitfires pelted the Confederate warships, but the shields could not be penetrated. The small Confederate fighters retaliated against their Allied analogues, forcing the swarm to take evasive action.

"White Alpha," said Ray to the nearest squadron leader, "this is Black Alpha, do you copy? Over?"

"Copy, Black Alpha," White Alpha replied. "Over."

"Warship's front shields have to drop to fire the cannon," said Ray. "Cannon mouth is tender. Hit 'em there, take 'em down. Over."

"Copy that, Black Alpha, but we need more weight," White Alpha answered. "Over."

"Copy that, White Alpha," said Ray. "Over." He opened a channel to the nearest Allied gunships, two daring-class vessels. "ANVs *Carlisle* and *Lyon*, this is Black Alpha, do you copy? Over."

"The *Carlisle* reads you loud and clear, Black Alpha. Go ahead. Over."

"This is *Lyon*. We copy. Over."

"Unload on the warship, right into that cannon. Shields drop to use it and we gotta hit 'em while they're down. Confirm. Over."

"Roger that, Black Alpha. *Carlisle* armed and ready. Over and out."

The *Lyon* responded with its own affirmative.

The White and Black Squadrons ducked and weaved around the Confederate warship, avoiding its smaller guns while dodging both the trailing and incoming stingers and speeders. The *Carlisle* and the *Lyon* took fire from the smaller Confederation vessels, but their shields held. The squadrons laid down cover fire.

The two Allied gunships set upon the Confederate warship, coming at it from ten and two o'clock. The warship fired its smaller guns while the front cannon charged. The warship artillery was considerably more powerful than that of the speeders and stingers pestering the *Lyon* and the *Carlisle*. Their shields drained with each direct hit.

"White Squadron, Black Squadron," said Ray, "take out the warship's battery or our boats are toast. Over."

Confirmations came in over the comm. The swifts and spitfires swarmed the warship.

Against the barrage from the warship's smaller arms, the *Carlisle*'s shields dropped to 20 percent. The *Lyon*'s held at 50. The small Allied fighters attacked the warship, taking out its lesser guns, giving the Allied boats some relief.

The warship's front cannon fully charged. The *Carlisle* and *Lyon* lay in wait for the shields to drop, guns trained upon the perimeter of the hulking ship's devastating weapon.

"White and Black Squadrons, get clear. Over," Ray ordered. He sped away from the warship, the *Carlisle*, and the *Lyon*.

The warship dropped its shields. The Allied gunships fired. Their pulse cannons and torpedoes exploded against the hull of the Confederation vessel. It turned to face the *Carlisle*. The blinding white beam shot out, obliterating the *Carlisle*, but the Allied gunships had succeeded. The cannon collapsed on itself, imploding into the guts of the Confederate ship until it burst apart in a bright flash. Debris and shrapnel scattered across all axes, striking Confederation and Allied craft alike. The *Lyon* backed away, taking heavy bombardment from the debris, depleting its already battered shields.

Raucous cheers erupted over the Allies' shared comm, followed by Admiral Howe's voice.

"Take out the other warship! Remember the *Carlisle*!"

The *Lyon* limped away from the wreckage but was set upon by a Confederate battleship and a swarm of fighters. They bombarded the hobbled Allied craft until its shields failed. The attack persisted, breaching the hull. Minuscule bodies were sucked into space. The gunship silently exploded in a bright flash. It extinguished almost instantly in the absence of atmosphere.

During the melee, the other warship had recharged its cannon. It fired, cleaving Admiral Howe's ship in half.

The *Britannia* listed. It careened through the debris field until caught by Earth's gravity. Even rent in two, each half of the giant ship was bigger than an entire Allied gunship. The wreckage hit the atmosphere. It streaked across the sky, burning up as it plummeted to the surface.

While the warship's forward shields were down, the thirty women and men of the Allied Blue Squadron flew their ships into the exposed hull in a mass suicide attack. The five two-man spitfires and five four-man swifts exploded against the warship's hull, breaching it. The warship lost propulsion and drifted off its axis. The breach vomited scores of tiny humanoid figures. One of the frozen, asphyxiated bodies bounced off Ray's shields, burning on contact before freezing again as it changed course, spinning through the void.

Allied Naval Vessels *Imperial* and *Relentless* unloaded their arsenals on the disabled warship, blasting it to bits. As they fired, two Confederation gunships countered, destroying the distracted Allied craft while simultaneously coming under attack from the Allied White and Gold Squadrons who were, in turn, dogged by swarms of speeders and stingers.

Ray turned his head from his left shoulder to his right as he rolled and yawed, taking in as much of the scene as he could. It was a chaotic mess. The two fleets were enmeshed. Both Allied command ships were gone. Only a handful of their gun- and battleships remained. Smaller craft comprised the majority of surviving Allied ships. Even with its two warships destroyed, the Confederation had the better of the outcome. The Allies couldn't hope to prevail.

Ray, his fellow Black Squadron pilots, and the White Squadron all flipped and burned, pitched, rolled, and yawed. They fired on each enemy bird they encountered, attempting to evade the debris of wrecked ships and the tireless pursuit of the stingers and speeders.

Wreckage from the Confederate warship cleaved White Bravo in two. Ray executed a barrel roll to avoid the tail of the destroyed swift. White Bravo's pilot and copilot, the WSO, and radio intercept officer were flung from the shattered cockpit. For sport, one of the speeders blasted two of the men to bits. The frozen flesh and gore struck Ray's shields and vaporized into molecules and atoms, which refroze, too small to notice.

The speeder set a collision course. It assaulted Ray's front shields with blaster fire. He ground his teeth. "Take him down, Major!"

Gardiner fired a missile, obliterating the tiny one-man vessel. Ray nose-dived to avoid the wreckage. His console beeped. He looked down to see that they were being hailed.

Gardiner opened the channel. "This is Black Alpha, go ahead. Over."

"Black Alpha, this is A'arilon Daedalus. Over."

Ray blinked once. "Daedalus."

"No time to chat, brothers," said Derovias, piggybacking on Daedalus' comm. "Break for the station, now. Over and out."

"Who is this?" Ray asked the strangely familiar voice.

"No time for that, Raymond," Daedalus interrupted. "Focus. Make a break for Overground. Find any open bay in the outer ring, land hard, and keep moving. We'll link up inside. Over and out."

"Wait! Link up how? How do I find you?" Ray asked desperately, but the channel was dead. He hesitated just a moment before calling in his birds. "White, Black, and Gold Squadrons, this is Black Alpha. Bug out and proceed to Overground. I repeat, proceed to Overground. Confirm. Over."

A flurry of confirmations came over the comm. The Allied swifts and spitfires sped toward the station in the wake of the four stingers flown by Derovias, Daedalus, Falco, and Ji'ilaad.

Kir had already breached the station.

"Stay tight as you can," Ray ordered, "and don't get got. Do whatever you must to stay up. Find an open bay, breach with the frequency modulations provided. Land hard and take care. See you on the inside. Black Alpha over and out."

Ivan tried to outmaneuver a trailing speeder to shake the small craft from their tail, but it stuck with them.

"Uh, Captain," he said to Carina, "I can't just bug out without orders from my squad leader . . ."

"Gold Alpha is down, Ivan," Carina replied. "Did you miss the chatter?" She opened a channel. "This is Gold Echo to Gold Alpha, do you copy?"

"Gold Echo, this is Gold Charlie. Gold Alpha is down. Over."

Carina glowered at Ivan even though his back was to her. "Our squad leader is dead. I swear, Lieutenant, if you don't bug out I'm gonna space us both."

"Gold Charlie, this is Gold Echo, copy that," said Ivan. "Over and out. Hold on to your guts, Captain."

He cut the engines, did a sharp right-angle thrust, and burned toward Overground. Carina's stomach ping-ponged around her torso. As they accelerated, she felt her eyeballs being pressed into her head. It felt like someone had reached inside her and was squeezing her ovaries.

The speeder stuck with them.

She deployed a mine and detonated it immediately. The blast destroyed the pursuing speeder and rocked their boat as well.

"Dammit, Captain!" Ivan barked.

"What would you prefer?" Carina spat back.

Ivan said nothing. He sped after the receding forms of his fellow Allies as they chased toward Overground.

Ray and his expanded Rogue Squadron—Carina with Ivan, Patrick with Jimmy Gray at the helm, and the rest of Black, White, and Gold Squadrons—overtook the Confederate ships in pursuit of Daedalus, Derovias, Falco, and Ji'ilaad.

Gardiner destroyed a speeder. The remaining Confederate craft scattered, yawing port and starboard to avoid being picked off. The Allied rogues outnumbered the nine remaining Confederates, but the corren pilots in their superior ships refused to be taken down easily.

The Allied spitfires and swifts danced with the stingers and speeders. The more maneuverable Red craft eluded weapons lock. They forced the Allied pilots to rely on sight and anticipation. With the stingers and speeders in full evasive action, the Allies had the tactical advantage. The Confederates jockeyed for the upper hand, luring the Allied craft back toward the Red fleet.

Ray called out orders over the comm. His birds grouped into trios to triangulate their targets. The stingers were easier to catch, but the speeders were too quick and agile. One of the small Confederate ships flipped and burned onto a collision course. The White Squadron ship in pursuit couldn't adjust in time. Both ships exploded into scrap.

Jimmy couldn't avoid the debris. It peppered his and Patrick's spitfire, draining the shields.

"Shields are at 15 percent!" Patrick exclaimed, panicked.

"We gotta bug out!" Jimmy replied, plotting their escape.

Patrick looked around, desperate. As he jerked his head in every direction, he caught motion from above. A stinger dropped precipitously toward them, its dorsal thrusters at maximum. Before he could cry out to take evasive action, the stinger slammed its belly down atop the canopy of the spitfire, rupturing the cockpit seal. Patrick's and Jimmy's insulated suits and oxygen supply were all that saved them.

The Confederate ship rose to mount another slam attack. Patrick looked around helplessly as the atmosphere leeched from the cockpit. His flight suit and helmet would keep him alive for a few hours in the vacuum, but he knew no one would retrieve them.

The stinger crashed down again. The spitfire's canopy buckled and rent, crushing Jimmy into a tiny, inescapable prison. His ribs burst through his skin and punctured his flight suit. His lungs, blood, and innards froze.

Patrick panicked, looking at Jimmy's slumped, dead form. The stinger came around, sighting the vulnerable, motionless ship. The corporal began to hyperventilate. The cockpit seal expanded to conform to the twisted new perimeter and keep the vacuum at bay.

Ivan came up behind the stinger and Carina fired. The Confederate fighter exploded in a burst of twisted metal, propelled forward from the blast. The razor-sharp shards pelted Patrick's spitfire.

"Oh, fuck . . ." Ivan murmured.

Carina put her hand atop her respirator. They watched as the debris chewed Patrick's ship, but the battered canopy held.

"This is Rogue Bravo. Rogue Charlie, please respond," Carina implored. "Private, do you copy? Over."

"I copy, Rogue Bravo," said Patrick, dazed.

"Do you have thrust, kiddo?" Ivan asked.

"Thrust?" Patrick replied.

"Take the stick," said Ivan. "Put your left hand on the throttle and give it a little push."

Ivan rolled away from attacking fire. He gritted his teeth against playing flight instructor and fighter pilot at the same time.

Patrick pushed the throttle and the ship shot forward. "I've got thrust!" he blurted in elation.

"Okay!" said Ivan, smiling at the good news. "Get on my tail, buddy. You gotta follow me."

Patrick brought his crippled vessel around. He pushed the stick forward and nose-dived, making his stomach lurch into his throat. He pulled back and cursed himself, pushing instead on the throttle.

"Okay, he's on our six," said Carina. "Punch it, Ivan."

A stinger screamed in behind Patrick and opened fire. He clenched his teeth against the barrage. The canopy broke free. The impact ejected him into the infinite black.

"Fuck!" Ivan howled.

Carina said nothing. She had no words. The battle raged all around. She gave her head a sharp shake and collected herself.

"Get us to the station, Lieutenant," she ordered.

"But . . ." Ivan hedged.

"Now, Lieutenant! There's nothing we can do for him!"

Ivan scowled. He raced away at full throttle.

Patrick hung, weightless in the expanse. He played dead, hoping the Confederate pilot wouldn't shoot him to pieces. He noticed he was moving, being propelled. Looking at his oxygen monitor, the level plummeted. The stinger sped over him in pursuit of Ivan and Carina. Patrick watched it go. He floated, ignored. As the oxygen leeched from his pack, it became harder and harder to breathe.

He turned.

He could see so much of Earth. It seemed so small from so high above.

The sun peeked out from behind the black orb. Patrick's visor tinted automatically, but he still had to hold up his hand to shield his eyes against the brilliant sight.

The last of his oxygen escaped. His eyelids felt heavy.

He brought his hand down for one last look at the sun.

He closed his eyes.

TWENTY-SIX

KIR DIRECTED HIS stinger at the nearest bay. It had sent back a confirmed friendly signal, signed by Asharan Lután. As he approached, the artillery guarding the port opened fire, belying the welcome. He took evasive action and gunned the throttle.

Touching down hard, the vessel crashed into the hangar floor at speed. The impact rattled their bones. The ship skidded along the metal deck, spewing sparks. Kir's helmet smashed hard against the back of his chair and then against the console. He blacked out. The craft crashed into the far wall, rending the starboard wing from the fuselage.

Sargas opened the canopy and climbed down. He surveyed the carnage and observed evidence of a firefight, coupled with the consequence of the crash landing: bodies strewn about, in pieces. Countless small fires burned. He made no attempt to look after Kir.

The stinger and speeder in pursuit of Kir and Sargas were met by fighters piloted by Marseh's loyalists. With the element of surprise on their side, Marseh's pilots neutralized the threat. The wrecks crashed into Overground, disabling the perimeter of the force field. The atmosphere leeched from the bay.

Sargas flew from his feet. He grabbed at the ladder on the side of the speeder, wrapping his arm around a rung to keep from being sucked into space. Surviving members of the hangar crew were vacuumed into the black.

The blast doors slammed closed. The pressure equalized. Sargas relinquished his hold on the ladder, checked his weapons, and set off to hunt down his target.

***

The Rogue Squadron dispatched their Confederate attackers, but at a heavy cost.

Only two ships from White Squadron remained. Ray and Gardiner were the sole survivors from Black. The three Allied vessels raced off, on the tail of Ivan's and Carina's Gold Squadron spitfire. They'd avoided the fray and gained the lead.

The Allied fleet was routed. The hulks of battered ships and a flotilla of estranged, frozen bodies littered the space between Earth and Overground. Though crippled, the Confederates were the victors. At any moment, the surviving ships would come about to return home.

Overground loomed. Ray couldn't see Daedalus, Derovias, nor the other dissident craft. He hailed them but received no response. He didn't know where to go.

"Where do we land?" Ivan asked.

"Just stay the course," Ray replied. "Find any open bay and land hard. Bail out and find cover. Turn off your transponder when you touch down."

They flew into Bay 11, passing through the force field uninhibited, thanks to the stolen plans. From within the hangar, Arak Matar's loyalists fired upon the ships. Ivan spun the spitfire around with its thrusters. He burned the engines again, incinerating two of the shooters. The thrust slowed the ship, but it crashed hard into the hangar wall and bounced back a few feet. Carina's teeth rattled as she slammed against the side of the cockpit.

The canopy popped open. Without a word, she and Ivan pushed upon the heavy lid and threw it aside. They clambered down the side of the spitfire, using it as cover.

Ray and Gardiner came crashing in. The blast doors slammed down behind them. One of the White Squadron ships couldn't pull up in time. It crashed headlong into the station, exploding in a silent ball of fire. The other spitfire pulled up in time but was cut down by the gun battery protecting the bay.

Inside, Ray spun his craft ninety degrees. It slammed upon the floor, skidding toward the back wall. Halfway through the hangar, the ship collided with a parked speeder and flipped over, grinding to a halt on its canopy. Carina and Ivan ran from their hiding spot with guns blazing. They hurried to Ray and Gardiner and pulled the men from the wreckage. Gardiner's tibia and fibula were broken. His left leg bent at a sudden, unnatural jag, but he didn't cry out. He threw his left arm over Ivan's shoulders. They hobbled toward the station's interior doors.

Gardiner used telekinesis to fling wrenches, crates, and any other loose item at the Confederates who blocked their way. He knocked the weapons from the correns' hands, knocking the men to the ground beneath the barrage of objects moved with his mind.

To witness such a display stunned Ivan.

Gardiner slumped against him, physically drained by the mental effort, but Ivan kept his balance and his wits about him. He kept his mouth shut, awkwardly firing his pistol with his weak left hand. He hit no living targets but came close enough to send them scattering.

He and the major reached the doors first. Ray and Carina followed a few meters behind. The portal refused to open.

Confederation soldiers also wore subdermal implants, but the Allied chips were useless on Overground. The soldiers scattered by Gardiner's debris storm and Ivan's sloppy shooting regained their bearings.

"Can't you throw some more shit at them, Major?" Ivan asked.

"No; I'm drained."

Ray and Carina fired, drawing the Confederates away from the hobbled Gardiner. And from Ivan, acting as his crutch.

***

Marseh remained incorporeal. He knew, in so dire a situation, that he needed free rein to cast himself about the station, materializing before any of his men who needed counsel. He worried that the ease with which he appeared on cue might inure his charges to his powers, but it served only to reinforce their awe.

As Marseh appeared before them, Lután came to a sudden halt with Miro, Skal, and Ishka.

"Emperor!" said Lután. "The Allies have breached the station."

Marseh deduced that the Allied soldiers who landed would need access to the station to be useful against Arak's loyalists. He cursed himself for not preempting the situation.

"Lután. Gentlemen," Marseh said, addressing the four correns.

They stood at attention.

"You must make an exception to our security protocols."

"My Lord?" said Lután.

"Give the Allies unfettered access to the outer ring, anywhere Arak Matar's men have dug in."

"Emperor," said Miro. "These are our enemies! We should eliminate these intruders!"

Marseh held up his hand. "Dearest Miro, there is an expression: the enemy of my enemy is my friend. Governor Arak is our enemy. The Allies, now . . . those who have breached the station . . . are our friends."

Marseh looked at Lután.

"Give them access. Their chips must work much the same as ours. Grant permissions to any foreign near-field broadcast. Keep the inner rings locked down. I want Shaula and the others to remain unmolested. And keep this action to yourselves. No one needs to know we give comfort to these Allies."

***

Ivan and Gardiner stood with their backs against the hangar exit. The lieutenant fired at the Confederates. His weak-hand shooting was getting steadier. Ray and Carina added crossfire.

The correns fell back.

Ivan leaned against the door. His left hand dropped near the sensor. The door slid open. He tumbled backward into the hallway, letting go of Gardiner who hopped on his good foot as Ivan fell onto his backside. The major clenched his teeth against the pain that jolted through his broken limb with each bounce.

Carina came and steadied him with her right arm.

"I said I'd carry you," she said. "And I can shoot straight." She smiled at Ivan to indicate the jest.

He returned to his feet and frowned anyway.

The four Allied infiltrators crept down the corridor, their pace hobbled by Gardiner's handicap. Ray and Ivan cut down the resistance, but after a while, the Allies found themselves alone and unbothered.

"We have to set his leg," said Carina.

"You're in charge now, Captain," Ray replied. "This is an army mission. We follow your orders."

Carina set down Gardiner and examined his wound. She palpated his shin, assessing the direction of the break and how best to realign both bones.

"Technically, I'm in charge, agh—!" Gardiner grimaced as Carina set his leg. He exhaled a shuddering breath. "But, in this case, I defer to the captain's good judgment."

Honestly, Maks, Carina thought, *we need to stash you somewhere. You're slowing us down and we can't afford that.*

Gardiner heard her as clearly as if she'd spoken. She couldn't see his face, hidden behind his opaque visor, but he stared daggers at her.

How dare you, he thought, yet said nothing to betray his disappointment.

Her thoughts angered him, but he tried to console himself that she hadn't said it aloud. Insight into the workings of a person's mind was a curse. He hated to be reminded that, fundamentally, people were selfish. It mattered little to him that, at very rare times, someone might act contrary to their base instinct. But it mattered some. The ability to contradict one's own greed was the only evidence he had of goodness.

Silently, he begged not to be left behind. He thought of telepathically forcing Carina to change her mind, but he was distracted by Ray.

"I wonder if there is somewhere safe we could put you, Major."

"We can't leave him behind!" Carina exclaimed. "That's a death sentence! Besides, he's far more valuable than any of us. We can't afford to lose him."

"That's kind of you, Captain," replied the major, grateful that Carina's actions belied her desires. "But my mind isn't of much use at the moment. I can't concentrate through this pain. All I could do is force one of you to shoot me, like a lame horse."

"That's not acceptable!" Carina admonished. "No one's going to do that, Major."

"You act as if you'd have a choice," said Gardiner.

Ray frowned. He looked at Carina. "Captain . . ."

She looked at Gardiner. "Come on, Maks. Be serious."

"I prefer not to be abandoned," he replied.

Carina sighed heavily. "Of course."

She wanted to fight. She rued being amid the enemy she had hated her entire life and yet unable to engage them. But her first duty was as a doctor, and Gardiner needed one.

He resented her ambivalence, thinking of Sotillo. *I saved you from him.*

Carina couldn't shake that Gardiner was the reason she hadn't been raped, yet again. Guilt bloomed from her core to the tip of every extremity. She recalled their conversation at Heathrow.

"You've always had my back," she said, smiling at him. "I won't leave you."

Gardiner rolled his eyes behind the cover of his visor. He ground his teeth but bit back a torrent of invective. He reverted his visor to transparent and offered his closest approximation of a smile.

TWENTY-SEVEN

KIR AWOKE IN the cockpit of his battered stinger and tensed. He sat up fast and regretted it. His skull throbbed. He looked over his shoulder. Sargas was gone.

Staggering from the cockpit, Kir set off into the station, hoping to catch up with Marseh's pet assassin. He tried to contact Derovias but the comm refused to function, broken in the collision that concussed him.

Hiding behind his own mirrored shield, a faceless Confederate—human, by his size—raised his rifle, but Kir shot first. Even with the pain in his head, his draw was second only to Derovias. That Kir's centurion uniform incited the human to violence meant the man was loyal to the emperor, but there wasn't time to discuss their mutual allegiance. Kir stepped over his victim.

Killing Inishi still haunted Kir, but he knew the first kill was always the hardest. His first human had been hard on him, too. The second had been easier, but guilt still followed him through the next few until he'd come to enjoy it. He'd thought that killing humans was one thing, correns another, but it wasn't. Killing was killing. The enemy was the enemy, and so, too, was a confused ally.

He doubted he would ever again derive joy from dealing death, but he couldn't put himself and his fellows at risk over pangs of conscience. His adversaries would not be equally troubled.

Kill or be killed. The directive took him over, and he went to work.

***

Derovias, Daedalus, Falco, and Ji'ilaad landed in a friendly bay in the outer ring. Unable to reach Kir, Derovias ordered the group to form up and move out.

He, Daedalus and René, Ceres and Andre, Falco and Ji'ilaad stalked the corridors in impeccable formation. They worked in seamless concert, mowing down adversaries with deadly force. Derovias and his column checked the bays, looking for Kir and Sargas, for Ray and his band of Allied rogues, and for Arak Matar. They found nothing.

In the chatter over the open comm, it was bedlam.

Both sides shared some of the same frequencies where combatants hadn't taken the time to sync to a private, sympathetic channel. Derovias cycled through the bands, listening for anything useful.

"Bay 44 . . ." he heard as he skipped to the next frequency.

It was the first specific place he heard mentioned that wasn't a junction. An interior cargo hold with no port. The large, open space provided little cover. Not ideal for combat, it suggested a show. Theater. Something in need of an audience. And it was close to Arak's quarters in the central ring.

Derovias opened a shared channel to his small group. "Anyone else hear 'Bay 44' on the chatter?"

"Yes," said Ji'ilaad. "A few times."

Falco confirmed.

"It's as good a place as any," Derovias pondered aloud. "I think that's where we'll find the Butcher. With me."

They regrouped into formation, taking the shortest route to the central ring, to whom they hoped to find.

***

Upon losing the Allies in the Hugtaender i Nord, Mag'err and Skru'ul retreated back to Blackwing manor. They arrived on the heels of Derovias and Kir taking off in apparent pursuit of Daedalus, the traitor Asharan Antal.

Pongsrion Klahan met the two oft-mute centurions on the tarmac and encouraged them to fly to the station. He told them that Arak Matar had absconded to Overground and needed loyal men to come to his aid. They didn't hesitate to suit up and fly off to aid their master.

Mag'err piloted a stinger into Bay 15, manned by Arak's loyalists. Upon landing, the two centurions hurried to the deck. The hangar's handler came over to provide a quick rundown. The correns learned that Arak was in open rebellion against Marseh. Their only thought was to join the fray.

Alesh and Inishi had been one of the most famous centurion tandems, feared for their cruelty and brutality. Alesh had been known, too, for his mouth. Inishi, less so, but had spoken whenever the need arose. Mag'err and Skru'ul were known for being taciturn. Few knew if they even could speak, but the men were equally famous killing machines. They struck even more fear than Alesh and Inishi, because they never taunted, never gloated, never threatened.

They acted.

TWENTY-EIGHT

IT WAS SLOW going with Gardiner's arm draped across Carina's shoulders. Ray and Ivan grew visibly impatient, although neither said a word.

"Stop, Captain. Please," Gardiner ordered.

Carina came to a halt and helped him slide to the floor. He rested against the bulkhead. Ray and Ivan turned around to face them.

Gardiner looked up at the two men. "You go on. We can't keep moving like this; we're putting you both at risk."

Ray flipped up his visor. "And what about you, sir? We can't just leave you here."

"The captain will stay with me. We'll find some place to hole up. There's got to be somewhere she can treat me."

The look on Carina's face betrayed her disappointment but was mercifully hidden behind her visor. Although she had made up her mind to stay, she didn't want to babysit her crippled CO. She wanted to run and gun, take out as many Confederates as she could. She wanted to see some action. Make a difference.

As much as Gardiner wanted to judge her for her actions, he couldn't ignore her inner conflict. And he couldn't stem the bitterness it elicited in him.

Ray looked at Carina. "What do you say, Captain?"

"I can't leave him," she replied. "You two go on. We'll be fine."

Ray nodded, then walked over to Ivan. The two of them double-timed it out of sight.

"Come on, Maks," said Carina. "Up. We've been lucky so far, but we can't bank on that."

After a long while of limping around, unchallenged only because they had not encountered another soul, they hobbled to a lift. Carina waved her chip in front of the panel and their good luck continued.

"Someone is looking out for us," said Gardiner.

"Yeah, it's creepy," Carina replied. She wondered how far Ray and Ivan had gotten.

The lift came to them and they got in.

"Computer," said Carina. It beeped its affirmative. "Where is the nearest medical bay?"

The computer replied with the location and the ETA.

"Take us there."

The computer beeped and began the horizontal portion of their trip. Gardiner pushed away from her and slid down the wall to a seat. Carina gravitated to the opposite side of the lift.

"You're disappointed," he said.

"I'm here, aren't I?" she replied. "Don't read my mind, Maks."

"Don't need super powers to see that."

"Aren't *you*?" she asked, turning the question back on him.

"Of course I am . . . I'm helpless, like a fucking child." He swiped at the air. Through no intent of his own, he lashed out telepathically.

Carina felt as if she'd actually been struck. She flinched. She eyed him, wary and sullen. But Gardiner remained oblivious to his psychic effluvia.

"You think I want to be useless?" he complained. "Be at your mercy when I could be tearing this fucking place apart like nothing they've ever seen?"

"I'm sorry," Carina blanched. "I didn't mean to upset you."

He waved his hand at her. Again, she felt physical contact though none had occurred.

"Please stop," she said.

He glowered at her. "Stop what?"

"Whenever you bark at me or wave your hand, it feels like you're hitting me."

He blinked in surprise, but he didn't apologize.

"Fuck," he said, looking at his broken leg. "I'm not upset at you. I'm just . . ." He set his eyes upon her with a hard look. "What's the fucking point?"

She frowned. Her brow furrowed in discomfort. Her full lips nearly disappeared into a taut line.

He smacked the floor of the lift.

"We get so close to something satisfying, and here we are," he said, "looking for bandages while everyone else runs around taking the fight to the enemy on his own turf. It's the first time in my lifetime we've ever mounted an offensive, and I'm missing it."

He growled the last few words through his clenched teeth.

"I know what you mean . . ." Carina replied.

"Sure you do," he replied. "Except for you, it's worse, right?"

"I didn't say that . . ."

He ignored her protestation. "Because there's nothing wrong with *you*. You could be out there . . . a part of it . . . not stuck playing nanny to a fucking invalid!"

"Maks," she pleaded. "You need to calm down."

"You want me to be *calm*?" he blared.

Again, Carina felt his telepathic attack. "Stop it! Stop doing that!"

"Am I hurting you, Carina?" His tone was cruel. "Really? I am *sick* of keeping it all together. I am *tired* of having to manage myself in the company of weaklings with delusions of power. You're all just fucking *ants* to me."

Carina's mouth fell open, just barely.

A twinge of regret flickered over his face. "I'm sorry. I don't mean you. You've been good to me . . ."

She said nothing.

Sliding to the floor, she wished she were anywhere else. She was truly afraid, and her fear terrified her because she never trembled in the face of danger. She welcomed the physical aggression of anyone who wished her harm, confident she could handle herself. But, in Gardiner's company, trapped in the small lift with his rage and his supernatural power, she was helpless.

She hated being at his mercy. He hated himself for making her feel that way. He thought of her as one of his only friends, this woman who despised everyone, especially men. Yet she had been uncharacteristically kind to him. All of the social capital he'd accrued with her, all the friendship and camaraderie they had built, he'd stripped away in seconds.

"I'm sorry, Carina," he said.

She smiled, but not from humor. Incredulous, she shook her head. She didn't know what to say.

"I know you know how it feels to hate yourself," he said.

"Stop that. You don't get to steal things from my mind. That's worse than hitting me. That's rape, Maks."

He flinched at the word but couldn't argue. What else could one call an uninvited intrusion into a person's most private place? He did it regularly. Daily. Hourly. He thought back to that day when he lay with his burned face in the cool mud, after those men had used his body for their pleasure. He didn't want to believe that only semantic, philosophical difference existed between those rapists and his own surreptitious burglary of private thoughts. He didn't want to be like those men.

"I know what rape is, Carina," he said.

"And so do I," she sneered. "Just because someone took something from you doesn't mean you get to pay it forward."

"How many men have you killed, Karin?" he said.

Hearing her birth name jarred her. She wondered if it was a tactic. It made her angrier. "What the fuck does it matter, *Maksim*? How many men have *you* killed?"

"What is it like to revenge yourself on everyone you meet," he asked, "whether or not they did you harm?"

"I have *never* been the aggressor. I've never *preyed* on anyone!" She shook with indignation.

"What about your women?"

"Fuck you. You don't get to put me on trial. I'm sorry you're upset, but get the fuck off my back. Don't push your shit on me."

He smirked and, at the same time, screwed up his face in disgusted disappointment. "What is the *point*, Carina?"

"There is no fucking point! Live until you die. That's it!"

"I've never enjoyed this. I never asked for it."

"None of us did. Our fathers couldn't keep their dicks in their pants. We're here because they just *had* to come. They just couldn't *help* themselves. That's the definition of selfish. For a moment's pleasure you bring a child into this fucking world. It's fucking contemptible."

"And what about our stupid cunt mothers who couldn't keep their goddamned legs closed?" he retorted. "It takes two."

Carina ignored the remark. They sat through a prolonged silence.

"Why do you even bother?" he asked.

She glared at him, but she couldn't maintain the expression. Exhausted with being angry, she wanted to rest. She wanted peace.

"Because as much as I think I want to die," she answered. Tears welled in her eyes but she fought them back. "I don't. I've thought about it." She shrugged. "I can't bring myself to do it."

Gardiner chuckled to himself. "It's sad, really," he said. "That even when there's no reason to go on . . . you can't even bring yourself to stop."

Carina looked at the monitor. A few minutes remained until they reached their destination.

"It's just not worth it," he declared.

Carina's left hand twitched involuntarily.

"What are you gonna do?" he asked. "Put me in a brace and leave me in a bed to get shot, helpless and crippled, by the first snake who walks in the door?"

Carina pulled her Mateba from her hip holster. She looked at her hand in horror. She was not in control.

"What are you doing?" she asked, panicked. "Maks?"

He forced her to raise her arm and aim the pistol at his face. "I asked you to do me and you said you would."

"Not like this . . ." she protested, helpless. She fought to bring her arm down but couldn't.

He smiled at her. "Just do me this mercy. Okay?"

There was no malice on his face. He was the picture of calm.

She fought with every ounce of strength to take control of her body away from him. She failed. Her finger squeezed the trigger. The bullet struck Gardiner's forehead, blowing out the back of his skull. His brains spattered the wall.

Released from his thrall, Carina screamed.

She threw away the gun. She screamed. She screamed and screamed, unable to withhold the grief. Tears flooded from her eyes. Raising her shaking hands to her face, she blubbered in shock. A heavy sob wracked her body. She retched, but nothing came out. She retched again, but her stomach was empty. A third time, she retched and spat bile and blood onto the floor. Her insides hurt from the effort of expelling the nothing in her guts.

The lift came to a halt and the doors didn't open.

The computer beeped and then spoke.

"Life support to this block has been disabled. For access, you must request an override."

Carina looked around, confused. Her eyes fell upon Gardiner's corpse. The peaceful look on his face was incongruous with the .44-caliber hole in his forehead. He looked asleep. He was. Asleep forever.

She shuddered at the sight of him and then couldn't stop shaking.

Rising, she looked around again, as if seeing her surroundings for the first time.

The computer beeped again and repeated its message.

"Life support to this block has been disabled . . ."

She opened the collar of her armor and zipped her leather jacket as high as it would go, to shield herself from the cold, but it came from within. Her skin crawled. She shuddered again. Her teeth chattered. The smell of Gardiner's bowels reached her nostrils and she retched again, spitting more bile, more blood onto the floor. It felt as if her organs would erupt from her mouth.

Replacing her armor collar, she donned her flight helmet, creating the seal to protect her from the vacuum. The heads-up display in her visor indicated that an hour of her oxygen supply remained.

"Computer," she said, her voice muffled by the respirator. "Let me out."

The computer beeped. "Override requested. Please confirm."

"Confirmed," Carina said. Her voice was small. "Open up. Please. Please . . ."

A hot tear streamed from her right eye and down her cheek.

"Let me out."

The computer beeped again and the doors opened. The air rushed from the lift. Carina took a step and inadvertently kicked her revolver. She looked down at it. She had loved that gun from the moment she found it, had cared for it meticulously. It had served her well. Saved her life. She'd killed with it more people than she could count. Now, the last body on it was her friend.

Her friend, who made her murder him.

She couldn't bear to look at the pistol. She stepped over it and into the hallway, leaving both the Mateba and the major behind.

TWENTY-NINE

MARSEH HAD LET their presence slip, so Reyevas sought out the refugees from Lambda Scorpii.

He inferred that Marseh had rescued them and brought them to the station. Inference was the best Reyevas could do; Alitán couldn't read each other's thoughts. They could meld their incorporeal forms to create a shared consciousness, but only through a willful act. Their thoughts could not be invaded from afar.

Left to guess whom Marseh had saved, and where on Overground they were kept, Reyevas projected himself around the station. He felt for a mind or minds out of place amid the bellicose bustle of correns and humans. They fought their former compatriots because their masters could not agree.

And then Reyevas felt it. Dozens of minds. Some of them unlike any he had encountered: animal but intelligent—sapient—and then some that were unmistakably human. Except, these human minds were not preoccupied with the strife that gripped Overground. They were insulated. Only one of them seemed to know about anything beyond the environment to which she was confined.

Reyevas focused on her. When he appeared before her, he projected himself to look like Marseh. Shaula could not tell the difference.

Reyevas read her mind. He picked off her name as it bubbled up in her own consciousness in response to seeing, or so she thought, the man who had named her.

"Hello, my dear," said Reyevas, mimicking Marseh's tone and his gentle, grandfatherly comportment.

"Hello, Darek," she replied.

She suspected nothing; Reyevas presented a perfect illusion.

Shaula still wore the armor in which she'd raided the Dorance facility with Lután, Miro, Skal, and Ishka. Her gray cat stalked nearby, its long tail snapped soundlessly through the air. It looked at Reyevas and bared its teeth. Before the cat could growl, Reyevas struck at its mind and knocked out the feline. It slumped to the ground in deep slumber. To Shaula, it seemed like any other gesture from a lazy cat without a care in the world.

A few other humans lurked in the distance. They watched Reyevas interact with Shaula. Other animals stood near the eavesdropping humans. The creatures' eyes exhibited keen, wary intelligence but the impostor refused to let the curiosities distract him.

He searched Shaula's mind for something to use as a lure and he found Sargas. He didn't know who the man was, but Shaula's own thoughts surreptitiously revealed it. In the chaos of the battle between the Confederate and Allied fleets and the hard landings of rogue fighters, Reyevas wondered if her Sargas might be among the infiltrators. It didn't matter whether it was true. Shaula only needed to believe that it was.

"Sargas has returned," said Reyevas.

Shaula's face lit up. Her hand went unconsciously to her belly. Its roundness was incongruous with the fitness of the rest of her body. Without needing to confirm, Reyevas knew she was pregnant with Sargas' baby.

"May I see him?" she said, excited like a child. "Will he come here?"

"No, child," said Reyevas. It amused him to copy Marseh, and to do it so well. Shaula believed Reyevas was him. "You must go to him."

"Really?" she said, surprised.

Reyevas sensed that she was suspicious. He worked to allay that suspicion.

"I know I've kept you here, to keep you safe . . ." Flashes of her mission to Orchard City appeared before his mind's eye. "But you have proven that you can handle yourself."

He mimed Marseh's wan, beatific smile.

"War has erupted, Shaula. Arak Matar and his forces move against me. I need your help."

Shaula beamed with pride.

Reyevas inwardly derided her naïveté. She was his puppet. The doors to the private bay opened, bidden by his will. She looked at Reyevas, who nodded at her. She ran into the lock, activating her boots to bind her to the lesser gravity as it transitioned.

Reyevas closed the doors behind her and winked out of sight. Knowing now what Sargas looked like from the picture in Shaula's mind, Reyevas cast himself here and there, not even bothering to pop into full view if he did not encounter whom he wished to see. He appeared like a swirl of opalescent dust buffeted by an unfelt wind. Anyone who noticed him may have startled in momentary disbelief, but no one on the station could afford to wonder at what they saw, lest they be cut down by an opportunistic, corporeal enemy.

Reyevas delighted in impersonating Marseh. When he found Arak's wayward centurion, Derovias, he materialized before him.

The dissident band all halted. Daedalus and René stood agog. Neither could believe what they saw. Neither had really believed Marseh was anything but an idea invented to inspire fear of a godlike creature. To see Reyevas' perfect illusion of the emperor, they didn't know any better that he wasn't the genuine article. They were stupid with awe.

Andrei grabbed Ceres' arm in shock. She shrugged him off and sidled closer to Falco. Andrei bristled and Ji'ilaad forced himself between the estranged partners.

"My Lord," said Derovias, fooled by Reyevas' disguise.

"Hello, Derovias," said Reyevas. "I've come to inform you of Arak's whereabouts."

"Bay 44," said Derovias. "That's where we're headed right now."

Reyevas pondered whether to mislead them, but a certain curiosity afflicted him. The Alitán were, more than anything, fascinated by behavior. Looking over Derovias' party, the impostor noticed that Sargas was not among them.

Reyevas remained unconvinced that destabilizing the Confederation—the only power strong and cohesive enough to potentially govern a unified planet—was an acceptable course of action. He believed the Allies were the bigger threat to Earth's recovery and future prosperity, and that Arak was the best hope for defeating them.

Alitán directive forbid insinuating oneself into the fabric of a society. Marseh had defied it countless times. But Reyevas prided himself that he was not Marseh. That he would not go to Earth and kill the Allied bureaucrats and commanders blind to the big picture. Despite that they focused only on their petty, egomaniacal lust for individual power. He had to let them be.

Yet, as he inwardly judged Marseh, Reyevas hedged. He refused to acknowledge his own hypocrisy. He excused his own behavior as necessary, minor enough in scope to be excusable. He rationalized that to move a few pawns was not to infiltrate the fabric of a society. And, besides, society on Overground was tearing itself apart. He intended his machinations to mend those tears. He believed that Arak could dispatch these nuisances. Reyevas was fixing, not destroying.

"Yes," he said. "Go there. Confront him." He stood aside, allowing them to pass.

Derovias took point with Ji'ilaad and Andrei behind him. Falco and René came next, with Ceres and Daedalus as the rear guard.

Reyevas winked from view. He continued to cast about the station until he found Sargas.

"Hello, Sargas."

"Emperor." He looked shrewdly at Reyevas, in a way that seemed as if he doubted what he saw, but his eyes told him that it was Marseh.

Reyevas knew Sargas was unconvinced. "Why do you roam the corridors when you have an objective to accomplish?"

"I *will* kill him, Lord," said Sargas. "If you'll just tell me where he is."

"Despite reports of his presence, my dear boy, the governor is not on the station. We believe he's gone to Mars."

Sargas screwed up his face in disbelief.

"Shaula, however, is roaming the corridors," said Reyevas. He wondered how stupid or, at the very least, lovesick and foolish Sargas might be. To Reyevas, such things were equivalent.

The large man's stony expression wavered for a split second. He was confused. He had a mission to fulfill but was worried for Shaula, and for their baby.

"Why is she roaming the station?" he demanded.

Inwardly, Reyevas smiled at his attempt to undermine Marseh's pet. "She refused to remain captive while the battle raged all around her. Dearest boy, you know how she is."

Sargas' resolve wavered completely. A slight panic overtook him. "I have to find her."

"No!" Reyevas commanded.

The emphasis shocked Sargas. He had never heard Marseh raise his voice. It might have given him further cause to wonder, if Reyevas' illusion had not been so complete, his manner so convincing.

"You have a job to do," said Reyevas, his voice stern. "You have one purpose, and it is not Shaula. Wherever Arak Matar is, it is your duty to find him. To kill him. Don't disappoint me."

Sargas nodded and Reyevas winked out of view, satisfied that the distraction of worrying about Shaula would derail the assassin.

THIRTY

CARINA SAW THE bodies the instant she left the lift, dozens of them. Many wore no armor, nor respirators. Civilians. They had suffocated where they stood.

She kept her eyes straight ahead, not wanting to see the tortured, terrified faces. Gardiner's own dead face still swam in her vision as if she'd stared at a light for too long. She moved slowly, noticing the bodies in her peripheral vision, stepping over and around them as she made her way toward the medical bay.

And then she realized there was no point.

She looked around the deathly silent corridor, not knowing what to do.

Following the endless leftward bend of the circular hallway, she pressed onward until she reached another sealed door. The computer informed her that her current compartment was devoid of air, as if she didn't already know.

"Just open the fucking doors, please," she said.

The computer beeped in affirmation. The atmosphere on the other side rushed in to fill the vacuum, whooshing past Anjali who stood, surprised, with her weapon pointed at Carina. The captain's green and black armor gave Anjali pause.

Carina held up her hands and walked through the door. Her visor turned transparent, revealing her unmistakable eyes and her angry face. The door closed behind her and the atmosphere was restored.

Anjali clarified her own visor.

"Don't point that fucking thing at me," Carina said. Her voice sounded tinny through her helmet's speaker.

Anjali frowned and lowered her weapon.

Of all the people to find, it's her.

***

Ray and Ivan ran through corridor after corridor, trying to reason where to go, thwarted at every attempt to reach the inner rings of the station. Their mystery clearances didn't extend beyond the outer ring.

"We're completely fucking adrift," Ray finally admitted over the private comm.

"We should get back to the main drag," Ivan suggested. "I don't think we can get to the center ring on foot, at least not the back way."

Ray was sure they couldn't get there at all but saw no point in saying it. He nodded. They worked their way toward the central corridor. At the bottom of a service ladder, the stencil on the wall told them their location.

Ivan began to climb. Ray looked down. He couldn't see the bottom of the shaft. It gradually curved, following the contour of the tubular ring. He climbed. Each level was at least two stories tall, but they made good progress. Looking up at Ivan, Ray hoped the lieutenant wouldn't slip.

***

Anjali and Carina walked the abandoned corridor.

They left their visors transparent, to see each other's faces. Neither understood why the outer ring was deserted. Carina surmised that, like the docks of any port city, if attack came from the water, the stevedores would retreat. It explained the lack of civilian traffic, at least, but not of soldiers. The only enemies she saw were those already dead, lying in various poses, strewn everywhere.

"I guess the battle's moved on," said Anjali. She gripped her rifle.

A rat darted out and she took aim at it, but her finger relaxed from the trigger as the scared rodent scurried away. She turned to Carina and smiled self-consciously, but her expression turned to dread. She saw movement from a maintenance shaft over the captain's shoulder.

Anjali pushed Carina aside and fired.

Ivan threw up his hands in a futile attempt to defend himself. The blast struck him and he fell backward into the shaft, slamming against the back wall, screaming as he fell. He crashed into Ray and knocked him loose.

Ray's helmet banged against the wall. He flailed for purchase, slapping his hands on the opening to the level below, slowing his descent only slightly. Gravity pulled at him as he scrabbled for purchase on the smooth floor. As he went over the edge, he turned and made a desperate grab for the ladder behind him.

He snagged a rung but his hand slid free, slapping against the next. Reaching out with his other hand, he grabbed firm hold of another rung, putting his free hand and his left foot against the wall opposite the ladder.

He stopped his descent. He looked down.

Ivan was gone.

***

"Who was that?" Carina accused.

"I don't know . . ." Anjali replied. A faint whine crept into her voice, like a child who knew she'd done something wrong. She frowned in guilt-ridden distress.

Carina moved cautiously toward the shaft and looked down. She couldn't see anything, so she switched to night vision. A few stories below, she saw a person on the rungs but couldn't make out any detail.

"There's someone down there," Carina said to Anjali.

"Really?" she said, moving toward the shaft with her gun at the ready.

"Don't!" said Carina, using her body as a barrier. "They're not moving. Put that gun away before you shoot me, too. Come on. Let's get out of here. I don't want to know who you hit. And I doubt you do, either."

***

The recent encounter with Marseh still gnawed at Sargas.

He didn't know where Arak Matar would be, only that he didn't believe the Butcher had absconded to Mars. Sargas knew something was amiss, but he couldn't put his finger on it. When the real Marseh appeared, the emperor sensed something was awry. He searched Sargas' recent memories and saw the encounter with the disguised Reyevas.

"It wasn't me," Marseh said. "But it seems you already suspected that."

"Tell me something I can believe, then," Sargas replied.

"Arak is here," Marseh admitted. "Making his stand in Bay 44. I am going there now, to eliminate him."

"But . . . that's my job," Sargas said, surprised to feel so bereft to be relieved of his responsibility. "Why go through all of this just to do it yourself?"

"If you wish to fulfill your purpose, I suggest you head there now. But I can't wait a moment longer. I can't let this cancerous fool continue to ruin *everything*."

Marseh disappeared from view. Sargas ran as fast as he could to reach his enemy in time to be the one.

THIRTY-ONE

ARAK STOOD IN the midst of the cargo hold clenching and unclenching his fists.

Tolon Intiri, Uron Irva'a, Soleron Besucher, and Uron Absalom maintained reverent silence in the presence of their master. Each corren wore a rifle slung across his back, a pistol in the holster on his thigh.

Arak began to pace.

"I'm *here*!" he shouted into the air. "You want to end this? Then do it!"

Reyevas appeared first. His sudden materialization surprised Arak, but the Butcher composed himself.

"It isn't you I want," he groused.

"I'm just here to watch," Reyevas replied.

Marseh appeared between them.

"There you are," Arak stated.

"All that shouting is hard to ignore," Marseh replied.

"Where are your men?" Arak asked. "Your man."

"I've brought no one," said Marseh. "I don't need them."

Arak sneered in reply.

***

Derovias led his charges through the station. His intimate familiarity with Overground was better than a map.

Where they met enemies, they dispatched them. Bedecked in the unmistakable markings of a Blackwing detail, the group encountered resistance from both sides. They became practiced at switching their weapons from kill to stun, knocking out comrades who mistook them for enemies.

Arak's core centurions were either dead or in his company. What remained of his loyalists were Red Guardsmen and footsoldiers. The guardsmen in the Butcher's service acquitted themselves well in battle but were spread thin on command duty. It left grunts and pukes to carry the combat load.

The noncommissioned soldiers were no match for the elite skills of Derovias and Daedalus. Falco and Ji'ilaad were well-trained, seasoned fighters. Ceres and Andrei were battle-hardened mercenaries. René, the weak link of the group, was no slouch. He knew how to stay cool under fire. His marksmanship far surpassed his combatants.

René marveled that he found himself at Overground but didn't allow bemusement to cloud his focus. The action excited him. Only days prior he'd worried that the blaster-pocked walls of the Dorance facility were the last things he'd ever see.

Beset by Marseh's men, they dispatched all but one. He dropped his gun and put up his hands. Daedalus, René, Ceres, and Andrei watched as Falco and Ji'ilaad set about checking that the fallen men still lived.

Derovias flipped up his visor. "Do you know who I am?"

The human looked small compared to Derovias. He nodded.

"I'm on your side," said Derovias.

The human shook his head in disbelief.

"They're alive, sir," Ji'ilaad confirmed.

"See for yourself," said Derovias.

The man tentatively felt a few of his comrades for signs of life. He was surprised when he found them.

"We're hunting the Butcher," said Derovias.

The man looked at the mixture of corren and human faces. He only recognized Derovias and couldn't quite reconcile his disbelief.

Derovias shook his head at the dumbstruck human and ordered the party to form up and move out. They marched past. Daedalus and Ceres backpedaled, keeping their guns on the man in case he thought to shoot on them as they went.

"Arak's men are shutting off life support," he called.

Derovias put up his fist and the column halted. He looked back.

"Not just for us," said the man. "They hit civilian quarters, too."

Derovias pictured the asphyxiated bodies of men, women, and children, dead in their homes. Collateral damage of Arak's desperation to retain his power. He ordered the human to shelter in place, revive his fellows, and hold the line.

The man saluted. Derovias twisted his mouth into a wry smile.

They reached the lift connecting the outer ring to Bay 50, the tenth of the bays in the central ring.

Arak loomed closer with every step.

***

"What do you hope to do?" Arak asked. His lip curled behind the upper jaw of Jack Mason's broken skull.

"I'm going to end you," said Marseh.

Soleron Besucher didn't wait for an order. He fired. The blast flew right through Marseh. It struck Uron Absalom, blasting the corren from his feet. He fell to the floor. Besucher looked dumbly at Marseh as Absalom coughed and sat up. Smoke rose from his melting breastplate and he fumbled with the straps. He hurled away the ruined armor and shifted his visor to transparent. He glowered at Besucher.

"Get out of the way, Absalom," said Intiri.

Absalom struggled to his feet with a cough. He came around so that the centurions flanked Arak and all faced Marseh.

"Care to try again?" Marseh taunted.

All four centurions fired on Marseh with their pulse rifles. Their volleys screamed harmlessly through him. Marseh's projection never wavered. He waved his hand in dismissal and the weapons flew from the centurions' hands. The rifles skittered across the floor, well out of reach. He took a step toward Arak. The centurions, reflexively, took a step back.

Arak looked to his left and then his right, regarding his men with disdain.

Marseh took another step.

"Don't do it," Reyevas warned.

Arak looked at Reyevas, trying to understand what "it" was. Marseh gave Reyevas a look that seemed almost like an apology.

The image of Marseh, the giant man, his lipless mouth and noseless face, the sharp, skin-covered bones that jutted upward from his forehead, all dissolved into shimmering particulate, like a broken stained-glass window, pulverized and suspended in time. The brilliant ether rushed into Arak's body.

He clutched at his armor, grabbing in futility at his abdomen, his chest, legs, arms, hands, and head. Reyevas disintegrated just like Marseh. The shimmering cloud that Reyevas became, colors distinct from Marseh's, rushed toward Arak.

The centurions took another step back, circling their master in impotent confusion. Arak tried to yell, but it came out as a strangled yelp. Reyevas disappeared into Arak's body, forcing Marseh out.

Marseh reappeared within the bay, forming into an almost-complete version of himself, an outline of his usual shape, but he remained fractured. A suggestion of a solid man, wrought from brilliant points of light.

Reyevas reappeared a picosecond afterward. Marseh wasted no time diving back in to continue his assault.

Each blow delivered by Marseh pushed Arak closer to death, and every parry to force Marseh out dealt another debilitating—albeit necessary—cut. Reyevas had to hurt Arak to save him, to keep Marseh from snuffing him out more swiftly, but every attempt to thwart Marseh nudged the Butcher just a little bit closer to death.

Yet the Alitán fought, with Arak as the battleground.

Neither Marseh nor Reyevas could interact with each other in their incorporeal forms, but they washed through Arak's nervous system, his ganglions, neurons, and synapses. They plunged into his body like stones into water, but occupied it like oil, polluting him with their presence. His body could only hold one intruder at a time.

When Reyevas hurled himself into Arak, Marseh splashed out. Reyevas became the corruption, but he extracted himself to mitigate the damage. As soon as he retreated, Marseh attacked anew. With each attack and defense, yet more of Arak's consciousness, his energy, his essence, was displaced.

His quintessence sloshed from its vessel, draining him of life.

Sargas burst into the hangar. He rushed toward the surprised centurions and the debilitated Arak. The centurions hurried to head him off. They fired at him with their pistols, but he was impervious. They came to blows, four against one, but Sargas was up to the task. He grabbed Besucher and threw him like a toy at Arak's feet.

Reyevas struggled to find a way to buy Arak time to escape. Forcing out Marseh, Reyevas reformed and hurled Arak across the hangar. He pushed Besucher along as if both men were mere leaves in a gale wind.

Run, Reyevas commanded telepathically. *Run, dammit!*

He surged into Sargas. Marseh rushed to dispel the attack. They went to battle inside a new host, but the roles had reversed. Now Marseh tried desperately to save his prized creation. He thought of Shaula and couldn't imagine explaining that he had let Sargas die.

Reyevas pushed Marseh out.

As Marseh reformed, he summoned the four discarded rifles to him, and forced Reyevas from Sargas. He hurled Sargas' body far across the hangar, opposite Arak and Besucher. Marseh overloaded the four weapons. They exploded in a brilliant flash.

The remaining centurions retreated behind Besucher, who carried Arak toward safety. The Butcher staggered like a drunk. Absalom rushed up to help carry the weight.

The explosion could not harm Marseh or Reyevas; they weren't physical beings, but the energy of the blast disrupted them. It disoriented them. Marseh lost sight of his prey. He tried casting his perception around the station but found his own mind addled by the intense jolt of energy. He tried to coalesce into his regular projection but could not.

Reyevas was similarly hobbled. Stunned.

They each remained suspended as they were: out of phase and unable to interact with the environment. Trapped.

Sargas lay still upon the floor.

THIRTY-TWO

DEROVIAS HEARD THE explosion. So did Kir.

From their different locations, they quickened their pace, dashing past hangar after hangar, down corridors interspersed with living quarters and canteens, storage bays and administration offices. They shot down every man who dared to raise a weapon.

Ji'ilaad and Andrei, Falco and René, Daedalus and Ceres all chased Derovias. He hurried to Bay 44. Outside the doors, Kir stood over the bodies of two centurions whose necks had been broken.

"Where have you been?" Derovias demanded. "I tried hailing you. Nothing."

"My comm is broken." Kir looked up, annoyance plain on his face.

He swiped his hand over the sensor. The bay doors opened, revealing Sargas upon the floor and two brilliant, shimmering clouds of particulate hovering in the center of the room. Kir tore his attention away from the odd spectacle of Marseh and Reyevas' fractured forms. He looked instead at Sargas.

"Son of a bitch," he said. He knelt to feel for Sargas' pulse.

"Is he dead?" asked Derovias.

Kir shrugged and shook his head.

"How the fuck did he beat us here?" asked Daedalus.

"Obviously, he knew his way around," Kir replied, dryly. "He left me for dead in the hangar, after the hard landing knocked me out."

"Well, what's wrong with him?" asked Daedalus. "I thought he was indestructible."

Kir shook his head again. "Don't know. I'm not a doctor. And I don't quite understand humans, anyway."

Countless of the nanomachines pervading Sargas had been casualties of the battle waged within his body. He remained in a state of shock, a coma induced by billions of the tiny robots going haywire in his cells. Some tried to repair themselves, others ran amok.

Derovias looked around, noting the evidence of the large explosion and the hallmarks of blaster fire. The floor and part of the wall were charred. A few small fires burned among the cargo. He looked again at the two shimmering figures in the epicenter of the blast site. One gleamed almost pure gold, mixed with opalescent streaks of black and brilliant white. The other was a vibrant mixture of color.

He approached in wonder and caution, treading lightly, panning the room for hidden threats.

Ceres followed. "What is that?" she asked, awed.

Her voice jolted Derovias back to reality. His awe shamed him.

"Who knows." His lip curled. "And who cares? The bastard isn't here. Put away your wonder. We've got work to do."

The corner of Ceres' mouth ticked into a snarl, but she fell back into formation. She hazarded a glance over her shoulder at the two shimmering forms. Sargas remained upon the hangar floor, unmoving but for the ragged rise and fall of his breath.

Derovias and his cohort hurried into the corridor down which Arak had escaped. "Move! Move! I don't want to lose them!"

Black shadows along the bulkheads swallowed up the red lights of high alert. At junctions in the corridors, bright white-yellow light blared out, washing the oppressive, brutalist environment in fiery tones.

Intiri and Irva'a heard the clomp of pursuing boots. Arak rested with his arms across the shoulders of Besucher and Absalom.

"Keep moving," Irva'a urged, catching Besucher's backward glance. Irva'a looked at Intiri. "We'll hold them off."

Intiri nodded.

Absalom and Besucher hefted Arak, who still struggled to walk but was getting stronger. The three men continued their retreat.

The clomp of boots swelled, echoing off the walls. Irva'a and Intiri shared a look. They readied their rifles. Derovias rounded the corner and Irva'a fired, striking him in the chest. The blast threw Derovias backward. He slammed against the wall, crying out in pain and surprise. He fumbled to remove his breastplate before it melted through to his body armor and skin. He scrambled back to safety.

Kir took cover behind a jutting bulkhead. He transferred his gun to his weaker left hand. Peeking out, he was forced back by Intiri's rifle fire.

Derovias slid lamely toward cover. He looked at Kir and coughed. "He's going to get away."

Kir shook his head, exasperated.

Derovias crawled to the rest of the column, who stood safely around the bend.

"You have to hold them here," he said to Falco and Ji'ilaad. He turned his gaze upon Daedalus, René, Ceres, and Andrei. "All of you."

Kir slowed the centurion advance with his palsied shots, but they drew nearer.

"Need some help here!" he implored.

Derovias looked at Falco and Ji'ilaad. He nodded in Kir's direction. "Go. Send him back to me."

Falco and Ji'ilaad crept up, laying cover fire for each other as they each claimed a sheltered spot behind a bulkhead.

Kir retreated to his partner's side.

"We're going," said Derovias. "Daedalus, you're in charge."

"What?" said Daedalus, but Derovias and Kir were already heading back to the last junction. Daedalus looked at Ceres and Andrei, neither of whom was impressed. "Don't start."

He looked at René. "Ready, *mon ami*?"

René drew his gun and they took the fight to Intiri and Irva'a. They forced the centurions back, but slowly.

All the while, Arak Matar grew in strength, buffeted by Absalom and Besucher.

***

Sargas stirred. He pushed himself up from the floor into a sitting position and massaged his throbbing forehead. After rubbing his bleary eyes, he took stock of the hangar. He noticed the frozen, shimmering forms. He didn't know that they were Marseh and Reyevas.

Arak had retreated. It was obvious the venue had changed.

Sargas inferred the direction in which his quarry would have fled and, rising unsteadily to his feet, he gave chase.

THIRTY-THREE

KIR NOTICED SARGAS on their tail. The corren made up his mind. He believed he and Derovias could take out Arak Matar by themselves. That they should.

At a right-angle junction, they cleared the intersection and Kir went right to the control panel. Derovias turned the corner, not stopping for his partner. Sargas ran after them, full bore, but not fast enough to beat the doors. They slid closed. Kir locked the portal.

With no idea what kind of overrides might be swimming in Sargas' artificially educated brain, Kir pulled the panel from the wall and shorted it. He could hear Sargas banging against the door in frustration, but Kir didn't care. There was only one goal.

Derovias was gone. Kir hurried after him.

***

Reyevas' attack had left Sargas near death, but he'd mustered every iota of his energy to pursue the Butcher. Locked out, on the wrong side of the door, Sargas felt his power slipping. He turned, slamming his back against the obstruction. Sliding to the floor, he began to lose consciousness.

He forced himself awake and climbed to his feet, waving his left hand in front of the sensor. It didn't respond. Knowing that Kir must have shorted it, Sargas popped free the reciprocal panel on his side of the doorway. He drew his knife and snicked it across his palm. As expected, his flesh yielded. The nanomachines were too preoccupied with their own repair to function in their normal defensive capacity.

Sargas squeezed as much blood as he could onto the panel before his wound coagulated. The combined effort of his biology and the alerted nanobots addressed the new injury.

The machines in the extracted blood went to work on the control panel, repairing the damaged circuit. They culled resources from the surrounding materials: iron, carbon, and other elements in their former host's blood, as well as the metal and polymers within the circuit itself. The bots recognized what was essential and what could be repurposed.

Seconds dragged as he swiped his left hand near the panel, repeatedly testing it. The grating notification of the door's refusal was its regular retort. He closed his eyes and inhaled deeply, smelling the burnt metal.

He tried again.

The computer chimed and the door opened. He staggered through, pushing himself to catch up with Kir and Derovias, refusing to let them do his job for him. As he turned to his right, he failed to notice Mag'err and Skru'ul stalking from his left.

The centurions fired their rifles, striking Sargas twice in the back.

He flew forward, crashing to the floor in pain. It was a mostly unfamiliar sensation; he'd grown so accustomed to being invincible. Droves of the tiny, self-replicating machines that gave him his superhuman powers had been disabled or destroyed. Those that remained functioned far from optimally. They were enough to keep him alive, but not to keep him impervious.

Sargas tasted his blood. The searing pain in his abdomen told him that something had burst. His eyes wanted to close, but he fought them open. Blood poured from his nose and mouth. It dripped from his chin. He climbed to his hands and knees and tried to crawl away.

Mag'err and Skru'ul took their time as they moved in, weapons poised to finish the job. Sadism kept their fingers off the trigger. Neither corren saw fit to speak; no words were required. Walking aside Sargas, Skru'ul kicked him over. Pain exploded through Sargas' torso. He vomited blood, bile, and what remained of his meal from Coventry.

Skru'ul aimed his rifle at Sargas' head.

A blue flash washed the red corridor in purple light. Skru'ul crumbled to the floor. Mag'err turned, his rifle raised, but Shaula cut him down as well. She closed the distance and shot him again, then kicked off his helmet and shot him dead.

Skru'ul attempted to rise. She unloaded on him, firing into his chest until he collapsed, his melted armor a smoking crater. The smell of burnt metal and cooked meat wafted to her nostrils. Shaula took no chances. She knocked off Skru'ul's helmet and bashed his head into pulp with the butt of her depleted rifle.

Sargas put his cheek upon the cool floor and closed his eyes. Shaula threw down her weapon and turned to him. "Sargas!" she yelled, panicked.

She knelt and shook him, but he didn't respond. She touched his face and jerked her hand away, then touched him again. Her entire body trembled beyond control.

Falling back onto her seat, she tucked her knees under her chin. She gazed in helpless despair at his battered, bloody, broken form.

THIRTY-FOUR

DEROVIAS CAUGHT SIGHT of the fleeing Butcher. The rogue centurion cut down Absalom, left vulnerable without his breastplate. Two more quick shots and Derovias dropped Besucher to his knees. Arak stumbled but continued under his own power. He turned the corner, abandoning his men.

Derovias ran toward Besucher to deliver the killing shot at intimate range, but the loyal centurion kicked Derovias in the knee, sending him toppling.

Besucher pounced, bashing Derovias' helmet against the floor.

Kir leapt, leading with his foot. He kicked Besucher in the head, driving him from Derovias. Besucher shook his head clear. Kir unleashed another kick with the other foot. His adversary hit the floor and Kir drew his knife. Climbing atop Besucher's back, Kir stabbed him through the nape.

Derovias clapped Kir on the shoulder. He looked up with a craze in his yellow eyes, the bones of his face prominent.

Derovias startled. "Come on," he urged.

Kir shook his head, blinking away his berserker rage. They continued pursuit.

Rounding the bend, Derovias ran at full speed. He caught a glimpse of his target ducking into another junction, into a straightaway. A foolish move. He turned the corner and shot Arak in the back.

The Butcher fell to his knees.

Slowly, Derovias approached.

"You craven . . . cowardly little bastard," Arak coughed, turning around. He collapsed into a sitting position.

Derovias raised his rifle, aiming it at Arak's helmeted face.

"You shot me in the back. But . . . why should I expect honor . . . from you?"

"Only a fool would fall for talk of honor from a charlatan like you. You have none. Why should I afford you any?"

"Because you want to kill me with your bare hands," Arak replied, taking off his helmet and throwing it aside.

He rose to one knee. Derovias took a cautious step backward.

"That's why you took down Besucher and Absalom when you could have taken me. You expected me to fall. To lie there, helpless, while you beat me with your fists."

Kir ran up behind Derovias with his pistol drawn.

"Well," Arak laughed. He coughed and sputtered. "I am not helpless."

He rose to his feet.

"I am not my best self, but I reckon I'm a match for you. Face me like a man, Derovias. Surely you can defeat a cripple . . ."

Looking at Kir, and then at his gun, Derovias believed his partner would have his back. That if, somehow, Arak were to gain the upper hand, Kir would eliminate him.

Derovias threw his rifle aside.

Arak grinned broadly. He unfastened his cloak. It puddled upon the floor in deep black and vivid vermilion red.

Derovias put up his fists and stepped in. Arak met him, swinging a wide left hook.

The corren struck first, straight ahead, connecting with his opponent's chin. Then, Arak's gauntleted fist smashed against the side of the centurion's helmet. The visor cracked. Light exploded behind Derovias' eyelids. He tore off the lid and tossed it aside.

Arak landed a right-handed uppercut. It lifted Derovias from the floor. The sharp metal edge of the Butcher's gauntlet cut through the corren's chin, exposing bone. Derovias bit into his tongue as his teeth collided. He fell onto his back. The wind rushed from his lungs.

Arak raised his foot to stomp, but Derovias rolled away. He spat coppery blood onto the floor. Arak kicked Derovias in the small of the back, then reached down, grabbing the smaller man with both hands.

"Get up!" growled the Butcher as he hauled Derovias to his feet.

A stream of green gore poured from the laceration under his chin. It looked black in the red light. He jabbed at Arak from between those massive arms. The Butcher barely flinched. He shoved Derovias back and advanced, appearing little worse for wear despite his near-death experience, nor for that Derovias had shot him only moments prior.

"I'm half-dead, boy, and you still can't beat me," Arak taunted. "Who here is the better man?"

Derovias screamed a wordless battle cry. He stepped into Arak, unleashing a flurry of punches. Arak staggered back. He shook his head clear, brought up his foot, and kicked Derovias in the midsection, sending the centurion backward. Losing his balance, Derovias tumbled. He tried to rise, but Arak pounced, backhanding him hard across the side of the face with a gauntleted hand, sending him reeling.

Stars again burst before his eyes. A fog shrouded his consciousness.

Arak took his time, closing the distance as if he lacked a care in the world. He ignored Kir as if he were of no consequence.

Heavy, booted footsteps blasted like thunder in Derovias' ears.

"Of all the men to betray me . . . I never thought it would be you."

Arak grabbed Derovias by the hair. The Butcher reared back his fist. The sharp metal edges of his gauntlet glinted in the fiery light, poised to rip the flesh from Derovias' face and dig into his skull.

Kir fired.

Arak staggered from the point-blank blast and fell to the floor. He rolled into a heap.

Kir helped up Derovias.

"You waited long enough," Derovias rasped. He tried to speak at a normal volume but could only manage a hoarse whisper. He held his hand beneath his chin, trying to staunch the bleeding.

He staggered, heavily concussed. Steadying himself against the wall, he limped toward Arak, who coughed and sputtered as he tried to sit up.

"You asked me a question . . ." said Derovias. He tested his jaw. It was tender, but unbroken. His flesh slowly mended. His blood congealed. His voice grew stronger.

Kir kept his gun trained on the Butcher.

"But didn't wait for my reply."

Arak said nothing. He coughed again, retching up blood.

"I thought . . . you were a great man," Derovias struggled to say.

He looked at Kir, whose face twisted in regret, disappointed at the loss of his own blinders and the full force of the truth.

"We revered you," Derovias continued. "Our father. Our god. We believed in you. We were wrong . . . How could you expect us not to change our minds? We live so long. We see so much. After seventy-five years, why wouldn't I wonder what the point was?"

Arak growled. It seemed as if he tried to speak, but no words spilled forth. He spat blood at Derovias.

"You've lived so much longer," said the centurion, ignoring the petulant gesture. "How could you never waver? How could any man be so convinced how right he is . . . when he is so wrong?"

Arak tried to rise, but Derovias kicked him down.

"Stay down!" he growled. "You're going to listen! For once you're going to fucking listen to someone. To *me*."

Arak vomited. Nothing came out but a slow dribble of gore. He was nearly drowning in his own blood. He wheezed for every sip of air.

"I killed for you," Derovias continued. "I raped in your name—"

"Don't . . ." Arak choked out the word. He coughed, spat more blood, and drew another ragged breath. "Don't dare . . . throw that . . . at my feet."

He snarled. His voice came back to him.

"You raped . . . because you *could*. Because you had *power* . . . had people . . . at your mercy. I gave no order . . . You *chose* . . . to abuse your authority. That's . . . on you!"

A disgusted frown perturbed Derovias' face.

"I know I'm not blameless," he replied. "I stole women from their homes for you to fuck. You led by example, and we followed it. I made orphans of children . . ." He looked at Kir, aggrieved. "We all did. We did it for *you*. We did it *because* of you. Because you led us to believe we're somehow better. That we had a calling . . . a cause. That we were *righteous*. That the world was sick, the humans the disease . . . and you, the cure."

He hung his head.

"I was such a fool," he said, his voice quiet.

"We all were," Kir offered.

Arak turned his amber eyes upon Kir, bugging them out in vehement hatred.

"How could one man hate so much?" Kir asked.

Arak retched again. This time, he spewed blood. He tried to come forward onto all fours, but Derovias kicked him back again. Turning with the kick, Arak rose to his hands and knees. His backside faced the two men. He coughed and spat and vomited. His breath whistled through his skull, but it came more easily. His insides were healing.

"You are both," he croaked, "so . . . *ungrateful*."

"Ungrateful!" Derovias exclaimed, incredulous.

Arak turned over and sat, leaning weakly against the bulkhead. "I gave you *life*! You *exist* because of *me*. You *belong* to me . . ."

"We are *not* your property!" Derovias fumed.

"I gave you life and you treat me with such ingratitude." Arak chuckled to himself and shook his head. "Is it the fate of every father to be disappointed by his sons? You are both . . . such failures. So weak. So soft. So beset by . . . what? Conscience?"

He laughed. It sputtered into a cough. Green spittle oozed from his mouth.

"Spare me." Arak spat. "What meaning is there to life but to do what you must to preempt the man who'll prey . . . upon your weakness? Fuck or be fucked. Kill or be killed. You act as if Darek Marseh is righteous."

"At least Marseh has changed," Kir retorted.

"Has he?" Arak laughed again. "Or have you just fallen . . . for his magic? In awe of his sorcery. Blind to the reality that he is the architect of all of our lives. He is the reason for this dead world. A passive engine in perpetual motion, driving this never-ending war."

"And so," said Derovias. "What are you? His lackey? His pawn?"

Arak's face twisted with indignation, but he had no rebuttal.

Derovias laughed. He looked at Kir. "We are all such idiots."

Arak looked from Kir to Derovias and back again.

Kir frowned, keeping his weapon trained.

"Hundreds of years," said Derovias to Arak. "All of that life and, yet, no wisdom. How could you be so stagnant? What have you ever done that wasn't to satisfy your illusions of how important you are?"

"Marseh . . . has an apt pupil in you, Derovias. How quickly you've become . . . so sanctimonious. So righteous."

"I am not *righteous*!" Derovias growled. "I couldn't have been more wrong!"

Arak chuckled. It was deep and throaty, but also sickly wet.

"That's the first bit of sense I've heard from you . . . in this long, tired farce of a conversation. You simple, foolish, idiot boy. You could have had . . . all the power in the world."

Derovias put his hands to his head. "I don't *want* it! I don't want any of it! I don't want life and death in my hands. I don't want to do the bidding of a venal, petty, small-minded egotist! I've wasted my life for your benefit, and what's my reward? A pittance! Food, shelter, clothes. What else? Nothing! I exist to satisfy your whims, for the sake of your vanity . . . Every fucking day of my life has been arbitrary . . . useless . . . wasted on you . . . who, somehow, seized a handful of power and, like a child with a gun, wielded it with infantile stupidity."

Derovias looked at Kir. "Shoot him."

Kir hesitated.

"*Shoot* him!" Derovias demanded.

Arak looked at Kir.

"All of that high-and-mighty posturing and he orders me to death so capriciously. How is he any different than what he decries? Do you want to be that to him, Kir? What he complains about being to me?"

"Give it to me!" Derovias said, grabbing for the gun.

Kir refused to relinquish it.

"What the fuck is wrong with you?" Derovias fumed.

"Death is too good for him," Kir replied. "I want him to *suffer*."

A blue pulse struck the wall, scattering Kir and Derovias. Intiri and Irva'a closed on them. Daedalus, René, Ceres, and Andrei gave chase.

Derovias pushed Kir into the adjacent corridor to escape the barrage. They fell to the floor together.

"What are you doing?" Derovias heard Intiri demand of an unseen figure. A flurry of Confederate blaster fire erupted. Then a sickening gurgle followed by a loud retch.

Derovias thought to rise and to run, but the corridor from which they fled fell eerily quiet. He crept back to see Darek Marseh standing over the corpses of Intiri and Irva'a.

Intiri had been shot full of holes. Irva'a lay facedown in a pool of his own blood. Arak Matar, on his knees, glowered up at Marseh.

Derovias looked to his right. Daedalus and the others stood rapt in stunned disbelief.

Reyevas winked into existence opposite Marseh.

Without a word, Marseh disappeared into Arak. A warble welled up in the Butcher's throat, as if he couldn't decide whether to vomit or scream.

Reyevas separated into a swarm of opalescent dust and poured into Arak's body, forcing Marseh to coalesce into a fractured-but-recognizable facsimile of his complete form.

A similarly incomplete version of Reyevas appeared the moment he expelled Marseh from Arak's body. Reyevas still wanted Arak alive. To stay within would kill the man. Reyevas' only aim was to keep Marseh from remaining within Arak until he died, but Marseh resumed his assault.

Arak moaned in pain. His head felt like it would burst. His invaders coursed through his being like poison in his veins. He put his hands to his head and pulled at his braids.

"Help me!" Reyevas' ghostly form implored the spectators. "Don't let him die!"

If he were hoping to appeal to some deep compassion within Derovias, Kir, and Daedalus, or Ceres and Andrei, he was sorely mistaken. René felt a pang of sympathy for the dying Arak but reminded himself that the man was a murderous dictator. Falco relished the sight. Ji'ilaad betrayed no feelings.

Kir had only wanted Arak alive to face punishment, but not enough to interfere in a fight between two gods. He wanted the Butcher to suffer, and he was suffering.

All watched as Arak's eyes rolled back into his head. He screamed and howled. Blood streamed from both of his nostrils, his mouth, and ears. It seeped from his tear ducts.

The flashes of Marseh and Reyevas grew brighter. They became harder and harder to discern, surging with blinding velocity into and out of Arak Matar until both men reappeared, apparently solid.

The Butcher fell to the floor.

THIRTY-FIVE

REYEVAS STOOD IN silence over Arak's corpse. Marseh remained rooted to where he had materialized. Neither Alitán spoke for a long while.

"I don't know what you are," said Reyevas, finally. His tone was almost sad. Gone were the notes of mockery, condescension, antagonism.

Marseh said nothing.

"You've violated every tenet that makes us what we are," Reyevas continued.

Marseh looked at him. "And what *are* we?" His tone was tart, defensive.

"A society of laws, Darek."

Marseh expressed disagreement with his face. "The policemen of the galaxy," he said with disdain.

"You don't think the galaxy needs policing?" asked Reyevas, his sadness and disappointment waned. As his shock subsided, he remembered that he didn't like his contemporary.

"Who are you to meddle in the affairs of a world you've almost entirely ignored?" Marseh asked. "Who are you to come to my house and tell me to clean it up?"

"Your house?" Reyevas retorted, aghast. "This is *not* your home!"

"It is the only home I have!" Marseh replied.

"You are *lost*," said Reyevas. "And you must be displaced."

"Don't threaten me, you insufferable pain."

"That is not a threat, Darek Marseh. *You* are the threat. You are as much the enemy as the Gur, you . . . destroyer of worlds."

Marseh laughed.

It astonished Derovias and Kir, Daedalus, and the others. They watched the conversation between the two inscrutable beings, enthralled.

Reyevas blanched at Marseh's guffaw.

"You self-important jackass," said Marseh. "*We* destroy worlds! That is what we do! *Our* people. We go from planet to planet imposing our will upon civilizations, demanding they abide by our wisdom and we *eradicate* them if they refuse! *We* are the Gur, you fucking cunt!"

Daedalus couldn't help but smile at Marseh's use of Earthly pejoratives.

Reyevas, realizing the futility of further discussion, vanished from the scene.

Sensing the area for any hint of his adversary, Marseh found none. He assumed Reyevas would return home, inform their kin of their wayward steward's crimes, and bring back the wrath of the Alitán.

Marseh wondered how much time he had before his people would come for him. He wondered if they would come at all.

He turned to his audience.

"Derovias, show our Allied friends to a safe place. A canteen, perhaps. I will direct Lutan to find the others and send them there as well."

Marseh disappeared as instantly as had Reyevas, leaving Derovias to shepherd his unlikely companions.

He much preferred his role as a fighter. He tried to imagine life without war, without the constant threat of physical violence and death. That world was a long way off. Overground might be easy enough to corral. Venus, Mars, and the belt would eventually fall into place, but establishing order on Earth would be the biggest task.

While the Allies were crippled and much of their fleet destroyed, their resistance on the ground remained. And, now, the Confederation faced war on two fronts. Arak's loyalists would learn how he died. Even if Marseh tried to spin it some other way, many would not believe him. They would not simply lay down their arms. They would know that death awaited them if they surrendered, that their only chance to live would be to fight.

Derovias swallowed his pride and played his role. He knew that more fighting awaited him and was pleased to think that, finally, his cause might be just.

THIRTY-SIX

ANJALI AND RAY sat in the canteen with a table between them.

"I expected to be a part of it," Ray said, drawing Anjali's wandering attention back to him.

"You were a part of it, Ray," she replied.

His face conveyed his disappointment.

"You wanted to be the one," she stated.

He looked away.

"I'm grateful you're here," she said, and he looked back at her.

"I almost wasn't. When Ivan came crashing down on top of me, I thought it was over. I'm glad I held on."

Anjali blushed as she put together that she'd killed the lieutenant. The added color was hard to notice on her brown face, but her innards churned with guilt. Ray failed to see her reaction; the opening door diverted his attention.

Anjali looked over to see Lután usher Carina into the canteen. She wondered where the captain had been since they'd argued and she'd stalked off alone. Carina glanced at the couple. They looked at her expectantly, almost amiably. She gave them a weak smile but said nothing. Walking to the far side of the room, she sat down alone and crossed tight her arms. She shivered imperceptibly, trying still to blot the image of Gardiner's slack, dead face from her mind.

"I understand that there are more of you," said Lután. "They'll be brought here as well."

He offered a slight bow in no specific direction and left.

Anjali got up and walked over to Carina. "Can I sit with you?"

Carina looked up and frowned. Her eyes were tired and troubled. She wanted to tell Anjali to go away but, at the same time, wanted more comfort than anyone could offer. Ultimately, she said nothing.

Anjali sat. "I'm sorry I upset you earlier."

"It's no big deal," Carina replied, not making eye contact.

It wasn't the response Anjali expected, but she didn't know why she expected reciprocity. She shrugged. They lapsed into silence. Ray watched from across the room.

The door opened again. He and Anjali looked up to see Derovias guiding Daedalus and René. Seeing Ray, Daedalus' face lit up into a broad smile. He walked over with his arms spread wide. Though Ray still held a grudge for the beating in the wreckage of the *Filomena*, he rose and accepted the embrace. He decided it was wiser to repair the relationships he expected to need; his entire reality was poised to change.

Falco stood just outside the door with Ceres. Both remained out of view although he could see within. His heart leapt into his throat at the sight of Carina. She stared at nothing, directing her eyes at some point on the floor, meters away, and miles more beyond. Anjali looked at her but remained quiet.

Falco, confused and torn, looked at Ceres. He wanted so much to see Carina but couldn't bring himself to interfere with the sisters' reunion. Ceres didn't know that her sister was inside. He refused to spoil the secret.

Andrei glowered at Falco, refusing to let go of the tryst in Coventry. The Red Guardsman, preoccupied with his budding feelings for Ceres and the torch he still held for Carina, paid no attention to the simmering mercenary.

Ceres moved into the doorway. The change in light diverted Anjali's attention. She looked up to see a beautiful medium-brown woman with unnaturally pale hair and rust-colored roots. Behind her was a stubbly human as tall as Ray, with a few days growth upon the head he appeared to regularly shave. Anjali looked from the newcomers to Carina and back again. She looked at Carina one more time.

"Captain, do you know that woman?" Anjali asked.

Looking up at Anjali, Carina made a face that seemed to say: *Why are you bothering me?* with the body language to drive it home. She didn't look toward the door.

Anjali tried to rein in her annoyance. She had no idea what Carina had experienced on the station before they linked up nor after they parted. She knew nothing of Gardiner's demise. All she could go on were her memories of the mean-spirited doctor from the Dorance facility. And, now, the rude petulance. Remembering that she didn't like the nasty woman across the table, at all, Anjali rejoined Ray as he caught up with Daedalus.

The loud-mouthed corren was flapping his gums and waving his hands. "And then I said: 'Oh, yeah? Think you can take us both?' Oh, hey, Angie . . ."

Carina sank back into her sullen, unfocused stare. René watched her from across the room but knew well not to disturb her in such a mood. He turned his attention back to the bragging corren.

Ceres scanned the canteen, wondering why Derovias and Falco had brought her. She froze at the sight of the redhead sitting alone in the farthest corner. The image struck her like lightning. Slowly, she approached. Carina sensed movement. She looked up in annoyance but, at the sight of Ceres, her face melted into abject surprise. It was like looking into a strange mirror at a younger, punkier version of herself.

"Karin?" said Ceres, her eyes welling.

Carina's mouth opened and closed. She made no sound.

Ceres dived in, enveloping Carina so swiftly she nearly tackled her from the chair. Carina steadied herself and sat, stunned, with her arms at her sides.

"Michèle?" she said quietly.

Ceres nodded. She crowed and laughed and cried in Carina's ear.

Carina wrapped her arms around her sister and rose from the seat in the embrace. Ceres moved with her, refusing to let go.

"Michèle," Carina said, as it sank in. She realized that her face was wet. She squeezed tighter and Ceres squeezed back.

Anjali and Ray, Daedalus, René, and Andrei looked on.

Carina extracted herself and moved toward the door, tugging Ceres' hand.

"Where's the kid?" Daedalus asked, turning his attention back to Ray.

"What kid?" Ray looked at him, arching an eyeridge.

"Patrick," Daedalus clarified.

Carina stopped at the sound of Patrick's name. "He . . . didn't make it."

"What happened to him?" Daedalus asked.

"Reds attacked his spitfire." She frowned and looked around in obvious discomfiture. "They spaced him."

Daedalus made an "o" with his mouth and looked away for a second.

She shrugged in a lame attempt at punctuation and pulled at Ceres, beckoning her toward the exit.

"Ceres," said Andrei. "Wait."

She positioned herself behind Carina, who gleaned that her sister wanted nothing to do with the man.

"Why don't you back off," Carina warned.

"Or what?"

"Or she'll pump you full of holes," Daedalus said, recalling the alley in Orchard City. "You don't wanna fuck with this chick, baldy."

Andrei diverted his attention toward Daedalus. Carina and Ceres used the opportunity to leave the canteen.

"Fuck," Andrei exclaimed, marching toward the door.

Daedalus and Ray both intercepted him.

"Let go of me!" he demanded. "Get out of my fucking way!"

"Not gonna happen, man," Daedalus replied, blocking the exit. "You need to take the hint."

Andrei sneered in reply. He shook off Ray's grasp, then stalked to the farthest corner of the room and sat facing the wall. He kicked it in anger, muttering to himself.

Daedalus looked at Ray. "So, Patrick's dead, huh? He got spaced?"

Ray shrugged. He had no idea until Carina brought it up.

"Fuck," Daedalus rued. "That was no way for him to go; he was a good kid."

"Who you pretty mercilessly tormented," Anjali retorted.

"He was a cupcake," Daedalus replied, unabashed. "He needed a hide. You think I should have hugged him and told him how special he was? Kid's head was all over the place. I put it firmly in the here and now."

"Well, here and now, he's dead," Anjali replied.

Daedalus shook his head at her. "Yeah, and probably a lot later than his green ass woulda gone if I hadn't laid into him." He looked at Ray. "We need to retrieve him. Get his body. Give it to his wife."

"And how would you like to do that?" asked Ray, crossing his arms.

Daedalus shook his head again. "You're both fucking useless."

He walked out of the canteen before they could respond. They looked at René, who blushed and shrugged.

It pleasantly surprised Daedalus that neither Lután nor Derovias had bothered to leave a guard, even if it were stupid of them. He set off to find a ship. It was up to him to track down Patrick's transponder amid the wreckage and bring the man home.

THIRTY-SEVEN

THE SISTERS DUVAIS walked down the Overground corridor. They saw Falco only steps ahead. Ceres called to him.

He froze.

At the sound of his name, cold radiated from Carina's abdomen to the tips of her extremities. Falco turned slowly. Laboriously. He looked meek and apologetic as he caught Carina's eye. Her breath caught in her throat.

"*You know him?*" Carina asked, tugging Ceres' arm to capture her attention.

"*Uh … yeah,*" Ceres replied with a knowing smile that felt like a slap. "*Do you?*"

Carina let go of Ceres' hand and exhaled a heavy sigh, putting a hand to her head.

"Karin?"

"Carina?" said Falco at the same moment.

Ceres looked at him, shocked and confused that he called her sister by the strange but similar name.

Carina gently pushed them both away. "I'm fine."

They continued to dote on her.

"I'm fine!"

She looked at Falco and had trouble parsing her feelings. In his face, she saw the resemblance to Lieutenant Pablo Sotillo and felt repulsed. But she saw, too, the boy she was sure she'd loved. Atop it all, she knew something now existed between him and her sister. She wanted to laugh, cry, vomit, and slap them both.

"Are you okay?" Falco asked.

She pushed his wretched older brother from her mind. Ignoring her sister for the moment, Carina transported herself back to the slave colony.

She remembered how safe she had felt in Falco's arms, half a lifetime ago. She stepped into him, put her arms around his waist, and rested her chin on his shoulder.

Ceres watched, trying to understand. It was clear that they knew each other. She looked hard at Falco and, though no amount of scrutiny could reveal a face she'd never seen as a child, the revelation struck. She remembered her older sister as an over-the-moon sixteen-year-old.

"You're the boy from Tripas," Ceres said.

He looked at her and flashed a weak smile.

Carina let go and took a step back. "This is too much . . ." She looked him in the eye. "I want to see you again. I really do. But, right now," she looked at Ceres and then back at him, "we need to be alone."

The dismissal left a yawning hole in his guts. His face flickered, but he tilted his head at her, glanced at Ceres, and departed.

Daedalus intercepted him. "Yo! Birdman . . ."

"*Walk with me,*" said Carina to her sister. She offered the crook of her arm and Ceres took it.

They wandered back toward the canteen. The corridor was vacant but for guards posted at certain doors. The men paid the women no mind. The sisters found it strange to be strolling the halls of Overground, unmolested by the Confederate soldiers, as if on some fictional street in some nonexistent friendly town.

"*I'm guessing you want to know . . . what happened to me,*" Ceres said in French, breaking the silence.

Carina nodded. "Oui. Bien sûr."

"*When you let go of me,*" Ceres said, and Carina grimaced at the statement, visualizing how she had relinquished her grasp of Michèle in the cold Atlantic water because she couldn't hold both her and Agnès. She had chosen to save the youngest child.

"*The current carried us apart,*" Ceres continued, "*and I grabbed onto the first bit of wreckage I found. I washed up on Madeira with a bunch of others. We were all dazed, confused, but I knew the Reds would come for us, so I . . .*" She blushed. "*I figured out how to get off the island right away.*"

"*A man . . .*" She blushed again.

Carina furrowed her brow, knowing that her sister had been ten years old. She didn't want to think about what "a man" might have done to a vulnerable little girl, but her imagination wouldn't let her ignore it.

"*. . . took me to Essaouira and I stayed there for a little over a year before I got restless. I fled on foot, working my way along the coast. It took me a* long time . . . but I made it back home. It was stupid to go there . . . It was crawling with Reds."

"Don't say that," Carina admonished. "I still think of Algiers. It's not stupid. It's home. On es algériennes."

Ceres made a sharp, negating motion with her hand. "It's not. And it wasn't then, either. It was stupid to go back. It was childish. I . . ." She looked at Carina, unapologetic, and managed not to blush. "Bought passage to Marseille."

Disgust crept across Carina's face. She hated the idea of her prepubescent sister whoring her way hither and yon. Worse, Carina wondered if they had been in Marseilles at the same time. After washing ashore on Isla Sangrante, it had taken Carina a long time, too, to trek across the island, then through Portugal and Spain before arriving in France.

"I tried settling into one of the camps," Ceres continued, "but it was rough. I was thirteen. I was tired of fucking through the meanest, toughest men. Each one kept me safe from others, but nothing kept me safe from them."

Carina clenched and opened her fists. She gritted her teeth but didn't interrupt.

"So, after a while, I left. A few of the guys taught me to fight. Some with my hands, others with weapons. I guess they never worried about me posing a threat. I mean, some of them did . . . the ones who only used me for a fuckdoll."

She smiled wryly. Her expression betrayed no hint that she was wounded by her experience. Carina felt a pang of jealousy at her sister's apparently uncomplicated view of sex.

"But at least I got something practical out of the others," Ceres added. "I had a gun, a knife, a short sword. I killed and fucked my way to Britain, made good money along the way, doing both. Cast about the isles for a couple years. But living in the badlands and still being under the Allied boot heel is about as bad as being a Confederation slave. Maybe worse."

Carina again ground her teeth but kept her mouth shut.

"I roamed around, stayed out of people's beds for a while . . . until I got wind that Nova Spes was the best place to make a living with a weapon. Practically lawless, almost free of influence from either side of the war. And that's where I met Manon—"

"Manon?" Carina could no longer contain herself.

Ceres' face lit up. "*Oui*, Karin." She slipped back into English. "We have another sister!"

"I know that," Carina snapped, wiping the smile from Ceres' face.

Carina was angry and Ceres couldn't understand why.

"What's wrong—?"

"Why the fuck didn't she tell me about you?" Carina said, livid.

"You . . . know her?" Ceres couldn't hide her shock.

"Yes. I fucking know her," Carina's lip curled. She balled her fists. "She kept you from me. How could she *keep* you from me?"

Ceres' creased her forehead. "I . . . don't know. I'm sorry. I don't know why she'd have done that. She never said she knew you."

Carina closed her eyes and sighed heavily. "So she kept me from you, too. I'm gonna talk to her about that." Her tone turned the benign remark into a threat.

Ceres looked around. "If we can leave this place."

"We will," Carina replied. "I'm not leaving Agnès down there alone . . . God knows Manon won't look after her."

"Agnès is alive?"

"Of course she's alive," Carina snapped, taking Ceres' surprise as an insult.

Ceres frowned. "I thought you both were dead. I think it was easier, that way. I . . . never thought I'd see you again, even if you *had* lived."

Carina frowned and shook her head. She scoffed, unamused. "I never wished you dead, 'chèle."

"I didn't *wish* you dead."

"No . . . you just blame me for saving the baby."

Ceres flared her nostrils. "Don't make this ugly. I haven't blamed you for anything. If you feel guilty, just say so. *Ne te caches pas derrière des conneries.*" *Don't hide behind some bullshit.*

Carina frowned and her expression softened. Tears welled in her eyes. *"I do feel guilty, honey,"* she replied in French. She sniffled and ran the back of her hand across her nose. *"I really do."*

Ceres opened her arms and they embraced.

Carina pressed her head against her sister's. "You have no idea *how* guilty I feel."

THIRTY-EIGHT

DAEDALUS PILOTED THE stinger through the debris and corpses that littered the celestial battleground. Falco surveyed the scene, searching for Patrick's transponder.

"I've got him," he said, locking in on the signal. He transmitted the coordinates to Daedalus' terminal.

He crept toward Patrick's corpse. It drifted through the emptiness along with thousands of other dead, millions of bits of shrapnel, and mechanical wreckage.

"You don't think we should get anybody else?" Falco asked.

"Do we have room for anyone else?" Daedalus answered.

"Well, no."

"Then shut up and pull him in already."

Falco frowned. He used the joystick to control the retrieval claw, grasping Patrick. He pulled the corporal's frozen body into the small hold of the two-man Confederation fighter.

"He's aboard."

Daedalus nodded. He flipped and burned back toward Overground.

Lután waited in the hangar with a nurse, who stood next to the gurney.

Daedalus and Falco climbed down from the cockpit to the hangar floor and retrieved Patrick's corpse from the ship. The nurse took it to the morgue.

Lután looked at Falco, tacitly dismissing him.

As Falco left, Daedalus met Lután's gaze.

"This is where one of us is supposed to say, 'It's been a long time.'"

"Looks like that's you," Lután replied.

"So, big deal. What do you want?"

"Aren't we supposed to be even more like brothers, coming from the same batch?" Lután asked. The question was not in earnest.

"I don't feel kinship with any of you," Daedalus replied.

"That explains why you abandoned us," said Lután.

"I really don't need this bullshit, Lután. I need to take that body you just whisked away back to his family."

"That's not going to happen, Antal. We can't very well let you go back to the Allies to take up arms against us again."

"Don't be a dipshit, asshole. I deserted. I can't *go* back. And if I'm such a problem for you, why let me take one of your ships out for a spin just now? Why let me get the kid if you won't let me deliver him?"

"It was a gesture of good will."

"Fucking useless if you won't go the distance," Daedalus replied.

"We'll have someone deliver him for you," Lután offered, unbothered by Daedalus' insults and manner.

"Oh, I'm sure that'll go well. 'Hey, enemy mine, got one of your boys here. We killed him. Corpse delivery.'"

"There is a long history of peace offerings."

"No one knows history, Lután. Most people can't even read."

"The Allied High Command knows how to read."

Daedalus shook his head and rolled his eyes. "You done wasting my time?"

"Not quite," said Lután. "I'm to escort you to quarters and confine you there."

"Swell," Daedalus replied. "Think you can make me?"

"I know I could shoot a hole in you that you won't come back from. Does that sound better to you?"

Daedalus frowned.

Lután stood aside, indicating that Daedalus should walk ahead of him.

"It's up to you," said Lután. "Prove that you can go along, and we'll let you move freely. You can integrate back into the society you forsook. But be a contemptuous, difficult shit and you can just stare at the walls in your quarters until you go mad."

***

Andrei looked up as the door slid open. It revealed Miro and Skal, fully armored and armed with pulse rifles. Their visors were raised.

"What the fuck is this?" Andrei said, rising to his full height.

Both Miro and Skal had to look up to make eye contact with him, but neither corren was intimidated.

"You're to come with us," said Miro.

"And what if I don't?"

"We really have no use for you," Miro replied. "So, you can either come with us, if you want to live. Or die, here, like an asshole." He cast Skal a look that said: *Can you believe this prick?*

Skal shrugged in boredom.

Andrei set his jaw and rolled his eyes. "Where is Ceres?"

"That doesn't concern you," said Skal.

"Fuck you, it doesn't concern me. She's mine. I want to know where she is."

Miro and Skal exchanged a knowing glance and both correns smiled.

"Listen to this guy," said Miro. "You want to tell him, or should I?"

"Tell me what?" Andrei asked, losing some of his bravado.

"The woman doesn't want you," said Skal. He smiled without showing any teeth.

Miro furrowed his brow in recollection.

"Let me try to remember her words, exactly . . . 'You can space him, for all I care.'" He looked at Skal. "That was it, right?"

Skal thought about it. "The bottom line, anyway." He looked at Andrei, who appeared stunned, but whose face contorted into adamant disbelief.

"She didn't say that," he insisted. "Let me talk to her."

"Don't be pathetic," said Miro. "We barely ever see women and even we know, when a girl says she doesn't want you, it's time to move on. Have some fucking dignity."

"I'm supposed to believe you assholes?" Andrei despaired.

Skal primed his pulse rifle. "I don't care what you believe, human. I am *tired* of you. You can be shot, spaced, or you can accept our very gracious offer to get on a ship and go the fuck away."

Miro primed his gun. He looked at Andrei.

"So, what'll it be?"

***

Anjali sat on the edge of the bed, looking up at Ray.

"I don't want to be here," he said. "I don't want to be a part of this."

She shook her head at him.

"I'm here because of you," he pressed. "You don't have anything to say to me?"

"What the hell do you want me to say?" she snapped. "Grow up. You don't always get what you want. This is how it is . . . You have to deal with it. I can't wave my magic wand and send you back. I can't make everything all right for you."

"Because what I want is clearly none of your concern."

"Don't fucking do that. Don't turn this into the most banal couple's disagreement. I'm not going to indulge you, Raymond. Don't be a child."

"Don't chastise me like I'm unreasonable to be *pissed*. You duped me into this mess. I'm trapped behind enemy lines, being told I can never go home. How should I feel, Angie? Huh? Tell me."

"You're supposed to feel like shit, babe. And I'm sorry that you do. Really. But this is how it is. Complaining does nothing. The sooner you accept it, the sooner we can make the best of it. Together."

Ray glowered at her. "So, now you're about us. Now we're a team."

"Fuck, Ray. Please. What do you want from me? You can't put the blinders back on once you've laid bare the big lie. It wasn't our home and you know it. There's no going back. Maybe . . . maybe we could make a home here. But I can't do it without you. How many times do I have to apologize before you'll accept it?"

He crossed his arms and pouted. The expression was incongruous with his brutal features. Anjali had to suppress the amusement that bubbled up at the sight of him acting like a spoiled child.

"I could stand to hear it one more time," he said.

She smiled, unable to keep the amusement down any longer, but she gracefully disguised it as incredulity wrapped in warmth and understanding. She rose from the bed and approached him.

"I'm sorry, baby. I am. I never meant to betray your trust. I know this hasn't been . . . pleasant."

He looked at her, trying to be angry. "You're a master of understatement." He winced a sad smile.

THIRTY-NINE

MANON, ROZHENKO, AND Adnan sat around the huge banquet table in her island hideaway's great room. Jack stood motionless near the wall, looking like an armor exhibit.

"Will you return to the service?" Manon asked Rozhenko.

The conflict was plain on his face, but he had made up his mind. "No. I am having quite enough of being useful tool, I think. I am remembering when the angry corren says, 'Fuck the Allied military' and I was being very offended. But I am having time to be thinking . . . and I am thinking he is right."

"So, then, what now?" she asked.

"This, I am not knowing. I—"

"You're welcome to join us," she interrupted.

Jack looked at her. He animated his robotic face into a perfect facsimile of human expression. Surprise.

"You are meaning this?" Rozhenko asked, wary. "Just before, you are saying it is just you and just him," he indicated Jack. "Just so."

"Don't be like that," she replied. "What kind of idiot trusts a stranger? Especially in this awful world. I needed to know you first."

"So I am not being stranger now to you?"

"I think you've proven yourself trustworthy . . ." she replied, looking at Jack, who nodded, crossing his huge, metallic arms.

"And that's rare," she added. "It's not every day I meet a man who cares about the fate of a boy he doesn't even know." She looked at Adnan, who rolled his eyes at her. "Who's not the fluffiest of cats."

"He is just boy," Rozhenko replied. "What are we doing if not defending who is needing defense?"

Manon looked at Jack. "He's wonderful. I love him."

Rozhenko blushed. He couldn't help but beam at her praise.

"So, what do you say, Vasily?" She held out her right hand. "Friends?"

He considered her hand for a moment, then grasped it, taking care to be firm but not squeeze too hard lest he break her delicate fingers. Despite the elegant appendage, her grip was strong.

"I am very happy to be being your friend," he admitted.

Adnan emitted a mock retch.

Manon stuck out her tongue at him. He shook his hair in front of his face to hide the smile he fought to suppress.

"No matter what happened up there, things are going to change down here," Jack said. "I can't see the Allied fleet beating the Reds . . . and if they *were* routed, there's no way they can hold any city here. Maybe they keep Klippeborg . . . but if the Ingili and badlands humans get wind the Allies have no ships? I could see the tribes uniting, mounting an assault on the North."

"I don't care about the Allies, or K-borg," Manon replied. "But Karin said Agnès is in Ulterboro. And, if the Allies can't hold their claims, she'll be in even more danger than she already is."

Both Jack and Rozhenko looked at her expectantly.

"I want to get her," said Manon. "Because fuck the Allied military. We're not the only ones who feel that way. And with her wearing those colors . . ." she bit her bottom lip and set her blue eyes on Jack. She shook her head.

"So we get her," Jack said. "All in?"

"I am in," Rozhenko replied. He looked at Adnan. "You, too, little man?"

Adnan shrugged.

"There is being lots of fighting," Rozhenko said in a tone of voice intended to sound extra enticing.

"And I bet the armory here'll put a smile on that sour face," Manon added.

Adnan looked at her. He couldn't help himself. He broke into a grin.

FORTY

ADA PACED THE opulent Buckingham Palace rug while Tuah watched from the bed.

"Will you please sit down?" she insisted.

"Sit down?" Ada replied. "How the hell am I supposed to sit still? They arrested my father!"

"Is wearing out the carpet going to solve anything?"

"Sitting sure as hell won't," Ada retorted.

"Well, what can we *do*?"

"I don't know . . . I don't know. But I am *not* taking this on my back. Courtois doesn't get to consolidate power like that. We have to fight back."

"How, though?" Tuah pressed. She had no answers and felt lame just throwing out questions.

Ada stopped pacing. "We've gotta get to Venus. Get Heston and Adeola to back us up. I don't know who else could. We can't leave Courtois and Hastings in charge."

"Baby, Heston is here . . ."

"What? He is? But the field marshal sent him back to Venus after the council."

"Have you talked to anyone but me since then?"

"Obviously, Tuah! How do you think I found out about my father?"

Tuah held up her hands in apology. "Okay, okay . . . Well, that cute cook in the mess, you know the tall one with the tattoos? He told me Heston came back with the First and Third Fleets but the battle was already over."

"They destroyed us," Ada said, shaking her head in dismay. She wasn't in the mood to think about handsome cooks. "And my father encouraged the offensive. They're gonna execute him, Tuah! They won't even need help making him look like a traitor. And I'll be next."

"Calm down," Tuah said. "Getting worked up won't help anything—"

"How the hell am I supposed to be calm? They're coming for me, too—!"

"Ada!" Tuah said, her voice firm and sharp.

Ada exhaled a deep breath and tried to calm herself.

"What we need to do," Tuah said, "is find Heston. We can't fight back without him. We're not just gonna sit here and wait for them to take you. I promise."

FORTY-ONE

IN THE MORGUE of one of Overground's medical bays, Carina flipped open the rectangular metal door. She pulled the long tray from within.

Gardiner's body rested upon the slab, covered by a sheet. Patrick was ensconced nearby, but she couldn't afford him the attention.

Her breath fogged in the cold.

Pulling back the sheet, she looked at Gardiner one last time. She could never forgive him for what he'd done to her, for what he forced her to do, but she decided that she understood.

It was a start.

Marseh stood across from her. No condensation plumed from his mouth. His telepathic suggestion of himself didn't need to breathe, and he didn't care to present the illusion.

"I understand that this is hard for you," he said.

She looked at him. She smiled without showing teeth. It never reached her eyes. *Do you?*

"Yes," he replied. "He'll be cremated. I just need you to approve."

She nodded and pulled the sheet back over Gardiner's ruined skull.

Adieu, Maks.

She returned to the medical bay and Marseh followed her.

"Do you wish to return home?" he asked.

She almost instantly replied, *Of course,* but then bit back the words, wondering if she actually did wish to go back.

Michèle was on the station with her, though she bristled to get off. Agnès was still on Earth, as was Manon. Carina realized that she cared so little about the war. Being reunited with Michèle had altered her paradigm. All she wanted was to bring her sisters together and to find some way to bring Tuah and Ada along. She had forgotten how it felt to have a family.

"No," she said, finally. "What home? When was that place ever home?"

Marseh bowed his head. "Will you join us?"

Carina's lip curled. "I don't want to be a part of your war . . . no. Not anymore. I'm *tired* of death."

"What about as a doctor?" he suggested. "You could practice here. We have a significant civilian population. A lot of expectant mothers in our midst and very few obstetricians."

He led her to the large bed in which Sargas lay, unconscious but alive. For a long while, he'd hung at the brink of death, but the nanomachines replicated like bacteria. Their stem-cell payloads could regrow anything with enough time. When he finally rises from the bed, he'll have grown a brand-new spleen and an appendix. His internal injuries will all have mended, as if no physical trauma had taken place. The sole trauma the nanomachines could not eliminate was his memories of the assault.

Shaula stood over him. Carina looked at the small pregnant woman. Shaula knotted her brow. When she looked up, her incongruous, brilliant blue eyes startled Carina. They looked fake, especially in contrast to Shaula's dark skin, but the doctor recognized the symptom.

"Carina Duvais, this is Shaula," said Marseh.

"Hello," said Carina, smiling awkwardly. She wondered if the Waardenburg syndrome had rendered the woman deaf.

Shaula clicked and vocalized at Carina.

"Shaula doesn't speak the common language," Marseh explained. "She's from . . . elsewhere. Normally, she wears a translation collar but," he looked at her, "I guess she didn't feel like talking to us today."

Shaula pouted at Marseh and shook her head. It was clear that she heard, and understood, him.

"I am learn," she said.

"When are you due?" asked Carina.

Shaula looked at her, confused, then at Marseh. He pointed at her belly. Shaula's face lit up with understanding. She held up one hand and splayed all four fingers. "Four . . . four . . ." She tried to think of the word, but it eluded her.

"Four months?" asked Carina.

Shaula nodded, smiling. "Yes. Month. Four month."

Carina looked at Marseh.

"Maybe I could stay. For a little while. But only *after* I get my girls."

ACKNOWLEDGMENTS

I offer heartfelt thanks to the many people who made this work a reality, especially to those who provided encouragement and feedback during this odyssey.

Thank you to Ray Bradbury, George Orwell, Philip K. Dick, Arthur C. Clarke, and Isaac Asimov. They revealed to me the limitless possibilities of science fiction and profoundly influenced my worldview. Mr. Asimov has a special place in my heart as a fellow Brooklynite. I remember walking through the Botanic Gardens and smiling every time I encountered his name, thus the namesake character. Speaking of Brooklynites, I must also mention Carl Sagan. He was the kind of man I aspire to be: rational, thoughtful, curious, intrepid, erudite, and articulate. His patience and calm inspire awe. It pleases me that we share a middle name. Mr. Bradbury earned his own namesake character for being my gateway author to the wonders of the genre.

Without Tijuana Ricks, this book never would have happened. The impression she left on my life is indelible. I can't thank her enough for her love and support.

Michael Haase, Richard Cernese, Jeff Adams, Michael Williams, and Ken Soldwedel made excellent suggestions and kept me motivated. Their input was integral to the finished product. They made *Disintegration* a much better book.

Ben Macaluso, Christopher Grady, and Lauren Turner provided immense support in proselytizing for this novel. Thank you.

Seamus Scanlon infused hope into my quest to be published with his many tweets and his generous outlay. Our mutual love of pulp noir and similar dispositions helped get me through the workshops at City College. Speaking of CCNY and noir, thanks, too, to Larry Hanley for teaching me to surf. And to Salar Abdoh for being himself, which earned him a cameo.

Carl Scott is one of the coolest cats I know, and talented as hell. Thanks to him for my reel, and for our friendship. To Dan Broyles, Todd Dubester, and Dan Paskell: as promised, your namesakes appeared in the original manuscript, but I had to cut 40,000 words and you three were casualties of that cull. My apologies.

Stephen Carl Arch and Robert Ruffalo believed in me, at different times, when no one else would. I can never repay my debt to them, but they have my most profound gratitude. I would never have made it to where I am without them.

Nickelina Noel was my sounding board and traveling companion. She encouraged me to get the book done and taught me a lot about myself along the way. Rick and Ilsa will always have Paris. We have Budapest. And, Nina, while I fear it may not amount to anything, I am sorry.

Deep thanks to Diane Sanlatte-Suero for her patience, generosity, and too many other things to list. My life is richer with her in it.

To my parents, thank you for the myriad things you provided, my existence paramount. Without you, there would be no me.

I'd be remiss not to mention the music of Mastodon and Baroness, particularly the albums *Crack the Skye*, *The Hunter*, *Yellow & Green*, and *Purple*. Both bands provided much of the soundtrack of *Disintegration*'s completion, as much as KMFDM and Pop Will Eat Itself played during its earliest incarnations.

To anyone I haven't mentioned by name but who played a role in my development as a writer and an artist—and, most of all, as a person—please know that you, too, have my gratitude.

Yes, even you.

GRAND PATRONS

Jeff Adams
Nicolas Agrait
David C. Andersen
Ivan Anderson
Katrina Anderson
Rachael Berkey
Nicholas C. Booth
Bob Broad
Daniel J. Broyles
Cathleen J. Burke
Tabi Card
Maurice Courtois
Richard Curwen
Andrei Dan
Todd Dubester
David Gage
Janna Grace
Christopher M. Grady
Alex M. Gray
Bonita Gray
James J. Gray
Timothy Holst
Jason Lindner

Benjamin J. Macaluso
Sean P. Mahoney
Alexander Maisey
Nat Milner
Erik Nergaard
Kay Prunty
Rudi J. Prusa
Dan Paskell
Seamus Scanlon
Wendy L. Schutte
Kenneth J. Soldwedel
K.W. Soldwedel
Lauren S. Turner
Nicole Van Destienne
Janu Vanier
Erik Venetsky
Brian Whiton
WilHelmus.! ([Bassist At Large])

INKSHARES

INKSHARES is a reader-driven publisher and producer based in Oakland, California. Our books are selected not by a group of editors, but by readers worldwide.

While we've published books by established writers like *Big Fish* author Daniel Wallace and *Star Wars: Rogue One* scribe Gary Whitta, our aim remains surfacing and developing the new author voices of tomorrow.

Previously unknown Inkshares authors have received starred reviews and been featured in the *New York Times*. Their books are on the front tables of Barnes & Noble and hundreds of independents nationwide, and many have been licensed by publishers in other major markets. They are also being adapted by Oscar-winning screenwriters at the biggest studios and networks.

Interested in making your own story a reality? Visit Inkshares.com to start your own project or find other great books.

CPSIA information can be obtained
at www.ICGtesting.com
Printed in the USA
FSHW010851160719